Their Twisted Rules

UNTOUCHED BOOK 2

C.S. BERRY

Author Note

Dear reader,

IMPORTANT NOTE: This is book TWO in a serial, meaning if you didn't read book one, you will be super confused. But if you are just skimming for sexy times, you've come to the right place.

Hopefully you've read Their Dangerous Game and are prepared for the next leg of the roller coaster. Well, strap in. Their Twisted Rules is the longest book of the series so far. That being said, things have been shortened in places and scenes from the original serial were cut.

If you have a close relationship with me, you probably shouldn't be reading this. I'm that reader who gets miffed when the author yadda yaddas over a sex scene. So there is sex, loads of it.

There will be a bonus download of a whole chapter that got the axe (and this is still a monster of a book).

Now here's your fair warning: this series is six books that have been published as a serial and are currently being reedited to tighten them for book readers. They all end on a cliffhanger. The sixth book ends with a happy for now that closes almost all the loops and a surprise that will open the door for future books. I am 100% committed to the journey of Harper and her guys. If you ask who, please refer to paragraph one.

But, it's also a spot to get off the ride if you're happy.

This book does have some darker themes so please see content warning on next page if you're concerned. Your mental health is important and if you need to know, it's there for you. Or on my website.

This is a steamy series not meant for readers under 18 (or anyone related to me, seriously, no).

On a personal note, I'm thrilled to finally have this in books! Untouched was first a serial only available on Kindle Vella – if you got it somewhere else, that wasn't me (pirates).

This was the book that started the amusement park that is the Berry-verse. Untouched started out as a passion project. Meaning at first, I wrote this story for me and I'm so happy I'm not the only one who loves it.

If you're new to the Untouched books or only read part on Vella (this ends on episode 124), buckle your seatbelts. The ride's about to get bumpy.

XOXOXO,
C.S. Berry

Content List

Content Warning for the series:
Bullying
Stalking
Dubious consent
Spanking/bondage
Public humiliation
Group scenes (No swords crossing)
All characters are of age

Later books:
Attempted sexual assault (not by heroes)
History of child abuse - victim
Sexual assault (told by character as part of their story)
Stalking/threats
Being drugged
Kidnapping
Panic/sounds like guns, but no firearms are discharged in school
Trafficking is discussed
Death (not main characters)

CHAPTER 1

The Petition

Nico

Of all the things I thought I'd return to, a standoff between my friends and cheerleaders wasn't one of them. The guys I've seen at football camps over the years, but the girls I only remember from when I was in sixth grade.

"Nico will join the football team," Luke says. "He's one of us."

Sidney's calculated gaze turns to me. "You don't let just any football player hang out with you."

"Nico isn't just some football player." Eli steps forward. "He's a horseman."

Sidney's mouth drops open and she hesitates. Everyone knows you don't fuck with the horsemen on the football field. We've used the name every year at football camp, the only time I get to see the guys. It was one of my parents' concessions when we moved away.

The five of us have been connected almost since birth, but the horsemen is ours. It's who we are. They told me they used the name at school too. But I had no idea how far they've taken it.

When the opportunity to come back for my senior year presented itself, I seized it. To get to be part of the horsemen again. To finally return to the place that feels like home. To return to the girl that feels like home.

1

Harper. I was also hoping to rekindle my friendship and more with her. Especially after seeing her at the football game. She's always been pretty, but now she's gorgeous.

I'm not surprised they've claimed her.

I don't turn around to look at her with Caden. Watching Luke paw her was enough to make me burn inside. I knew coming back was a gamble, but I hoped Harper would still be free. That we could find something new together. Best friends with something more.

So many times before this year, I thought about reaching out, but what would be the point? I was in New York and she was here. Part of me didn't want to hear about how she was getting by without me. Who she was dating. I could have reached out before we moved back, but by then it had been so long...

Tonight, she didn't mention a boyfriend. Even though Luke has kept her on his lap, the way Caden holds her I can't tell which one of the guys she's with.

"There are only four horsemen," Emma Garcia says with her hand on her hip and a welcoming look in her eyes for me. These girls didn't look twice at me when I was a scrawny sixth grader.

Sure, they're hot and they know it. The scraps of fabric they call clothing flaunt their assets. If I give them even a hint I'm interested, I could be balls deep in any of them before tonight is over.

I never really had to work hard for female attention at my old school. But there's only one girl who I've thought about for years and couldn't have, until now. These bitches don't hold a candle to her.

But I don't know where I stand with Harper. If it's too late.

"Nico is Apocalypse." Luke steps closer to the group of girls. He's a cold bastard. Death always suited him. "He's one of us."

"Does that mean he gets to play with your pet? Or is he eligible?" Hannah raises her eyebrow. She twists her finger into her curly black hair and gives me a wink.

A stone sinks in my gut. Pet? Fuck, is that what Harper is? Their goddamned pet? What the fuck happened while I was gone?

I can't help but glance back at Harper. Caden's hand is dark tan against the pale skin of her midriff. She's relaxed in his arms like this is a normal thing. I noticed her tension when Luke held her, but right now, she appears content to let Caden touch her.

That spark of jealousy rips through me again. How can she be with them? Is she with all of them? What the fuck happened to the girl I knew, and who is this gorgeous creature before me?

And why doesn't their claim make me want her any less?

Luke glances at me with a smirk. "Apocalypse just moved back. For all we know, he's already taken."

"Are you?" Hannah asks. She wets her red lips.

Fuck. Way to put me on the spot. If I say no, these chicks will assume I'm fair game. But I came back with one girl in mind, and that might not be possible if she's their pet. Fuck.

Luke's eyes narrow on me, but he turns to the girls with no expression on his face. "We'll get back to you on that. Now state your business."

Sidney smiles as she tosses her blond hair over her shoulder. Her green eyes are shrewd. "We figured you could use more company. After all, there doesn't appear to be enough Harper to go around."

Eli steps up to her. "Why do you always make assumptions, Sidney? You keep acting like you know what we need." His gaze rakes her up and down before he gives her a dismissive look. "Why don't you go find the rest of the football team? I'm sure you could get someone to stick their dicks in you for the night."

Sidney's lips press together. "Maybe we want to play with the new horseman. Break him in. I'm sure he wouldn't mind four on one since your pet has the four of you."

The tips of my ears burn. Fuck. Would I lose my man card if I say no? Because while it sounds fascinating to have four women at once, I'm not sure I'd be able to keep up. And the women in question, while attractive, aren't the woman I want.

Luke gives me a look that asks if I want to. I'm sure he'd allow it to happen, but I give him a slight shake of my head to indicate I'm not interested.

Luke must have noticed my earlier interest in Harper. I don't know what he wants to do with that information, but I'm not backing down until I know Harper doesn't want me.

"For now, our friend will pass." Luke holds his hand back toward Harper and Caden.

Harper comes forward and takes it without hesitation, but her gaze flicks to me as he pulls her into his arms. Caden joins us.

"If you'll excuse us, ladies, we have a previous obligation to take care of." Luke nods to them and his gaze falls to me. "Are you joining us?"

I look at Harper, and I see a spark of hope in them. Whatever they're planning, she seems to want me there. I wish I could read minds, to tell if she wants me to join in or stop whatever this is from happening, but it's been too long and we can't read each other the way we used to. But if there's even a chance I can be her hero...

"I'm in." I lift my gaze to Luke's, and he nods.

HARPER

Luke leads us away from the Cheermonsters, and their hate-filled gazes dig into my back. Like any of this is my decision. Like I knew being the last virgin would paint a target on my back.

I don't dare look at Nico, but I'm glad he's coming with us. Honestly, I'm surprised he didn't take the girls up on their offer. Most men would be happy just with a threesome with two women, but they were offering all four of them. I can attest four is a lot.

The only reason I have the horsemen's attention is because of an intact hymen. Yay. That's how to get a man. Or four. Or is it five now?

Nico is a horseman after all. Though I still don't understand how that works. In fifth grade he was still my best friend. I didn't even know he was friends with these guys. Of course, the guys didn't really claim their titles until sometime in sixth grade and didn't make waves until high school.

Caden pushes open a door, and we all go through it. The noise from the party ceases as he closes it behind us. Suddenly I'm on high alert.

Dammit, I'm alone with them, but they won't do anything with Nico here, right? I mean, I belong to the four of them. Not five.

My insides soften as I wonder how it could work with five of them. The four of them overwhelmed me this morning. Their hands everywhere. I couldn't lock on a single sensation, dissolving into a mass of liquid desire at their touch.

I'm so not ready for this.

As we walk through the darkened, quiet household, no one speaks. I kind of expect Nico to ask some questions, but it seems like everyone is waiting. I'm not sure what for.

We climb stairs and turn down another long hallway. When Caden opens a door, we walk into his bedroom that I've only seen online. My heart jumps at the familiar room and enormous bed. Awareness floods me even as I swallow down the burst of nervous energy.

The room is huge with a couch and chairs. An open door leads into a bathroom.

When I freeze, Luke tightens his hold on my waist. Once again, I'm a hare trapped with hungry wolves, and now there's a fifth one, and I don't know how hungry he is. Will he help them tear me apart?

"We need to talk." Luke leads me to the chair and lets me sit in it by myself. I release my breath. The guys claim the couch and the other chairs. I slip off my shoes and pull my feet up, trying to make myself as small as possible.

This time I'm not the center of attention.

"I think I'm missing some details." Nico's gaze meets mine, and I almost feel sorry for him. If he'd gotten here before school started, I would have begged him to claim me, even if he didn't feel that way about me. I could have started the school year with a boyfriend and protection from the horsemen.

Except part of me doesn't want that. Part of me really enjoys owning four guys. They're mine and mine alone. I enjoy their touch and attention. But maybe if I had Nico, it would have been enough. I'll never know.

"We have an arrangement," Luke begins. He rubs his finger over his lower lip. My traitorous body softens, knowing what those lips can do.

Arrangement? More like ownership. Scoffing, I fold my arms over my chest.

Luke lifts an eyebrow. "You have something to say, princess?"

"It's not like I had a choice in this *arrangement*." I feel a little braver with Nico here. Of course, that won't stop Luke from punishing me. But I can't say I haven't liked some of his punishments.

"You had a choice, kitten." Eli leans back on the couch, but his dark eyes track me.

A sharp laugh bursts out of me, and I feel the glares of the horsemen. Not Nico though—he seems confused.

"The horsemen made it a mission to leave no virgin behind, with a few exceptions." I settle back into my chair and look only at Nico. "Other than when we were freshmen, they leave the freshmen alone. They also don't go after girls with boyfriends. And of course, there is a class of *unfuckables*."

Nico's gaze narrows on me as I continue, but fuck it, he needs to know the whole truth of who these guys—who apparently are his friends—really are.

"However, they've worked on our class, and it's a point of pride to have cleared the senior class of their virginity, except for one." Heat licks my cheeks. "So first day of school, as the lone senior virgin remaining, the horsemen claimed me. Of course, I've always hidden from them and avoided them since early freshman year, because they're bullies, and everyone knows to get in their way is to have hell rain down on you."

Someone scoffs but they don't deny it. They are who they are.

"So when I decided I didn't want to be *claimed*, I hid from them. Of course, when they found me, they spanked me in front of the entire cafeteria."

Nico's eyes widen, but there's also a flash of heat in his dark eyes. Interesting.

"Keep telling your story, princess. Understand you'll be punished for it." Luke draws my gaze as he rubs his hands together.

My panties dampen in response. Fucker.

I turn back to Nico. "The next morning, Caden and Jack showed up to take me to school and forced me to change my shirt in front of them. At lunch, in the cafeteria again—which I hate—they told me they own me, and I demanded a choice. Not my finest hour, but at least I tried."

"What choice?" Nico leans forward with his forearms on his knees.

"I asked them to let me find a boyfriend for the year and if I couldn't, I'd submit to their ownership." I swallow and look down. "Of course, Luke only gave me five minutes to find anyone in the cafeteria to be my boyfriend. So I got up on the table and humiliated myself a second time to ask anyone to step forward and be my boyfriend."

Nico nods thoughtfully. "And no one did."

I smile warily. "Nope. It didn't help my case that the horsemen were mean mugging everyone in the cafeteria." I take a deep breath. "So no boyfriend, and now I'm owned by the horsemen for the entire year. They aren't allowed to touch or fuck any other girl, but I have to give them my virginity, so it's my choice when I give it up."

"Come on, little nympho. We all know you'll give it up to us." Caden smiles, but it's not a friendly smile. It sends a jolt through me. "Harper hadn't even kissed a guy before last Wednesday, and we had her naked in a closet with our hands all over that fantastic body this morning. She came so hard I'm surprised she didn't pass out."

Nico's lips tighten, and my whole face burns. Yeah, I wasn't going to give him that information. This is pretty fucked up as it is.

CHAPTER 2

A Tactical Liaison

HARPER

Nico's gaze leaves me and goes to each of the horsemen. "So what? You're going to take turns with her?"

I grow hot all over, mostly from embarrassment, but partly because the thought turns me on.

"Eventually." Luke spreads his arms over the back of the couch and crosses his foot over his knee. His cool gaze locks on me, making me want to squirm. "But as we take her firsts, we all want to be there. So far, we've kissed her all over."

Heat flows through me at the reminder of his tongue against my clit. Hot, firm, and so fucking wicked.

"And touched her all over."

My core aches and tightens.

"She hasn't made it past second base with us. Yet."

My gaze flies to Luke's. His earlier comment to Eli about not damaging my mouth rings through my head. My gaze drops to his erection and I clench my thighs together.

"Though last night when we all shared an orgasm over webcam, she gave us an idea of what else she could do with that mouth."

I don't think I can get any redder, any more turned on, or any smaller.

Luke's heated gaze slides over me, reminding me of what he can do to me with just a touch. Fuck, I wish I didn't want him. I wish I didn't want them all. It would be a hell of a lot easier to resist.

He smiles at me before turning to Nico. "So our question is what do you want to do?"

Nico straightens and his gaze flicks to me before he meets Luke's. "Harper has been mine since kindergarten."

His words send sparks flooding through my veins and make my heart feel lighter. Kenz was right. He wants me. What the fuck does that mean?

"You may have claimed her in my absence, but I came back for her. You guys are a bonus, but I could have stayed in New York for my senior year. I planned to come back and claim my best friend."

Luke nods thoughtfully. "Harper?"

I whip my gaze to Luke's. His eyes are narrowed on me with a fire threatening to burn me whole.

"Do you acknowledge this claim?"

The rest of the horsemen lean forward. I'm not sure what will happen if I tell the truth. But I know for any of this to work, I have to be honest. I don't look at anyone but Luke.

"If Nico hadn't left, would I have a boyfriend? Probably. Would he have stood up for me in that cafeteria? Maybe."

"Yes." Nico straightens and his dark eyes hold mine. "Not probably. Not maybe. Yes, Harper, if I hadn't left, I would have been more than your best friend. I had a crush on you, but knew I was moving and didn't act on it."

My heart throbs, but the problem is I'm no longer free to choose. Whether I made my choice or was forced to make a choice, it's still mine. They're mine, but for how long? And when they decide to leave me, will Nico still want me? After they're done with me?

I blow out a breath. He may have wanted more, but he never actually offered it.

"He was my best friend, but I haven't spoken to him since he left," I admit. He may have claimed me when we were children, but he didn't keep in touch. So it doesn't matter now.

"Harper is ours." Luke relaxes into the couch and looks between the two of us. "We've made our claim and she'll be ours all year, no matter how she tries to back out of it."

My cheeks are on fire. Besides the fake grounding and suggesting they get with the Cheermonsters and asking for a boyfriend... Well, shit, I have been actively trying to get out of this. Just nothing works.

When they put their hands on me, my mind shuts down and the horny bitch in me starts panting for more. I want them to want me.

"Do you acknowledge that, Harper?" Luke doesn't call me *princess*.

It may not have been what I wanted, but I want them now. Will I still fight? Probably. But I also accept their ownership over me and enjoy the benefits. "Yes."

Nico's gaze is on me, but what can I do? I don't want to fear punishment my whole senior year. As overwhelming as their attention is, I crave it. And I much prefer the kisses and the touches to being a social pariah.

"You have a choice to make, Nico." Luke leans forward with his elbows on his knees, hands clasped.

Nico straightens.

"You can remain a member of the horsemen and enjoy all the benefits that come with it." Luke's gaze flicks to me, so no one can mistake I'm a benefit. "Or you can become our enemy, which means Harper isn't anything to you. Not your friend. Not even your crush."

My heart falls into my stomach. I don't want to give up Nico as a friend. I'd love to explore our connection to see what more there could be. But I don't really have a choice, he does. This may be too much for him. I haven't known him for years. I don't know who he is now.

But if he came back for me, this is the only way he can have me.

"If you're with us, then you play by our rules. Harper has limits. Until we push the limits as a group, you stay within those limits. No one goes beyond what has been shared by the group. When we play our games, you respect everyone's turn."

Caden scoffs. "Even if the fucking bottle plays favorites."

I almost laugh at his pout. The bottle didn't like him last night. I give Caden a smile, and his green eyes light up, sending a burst of heat through my insides.

"We take care of what's ours. When she steps out of line, we punish her," Luke continues.

I squirm in my seat.

"Her virginity is still intact. When we take it, we take it together and only when she begs for it."

Yeah, probably not going to happen. We can all come without anyone penetrating my body. Though their fingers thrusting inside me feels really good.

Luke's blue eyes capture mine. "She was untouched when we found her and she has yet to do more than kiss us, grind on us, and kiss our chests."

"Which she only got to do to you," Eli complains. While the bottle liked Eli, the coin didn't last night.

"I don't control the bottle or the coin." Luke smirks. "Or I would have been the first to kiss her breasts."

Heat engulfs me as I think about the first he took this morning. His tongue on my clit and his finger inside me. I'm going to need a fan just thinking about how amazing it felt when I finally let go. They must have all agreed to what they would do to me in that closet for it to work so effectively.

"We also have a webcam set up in the evenings when Harper is away from us." Luke's gaze gentles. "She likes to watch us sleep, amongst other things."

If human combustion were a thing, I'd be ash. I can't even look at Nico. What he must think of me. Why would he want any part of me when I'm just the horsemen's whore?

"Are you in or are you out?" Luke raises an eyebrow at Nico. It feels like bargaining with Death himself.

Nico rubs his hands together and gives me a searching look. "Can I talk to Harper alone for a few minutes?"

"You may, but remember Harper has limits. If you're even considering not being a horseman, don't touch what's ours. We won't stand for disobedience." Luke gestures to Caden.

Caden comes over to me and offers me his hand. When I slip mine into his, he helps me to my feet. He nods to Nico, who follows us. We leave Caden's bedroom and cross the hall. There's a small study with leather chairs and leather-bound books lining floor-to-ceiling shelves.

"You have five minutes." Caden kisses me gently. "Behave, little nympho."

I'm pretty sure if Nico crosses any lines, I'll be the one punished. When Caden closes the door, I sink down in a chair and put my feet up under me. I watch Nico curiously. He's attractive, and I definitely feel sparks with him. It wouldn't be a bad thing if he wanted to join in.

He sits on the edge of the chair next to mine and stares at me for a few seconds. "Do you want any of this, Harper?"

I hold my breath for a moment, trying to figure out how to make him understand.

"Honestly at first, no. I thought I could find someone to pretend to date me, but not in five minutes." Releasing my breath, I bite my lip before confessing, "I'm not saving myself for anything in particular. I just never found someone I liked. It's really hard to get to know someone when you're always hiding."

"And you *like* them?" His question sounds a little bitter.

It's so hard to explain what I feel for them now. I meet his dark eyes. "I won't lie to you. At first they scared me, not because of potential sex, but what they could do as punishment. That first day, they paraded me into the cafeteria and had me on a table over Luke's lap with my skirt up. The whole cafeteria counted along with Luke's spanks. That was mediocre compared to what they can do."

"What have they done?"

"Sophomore year, they had a project like me, but she fought against them. It got so bad she transferred schools. Guys get beat up. They made a guy take his underwear off and put it in his mouth before covering his mouth with duct tape." I meet his gaze and hold it, trying to make him understand. "You don't want them as an enemy."

Nodding, Nico settles into his seat. "What about me?"

My heart thumps and my insides feel crazy. "What about you?"

"Do you want me to join them or fight them?" His gaze drops to my lips, and I throb between my thighs. It's like the horsemen awakened something inside me and it likes what it sees in Nico.

"I don't want to see you hurt," I admit. "And if you fight them, they will hurt you."

"But do you want me to take part in this?" Nico stands and lifts me off the chair.

I squeal and grab his arms, but he settles into my seat and puts me on his lap, facing him. I swallow as I straddle his legs. The guys didn't really approve him touching me. I glance toward the door nervously.

"Do you want me, sunshine?" His hands come up and cup my face. He searches my eyes.

Sparks race through my veins along with a throb in my heart. How different my life might be right now if he stayed. I would have lost my virginity already. For sure.

"Yes," I whisper, afraid if I say it too loud, he'll pull away.

He brushes his lips gently against mine. Tingles dance where he touches. "If I stay, will you give me all of you?"

"I—" I hesitate. I can't commit to just him. That isn't an option anymore. I don't know if I'd want to. I'm not ready to give up Jack, Eli, Caden, or even Luke.

He breathes out against my lips and smiles. "As much as the others. Will you let me share you?"

"Yes, but it's for the entire year. You can't touch or fuck another girl. You have to be all mine." These terms are nonnegotiable. Especially given the other clause. "The others are getting tested, because..."

Heat engulfs me. This is more embarrassing than anything else and so against everything I've learned.

"Because?"

"They want to have sex without condoms. I'm on birth control and have been for a while. And since they know I'm clean, they want to..." I can't say it.

He captures my lips. My heart races as I open beneath him. He tastes of beer and mint and something uniquely Nico. His kiss is gentle and respectful, so unlike the others. Is he holding back?

It's a sweet kiss and makes my insides soften. But I miss that edge the other guys have. That element of fear that they'll push too far. Want too much. That they'll make me *want* to give in.

He pulls away and searches my eyes. "I'm not a virgin, but I got tested before we moved. I can't promise I won't want to protect you from them. But I'll do what I can without breaking any rules."

"You aren't going to leave?" I push my fingers through his thick black hair.

"No. I'm here to stay. For you."

CHAPTER 3

The Initiation

HARPER

When the door opens, Caden holds out his hand to me. I search Nico's dark eyes one more time before I climb off his lap and join Caden. We cross the hall and return to our seats.

"Your decision?" Luke eyes my lips like he can tell Nico kissed me. I resist the urge to touch them.

"I'll play by the rules," Nico says.

Jack smiles and practically dives onto Nico's lap. "Dude, I've missed you so much. These guys don't know how to have fun."

Eli lifts an eyebrow, and Luke rolls his eyes.

"I guess I should have asked if this arrangement goes all ways." Nico lifts an eyebrow at Jack's enthusiasm.

"Most of us only go for females," Luke says without inflection.

I watch Nico's face to see how he'll react to Jack being bi.

"Hey," Jack says, "if a guy wants to tackle me off the field, I'm not opposed."

"But not with any of us," Caden assures Nico. "I'm thoroughly into pussy. Dick doesn't do it for me."

"Sorry, Jack." Nico pats his arm. "I'm not a switch hitter."

"Your loss." Jack winks at him. "I'm always open to experimentation, but don't spread it around school. Wouldn't want to break anyone's heart. Besides, I'm taken for the year."

All their eyes fall on me, and I squirm in my seat. Now that they've gotten the talk with Nico out of the way, that means everyone is in. Maybe I could have used him as an out, but I doubt they would have allowed it.

Besides, the more time I spend with them, the less I want out.

"Come here, princess."

I cross the floor to stand before Luke.

His gaze flicks to Nico's as Jack takes my seat behind me. "Take off your shirt."

Shit. I glance over my shoulder at Nico. Um. After that gentle kiss, he might not like how the guys treat me. I still have bruises on my ass from the way they grab me.

"Don't be shy, princess." Luke strokes his hand down my thigh, sending a shiver coursing through me. "Your new owner deserves to see what's his."

My heartbeat triples as I lift my shirt over my head. I've been naked in front of them so much. Last night, my skirt hid very little from them. My nipples tighten and I grow wetter, knowing someone will touch me soon. Stupid Pavlovian response.

"Take off your bra."

I inhale and release the clasp on my bra. I let it fall with my shirt to the floor.

Nico sucks in a breath. Heat curls its way up my neck. He just got here a few hours ago, and I'm already stripping for him. My life is pretty fucked up.

Caden leans forward and brushes his fingers over my nipple. My breath catches. He smirks and leans back on the couch beside Luke. Eli sits on Luke's other side, while Jack and Nico are behind me.

"Pants next." Luke's gaze holds mine as I undo the button and zipper before shimmying my pants down and off, leaving me in only my pale blue panties.

I reach for them, but Luke holds up a hand to stop me.

"First your punishment."

I cross my arms over my chest and ask, "What for?"

"You let someone else claim you, princess." Luke stands and his shirt brushes against my hard nipples. He grabs one of my braids and tugs gently. "We own you. You're lucky he's a horseman or the punishment would have been doubled."

I press my lips together, still not wanting to be punished, but at least it's not in front of the whole party downstairs. Small favors. I drop my arms and wait.

Luke palms my breast. I suck in a harsh breath as heat coils tight in my womb. Is this the punishment? When his thumb brushes over my nipple, I gasp at the electric flow of desire through me. If this is my punishment, I'm okay with it.

"Turn around," Luke says.

Blushing, I turn to face Nico. I can see the outline of his erection against his jeans. I don't cover my breasts because I know that will earn me another punishment.

Luke crowds me forward until I stand a foot in front of Nico. "Nico, put your hands on the arms of the chair and don't move them."

Nico narrows his eyes at Luke.

"You kissed our girl before she was yours. This will be your punishment too." Luke strokes down the side of my body, and I almost moan at the desire swelling inside me. My panties are soaked.

Nico puts his hands on the arms of the chair and clutches them. His gaze roams over my body freely, like he wants to touch it all. Everywhere he looks grows hotter.

Luke pulls my hips against his erection and puts his hand in the center of my back, pushing me down. "Put your hands on his knees and don't move them."

I follow Luke's directions and tip my face up to search Nico's dark eyes. The longing in them makes me even wetter.

Luke slips his hands into the sides of my panties and draws them down my legs. For a second, I almost resist. But like he said, they've seen everything and touched everything. Besides, I already have one punishment to face, I'd rather not have a second one.

After I step out of them, Luke puts a foot between mine and makes me spread my legs hip width apart. I'm spread open for him. I want to bite my lip, but the collar around my neck reminds me not to. This is a dangerous game, but they won't take my virginity.

"Maybe I should move to the couch?" Jack asks uncertainly.

"Your view might be better. All I get is Luke's ass." Caden sounds disgruntled. "At least you get to see her tits."

"Enough." Luke silences both of them. "No noises, Harper, or we start over. How many should she get?"

"Five," Eli says. Maybe he's still in my corner. "But we get to take turns checking how wet you've made her between spanks."

Oh, fuck, that makes me even wetter. My head drops to hang between my arms. I don't know how I'm going to keep from making noises.

"Brace yourself." Luke pushes my back down with one hand and swats me with the other.

I bite back the instinct to say *ow*. Luke rubs my ass cheek, taking away the bite of pain, stirring up that other feeling.

"Eli, since you had the idea, you can go first."

Eli steps behind me. Luke is still caressing my ass when I feel Eli's blunt fingertip slide inside me. My knees try to buckle, but I hold myself still and try not to moan. I clench around his thick finger.

"She's so fucking wet." Eli takes his finger out of me, and I hear him suck it clean. Fuck.

My pussy pulses and I can't do a damn thing about it. I've only come three times in my life, but I want to do it again. These guys will get me there. I lift my gaze to Nico's. His breathing is a little faster and his eyes have darkened.

Luke claps my other cheek. I suck in a breath, but don't make a sound. I hold Nico's eyes as Luke rubs my sensitive skin.

Caden steps behind me and slides his thick finger in with no resistance. He pumps it a few times. I tighten my grip on Nico's legs and try not to bite my lip to keep my moan inside. Fuck that feels good.

"Tight and wet," Caden says before I hear him suck on his finger. "Tastes good too."

"Fuck." Nico shifts in his seat, but his hands remain on the chair. His eyes search mine. "You like that?"

There's curiosity in his voice, not accusation. I nod before Luke's hand comes down again. A burst of pleasure flows through me and I almost cry out. My lips part and my eyes close as Luke rubs the pain away.

Jack is next. He slips his finger inside me, curls it toward the front, and presses down. My legs shake and a gush of wetness flows from me.

"Mmm, good girl." He sucks on his finger and I'm hopeless. There's no way I can get through this without crying out or coming or begging them to make me come.

Luke strokes down my back, and I want to arch into his touch like a cat. "Two more, princess. You think you can take it?"

Lifting my head, I meet Nico's eyes. He looks as shattered as I feel. I nod since I'm not allowed to vocalize.

Luke smacks my ass. He presses against my cheek with one hand while sliding two fingers inside me with the other hand. My hips move instinctively as he thrusts them in and out. I'm so close right now.

Nico clenches the leather as he watches my breasts sway with the motion.

"Tight and wet. You want us, don't you, princess." It's not a question, and he doesn't have to ask. I crave their touch. Luke sucks on his fingers, and my pussy pulses in response to the sound.

"One more." Luke rubs my ass. "You can be as noisy as you want on this one, princess. And then Nico is going to see how wet you get for your horsemen."

Fuck.

Luke smacks my ass, and I can't stop the cry that bursts out of me. It feels so fucking good to release all that pent up sound. Luke helps me stand straight and then turns my back to Nico. He bends me forward.

"See how wet we make our pet and how red her ass gets."

I'm beyond embarrassment at this point. Nico sinks his finger into my pussy, and I moan. His finger is so much thicker than mine. I want to come, but he pulls it out. Luke turns me around as Nico puts his finger in his mouth.

His eyes close like it's the best thing he's ever tasted. Luke's erection presses against my ass. Being naked makes my awareness of all these guys heightened. Nico stands and closes in on me. His heat envelops me. His erection presses against my stomach.

Nico tips my chin up. "I always knew you'd be mine."

When he lowers his mouth to mine, this kiss is anything but delicate. Like something unlocked in him, he claims my mouth with the aim to destroy any shred of innocence I have left. Luke kisses the nape of my neck, teasing, torturing.

They both caress my breasts while they slide their other hands between my legs. One circles my entrance while the other circles my clit. Their fingers tweak and caress my nipples, until I'm a writhing mess between them.

Luke thrusts his finger inside me and pumps it in and out a few times, before it trails back. Nico works his finger inside me while he continues to press his thumb in circles around my clit. Luke's finger stops at my puckered hole and presses in, using my own juices as lube.

I gasp into Nico's mouth as my eyes pop open. What the hell?

"Relax, Harper." Luke pushes a little farther inside. "Let me make you feel good."

I whimper as he pulls out a little and pushes back in, at the same time Nico thrusts his finger inside my pussy. It doesn't feel bad. It just seems wrong, but as they continue to move, the pressure builds.

Nico takes his mouth from mine and works down one side of my throat, while Luke sucks down the other. I can't catch my breath. They're the only things holding me up, because my knees definitely aren't working. My eyes open, and I meet Caden's and Eli's as they sit on the couch with their cocks out, stroking them.

"How does it feel, kitten?" Eli's darkened eyes hold mine.

I can't find words, and before I can even say that, Luke and Nico bite down on where my shoulders meet my neck. I shoot off into oblivion. My body clamps down on both of their fingers while they try to keep stroking me through the orgasm. Luke withdraws his finger from my ass and holds me against his body. Nico lifts his eyes to meet mine while his finger thrusts in and out of my pussy, fueling the aftershocks through me.

I sag against Luke as I stare into Nico's eyes.

Yup, I'm a horny bitch, because I want more.

CHAPTER 4

The Siege

Luke takes me into the bathroom and sets me on the double counter. He wets a washcloth and presses it between my legs. When he turns it to cold water and wets it again, he says, "Stand and turn around."

I do as he says, and he presses the cold cloth to my warm ass cheeks. I suck in a breath.

"We're not done playing with you tonight, princess." He presses a kiss to the nape of my neck as he slides the washcloth between my butt cheeks and wipes me. Heat fills my face.

"Uh..." What do I say at this point? He stuck his finger up my ass.

"It'll be a while before we can take your ass too." He washes his hands and dries them before meeting my gaze in the mirror. "You'll need prep, so don't think about it. I wanted to see how you'd respond and, as always, you did so beautifully."

I stand completely naked in front of him while he's fully clothed. I should grab a towel or insist on my clothes, but this is part of being theirs. They've had me stripped bare before them plenty of times.

Mostly with an internet between us, but not always. Especially with Luke.

He reaches out, making my breath catch in anticipation of his touch. He takes my hand before leading me back into the bedroom. The guys have moved to make a circle on the floor. My heartbeat increases as I see the bottle in the center of them.

I drip with anticipation and my breath quickens.

Luke hands me my phone. "Tell your mom you're staying at MacKenzie's tonight."

I lift an eyebrow at Luke.

"No cock in pussy action tonight, princess, but we don't want our game interrupted."

I've only spent the night with Luke one time. Now they want me to stay with them. Sleep with them all?

I clear my throat and open my phone. I could get out of this so easily, but do I want to? I watch the guys stand and disrobe, including Nico. I hadn't considered his cock size, but yeah, not exactly on the small side of things. Not a Caden monster size though.

Fuck it. You only live once, right? I text my mom I'm staying with Kenz. Not a lie because Kenz is here. I also text Kenz to let her know.

Kenz sends me four eggplant emoji and water drops. Should I tell her it's five now or wait to see her face in the morning? I glance at Nico's body. Yeah, definitely not the scrawny kid who left me behind.

My mouth literally waters over his cut abs and his lean physique.

Mom texts me back to be safe, and I assure her I will before putting my phone away.

Taking a deep breath, I walk up to the circle. There's a gaming chair off to the side that wasn't there before. I put my hands on my hips as I look them all over. Fuck, they're beautiful boys. I could do a lot worse for my first sexual experiences.

"What's the game?"

Luke leans back on his hands, and I can't resist dropping my gaze down to his hard dick. When I lift it back to his face, he smiles. "We're going straight to pussy and cock this time."

My thighs clench together and I swallow hard at the thought of taking each of them into my mouth. My curiosity is definitely winning out tonight. "The rules?"

He holds his hand up to me, and I take it. He leads me into the center of the circle and motions for me to sit down on the rug in front of him.

I slide down to my knees and face him. My hair is still in my braids from earlier in the day, and they fall over my breasts. The ribbons tickle my nipples.

"Two spins this time, princess. The first gives and the second receives."

I lift an eyebrow in question.

"You sit on the first's face, and while they eat your pussy, you go down on the second's cock." Luke's eyes sparkle. "Thirty seconds each, and we keep going until everyone has had a turn."

Fuck.

"By the way, we all got tested earlier this week. The results came today. We're all clean, but we'll still wait until you want to give your virginity to us. The reports are in your inbox." Luke smirks. "Well, except Nico."

"I got tested as part of my physical and haven't had sex in three months, so I'm clean," Nico says.

I meet Nico's eyes. I'm trusting all these guys to be naked with me and not take me until I say it's okay. While I can't trust the others, Nico was my best friend. Maybe if things go south, Nico will help me if someone tries something.

Of course, it might not be wise to trust another horseman.

"Then we're good whenever you are, princess." Luke's blue eyes take me in. "It won't be a game. You'll have to ask for it. You can even determine how it happens as long as we're all there."

I wish that didn't turn me on.

"Hands or mouths?" I ask and reach for the bottle.

"Both."

I spin the bottle and sit back on my heels. The bottle stops on Eli.

"Spin again."

It stops on Luke. I lift my eyes to both of them and wait for them to tell me what to do. Luke stands and reaches for my hand. It feels odd to be naked with all the guys naked as well. But I'm sure this is more conditioning.

Luke sits in the low chair. Eli comes up behind me and kisses the back of my neck. Shivers trickle down my spine and pool low in my gut. Eli lowers himself to lie on his back, his head between Luke's feet.

I can do this. But this is really fucked up.

Luke holds out his hand, and I hesitate.

"Have we done anything you don't like?" Luke asks.

I shake my head, but I still hesitate. I have no clue what I'm doing, and Eli will be a huge distraction.

"How about the guy in the chair doesn't use his hands?" Luke raises an eyebrow to ask if that's okay. "Come on, princess. Everyone has to have a first time. You'll get better with practice."

His smirk is almost insulting. He thinks I'm going to suck at this. Not suck at this? Be bad at sucking? Well, fuck him. I'll prove him wrong.

I take his hand and straddle Eli's face.

"Pillow," Eli says. Caden hands him one, taking a moment to caress my ass.

"Same rules as last night, sweetheart. We start timing when you start kissing."

I look up into Luke's eyes and feel something settle inside me. Eli's breath kisses my pussy, and I gasp at how intimate this is. My hands move to Luke's bare thighs, and Eli's hands do the same on mine.

This isn't like the closet where everything was out of my control. This is me choosing to do this. Me accepting this is how I want this to happen.

Wanting to go slow, I reach out and clasp my hand around Luke's cock. My fingers barely touch around his thickness. Eli parts my pussy lips with his fingers, and I suck in a breath, knowing the minute I touch my lips to Luke's cock, Eli's tongue is going to touch me.

I summon all my courage. Leaning down, I lick the tip of Luke's cock. It's smooth against my tongue, salty. I squeeze the base of his cock a little, noting the skin is a little rougher there. Eli closes his mouth over my pussy and thrusts his tongue inside me. My lips part at the heat coursing through my veins, and I lower my mouth over Luke's tip before sucking lightly just above the ridge. I trace the edge of his head with my tongue, exploring.

I moan as Eli works my pussy with his tongue and lips. He twirls his tongue around my clit. I lift off Luke and trail my tongue down the underside of his cock to his balls. My gaze lifts to his face. Wanting to see his pleasure at my hand. I stroke my fist over him like I've seen the guys do to themselves while I lick his ball sack.

"Fuck." Luke's outburst makes me smile while I draw one of his balls into my mouth and suck gently.

Eli's finger presses inside me, and I release Luke on a moan. His finger stretches me as it pulses in and out. Luke's eyes blaze down at me as I continue to pump his cock before lowering my mouth over the head again, taking him as deep as I can go. Deep in my throat.

"Fuck," Jack says. Eli scrapes his teeth on my clit, and I moan on Luke's cock. Luke groans.

"That's time," Caden says.

I straighten and wipe the side of my mouth. My eyes lock with Luke's, the heated pools of clear blue reflecting his desire and amping up mine. Eli flicks his tongue against me one more time, sending a shiver through me, before Luke captures the back of my neck and kisses me long and hard.

My breasts press against his bare chest as he claims my mouth. I swear my whole body feels like it's connected to a live wire. He pulls back slightly, and the fire burning in his eyes reaches out to scorch me.

"That was hot." Jack grins as I come back into the circle and kneel beside the bottle. My insides burn and I squirm, needing more.

I lift my gaze to Nico, wondering if he really thought this through. If he wants to leave? If he can really share me with the other guys? The others don't seem to have any issues with it, but Luke leads them and has for years. They also came into this knowing they would have to share.

Nico's eyes blaze with heat. He nods toward the bottle. "Spin it."

The dark tone in his voice makes my pulse race as I spin the bottle. It stops on Caden. His grin is positively wicked as he jumps up to settle on the pillow. I almost shake my head at his eagerness. Instead, I spin the bottle again.

It stops on Nico. My gaze lifts to his. The other guys have become familiar to me. I've watched them stroking themselves and had them touch me for days. But Nico... I knew him for years when we were younger. Now all this time has passed, when we grew up without each other. Somehow, he still feels comfortable to me. Even stripped naked.

We just kissed for the first time, and then he finger fucked me with Luke, so I guess he's good with this.

He takes my hand to lead me over to the chair. Before he sits, he rests his forehead against mine. His body heat calls to me. "You're perfect."

He sits, and I want to protest. I'm not perfect. I'm playing sexual games with five guys and really hope to come on someone's face. I'm not sure I'm ready for anyone to come on mine though. But I'm excited to find out.

And that's the messed up part. I don't know how comfortable I would have been doing this with one guy. It would be awkward, and I'd feel uncomfortable with all his expectations for me. But with all this attention on me, I feel powerful and freer than I've ever felt before.

With one guy, I would have to hold the line, but with all the guys, they hold the line for me. While they all want me, they won't let someone take the one thing I'm not ready to give. The only thing they want me to give them.

Nico takes my hands and helps me kneel over Caden. Caden doesn't waste any time. He grabs my hips and sucks on my clit.

"Holy shit!" I grab onto Nico's knees and try to breathe through what Caden is doing to me, but there are no words. If I thought him smelling me was hot, I might not make it through a day without him going down on me. Tingles race all through my veins. Delicious ripples of pleasure rock through me.

The noises he makes are obscene, as if he's devouring me. But fuck does it feel good. I can feel the tension wind tight inside me. I haven't even started the clock because I'm just sitting here, trying not to lose my fucking mind.

"Ticktock, princess."

I'm seriously five seconds away from telling Luke to fuck off and let me come already. My eyes meet Nico's, and he seems to understand what I'm feeling. I glance down at his cock and notice the precum pooling at the tip. Forgetting everything I said last night or wanted to do to rile them up, I lean forward and lick his precum, running my tongue along his head like Caden is doing to me.

I inhale as Caden's tongue penetrates me, thick and wet, and I'm pretty sure I'm going to explode. My eyes meet Nico's, and I feel that connection between us. I want to please him the way Caden is pleasing me.

Taking his tip into my mouth, I suck on him while stroking my hand down his cock. My tongue runs along his head while Caden tongue fucks me. Nico bucks against my mouth and he moans. I keep sucking until I can't hold back my release anymore.

I come off of Nico's cock, moaning hardcore, and squeeze his thighs as I ride Caden's face to climax. His fingers dig into my ass cheeks to hold me still as I come.

Fuck.

I rest my head on Nico's thigh. Nico runs his hand over my hair, almost petting me.

Caden swipes his tongue from clit to ass, and my body spasms once again. He chuckles against me, and I lift my hips to look down at him.

"I win, little nympho." He swipes at the juices on his cheeks. "We might need to grab a towel, because our girl is a gusher."

Jeezus, heat floods my face. Caden eases out from beneath me and tips my chin to the side.

"Don't be embarrassed. I love it." He kisses me almost as obscenely as he ate me out. All tongue and teeth. I can taste myself on him, and I swear things heat back up inside me. My hands are still on Nico's thighs.

"Did I miss the timer?" I lick my lips and look down at Nico's cock.

"Fuck, sunshine. You were a little occupied at the time, but yeah, the timer went off."

I grin up at him. He leans down and kisses me hard, then leans close to my ear. "I can't wait to make you come again."

My core clenches. Nico helps me stand, and I turn back to the circle and sit next to the bottle. I should feel a little embarrassed about coming so loudly, but not one of these guys seems to think anything bad about it.

Their eyes are all hot and watch me like I'm their next three-course meal. A little aftershock works through me. Caden comes out of the bathroom and hands me a towel. I scrunch up my face at the thought of wiping myself in front of these guys.

But I'm sitting here naked with a soaked pussy, so... As discreetly as I can in front of five guys with erections for me, I wipe a little.

"Spin the bottle." Jack eyes me while he strokes himself.

I throw him a kiss and spin the bottle. The first spin lands on Luke and the second on Caden.

"Fuck, little nympho. I'd hate to be the first to blow in your mouth, but I don't know how much I can take." Caden takes my hand and leads me to the chair. "What do you think? Think you can swallow?"

His dancing green eyes gleam as he strokes my throat. It's not something I've thought a lot about to be honest. I've been worried about getting kissed, and somehow we're already to third base.

He tugs on my braid. "I can tell you when to pull off if you want me to."

I look down at Luke and the others around the bottle. If I let Caden come in my mouth, they'll all expect it from me. Caden had to have swallowed a lot from me given how much coated his face. While they're being nice now, I don't think they'll give me the option long-term to not swallow, so I might as well get used to it.

"How about we see what happens?" I give him a cheeky grin as he lowers himself into the chair. He helps me down over Luke's face.

"That's what I like about you. Always so willing." Caden gives me a grin and puts his hands behind his head. That's almost a joke. I haven't always been willing. "Whenever you're ready."

My gaze drops to his cock, and I'm still uncertain that will fit anywhere in my body, but I can definitely try. Especially after the orgasm he gave me.

Luke takes hold of my hips and teases me lightly with his tongue. After Caden's ravishing mouth, Luke's touch heats my blood but more gently. I focus on the cock at hand.

I wrap my hand around him and stroke a few times, watching his eyes. He seems to like it rougher, so I squeeze a little tighter as I come down over him. He groans.

"Put your mouth on it, little nympho." Caden smirks.

I raise an eyebrow and lick the tip, tracing his slit and the head of his cock with my tongue, before I open my mouth and take him inside, seeing how much of him I can take down my throat.

Luke thrusts two fingers in me at the same time, and I moan around Caden's cock. Luke changes tactics entirely. No more gentle easing touches. He sucks on my clit and thrusts his fingers up into me hard and fast. I follow his rhythm, moving up and down Caden's cock, running my tongue along the underside.

"I'm going to explode," Caden warns.

I take as much of him into my throat as I can and suck. Luke sucks on my clit and adds a third finger, stretching me full. He curls his fingers, hitting a spot that makes everything burst. Caden comes down my throat at the same time I come all over Luke's face.

I swallow as much as I can before I come off Caden's cock and swallow the rest. Caden leans forward and takes my mouth in a brutal kiss, tasting himself on my tongue. His body presses against mine. Luke pushes me over the edge again. My lips part as Caden captures my moans.

My legs tremble as I lift off Luke. He gives me a wicked grin as he grabs a towel and wipes his face.

I raise my hand weakly. "I need a break."

"We need to work on your endurance, princess." Luke leans forward and takes my mouth, making little aftershocks ripple through me.

"I've only been doing this for like a week," I complain.

Caden laughs as he walks to his pile of clothes, then stalks to me with his t-shirt. "Put this on and maybe we can concentrate on something besides your body."

He helps me put the t-shirt on. It's almost a dress on me. His cinnamon scent engulfs me as his body warms me. I gaze up at his heated green eyes as he takes in his shirt on me. An answering pulse of desire throbs between my legs.

Fuck, these guys are going to be the death of me.

I head into the bathroom and clean myself up before returning to the guys. They all have their pants back on, but not their shirts. Seriously, the eye candy is so fucking nice.

"Are we going back down to the party?" I ask, looking at my pile of clothes.

"Nah, let them have their own rager." Caden sits on the couch and gestures for me to come over. He tugs me down next to him and puts his arm around me. "We can watch a movie or play truth or dare."

I raise my eyebrow and look at the bottle still on the ground. Nico claims the seat beside me, and Jack sits on the other side of Caden. Luke and Eli take the chairs as Caden leans forward to grab the remote.

"I don't think you guys can do dares that wouldn't involve sex of some sort." I give them all the eye.

Chuckling wickedly, Caden turns on an action movie and lowers the lights in the room. I think it's one of the John Wick movies, because Keanu Reeves has long hair. Nico takes my hand and plays with my fingers. I lean my head against Caden's arm, and the last thing I remember is Keanu shooting someone in the chest and the head.

CHAPTER 5
Famine

JACK

Harper fell asleep at some point during the movie and started to snore lightly. We really wore her out. Well, everyone else did. I didn't get to play tonight, which is bound to happen with five guys and only one chick.

My phone buzzes.

GREEK GOD:

You down?

I glance at Harper. This guy I met over the summer at a party. We hooked up a time or two, but then he ghosted me. I didn't bother to block him. Technically I know him, but he acts like he hasn't fucked my ass or sucked my cock.

ME:

New phone who dis

GREEK GOD:

Stop fucking around, Jack

ME:

Nah, fucking around is fun

GREEK GOD:

Fuck around with me then

Fuck if I'm not tempted. The guy is a guaranteed all-nighter. My gaze lands on Harper's sleeping face again.

ME:

I'm involved

I close out of the conversation and consider blocking it. But Greek God isn't a misnomer. The guy is cut and gorgeous and really shouldn't be messing with an eighteen-year-old like me. But the attraction is smoking and he's got a great cock.

He's also someone who would never acknowledge our fuck buddy status in real life. Not that I'm down for being public, but if I ever found a guy I wanted to make a permanent edition, I wouldn't want to be his dirty little secret. I'd be out and proud, consequences be damned.

All that doesn't matter. I can't fuck someone else while I'm with Harper. Those are the rules. Yes, she specified girls and I could wiggle out with semantics, but if I really want to do this with her and go bareback—and I really want to go raw—I have to be one hundred percent hers.

Clicking on Block Number, I drop my phone back down. Caden looks at me. We've been best friends since kindergarten and have shared a lot of things, not just women. He's straight as an arrow, but he accepts me for who I am.

"That over?" Caden's low voice rumbles in the dark room.

I glance around, and Luke's the only one still watching the movie. "Yeah, that's over."

Caden strokes his fingers up and down Harper's thighs. She turns into him in her sleep. His shirt covers her almost to her knees, but she's naked underneath it. Almost absentmindedly, his fingers keep trailing higher, revealing more of her thighs.

Nico sleeps behind her with her hand still held in his. I don't know their story, but I'd like to find out more. Especially since Nico has always been a part of us. Sure, during the school year, he's in New York and we're here, but the well-oiled machine we become on the football field during camp is breathtaking.

This season just got more exciting with him joining the team. There's no way Coach would deny him a spot. The sophomore on the team just can't match our energy.

The only curiosity is what Harper means to him.

Did he hide her from us? Or us from her? Or both?

Will he try to take her from us even while sharing her? Is he going to claim her with all of us without wanting her for himself? Nico said he came back for her. That's a lot for a girl he hasn't seen since sixth grade.

Harper's eyes open a little and she blinks. "Caden?"

"Shh. Don't want to wake lover boy," Caden says. His hand clasps around her thigh.

Harper blinks her large brown eyes and glances over at Nico. She nods and snuggles back against Caden. He's the last guy I would think is a big teddy bear for snuggles, but maybe for Harper he is.

"You think you're awake enough to help Jack, little nympho?"

Her eyes find mine in the dark, and I'm struck that we didn't see her before this year. How the fuck did we miss this girl?

"What does Jack need help with?"

"He didn't get to play with you tonight." Caden makes a sad face like it hurts his feelings, when he got to eat her out and get a blow job. Sometimes that bottle really sucks. "You think you can make him feel as good as you made me feel?"

She almost bites her lip, but she glances at Eli. I can almost see the wheels turning in her brain. Does she want to get out of this? Does she need to be forced and have no other option? Because that would suck. Or is she just deciding how much of herself to give to us?

I'm committed to this deal with her and I'm pretty sure the others are too. I'll be hers.

Finally, she smiles softly and nods. Slipping her hand from Nico's, she stands to go around Caden. He grabs her hips from behind, and she glances down at him with a question in her eyes.

"Can I play with you too?"

Sneaky bastard. I'm not at all surprised.

Her cheeks burst red, and she inhales sharply but nods. Is she remembering how he went down on her? Because I am. Watching her ride his face and that fucking moan. I pull at my jeans to make room for my erection.

"Straddle me and face out. I'll hold your hips and keep you stable," Caden says. Always the gentleman.

She does as he asks, and he nods at me to stand. I strip out of my jeans and boxers.

My cock is so fucking hard. I stroke it a couple times as I stand in front of her. Her gaze follows my hand. Reaching out, she covers my hand with hers.

Her brown eyes meet mine as she says softly, "Show me what you like."

Fuck, this girl is going to kill me. I thread my fingers with hers and move our hands over my cock. She has small, soft hands. I hold back a groan as she thumbs my slit before we move our hands down again. When a little precum slips out, she bends over and licks it away.

I suck in a breath at the feel of her warm, wet tongue on my cock. Fuck, it's been a while. I won't last long.

Caden pushes her shirt up over her hips and slides his fingers between her thighs. She sighs a breath over my cock. It twitches in reaction.

"She's so fucking wet," Caden says, knowing what I want to hear. I haven't gotten to play with her pussy much. Just during her punishment, but I know it wasn't enough. I want to spend some time with her pussy, using my hands and my mouth to draw all the various noises I can from her. Caden has set the bar pretty fucking high with how loud she moaned when he made her come on his mouth.

But I like a challenge.

She takes my tip into her mouth and swirls her tongue around my head. My mind blanks as all the blood rushes southward. She's a fucking natural.

Caden slips his finger inside her and she takes me a little deeper. "Hot and tight. It'll feel so good on our cocks to slide deep inside her."

Fuck, her mouth around me is close to heavenly. She whimpers on my cock and I grab the base to hold off my orgasm. Her mouth feels too good.

Caden rocks his finger in and out of her, rubbing the heel of his hand against her clit. Following his rhythm, she bobs up and down on me. I brush her braid back over her shoulder so I can watch my cock disappear into her mouth.

"Suck on him, Harper. Let him feel how much you want his cum inside you."

She moans like she loves that suggestion. Taking me deeper, she hums around my dick before she sucks, hollowing out her cheeks.

"Oh, shit." I'm not going to last.

"She wants you to come down her throat, Jack. Don't you, baby?" Caden's voice is like a fucking pied piper, luring both of us deeper.

Harper's darkened eyes lift to mine. She replaces my hand with hers and strokes while she sucks.

I can't take it anymore and come hard down her throat. She takes it all. When I withdraw, she swallows as she meets my gaze. Her dark eyes are still lust-filled as Caden continues to thrust his finger into her. Her hips follow the motion of his hand.

As I move away, Luke steps past me. His cock out, hard and throbbing. I settle back on the couch and watch as Harper takes him into her mouth. I could watch her give head all day every day. But I also can play with her body, so I lift her shirt until her breast is exposed and lean in to suck her nipple into my mouth.

She moans around Luke's dick and her hips follow Caden's thrusts. She arches into me, thrusting more of her breast into my mouth.

"Suck it harder, Jack. She feels it all the way in her pussy, don't you, little nympho?"

She's not going to answer with Luke's cock driving into her mouth. But I can feel all that beautiful tension in her body as she climbs toward release. I slip my hand over her clit. My fingers tangle with Caden's and she moans again.

She's dripping wet and on the edge.

I slide to the floor between Caden's legs and lean forward to swipe my tongue against her clit. She moans hard and I suck on her the way she sucked on me, drawing her clit into my mouth. She tastes fantastic.

"Fuck," Luke cries out as he comes down her throat.

When she comes off him, she moans loudly as my mouth and

Caden's fingers drive her over the edge. I lick her gently, easing her down from her climax. Her hand finds my hair and tugs me up until our lips collide.

She tastes like Luke's and my cum, and I'm sure she can taste herself on my tongue as we kiss like we can't get enough of the taste of each other. Fuck if that's not hot enough to get me hard again. This girl. I draw away from her. Her warm eyes follow me as I sit beside her. My hands stroke over my hard-on, and her eyes don't leave it.

She licks her lips like she's remembering how I felt in her mouth. I groan.

Caden pulls down her shirt and turns her to straddle him. He claims her mouth in a kiss that has me feeling like he's kissing me and her together, knowing he's tasting both of us. My balls tighten and I explode without warning all over my hand.

I lean my head back against the couch. Harper Davidson. Fuck me. There's no one else like her. I can't wait for her to be mine.

CHAPTER 6

Pestilence

I wake up to Harper coming. Caden turns our girl around to kiss her. My gaze strays to Nico, sitting beside Caden. We appear to be the only two excluded from this round.

Fuck that.

I give him a nod. He glances at Harper. Dude has it bad for our girl. I can't imagine wanting a girl, and coming home to find your four friends already training her to take them all.

It could have been messy if he decided against joining us. It'll probably be messier with him in if he feels protective of her.

"Come on, kitten, let's get you cleaned up." I cross over to lift Harper from Caden's arms. Reluctantly, he passes her to me with a feral look and a low growl. Fuck him. He got his earlier.

Harper turns in my arms and wraps herself around me. Her head rests on my shoulder as I hold her ass in my hands. I hope she isn't too sleepy. I gesture with my head for Nico to come with us as I walk to the bathroom.

"Did that feel good, kitten?" I set her on the sink and press a kiss to her forehead.

Nico closes the door behind us and leans in to start the shower. We're a unit. It's what makes us a force to be reckoned with on the football field. We almost know what the other is thinking without actually saying the words. At summer football camp, we played as a team, but Nico always had to return to New York. We got by without him during the season, but I'm glad he's back.

"Yes." Harper licks her lips as she watches me. I untie the ribbons on her braids and undo them. As I run my fingers through her hair, she leans into my hands.

Nico hands her a glass of water. Her dark eyes flick to him as she drinks. This girl could break all of us if we aren't careful. It doesn't make me want her any less.

"Thank you," she says, setting the glass down and putting her hands beside her hips on the counter.

I love her submission almost as much as I love her fight. I undo her collar and take off her shirt, leaving her naked on the counter.

"Spread your legs."

Harper takes a quick breath and does as I ask. I lean back against the door and study her pussy. She's bare. This is so much better than on camera. Her flush starts at her breasts and works its way up her neck to her cheeks.

"Are you sore?" I ask, curious. She's not used to having fingers inside her pussy. It won't stop me, but I want to know.

She shakes her head.

Stepping between her legs, I lift my hands to rub at her jaw in circular motions at the joints. "How about here?"

Her breath hitches, but she shakes her head again.

"Good. Shower first, I think." I strip off my pants and so does Nico.

I help Harper off the counter and lead her into the shower, which is big enough for all six of us. With two shower heads and a rain head, the shower is perfect to share. If the guys don't mind grazing each other. But we're all comfortable with each other.

Especially with a naked Harper between us. This situation is different from any other girl I've been with. There's this need to take care of her. To pamper her. To keep her.

Warm water flows over us.

Nico moves in behind Harper. "How are you feeling, sunshine?"

She leans her head back against him and closes her eyes.

"A little tired, but not too tired." Her eyes open. No hint of fear or worry about being naked with two men in the prime of their lives. I smile, loving that trust, but missing the fear.

I hand the shampoo to Nico and take the body wash for myself. Together we work on cleaning our girl. My hands slip down her arms and over her breasts, leaving trails of bubbles in my wake.

She releases a soft moan as Nico lathers the shampoo in her hair, and I spend a little extra time exploring her hard, tight nipples until she thrusts her chest into my hands, looking for more. We rinse the shampoo, and I hand the conditioner to Nico.

When I pour more soap into my hand, Harper holds out her hand and cocks an eyebrow. Smiling, I add soap to her palm. As I work it into a lather over her hips and stomach, Harper runs her soap-covered hands over my shoulders and down my arms, across my chest and abs.

As the water washes away the suds, she kisses my chest and trails her tongue over to my nipple. Heat pumps through me and my cock strains against her stomach.

I lower my hand between her thighs and slide my fingers between her pussy lips, feeling her swollen clit. Her moan reverberates against my chest. Nico draws her back into the shower to rinse her hair. I make sure all the soap is off her pussy. Then I drop to my knees before her and lift her leg over my shoulder.

I give her a wicked grin before I lean forward and suck her clit into my mouth. Her moan fills the bathroom. She leans against Nico as he kisses her neck. I went down on her once already tonight, but was limited in time. I plan on taking my time now as I explore her thoroughly with my tongue, teeth, and lips. Noting every gasp, moan, and catch in her breath.

My gaze remains on hers, and she watches me with her dark, fathomless eyes. Her lips part. Nico reaches around her to cup her breasts, teasing her nipples between his fingers. Her skin is so pale against his.

When I dip my tongue inside her, she grabs my hair. Even though I'm tempted to ask Nico to take her hands, she's not pulling me away, and with what I want to do to her, I'll allow it this time.

Using my hands, I part her pussy lips and stroke my tongue along her clit before plunging it inside her wet cunt. I do this over and over again until she's grinding against my face and tugging on my hair.

"Eli, please." My name slips out of her lips before Nico captures them.

My pretty kitty is all flushed with arousal, and it won't take much to drive her over the edge. This time, I'll let her come. Next time, I'll draw it out, keep her right there at the peak until she's a mess in my arms and begging for more.

I drag my tongue up to her clit and flick it as I drive two fingers into her pussy.

She cries out as she shatters around my fingers. Nico tweaks her nipples and her orgasm crashes through her.

I stand with my fingers still buried inside her dripping cunt and take her mouth, letting her taste how sweet her arousal is. She meets my tongue greedily with her own. Lifting my mouth from hers, I withdraw my fingers from her pussy and suck her sweet juices off them.

"Down on your knees, kitten."

She sinks to her knees and leans in to lick my cock while staring up into my eyes. I stroke my hand over her hair as she turns and does the same to Nico. When she comes back to me, I tighten my hand in her hair and tug her head back.

A trickle of fear bleeds into her eyes at the pain, making me harder.

"Use your hands."

Harper lifts her hands to my cock and starts stroking. Her eyes still on me.

"Don't leave Nico out, kitten."

She reaches her other hand to him and strokes both of our cocks.

I bring her face to my cock. "Lick the tips."

Her tongue licks my slit, gathering the precum that leaked out. She swallows it like a good kitten and then leans in to lick the head of my cock. When she tries to suck it into her mouth, I pull her head back, and she glares at me.

A rush of lust burns through my veins at that defiant look. I'll enjoy getting her to do what I want.

"You have two masters right now, kitten."

She turns and does the same to Nico. His hand strokes down her cheek as he watches her work the tip of his cock. Once again, she tries to suck on it and I pull her away.

She squeezes my cock a little harder as she works her hand down it. Fuck that feels good.

"I want to fuck your face, kitten."

Her hand pauses as she squirms on her knees. Her eyes light up. She likes that idea.

"Here are the rules: we decide how deep you take us in your pretty mouth. You can use your tongue when you can. Keep stroking our cocks. You'll swallow every bit of cum we give you. If you disobey, you'll be punished."

Her eyes narrow at the punished part. Good.

"If you need me to stop, snap your fingers. If you do anything else, I won't stop. Do you understand, kitten?"

"Yes." There's still that spark of anger in her eyes, but a little hint of fear too. I do like an angry kitten. But her arousal is all I care about, and she wants this.

"Your punishment will be slaps to your pussy."

Her eyes widen as she probably remembers when Luke slapped her pussy.

"How do you make it all stop?"

She glares. "I snap my fingers."

"Good girl."

"I want to deal out the punishment." Nico bends down on his knee and kisses Harper deeply before he holds her chin. "I won't go easy on your pussy, sunshine, so behave. Don't worry, I'll kiss it better until you scream your release."

Before Harper can say anything, he captures her open mouth.

When he pulls back, her eyes search his.

"Kneeling?" he asks.

"Definitely." I drop to my knees on the other side of her. She glances at us confused.

Nico reaches out and tugs on her already tight nipples while I stroke between her legs to see how wet she already is. She gasps and moans as my fingers explore, stoking that fire inside her.

"She's soaked," I say to Nico over her head.

"I haven't gotten a taste yet."

Her hot eyes find Nico, and I can see the want in them.

"On all fours. Face me," I command.

She hesitates. I tap her pussy, and she meets my eyes.

"Nico's going to suck your clit while I fuck your face." I slide my finger out from between her legs.

Without a word, she releases our cocks to get into position. Nico smacks her pussy. She cries out and jumps.

"What the hell?" She looks over her shoulder at him, and he smirks.

"No one said to let go of our cocks, sunshine."

"My bad." I chuckle. I worried about him, but Nico will be fun to play with our toy together.

"That's not fair." Harper glares.

"But it felt good, didn't it, kitten?"

Nico strokes his hand against her clit, rubbing the sting away. Her cheeks flush and her breath quickens. "Yes."

"You want to take us deep in your throat. Don't you?"

Nico pushes his finger into her cunt. She whimpers and nods.

"You'll need your hands to help stabilize yourself." I tighten my hand on her hair. "Open up, kitten."

When she opens wide, I guide my cock into her mouth again. She takes me in, and I guide her gently at first.

Nico lowers his mouth to her pussy and licks her.

She inhales sharply on my cock, and I go a little deeper, moving her up and down over me in a steady rhythm while Nico strokes his finger in and out of her at the same pace. His tongue slides over her clit and he sucks on it.

Her breasts sway and her hips push back against him.

Moaning, she draws my dick in farther and drags her tongue on the underside as I pull out. I won't last long and I don't want to, because as soon as we both come, she'll be mine to torment while Nico fucks her mouth.

Nico pulls his finger from her pussy and circles her asshole with it. She jerks forward away from his teasing finger, taking more of my cock into her throat. He thrusts his tongue into her pussy as he dips his finger into her puckered hole.

Harper whimpers on my cock, and I ease her back so I'm not as deep. Her tongue circles me and she sucks while making noises in the back of her throat that shoot straight through me. Nico fucks her cunt with his tongue while his finger glides in and out of her ass.

The visual is too much for me. When I push my cock deep in her throat again, she moans around me as we come together. I lift her off me and claim her mouth as she's still swallowing me down. Drawing her tight against my body, I love how her wet curves fit against me.

My cum makes her naturally sweet taste a little saltier. My cock begins to swell between us. I tighten my fingers in her hair and bite lightly on her lip.

When her lips open wider, I take advantage, claiming every inch.

Nico withdraws and I see him wash his hands with soap. The still warm water falls all around us.

"Hands and knees, sunshine." Nico moves on his knees and sits back on his heels.

Harper turns around and looks over her shoulder back at me. I give her a wicked smile while I lick my lips. I'm ready for another taste.

CHAPTER 7

The Logistics

HARPER

At the look in Eli's dark eyes, a little thrill of fear rushes through me along with the desire that has been flooding my veins. Everything they do makes me crave more.

When I turn back to Nico, he captures my mouth with his. His kiss aims to destroy the last of my defenses. It creeps into my blood like he never left me. As if this was always inevitable. Threading his fingers through my hair, he gathers the wet strands, wrapping them around his hand.

"You ready, sunshine?"

A little nervous, I swallow and nod, growing wetter with the thought of what's about to happen. I can't wait to taste him again. He lowers my head to his cock, and I open my mouth to let him slip inside, feeling his smooth skin against my tongue.

Eli grabs my hips and raises them. Stiffening, I feel horribly exposed and know if he really wanted to, Eli could take my virginity. I might have a moment to react, but it wouldn't take much to just thrust inside and be done with the whole thing.

He may have just come, but I've seen him recover quickly. I have to trust he won't. I have to trust they'll keep their word and let me choose when and where and how. Even though I'm really enjoying tonight and making up for all the orgasms I missed out on, I'm not quite ready to go that far.

I'm not ready to give them everything.

Instead, I focus on the feel of Nico's cock against my tongue. All the guys taste a little different, and each of their cocks are different in size, both length and width. Eli is a little longer, but Nico is a little wider, filling my mouth.

Eli massages my ass cheeks, lightly digging into the muscles. His breath is hot on my skin. I relax, expecting him to go down on me, anticipating his tongue on my pussy.

Nico keeps my head moving over his tip, pressing in and out of my lips. I'm sucking on him like a lollipop, rolling my tongue over the head of his cock, when Eli's teeth scrape along one of my ass cheeks. I startle away from Eli, taking more of Nico into my mouth. Eli's mouth stays hot against my skin, undeterred by my movement.

He trails his hand from my hip until his fingers skim over my pussy, and he rubs circles around my clit, making my whole body buzz. I hum around Nico's cock. Nico groans and drags me up and down over him. While Eli kisses and teases my ass cheeks with his teeth, his fingers slide inside my pussy briefly, pressing in and out until my hips rock, seeking his fingers, wanting them deeper.

Knowing he could push me to the verge of climax again. Craving that blissful euphoria that comes with an orgasm. However, I can't quite relax with him behind me. His tongue on my ass cheek keeps me on edge, not sure what he'll do next.

Distracting me, Nico bobs my head back and forth on his cock a little faster, pushing farther into my mouth and into my throat. I grab his thighs to steady myself.

Eli's hands spread my ass cheeks and, before I can register what he's about to do, his tongue flicks over my asshole. My heartbeat goes wild. I try to push off Nico, but he holds me still. His cock twitches in my mouth.

I can't get away from either of them. Eli holds my hips in place and his tongue flattens over my puckered hole. Heat pours through me. Nothing I've read could have prepared me for this.

Yes, blow jobs and cunnilingus, even a little anal sex in some of the romance novels I've read, but rimming? Not really. I'm having an eye-opening experience I wasn't expecting tonight. Or at all.

"Just relax, Harper," Nico says in an easy voice meant to calm me down, but Eli's tongue rims my puckered hole, making me not feel calm at all. Nico pulls me off his cock and lifts my head to look at him.

I draw in a breath. Eli flicks his tongue over my asshole again as he massages my ass cheeks. Nico smiles and his dark eyes draw me in.

"It's not like you haven't already had my finger in your ass. You liked it, sunshine. I could feel you pushing back to get more of it in you. This is just like that. Eli is going to make it feel better. It feels good, doesn't it?"

Eli chuckles as his mouth moves down to lavish attention to the sensitive skin between my asshole and pussy. My whole body feels like it's on fire, and I'm not sure if it's from embarrassment or desire. Then his mouth finds my asshole again. Sparks flood my veins and molten fire pools low in my stomach.

Nico's gaze goes to where Eli is. "Just imagine, sunshine. I could have my mouth on your pussy while Eli worships your hole. We could make you feel so good before you explode all over us."

My pussy clenches, empty, desperate for attention. Eli kisses and licks my puckered hole, spreading my ass cheeks apart to get at it. It feels naughty and wrong, but also kind of good. As much as I want to pull away, I don't want Eli to stop. My whole body buzzes with lust.

"Okay, time to play. You good?" Nico tips his gaze back to mine.

I swallow, but nod. I could snap if I want this to end. They did give me an out.

"Good girl." Nico guides my mouth back on his cock, making me take him all the way until my throat tightens and I swallow. At that same moment, Eli thrusts his tongue into my hole.

I moan at the sensation. All those nerves ping at once, sending an overload error to my brain.

"She needs more," Nico happily points out. He draws me back, but keeps me almost fully on his cock as he thrusts in and out of my throat. Tears leak out of my eyes, but it feels so fucking good. It makes me even wetter.

Eli's hand slips between my legs and his fingers glide against my clit, rubbing me, taking me higher. Until he thrusts two fingers deep inside my pussy at the same time he thrusts his tongue into my hole.

I moan, widening my legs for Eli. He could do anything to me right now, and as long as I get to come, I think I'd be all right with it.

The guys find a rhythm and soon, I'm rocking with them, taking Nico's cock in my mouth and Eli's fingers in my pussy and his tongue in my ass. Nico reaches down to tug on my nipples, and my body explodes into liquid sensation, shattering around them. The waves grab hold of me and toss me about as I convulse around Eli's fingers.

Every swipe of Eli's tongue feels like too much, like I'm on a live wire and can't let go. I moan through it.

"Fuck, Harper. That feels so fucking good." Groaning, Nico releases his cum into my throat. I swallow everything I can. Pulling my mouth off his cock, he keeps me in the same position with my head down and my ass up as Eli continues to work my overwrought body.

I lean my face against Nico's thigh as I breathe heavily, still rolling through the waves.

"One more time, kitten. I want to hear you scream." Eli thrusts his tongue into my asshole and his fingers fuck in and out of my pussy. Nico squeezes my nipple and reaches down to my clit with his other hand. He presses in time with Eli's thrusts.

White hot heat spreads through me as my body convulses around the intrusions in it. The sensations build inside me until they have to get out. The pressure is too much. Screaming, I come harder than I have before. My hands tighten on Nico's thighs and I'm sure my fingernails draw blood, but I'm beyond caring.

I shake as the waves slowly die down. My throat feels raw from the screaming.

Eli removes his fingers and mouth from my body, and Nico drags me into his arms. I sit on his lap with my arms around his neck, my face in his shoulder as he cradles me against him.

I become aware of our surroundings slowly. The water flows warm around us. I'm amazed it hasn't gone cold after all this time. Nico's hand rubs up and down my back as my breathing returns to normal. Even though awareness of my naked body against Nico's thrills through me, I'm so worn out.

Eli sits next to him, their backs against the tiled wall of the shower. Eli strokes his hand over my hair, rubbing my scalp where it's a little sore from the pulling.

"You okay, kitten?" Eli reaches out and takes one of my hands.

I meet his dark eyes and see the warmth in them. I squeeze his hand. "A little overwhelmed, but okay."

I'm done though. I feel like my body has been through the wringer. The guys cuddle me for a few more minutes before we all stand and wash off once again. Nico folds me in a fluffy towel, helping me dry off.

Eli walks out into Caden's room. He comes back with a t-shirt. It's huge so it must be Caden's, but this one smells like fresh laundry instead of Caden's cinnamon scent.

He also has my panties with him. I pull on the t-shirt and panties, and the guys wear their boxers. Nico wraps an arm around my waist, and I rest my head against his shoulder.

"Thank you, sunshine."

I glance up into his dark, smiling eyes. This is a really weird situation. He just came back to town and suddenly he was part of this. One of mine. I can't process any of it, so I just give him a smile as he leans down and kisses me softly. This time I like the softness, the comfort. Nico feels like childhood and summer vacations and sleepovers in a tent in the backyard.

Safe.

After I brush my teeth, we all head out to Caden's bedroom.

The rest of the guys are all in their boxers.

"You tired, princess?" Luke stops in front of me and tips my chin up. I'm almost immune to all the hot man flesh around me, but not even close to immune at the same time. My lady bits get a little excited, but even they're down for the count.

For a second, I search Luke's usually frozen eyes. He chose me. And gave me all these men for my own. He took me from invisible to being theirs.

I step into Luke and wrap my arms around his waist, resting my head against his heart. It pounds a little quicker beneath my ear as he wraps his arms around me and places a kiss on my hair. I don't know why I'm seeking comfort from Death, but I just want to be held.

"How's this going to work?" I lift my head to look up at Luke. He's our leader after all. "The sleeping bit of the night, because I need a good nine hours to recover."

His pale blue eyes look a little warmer as he smiles. "Caden's bed is big enough for whoever wants to sleep with you."

I glance around at all my guys. I can't think of them as anything but that tonight. Maybe tomorrow I'll fight some more for my virginity, but tonight I don't have to. All of us should be satisfied enough to sleep without fear of being manhandled in the night.

I slip from Luke's arms, but take his hand as I head to the bed Caden is already on. Caden grins at me and holds his hand out. I drop Luke's hand and crawl onto the bed until I'm next to Caden.

"Well, come on." I meet each of their eyes again as I snuggle against Caden.

"I like you in my shirts, little nympho." Caden wraps his arm around me.

"I like her in nothing at all." Luke moves onto the bed behind me and lies on his back with his hands behind his head.

Jack, Nico, and Eli all find spots on the bed as well. I catch hints of all of their scents. Apple, cinnamon, outdoors, rain, and sultry cologne.

And the warmth. I doubt I'll even need covers with all their heat around me.

"So is this going to be an every weekend thing?" Nico asks through a yawn. "Sleepovers at Caden's?"

"I don't see a problem with that." Caden holds me tighter. "As long as Harper is here."

Not sure what my mom will think of that. But that's something to worry about tomorrow. My eyelids are heavy as Luke wraps his arm around my waist and spoons me from behind, just like he did in my bed. I snuggle my cheek against Caden's bare chest and listen to the steady beat of his heart.

"Harper does belong to us." Luke's voice barely penetrates the fog settling in my brain. "She should always be with us."

I fall asleep to murmurs of agreement and, for a second, I let myself believe they'll always want me.

CHAPTER 8

The Reveille

HARPER

Hot and achy, I awake aroused with a head between my legs. My panties are missing, and Luke thrusts his tongue inside me. His hands hold my thighs apart. My whole body buzzes with electricity and fire scorches through my veins. I'm dripping wet.

Caden lifts my shirt and his mouth closes around my breast, sucking, devouring, tugging like a string is tied from my nipple to my pussy.

Jack takes advantage of the access to my naked body. Instead of sucking my breast into his mouth, his tongue swirls around my hardened tip.

My brain hasn't even started yet. All I can do is feel. And these guys make me feel good.

"Good morning, kitten."

My gaze finds Eli as I pant in aching need.

"Move her down on the bed," Eli instructs.

Luke drags me to the edge of the bed as he sinks to the floor and dives back into tongue fucking me, while I squirm with the need for release. Caden rubs my clit and growls as he sucks my nipple. The vibration racks through me, pushing me even higher.

Eli lies beside my head, removes my shirt from my neck, and kisses me upside down. Claiming my mouth with his in a battle of wills I'm not strong enough to defeat. I surrender to his kiss and he softens it.

Nico's hand slides under my ass. It feels slick as he circles my asshole and presses his finger inside easily. Lube.

As if they're one, the guys fall into a steady pace while Eli's tongue fights with mine for dominance.

Jack plays with my hand and my waist, while he teases and tortures my nipple with his tongue. I'm melting beneath them. Caden holds my other hand down on the bed. He torments my clit with pressure and tight circles while his mouth devours my other breast. Being held down, helpless to do anything but feel the pleasure they're giving me, makes my insides burn hotter than before. Luke holds my legs wide as his tongue penetrates me over and over.

Nico kisses my stomach, teasing my bellybutton with his tongue. He presses another finger into my asshole, moving them in and out with the same pace as Luke's tongue. I writhe beneath them, lost in the pleasure.

Winding me tighter and tighter. Maybe with one guy it would be just as stimulating but less overwhelming. Of course, I've only made out with Luke alone, and he's always overwhelming.

The string within me tightens before snapping. I arch into them as I cry out my release. My pussy gushes on Luke's tongue and my ass tightens around Nico's fingers.

They all slow down and remove themselves from me. Eli kisses me before edging off the bed. Caden moves up and kisses me possessively before heading off to his bathroom. My breath hitches. Jack cradles my face as he claims my lips.

"Good morning, sweetheart."

I try to smile at him as he moves away. Nico presses his lips to mine briefly before resting his forehead against mine.

"Thank you, sunshine."

When he leaves, Luke moves up over me. I have no strength to fight him, not that I want to. He lifts me and positions me like I'm a doll until I straddle his lap. He has on his boxers. My hands hold the back of his neck as I search his light blue eyes. My nipples rub his chest.

That craving starts deep inside again. Will I ever get enough of them?

"Technically still a virgin." He smirks as his thumb skims my jawline.

"Technically," I agree. It's barely been two weeks since the guys decided I'm theirs. They've blown through almost all my boundaries, not that I put up much of a fight.

He leans in and takes my mouth. His lips gentle against mine as he draws me closer. I'm likely soaking his boxers, the only barrier between us, as his hard cock presses against me intimately. He lifts his head and his thumb drags along my lip.

"Did you enjoy last night, princess?"

"I don't think I've processed last night." My body feels a little achy and sore. I definitely need a toothbrush or some mouthwash. But last night became a blur, moving from one searing moment to the next, almost like the closet.

Fuck, was that all yesterday? I feel like it's been a lifetime, but it's all happening so quick.

"Do you like us going down on you?"

My naked back is to the rest of the room, so the only horseman I can focus on is Luke. I don't even know if any of the others are still here. My fingers play with the ends of his blond hair.

"Yes." I would assume my orgasms would be answer enough to that.

"What about giving us head?" That makes me blush and I try to lower my face, but Luke's finger tips my chin back up. "This only works if we're honest with each other."

Whatever *this* is, it's just about sex. Did I feel an emotional connection to the guys during all of it? Yes, but I need that to be part of it, even if they don't feel the same. There's definitely an attraction between all of us, but my heart isn't just quickening in fear anymore. I'm starting to look forward to seeing them, to touching them, to feeling them touch me.

But that's not part of what we have.

Hardening my lips, I lock on his eyes. "Yes, I enjoyed sucking your cock."

His eyes spark at the hint of defiance in my tone. His fingers wrap lightly around my neck. "Swallowing?"

Fuck, he wants to know everything this morning. "Even that."

"Our fingers in your pussy? And in your ass?"

Heat floods through me. Even I can smell my arousal growing again. "Yes," I say a little quieter.

Keeping a grip on my neck, he slides his other fingers through my wetness to sink into my pussy. I gasp and can't help but move a little on his hand, needing more. The friction I know he'll give me.

"You're so wet for me, princess." He presses his lips to my ear and whispers, "I could sink my cock into your greedy cunt right now. It would feel so good. So much better than my fingers. So much fuller and deeper."

My eyes slide shut. His voice is like an aphrodisiac to me now. His fingers almost pull all the way out of me. I can't contain my whimper.

Adding another finger, he presses three fingers inside me, and the fullness takes a moment to adjust to. But it feels so fucking good, I want to ride his hand until I come again. His hand remains still in me.

"You want to fuck my cock, princess?"

His words make me wetter, and I know he knows that. My fingertips curl into his neck as he slides his fingers easily in and out of me. My hips rock, needing more, needing all of him. Part of me wants to give in so badly. To tell him to do it. Fuck me.

But I also know giving in fully would be the beginning of the end.

They only want me for my virginity. For that barrier inside me that means no one else was there before them.

Sure, they may keep me around for a while as a novelty. The woman who will let them all fuck her at the same time. The woman who is only theirs. But the entire year?

How long will that last before someone gets bored? Five guys to keep entertained with only one of me. How long before someone decides I'm not worth it, and then how long until they all leave me to find someone new to torment, to teach, to fuck?

I may be the last virgin in the senior class, but I'm not the last virgin in the school.

He leans back to look into my eyes, and whatever he sees there doesn't make him happy. He captures my lips with his, trying to claim my soul, and rolls me onto my back on the bed with his fingers still inside me.

My mind stops focusing on what ifs. I'm so close to the edge. My body wants this. It wants him. His thumb presses down on my clit, and the whole room bursts into stars as I topple over the edge.

He eases me through my orgasm and lightens his kiss. When he pulls his fingers out of me, I whimper at the emptiness.

"Time to get ready for the day, princess." He lifts off me, leaving me naked in the middle of the bed. I lie there staring up at the ceiling. I'm so fucked.

A door shuts, and I figure I'm alone.

I reach over and snag the t-shirt Eli removed from me and slip it on over my head. I glance around for my panties, but don't see them.

The guys have all disappeared, except for Caden. He sits on the couch, watching me. He put on a black t-shirt and a pair of silk athletic shorts. His dark hair is slicked back. He's beautiful and rough.

Did he watch Luke finger fuck me?

That's part of this. Them all taking turns watching each other with me. It shouldn't make my insides burn and crave more, but it does.

Taking a breath, I walk over to stand in front of him. "Is there a bathroom I can use?"

"You can use mine, little nympho."

I glance at the door. "Didn't—"

"Luke went to use the bathroom across the hall. We figured you might like some time alone this morning." His hand reaches out to brush my thigh. "I know Luke checked in with you, but are you doing okay?"

I feel tears well at the concern in his voice. God, I'm being stupid. These boys don't feel anything but lust for me. I'm just a very convenient hole to them. And I've let them use me however they want to.

"Hey." His soft tone brings more tears surging forward. He pulls me down to straddle his lap and cups my face in his giant hands. "It's a lot. We're a lot."

His green eyes stare into mine as tears drift down my cheeks. His thumb brushes them away.

"It's okay to feel overwhelmed, Harper. We've pushed you pretty far fast." The corner of his mouth tips up. "Not that I regret a minute of it."

I try to take a shuddering breath in and hold back the tears. I don't want them to see me like this. Vulnerable.

But the softness in his gaze undoes me. I collapse on him. His arms wrap around me, and I tighten my arms around his neck as I press my face against his shoulder. Quiet sobs rack my body.

His hand strokes up and down my back and he makes a soothing noise. "You're so strong, Harper. You may not think it, but you've taken everything we've thrown at you. You may not have wanted to play those games with us, but you didn't let that stop you from taking your pleasure from them."

The tears keep falling and I can't seem to stop them, especially with Caden of all people being kind to me. He's not the tough enforcer I thought I knew. He was a dick a few times, but he's softened to me since we've gotten to know each other.

"Let it all out," he says, rubbing my back in circles. "Get it out so you can come back a little fiercer for the next round."

I want to laugh. How can I be stronger if I'm falling to pieces? I don't know how to deal with four... now five horsemen. My body isn't built for this. It isn't ready for what they want to do or what they're already doing to it. I want to go home and hide under my covers for the rest of the year. But I also don't want to lose this attention. The feelings they stir beneath my skin. The pleasure they coax from my being.

"Come on, little nympho." As he moves to stand, I wrap my legs around his waist to continue to cling to him. "Let's get you ready for the day."

CHAPTER 9

The Jealousy

After showering and jerking off with the taste of Harper still in my mouth, I return to Caden's room. I find Nico, Eli, and Jack sitting on the couch, the TV playing low while they watch a highlights reel from a college football game.

Everyone wears the clothes they wore to the party.

I'm surprised Caden isn't here. The shower is on in the bathroom, but there's no other noise coming from there.

"Where's Harper and Caden?"

Eli jerks his head to the bathroom door. "As far as we know."

Clenching my fists, I want to barge in and find out what's happening. But I have no right to be jealous. He has as much right to be with her as I do. But she riles me up, and I don't understand it. I'm possessive of her, but also enjoy watching my brothers get her off.

That doesn't stop the licks of jealousy that burn across my chest. I want more of her. I can't explain it.

She and Caden seem to connect on a different level. Maybe she likes him more. She's brought him sandwiches every day since he stole hers. At lunch she sits on his lap. She even admitted her mom would like him best.

Over me.

Caden's one of my best friends, and I still can't help to ask *why him*.

I sit in the chair and try to calm myself. Try to tell myself it doesn't matter. This whole thing is about us owning Harper. That means we all share her. And eventually that will include spending time alone with her.

"So why Harper?" Nico's question draws me out of my obsession.

"She's the last." I note the flinch in Nico's eyes. It was a strategic move to bring him in. To let Harper believe she has a friend on the inside. To make sure Nico doesn't undermine our progress. He wants her as much as the rest of us do. It's plain to see and I can't blame him.

Nico narrows his eyes and his words are a little bitter as he tosses them out. "It could have been any girl then?"

"Harper is unique. She's never kissed anyone before us. Never had anyone else touch her. She is completely ours, unlike every other girl in our high school." I temple my fingers before my lips as I watch him react to my statements. I haven't forgotten he said he returned for her.

"She's not a sex toy." No emotion tinges his words this time. His tone is casual. Nico crosses his ankle over his knee. He's trying a new tack.

"We never claimed she was." I lower my hands and raise an eyebrow. "We own her for the year. The entire school year. She will only belong to us and fuck us during that time."

"And after?" Nico's voice is a little tight. He wants Harper to himself, but he never kept in touch with her. If he had, would she have claimed a long-distance boyfriend? Would he have found a way to see her? To claim her as his own?

My insides boil at the thought of him taking what's mine.

"I'm curious. If you still want Harper after all these years, why didn't you keep in touch with her?" I lean back in my chair, letting the fire ease from me. She's mine now. That's all that matters.

"When I left, I was twelve years old and didn't really think about keeping in touch. I didn't think we'd ever come back." Nico's gaze takes on a far-off look. "Honestly, I didn't expect to find Harper free. But I also didn't think you guys would *own* her." His eyes refocus on me. "What the hell happened after I left?"

"We took our rightful place as leaders of the pack." I straighten my shoulders and sit a little taller. "We were the most popular, the most desirable, and the most unattainable."

"We threw the best parties and fucked the most girls," Eli adds. "We dominated in sports. It didn't take much for us to become legends."

"The virgin stuff happened by accident." Jack rests his elbows on his knees and grins. "Caden's closet saw more action than we ever did. Kylie Elias thought she could lose her virginity to all of us, separately and we wouldn't figure her lies out. Too many girls took that shit too seriously. But then it became a thing, losing your virginity to a horseman."

"They either came to us, or we wore them down until they couldn't help but give in to us." Eli rubs the back of his neck and glances toward the bathroom. "Most girls are easy to convince. They've already done stuff. It's just taking them to the next level."

"But Harper—" I stop. I don't even know where to begin with Harper. I wasn't lying when I called her a freaking unicorn. "We've been working through our class since eighth grade. This summer the remaining girls either lost it to one or two of us or someone else, until only Harper remained."

"It was unlucky for her then?" Nico's mouth sets in a firm line. Fuck, if I had it bad for a girl and came back for her to find her being tag teamed by a bunch of dudes, even my friends, I'd be mad too.

"Yes, she's the last, but she's not like the other girls in our class." My eyes are drawn to the door where the shower is now off. "We created her. Our rule made her hide herself away from everyone. She submitted to us, but not because she wanted to. Instead of crying and begging, she got angry. She defies us when she can."

My lips twist up into a smile thinking about her defiance. The way she makes me feel inside is unexplainable, undefinable. I need to possess her. Control her. I want her to defy me and submit to me in the same breath. I want her to give in to me fully, completely.

I'm obsessed with her.

No, she's not like other girls. She responds naturally and beautifully to our touch. She's not shy about exploring and doesn't stifle the noises she makes when she's worked up. Not embarrassed of her sexuality, she owns it and she's curious as hell about it too.

Nico nods. "As long as you don't hurt her, I'm all in."

My insides tense at his promise. The threat those words imply.

"But if you hurt her…" Nico lets it hang in the air around us.

I nod in acceptance of his threat, but have one of my own. "If you try to take her away from us…"

He may not know us as well now, but he knows who we became the day we all decided to become the horsemen. At the time, Apocalypse was our leader, but when he left, as Death, I took over. I won't back down to him now.

Our eyes meet and he nods in acknowledgment. If I hurt her or if he tries to take her from us, we'll no longer be brothers. We'll be at war.

HARPER

Caden hands me a toothbrush and toothpaste. The tears finally dried up, but he continued to take care of me. He started my shower. While I showered, he sat on the toilet seat and talked about his cook and what a pretentious dick the guy is. He wouldn't even make Caden a peanut butter and jelly sandwich when he was eight, because in the cook's words, "It's too lowbrow."

What fucker wouldn't make a kid a peanut butter and jelly sandwich? That's pretty shitty.

Caden handed me a towel when I stepped out. He hasn't touched me the entire time. Just handed me my panties, bra, jeans, and one of his oversized t-shirts. And of course, my collar courtesy of Eli. I feel like a little kid swimming in his t-shirt while I brush my teeth with him watching.

After I rinse and wipe my mouth, Caden asks, "Doing better?"

I glance at my reflection. My eyes are still a little red around the edges. I don't have any makeup with me to cover anything. Including the still healing hickeys.

I don't feel the same as yesterday morning. But I guess that's just part of growing up. And being in a quasi-relationship with five guys.

"I'm fine." Moving to stand in front of Caden, I run my hand through his dark hair. Tugging his head back, I look into his green eyes. "Thank you for taking care of me."

His arms drape around my waist, holding me loosely. He gives me a small smile. "You take care of me. I figure it's only fair to take care of you."

I lean down and press a kiss to his lips before I back away and take a breath. Time to face the others.

Caden stands and opens the bathroom door, leading the way out. The guys all look over at me.

"What's the plan for today?" I stop myself from fidgeting.

"First thing is to get you out of those clothes." Luke's discerning eyes runs over me with a frown on his lips.

I almost shuffle backward. "Excuse me?"

Luke smirks as he meets my eyes. "You need to go to your place so you can change."

"We need to check the basement for strays first." Caden grabs his socks and shoes and sits in a chair to put them on.

"Strays?" I sit on the couch between Nico and Eli. Nico gives me a warm smile and I almost blush, remembering what happened last night and this morning. He and I went from zero to sixty in a few hours. Yeah, I didn't really process anything while in the shower. I'm not sure if I can.

"People who overstay their welcome." Luke rises and holds his hand out to me.

I take it without hesitation, and he smiles that evil smile of his. I'm beginning to trust them more. I don't really have a choice. Public humiliation or give in to the pleasure they offer me? That's easy.

If last night is any indication of what giving in feels like, I'm all for it.

"Whether they got too drunk to drive or found a place to fuck, we need to get them out before the cleaning staff arrives." Caden nods toward the door.

We head back the way we came last night. At least, I'm pretty sure this is the same way. I couldn't tell you how to get to the basement or Caden's room any more than if they had blindfolded me before leading me. This place is a maze.

Luke holds me back as the others go in.

Various sounds of *hey* and *what* come from the room. Along with some grunts, whines, and groans about it being too early.

"Why aren't we in there helping?" I finally turn to look at Luke.

"What were you and Caden doing in the bathroom?" For a second, Luke sounds like a jealous boyfriend, but that can't be right. I mean, he's the one who came up with the games for us. He never claimed me for himself; he claimed me for the horsemen.

"Umm, he was making sure I was okay." I'm not about to tell Luke I was crying and Caden helped me get through it. I can't even explain what I was crying over. Probably just overwhelmed with everything.

"You like Caden." It's a statement. Not a question.

"Caden..." Well fuck, what do I say? Caden is nice to me sometimes. Other times he likes to boss me around or force me to do things. But sometimes, I feel protected with him. "I guess sometimes I like him and he's nice to me. Sometimes."

Luke's eyes narrow, as if he's trying to read extra meaning into what I'm saying.

I give up. Putting my hands on my hips, I close in on him until my chest bumps against his. My gaze holds his. "What do you really want to know, Luke? Do you want to know if he went down on me or if I went down on him? Do you need to know every single second of interaction between me and any of the guys, or just Caden?"

He grabs the tops of my arms and tips his head like he doesn't understand what he sees when he looks at me.

"All clear," Eli calls from the game room.

CHAPTER 10

Flanking

Luke doesn't answer me, of course.

Pressing his lips together, Luke turns me in his arms and walks me into the game room. Kenz and Brandon sit on the leather sectional. My mouth widens into a grin at the sight of her, and I forget all about Luke being a possessive asshole.

Walking over, I drop next to her on the couch. I raise an eyebrow and ask her suspiciously, "What are you two still doing here?"

"Taking advantage of their host," Caden bites out, but when I look at him, he's not angry. He's also not smiling, so I'm not sure how I know. If I'd seen that look last week, I would have thought he was angry. I shake my head and return my attention to Kenz.

"Actually, Luke said we should stay here, so I could give you a ride home this morning." Kenz shrugs. "So we found a quiet spot to be alone."

"Hope you used protection." Jack grins.

Kenz blushes, and Brandon grins back at Jack.

"So Kenz is taking me home. Then what?" I look to my keepers.

"We all have practice, kitten." Eli brushes his hand over my hair.

A few hours to myself? I don't know how to feel about that. Should I be happy because I'll be free from them? Or sad I can't be with them?

Or worried I'm getting Stockholm syndrome? Fuck.

"I might be able to hang out." Nico sits next to me on the couch with a grin.

"Not so fast, lover boy," Luke says. "You wanted to talk to Coach. No better time than the present."

Nico frowns and reluctantly nods. "You're right. I didn't drive though."

"I'll get you home and then you can follow me to practice." Jack holds out a hand to Nico and hauls him off the couch.

"Coach might not let me practice, so if that happens..." Nico takes out his cell phone and holds it out to me. "Put your number in, and I'll text you if I can see you earlier. So we can catch up."

My cheeks heat as I put my number in Nico's phone. He just returned yesterday, and I've already had his tongue between my legs and his dick in my mouth. I hope there aren't any more horsemen I don't know about.

Standing, I hand him back his phone. He leans in to give me a kiss.

Kenz's mouth drops open, but before she can say anything, Jack reels me in for a kiss of his own.

"Tonight is Sidney's party. Make sure you wear something hot, sweetheart. In fact, send me a selfie so I can approve your selection." Jack kisses me again before heading to the door.

"Until tonight." Eli grabs me and kisses me before heading out with Jack and Nico.

Kenz's mouth is still open. Yeah, she hasn't exactly seen the whole everyone kisses me show. And Nico kissing me and not getting punched will be a whole conversation after we drop off Brandon.

"Yo, Caden." Brandon stands. "Can you give me a lift to my house on the way to practice?"

"No problem." Caden steps in and brushes my hair out of my face before he gives me a small smile. "Behave, little nympho. I'd hate to have to punish you tonight."

My cheeks get hot thinking of all of them using their fingers to see how wet Luke's spanking made me last night. Before I can respond, Caden sweeps me into his arms and kisses the fuck out of me.

My knees buckle a little when he releases me, but I catch myself.

He gives me a knowing grin as Brandon kisses Kenz. Brandon and Caden leave us alone with Luke.

"I guess we should go then?" I gesture to Kenz and the door.

"MacKenzie?" Luke's tone is nice enough, but we both freeze.

"Um, yes?" Kenz glances at me and then at Luke and then back at me.

"Would you mind waiting outside for Harper?" He's already closing in on me, and I don't like the cold look in his eyes. I don't know if I want to be alone with Luke in his current mood.

That angry, jealous vibe still lingers in the air around him. My insides must have all the signals crossed because instead of fear, I'm excited.

"Yeah, sure." Kenz smiles and backs away. "I'll just warm up the car and wait for Harper out there."

The door shuts behind her, and I'm truly alone with Luke again. Just like that time in the car.

"Have you thought about it, princess?" He closes the distance until I'm breathing in his sultry scent.

"About what?" I wish I knew what he was talking about, but he makes my brain fuzzy when he's this close.

He brushes my hair behind my ear and smoothly transitions to gripping the back of my neck, but not hard. Instead of being alarmed like I should be, my muscles relax and heat pools low in my belly. He tips my face up so our eyes can lock.

His pale blue eyes used to seem so cold to me, but now I see the barely banked fire that always threatens to consume me. It makes me want to burn with him, for him.

He brings his lips down to hover above mine. My breath catches and everything inside me turns to mush. I can almost taste him. I arch into him slightly, trying to get closer.

"About fucking us?" he says against my lips.

Oof, that makes my insides buzz, but I'm not ready. I don't know when I'll be ready. If I ever am. I can't tell him all that.

"I'm not—"

Luke's lips claim mine, and he draws me into him as he opens his mouth over mine. Unable to resist, I part my lips. He consumes me with his lips and tongue and teeth. His hands cradle my ass, pressing me into his hard cock. A moan releases in my throat as my panties dampen at the feel of him.

I'm tempted to climb up him so I can get even closer. Wrap my legs around his waist so his cock will rub against me where I need it the most.

He lifts his mouth from mine and kisses his way to my ear. His dark voice wraps around me as he whispers, "Until you open up more, princess, we'll need you to work your magic."

Before I can ask what he means, he pushes me down to my knees. His hands work on unfastening his jeans in front of my face while I stare up at him.

"Here?" I glance around, but it's only him and me.

"Anywhere I want." Luke pulls his erection out of his pants and strokes it once.

That kiss has me locked in a haze of lust. My tongue darts out to moisten my lips. My heart pounds in my chest.

"Until I can fuck that pussy of yours, I'll fuck your face as often as I can." He grabs hold of my hair like Eli and Nico did. His words may be a threat, but I'm so wet and ready to take him in my mouth. "Open up, princess."

When I part my lips, he jerks me forward. His cock fills my mouth as he presses deep into my throat. I continue to keep my eyes on him as he uses my mouth. Kenz could come back in at any minute. The cleaners could arrive. But I keep my focus on Luke as I suck and lick when I can.

Some books I read talked about giving head and how the woman would always get aroused by it. I didn't understand that until last night. Maybe it's the act. The intimacy of having someone inside your mouth, or the fact it mimics what he wants to do to my pussy.

But I like it. I didn't have to lie to him about that. I loved it all last night, even if it pushed me to my limits.

His eyes remain on me, and that fire inside of him ignites within me too. I lift my hands to his ass to steady myself. The muscles are tight and ripple beneath my touch.

He thrusts forward and pulls me against him until my nose touches his abs. For a second I can't breathe, but I don't panic as Luke brings me back a little. I breathe in through my nose and swallow around the head of his cock.

When I lift my gaze to his, his eyes hold mine. Luke's lips part, and I see the moment pleasure takes him. Power courses through me as he groans and comes. I swallow as much as I can as he holds me there. He pulls me off him and yanks me to my feet.

"Your mouth is divine, but I still want all of you, princess." He takes my mouth with his and undoes my jeans. I almost pull away, afraid he'll push too far and I'll cave. It would be so easy to give in to him. "Shh, let me make you feel good."

I relax when he doesn't push my jeans down. He slips his hand beneath my panties and parts my pussy lips. He glides his fingers over my clit, finding how wet blowing him made me. The fire inside me burns even brighter as he captures my mouth in a heart-pounding kiss. His tongue thrusts into my mouth as his finger thrusts inside me.

He captures my gasp and increases his speed, making me tighten on his finger. I grip his shoulders, holding on for dear life as he makes me shatter into a million pieces all around him.

It was fast, but I feel deliciously lethargic afterward.

As the tension eases, I collapse against him. He removes his hand and sucks my juices from his fingers. Tiny aftershocks flood my system even as he does up my jeans and then his.

I'm still leaning against him, not sure I can hold my weight yet.

His lips brush my ear as he says, "Think of how good my cock will feel inside you."

An aftershock rips through me, my pussy clutching empty. I'm beginning to see why so many let the horsemen tip them over that final ledge. I don't know how long I'll be able to hold out.

***

"YOU LOOK LIKE YOU'RE IN SHOCK," KENZ FINALLY SAYS, when we're about five minutes from my house.

"I—" I honestly don't know what to say. I think I am in shock. For a brief second, I wanted to chuck all my clothes and Luke's and ride his cock, feeling him deep inside me. Fuck, I need some coffee and something to eat. "After I get changed, do you want to go get some breakfast?"

"Yes, please." Kenz turns down my street. "I don't know about you, but I'm starving. I'll run home to change real quick."

"Sounds good."

She pulls into my driveway, and when I go to get out, she says, "Are you okay? They didn't do something you didn't want to do, right? Because if they did—"

I shake my head and give her a faint smile. "No. Everything was consensual. It was just a lot."

"Well, I can't wait to unpack that statement. Be back in fifteen." Kenz waves me out of the car.

I take a deep breath and walk to my door. I'm not ready to face my mother and her potential questions. One, I've never gone to a party since fifth grade. Two, I've never texted to stay the night at my friend's house while at a party. Three, what if she can smell what Luke did to me in Caden's basement?

Sure, I found a mint to suck on, but honestly, I don't know how I look or smell. And even if she doesn't smell or suspect anything, I'm not sure my mom won't get the truth out of me. It's practically bursting to get out.

Opening the door to the house, I walk inside and look around. It's all quiet.

I check my phone for messages and don't see any. The schedule up on the refrigerator says she's off today, but sometimes she gets called in. As I walk farther into the house, I hear the TV and follow the sound to the family room.

Mom is asleep on the sofa. I breathe a sigh of relief.

Hurrying upstairs to my room, I take another shower. What Luke made me do didn't make me feel dirty, but I still can't help thinking Mom will be able to tell. I don't bother washing my hair again. I change into one of my t-shirts and a fresh pair of jeans before putting on some light makeup. Mostly makeup to cover the hickeys, plus some ChapStick.

Who knew kissing five guys would make your lips chap? I blush at my reflection. Five. Fuck, four was already a lot. My reputation at school will be trashed, but at least I'll have a reputation now.

On my way downstairs, I hear some movement in the kitchen. I take a breath and head in to face my executioner.

"I thought I heard you." Mom lifts her gaze from the coffee machine. She takes in my freshly washed and clothed self. "What are you up to?"

"Getting breakfast with Kenz." I almost say to catch up, but I was supposed to stay at Kenz's house last night. "She didn't have anything at her house, and we wanted to be fresh in case we run into anyone."

Mom's eyebrow rises. "Like the boys?"

I shake my head and smile. "Nope. No boys. They all have football practice."

It's not like Mom doesn't know about the four guys in my life. I went to a party with Kenz last night. She has to know they were there.

"Nico Lee is back in town," I say, trying to distract her from asking about the party. I wouldn't be able to tell her much. I'd been too worried what the guys would do to Nico. Turns out nothing he wouldn't like.

Mom is busy with the coffee machine. I also want to keep her from commenting on the football players in my life. She didn't like Eli one-on-one, just like I thought she wouldn't. His charm offensive didn't impress my mom.

After she pours her cup of coffee, she smiles at me. "I always liked Nico. He called to see where you were."

"Yup, I ran into him at the game, and he came to the party with me and Kenz." All true statements. "We didn't get to catch up much, so I might try to hang out with him later. He went to practice to see about joining the team."

"Sorry, all I can picture is the scrawny little kid who used to tear into my kitchen with you looking for snacks." Mom's smile softens. "I can't imagine what he looks like now. You'll have to bring him by sometime."

"Of course." I edge toward the door. "He's one of my best friends."

I don't mention he's hot as hell and fantastic with his tongue. But I'm sure my face has turned red.

Mom's eyes narrow. "Do your footballers have some competition?"

My mind flashes with images of Eli and Nico in the shower. I swallow and try to remain normal. "He's friends with the guys too. Like I said, I'm not really looking to seriously date someone my senior year. It gets weird with everyone leaving for college."

Mom watches me closely as she sips her coffee. Her silence is a trick she found always makes me confess. Unfortunately for me, it usually works. And I have so much inside I need to unpack.

Before I can blurt anything out, a knock sounds on the door. Relief spills through me. I turn and open it. Kenz smiles at both of us.

"Morning. You ready, H?"

I glance at Mom. "I'm heading out. I'll probably see you this afternoon?"

"Go. Have fun with your friend. We'll see each other when we see each other." Mom waves her hand at me. "Harper, I'm happy you're getting out more. Really."

"Me too." I give my mom a smile and follow Kenz to the door.

I almost get out the door when Mom says, "Next week is third shifts. You could stay with Kenz if you want to."

I pause. "I'll think about it, but I've got a pretty heavy course load next week. We have tests in two of my classes, so it might be better if I stay home."

"Just let me know where you end up. See you later."

CHAPTER 11

Perfidy

HARPER

"Oh, wow." Kenz stares at me over her pancakes. Her fork is halfway to her mouth as she digests what I just told her. We have a booth back in the corner, away from everyone else, so I filled her in on everything that happened last night.

I take a bite of my French toast while she processes.

"Wait, so Nico is a horseman?" She gives up on her bite and sets her fork down.

"Apparently. I'm still not sure how that works." I'm starving, so I continue to eat while she gets this far-off look. Hopefully I burned off some calories last night, and I'm replenishing and not just stress eating.

"And they just let him join in?" Kenz focuses on me.

I nod and blush.

"And you were okay with that?"

I inhale and nod again.

"I knew he liked you." A smile pulls at Kenz's lips as she glances around to make sure we're alone. She leans across the table and whispers, "You blew all of them?"

I bite my lip to hold back my smile as I nod.

Her eyebrows shoot up almost to her hairline. "And they all ate you out?"

"Yes, Kenz."

"My god, how many times did you come?" Her blue eyes are huge and her voice is awe-filled.

"I didn't count," I admit. "But a lot."

Just thinking about last night has me squirming in my seat.

"You're my hero." She sits back and shakes her head. "I only came twice last night. I can't even imagine what having five guys on you at once must feel like."

"Overwhelming." I pick up my coffee and take a bracing gulp before looking around to make sure no one else is close enough to hear. "Has Brandon ever done anything to your... butt?"

Kenz leans forward excitedly. "One time when he went down on me, he slid his finger in my ass. I came so hard."

"Eli..." I bite my lip and glance around before leaning across to whisper, "He licked my asshole and stuck his tongue inside."

Kenz's eyes grow rounder. She's practically vibrating with excitement. "Holy shit. What did that feel like?"

I shake my head. "It didn't feel bad, but I was so self-conscious of him being there. I couldn't relax."

"Fuck, H, I think you're more experienced than me and you're still technically a virgin." Kenz relaxes into the booth. "What's holding you back from giving in to them?"

"Besides the fact it's five on one, and they all want to be there when it happens?" I bite out a laugh and then it all floods out of me. "It hasn't even been two weeks! What happens when I give in? Isn't that game over? Isn't that what this whole thing is about? The chase? So if that goes away, what keeps them from leaving me? And why do I even care if they leave? Sure they promised to be only mine for the whole year, but how can I keep them satisfied? Five guys, Kenz."

I hold up my hand with my five fingers extended and thrust it toward her. "Five. How does that even work? When do I have any time to myself? Let alone my studies. That time on the webcam, they all came twice. Luke is already threatening to have me down on my knees to service him constantly. Probably between classes, after school, after practice, before bed. When will it end?"

"Calm down, sweetie." Kenz holds up her hands, and I realize I'm practically panting.

My breath heaves in and out so fast. My head is spinning.

"Look at me." Kenz motions to her eyes, and I raise my gaze to them. "All right, easy now. Breathe in, slow. Breathe out. Come on, five more. In. Out."

I follow her breathing until my heart stops trying to race out of my chest.

"Okay, let's take this one piece at a time." Kenz takes my hand on the table and holds it. "Five guys, hmm. Obviously, you'd have one in your pussy, one in your ass, one in your mouth." She taps her finger on her lips. "I guess you could have the other two in your hands. Or they could trade off. But yeah, that would keep you kind of busy. But my guess is they don't have sex every night, and the whole all five at once would probably be more of a once a week or maybe all weekend type thing."

My mouth drops open. "They're all huge. My jaw is sore today from last night, and you think they'll take my pussy and ass at the same time?! They'll rip me apart."

"How do you think Jack and Caden do girls together?" Kenz gives me a look meant to calm me. "One takes their mouth and the other the pussy. Or for a more experienced girl, they do her ass and pussy. They make sure the girl is ready for it. So if other girls can take Caden and someone else, you'll be fine."

"That's not very comforting." My chest burns thinking of other girls with the guys. I know they aren't virgins and have been with girls I have class with. Even so, it's hard not to think of them as mine after last night.

"The question of will they stray after you give it up." Kenz squeezes my hand and her eyebrows pull down. "I don't know the answer to that. I don't think anyone can give you that answer either. It's not like you guys are all in love."

My lips press together to stop the denial, because she's right. We aren't. Emotions have nothing to do with our arrangement.

"But you have an agreement, and from what I know about the horsemen, they don't go back on their word. They may try to renegotiate, but they would definitely give you a heads up if something was going to change." Kenz's words sink into me.

I take a deep breath, trying to cool off the burning in my chest at the thought of them with someone else. "It's about trust then?"

"Doesn't it always come down to that?" Kenz smiles. "Fuck, I worried Brandon might dump me after getting what he wanted."

"Really?" I'm surprised because they've been together for the past two years. I figured they were solid.

She shrugs. "Sometimes men really want something and when they get it, they're done with the chase. I couldn't be sure with Brandon, but I'm not sorry I finally had sex with him. It's so much better than just fooling around."

I nod and look down at my plate. I've eaten most of my meal and I could use a coffee refill. The thought of them being done with me still circles my head. I guess as long as they enjoy sex with me, they'll continue to want me. At the beginning, I wanted them to leave me alone. But now... I don't know how I'd feel if I finally gave in and then they went back to how it was before.

Sighing, I admit, "I know it's a gamble, but you and Brandon have two years of being together to rely on. I've been with the guys since last Monday and haven't really fully committed to being *theirs*. If this is just a game, do I lose if I give in so quickly? Do I make them wait until they beg for it?"

"I don't have an answer for you. You've already gotten them to give you more than any other girl with the exclusivity. But that might mean they expect more from you." Kenz takes a bite of pancakes and chews thoughtfully.

"What if I'm not what they expect me to be?" I ask softly, afraid of the answer. Afraid that even my best friend knows I'm not enough for them. What girl could be? It would take a team of girls, like the Cheer-monsters, to keep them satisfied, and even they couldn't keep the horsemen. This crazy part of me wants to be enough though. Wants to hold onto their attention when no other girl could.

"If I were you, I'd enjoy it while I can and have some nice memories for when I'm old and gray and my husband can't get it up anymore." Kenz winks as she shovels another bite into her mouth.

I smile and shake my head. "I was afraid you were going to tell your grandkids about it."

"Nah, they don't need to know grandma got railed by five dicks at once." Kenz laughs.

"Talk about needing therapy." I join in her laughter and it feels nice.

"Okay, enough about boys," Kenz says. "What do you think about our classes for this year?"

Kenz finishes her meal while we talk about our classes and the potential hell our homework and studying will be this year. The waitress comes by and gives us more coffee and takes our plates. I take the opportunity to look around, as the place has gotten more packed. Penny and her crew are at a table across the way and she gives me an enthusiastic wave. I smile, but don't gesture her to come over.

I don't know what those girls want from me yet.

"What are you doing Monday?" Kenz asks.

Before I can answer, a female voice joins in. "Probably Eiffel Towering the football team."

We swivel our heads to see Sidney, Emma, and Ashley closing in on our table.

"You know me so well." I give Sidney a fake smile and make a note to ask Kenz what an Eiffel Tower is. "What's up, bit—uh, cheerleaders?"

Sidney's eyebrows pop up at my almost slip. Really, *what's up, bitches* can be a friendly greeting. I'm not sure it would have been coming out of my mouth to them. But they haven't exactly been friendly, so it's accurate.

"We stopped for breakfast and saw you guys hanging out." Sidney grabs the chair at the table beside ours and turns it to sit at the end of our table. Emma slides in next to me, and Ashley sits next to Kenz.

Kenz arches an eyebrow. "Please join us."

"You date Brandon Walker, yeah?" Ashley asks Kenz.

"Yes." Kenz draws out the *s* like she's wondering where Ashley is going with this.

"He's a nice guy." Ashley waves the waitress over. "Can I get a hot chocolate?"

The others order coffee. I guess they're staying? What the fuck is happening?

"No one thinks this is your fault by the way." Sidney leans back in the chair like the bad bitch she is. "I mean, no girl wants her first time to be with five guys. That's a fucking hamburger chain, not a relationship."

"I really didn't ask for this." Something settles in me, knowing they don't blame me. "I don't even know how they knew I was the only one left."

Sidney smiles. "The guys keep tabs. Really, I'm surprised they didn't clear the board before this year."

Kenz kicks me under the table. I glance at her and she raises her eyebrows like what the fuck am I doing. We should totally bounce.

But I'm curious what the cheerleaders want. Know thy enemy and all that. "Where's Hannah?"

"Still fucking bitter as hell." Emma scoffs. "She likes riding Caden's monster dick and bragging how big it is."

That burn starts in my chest. I remind myself I knew the guys weren't virgins. They have a past and each of the guys except for Nico were in at least one of these girls, if not more than one.

"Not going to lie," Ashley says. "Those are the best dicks in school. Most of the other guys think you should be grateful they have one and don't try to learn what to do with it."

"It's not just the status we're worried about." Sidney reaches across for the cream to add to her coffee. "We can find boyfriends, but if we do, we need to make sure the horsemen don't come back on the market."

I press my lips together. "I have no control over what they do."

Sidney's smile is not so nice. "We know about the deal to keep you for the whole year. We just need a guarantee you're willing to keep your end of the bargain and they don't start straying. But if they do, it better be with one of us."

"Wait," Kenz interrupts and draws Sidney's attention. "What exactly are you asking Harper to do?"

"Keep the horsemen close and satisfied while we raise our boyfriends up to their ranks." Sidney arches an eyebrow and blinks her eyes almost innocently. "The horsemen never wanted to be our boyfriends, but they definitely appreciated us being available. They tend to wander, but they always came back."

"How do you think we keep being top of the school?" Emma takes a sip of coffee. Her dark eyes meet mine. "We kept them satisfied, and that makes everyone happy."

"Look, you've been hiding for so long you can't possibly know what happens when they don't get sex on the regular." Sidney tosses her blond hair over her shoulder. "The guys are aggressive, and when they have pent up *needs*, they can get dangerous."

"So if you can't keep up, you need to let us know so we can step in and pick up your slack," Ashley adds. Her smile turns into a grin. "Think of us as a public service."

Hoes-R-Us?

It's taking everything in me to keep my mouth shut. What the hell have I walked into? I kind of want to pry into these women's minds to figure out what the fuck is going on.

Kenz doesn't have my reservations. "So you guys fuck the horsemen into the *decent* guys they are?"

The girls laugh.

"Oh, sweetie, yes." Sidney turns her eyes on me. "We keep them calm. Right now, they're focused on you, but the second their attention strays is when the punishments to the whole school ramp up. So if you haven't already popped that cherry, get on it and keep the guys in line."

The girls all rise as one.

"If not," Emma says, "free them up so they can get what they need."

CHAPTER 12

Preparing to Enter Enemy Territory

Harper

I stare at my face in the mirror as I apply eye liner. This will be my second party, and I hope to actually stay longer at this one. Nico ended up staying at practice with the others, but he texted me to say maybe tomorrow we can hang out, just the two of us.

Not sure that will be allowed, but it would be nice to catch up.

I don't know what to think about the guys and what the Cheer-monsters told me. It makes some sense that sex would keep them a little more chill. If denying them puts the whole student population at risk, who am I to hold out?

My life is so fucked right now. I can't decide whether to give in to them or not. What is best for me, and what is best for the school?

"Harper?"

I step out into my room to see Mom at my door. "Come on in." I wave her in as I go to the mirror in the bathroom to finish applying my makeup.

"So the party tonight is where?" Mom sits on the edge of my bed.

"It's at Sidney Brown's house." I dig through my new makeup, searching for the perfect lipstick. The dark red stain. Definitely won't smear.

"Two parties in one weekend. Are you a cool kid now?" Mom's voice is tinged with laughter. "Did I raise a cool kid?"

"I've always been a cool kid. The others just figured it out," I tease. I swipe on the stain and blot my lips.

"See, I knew you were a cool kid the whole time. That's why I always hung out with you." Mom's brown eyes sparkle as I walk back into my bedroom.

"Did you want to load me up with more condoms?" Raising an eyebrow at her, I walk to my closet to pull out the dress I plan to wear tonight. I'm currently in an old button-down shirt and shorts. I've already straightened my hair to leave it down.

"If you've gone through all the ones I bought you, we definitely need to have a talk. Especially about UTIs."

"Ew, Mom, no. I haven't used any of them and I don't plan to." Because apparently my mouth will work perfectly fine for the time being. There's no risk of pregnancy. I received copies of all the guys' testing results as Luke promised. She definitely doesn't need to know the guys want to fuck me without condoms.

"I don't want you to end up with more than you can handle because of some stupid teenage mistake." Mom picks at lint on my bedspread.

I wasn't a teenage mistake. Mom and Dad were married when they had me, even if they were still youngish, but it didn't work out. Dad left us, and we've been fine ever since. I don't even really remember a time with him in my life.

"Don't worry, I won't make you a grandma. I'm being safe and cautious. Last night, I didn't even drink anything but a can of soda."

Mom perks up and smiles. "See, that's my smart girl. If your designated driver drinks, you can call me to pick you up."

"Yeah, that's what all the cool kids do. Call their moms to pick them up." I give her a friendly eye roll. Pretty sure the guys are already planning another sleepover. Tingles creep down my spine. "How about I text you I'm staying if it comes to that?"

Mom's eyes narrow but she sighs. "I suppose it was inevitable everyone else would realize you're cool. I wouldn't want to damage your new rep."

"Thank you." I take my dress into the bathroom and shut the door to change. It's a black and red skater dress. Not as short as the skirt from the other day, but formfitting to the waist with a flirty swing skirt that reaches about mid-thigh.

When I come back out, Mom's eyes widen. "May I interest you in a chastity belt?"

I laugh. "Not hardly."

I sit beside her to pull on a pair of black Dr. Martens. "If anyone tries anything, I'll just kick them in the junk with my boots and run."

"Solid plan." Her eyes pause on my collar. She reaches out and touches it. "You aren't going to a BDSM party, right?"

I laugh so hard I bend over holding my stomach. When I can breathe again, I say, "No. God, no. It's just an accessory, Mom."

It could end up another sex party with me as the star, but I'm not about to say that. I still don't know if I want to have intercourse with the guys yet. I'm just getting the hang of all the other stuff.

But there is a real possibility of me ending up back in Caden's bed with all of them tonight. I'd pack an overnight bag, but that might be a push too far for Mom. And if I get myself grounded for real, Luke will dole out punishment. A shiver runs through me.

"If you get serious with one of these guys, I want to have him over, one-on-one." Mom stands and slides her hands down her jeans. "So I can inform him I know where every major artery is and how deep to cut. I also have a pharmacy worth of deadly drugs at my disposal. Though a needle of air to a vein might be less traceable."

"I'm sure you'd scare any guy who wanted to date me." Fortunately, none of them do. Well, maybe Nico would have, but he's now one of my owners.

"You ever need me to make someone back off, say the word, Harper." Mom puts her two fingers in front of her eyes and swings them to point at me and back.

"And what word is that, Mom?" I ask with a smile.

"Ah, honey, the word doesn't matter. I'm here for you no matter what." She looks me over. "Though maybe I should get you a Taser in case that future frat boy decides to get handsy."

I shake my head as she heads down the hall. I don't think a Taser would help me with Eli. He might get off on it. I keep thinking about the Cheermonsters and their offer to step in if needed. Was that a genuine offer or a threat?

Neither Kenz nor I could make heads or tails of it. I can't really talk to the guys about it. But what if the girls are right? If it's up to me to contain the horsemen, how am I going to do that as one girl?

Not that they were all that tame before me, but I don't have any special hold over them. Except I'm not willing to share. And I'm still not. Especially with no condoms, but even with, I don't want to have a guy who cheats, even if it's not technically cheating because we're not dating.

Ugh, they wanted a year; I wanted no straying. Of course, I hoped they would be appalled and back off entirely. But that didn't happen, so I guess I'm going to have to step up. At some point. Probably not tonight.

I drop my lip stain into my purse along with some balm. I don't know if all of them will use my mouth tonight, but I know Luke will. He has a point to prove.

As I step into the hallway, I hear a knock on the back door, and Mom opens it. I don't even know who's picking me up tonight.

The deep rumble of a male's voice is the only clue I have as I hurry down the stairs.

"I didn't know your last name was Ross. Like Emily Ross?" Mom says as I rush to intercept.

"That's my mother, Jennifer." Caden stands next to the door. He has on a black button-down shirt with the sleeves rolled up, showing off his massive forearms. His dark blue jeans are carpenter jeans that leave a lot of room in the legs. His black boots match mine.

He can't help looking like a mean son of a bitch even dressed nice. He's too big and too much of a presence.

"Hey, Caden," I say to stop my mom from asking more questions.

Caden's green eyes widen when he takes in my outfit for the night. Heat flows from them, and a blush creeps up my cheeks.

"So you get to take Harper to the party tonight? Without the rest of them?" Mom asks with her eyebrows arched. She's going to freak out if they keep rotating like this.

"Yes, ma'am. We'll meet them there." Caden steps toward me. "You look amazing, Harper."

Thank god he didn't call me *little nympho*. Mom wouldn't have let me leave the house ever again. Forget a chastity belt, she'd lock me in my room and throw away the key. She likes to think she's okay with me being a sexual being, but I'm not sure she really is.

"We should get going," I say to Caden. "Good night, Mom."

"Have a good night." Mom mumbles about a Taser on her way into the living room.

I walk up to Caden, intending to pull the door open.

"Did your mom just say she was buying you a Taser?" Caden whispers against my ear. Shivers wash down my back as his hands stop on my hips. The sparks whip up inside me.

"How else would I bring someone like you down to his knees?" I lean back so I can meet his eyes.

"All you have to do is ask, little nympho. I'll go down on my knees for you anytime. Especially in that skirt." His fingers start to lift it.

I slap my hand on his chest and glance over my shoulder to make sure Mom didn't hear. "Let's go before you get me in trouble."

We go outside, and he opens the door to his Mustang. I slide onto the leather seat and wait for him to walk around the outside and get in.

"Fuck, little nympho." Caden starts the car and throws it in reverse. "I'm going to be hard all night with you in that dress."

"You say the sweetest things." Giving him a fake smile, I shake my head at him.

"If you're looking for sweet, you've got the wrong horseman." His green eyes flash to mine as he shifts into gear and speeds down the street.

My heart races as he plows through our town like a man on a mission. I don't know where Sidney lives, but I just hope we make it there alive at this point.

Caden slows when he turns into a residential neighborhood close to his own. Down the street is a house lit up with cars parked all around it. He parks a few houses away from the last car.

I unbuckle my seatbelt and prepare to get out when Caden's hand wraps around my waist.

"Nah, little nympho. I need a taste before we go in."

I swallow in the dark of his car and glance toward the party and people walking toward it. If any of them turn, they'll see us. Hell, anyone at the party might notice Caden's car sitting here.

Caden slides his seat back and pats his lap. "You know the position."

I sigh and climb over the console to sit on his lap and straddle his hips with my knees. Anticipation hums through my blood. I've only been alone with Luke before. I don't know how different it will feel without the others' eyes on me. The others to pull us back if we go too far.

His hands come up to cup my breasts. "Are you wearing a bra?"

I shake my head as tingles rush down to gather between my legs.

"Fuck. How about panties?" His hands move up my thighs under my skirt.

"Yes, I'm wearing panties and I'm keeping them on." Even if he's already made them damp.

Caden's eyes flash in the dark. His voice is excited when he asks, "Are they the red ones?"

I lift my skirt for him to see the red lace panties.

"Fuck. I'm going to need those panties." Caden slips his hand into my panties and rubs on my clit. He growls low in his throat. "I love how wet you get for us."

More wetness rushes to meet his fingers.

"You can't take my panties. I'm going into a party with other guys, and I refuse to flash them what belongs to you." I already thought of this. It worked on Luke in the cafeteria. Of course, my voice is breathless given how fucking aroused he's making me.

"True." He furrows his brow. "Fine, kiss me and you can keep your panties. For now."

I lean forward and press my lips to his. His finger slips inside me, making me gasp, as his mouth opens over mine. Desire courses through my body as he thrusts in and out with his thick finger while his thumb rubs my clit.

His tongue tangles with mine as, unable to resist, I ride his hand.

He pulls his head back from mine. When I lean in to kiss him, he stops me with his words.

"No, little nympho. I want to watch you shatter. I want to hear your moan fill my car with your sweet song."

That's hotter than it should be. I cling to his shoulders as I ride his finger. It feels so fucking good, winding me up. I can feel the edge hovering just there. A little further.

"Imagine what this would feel like on my cock, little nympho. Stretching you out to take every inch of me."

I meet his eyes as I think of how thick he is and how that would feel inside me, buried in me as I rise and fall over him. A gush of wetness flows out of me to coat his hand.

"That must sound good." His deep voice strokes along my neck. "Soon I'll be able to take you here. You can ride me as often as you like. Come all over my hard cock while I thrust in and out of your tight pussy until you come again. You'll provide the chorus with your moans, and I'll give you the deeper, more penetrative tones with my groans."

"Holy shit, Caden." My pussy tightens, and I fall over the edge at the picture his dirty words paint and his thrusting finger. I stop moving to catch my breath.

Caden removes his finger from my pussy and moves it back until he touches my asshole. "This will be mine too."

He slides his finger inside my puckered hole with all the wetness he caused.

"Caden." I jerk forward away from his touch, but he holds it inside me.

His finger is a lot thicker than the others', and the sparks stir through me as he moves it deeper inside my ass.

"Shh, little nympho. You know you're going to love it. Taking me up your ass while Luke pounds your perfect pussy." His thumb slides inside my pussy, and he moves his fingers in and out of my ass and pussy together. "You can work on sucking off the other three while we fuck you so good, you can barely stand."

His words, the fullness, the pressure. I can't take anymore and I come again, moaning. I cling onto his shoulders as the orgasm swirls through my body, leaving me breathless and limp in his lap.

He removes his hand and reaches into the center console for some wipes. After cleaning his fingers, he grabs a fresh wipe and moves to wipe me under my skirt. I reach for it, but he uses his other hand to stop me.

"I take care of what's mine, Harper." His voice is practically a growl, and it keys me up inside. He moves my panties to the side and wipes my pussy and then my ass before righting my panties.

He gets rid of the wipes and then yanks me down to capture my lips again. His kiss is possessive and conquering. I give him everything I pent up inside myself today. All the worry and frustration and want. Though the two orgasms definitely helped to loosen me up.

"You and I are definitely sticking together tonight," Caden says against my lips. Happiness fills my heart.

I trace my finger over his lower lip. "If we don't go in there, someone might come out to find us."

He nips at my finger. "Wouldn't want an orgy to start in my car."

After opening the car door, he helps me stand before easing himself out. When he straightens, he adjusts his hard-on. I would offer to help him with that, but we've already spent too long on the outskirts of the party. Heads turn our way, even from the front lawn of Sidney's house.

Gah, I think I'm going to break out in hives. These girls barely tolerate me, and I'm walking in with a horseman like I own the place. If that's not a recipe for disaster, I'm not sure what would be.

"Come on, little nympho. Time to make everyone else jealous." Caden wraps his arm around my shoulders and tugs me in hard against him.

I take a deep breath. Here goes nothing.

CHAPTER 13

Inside the Enemy Camp

Nerves scatter through me as we approach the lawn. I swear the Cheermonsters got into my head with their talk of keeping the guys satisfied. Caden didn't make me suck him off. I mean, last night should be enough for now, right?

I almost open my mouth to ask Caden, but we reach the lawn and the masses are excited to see one of their rulers. With the arm not around me, Caden greets some of the JV football players. Their eyes stray to me for a brief second before their gazes skitter away.

Caden talks to them, holding me against his side. The hair on the back of my neck rises.

Grant Perkins draws my attention. He's leaning against the house below a window. There's no reason why I should notice him. His pose is relaxed, except his narrowed gaze doesn't stray from me. Seriously? Like it's my fault he decided to be a dickhead and the horsemen took it out on him. Frankly, he creeps me out.

But I guess that's part of being owned by the horsemen. People actually notice me now. A few girls say hi to me as we make our way into the house. I return their greeting but I don't really know who they are. This is where I need Kenz. She knows everyone.

The house is flooded with music, so loud it almost hurts my ears.

Bass thrums through my body. Caden doesn't release me as he walks into the kitchen. He leans down to my ear. "You want something to drink?"

"A soda." I glance around for a closed container of soda.

"Nah, little nympho, tonight you're drinking the good stuff." Caden grabs a bottle of rum and a two liter of Coke that haven't been opened yet. He also grabs a couple of cups.

"I've never drank alcohol before, Caden," I try to protest. It's not like I've been partying for years.

Handing me the soda and rum, he fills the cups with ice. I balance the bottles in my arms against my body.

"Good. I want to see what happens when Harper Davidson gets sloppy drunk. It's a first, and I want to take it." His green eyes capture mine. "I've got you. Nothing will happen. I'm not leaving that sweet ass alone tonight."

My cheeks heat. He leads me farther into the party. It feels weird carrying soda and rum, but I guess that's part of being owned. We head into a large room, normally a family room and breakfast area. The lights are dim.

A bunch of people sit at the breakfast table with a bottle between them. The family room furniture is around the outskirts of the room. The TV is on, playing dance music while high schoolers grinding on each other fill the empty space.

It's hard to recognize anyone with the lights so low, but I think I see Penny and Vicky. They texted today, and I let them know I'd be at the party tonight. Kenz should be here somewhere too. Caden leads me into a darkened corner. Hands take the bottles from me, and before I can see who took them, lips claim mine.

Jack. His tongue teases my lips, and I let him inside. The taste of something sharp and alcoholic fills my senses. Caden's arm remains around me, but he shifts behind me. His hard cock presses against my ass.

"I've missed your mouth," Jack whispers against my lips, and I barely hear him over the music. He presses another kiss against my lips before he steps back.

Eli steps into the space and tugs me down with him on the couch.

My hands on his shoulders, I straddle his lap as he captures my mouth. Whatever Jack drank, Eli did too, because they have the same flavor on top of their own tastes.

Pulling away, he leans back on the couch. Nico reaches out and grabs my hair to pull my mouth to his while I stay on Eli's lap. I'm not as used to kissing Nico. Tingles fill my body, as if kissing him is wrong, but at the same time, his lips feel so right against mine. His kiss is just as dominant, but there's a hint of sweetness the others don't have.

Nico and I have a foundation of friendship, while the other horsemen are just conquerors. He lifts his mouth and leans his forehead against mine. "I'm glad you're here."

His words spark something inside me. I lean in and kiss him. "Me too."

Hands lift me from Eli to stand. Turning, I meet Luke's icy eyes. He backs me up against the wall. My breath catches as his eyes burn with that cold fire. My pulse throbs in my veins, wanting what he gives me.

"Princess." His mouth falls on mine, devouring me. No gentle teasing from Death. No, he takes and takes. I do my best to keep up, giving in to the heat flooding me. His hand reaches between my legs and runs along my panties against my clit. I gasp and clench my thighs together around his hand.

Anyone can see what he's doing. Sure, it's dark, but people pay attention to what the horsemen do. And while everyone is aware of the horsemen owning me, the kissing is proof enough.

His mouth goes to my ear. "I'm going to take these later."

"Caden already called dibs," I dare the monster against me.

"Then I'll take what's under it." His finger slips under the edge of my panties and thrusts deep inside me. I gasp at the intrusion, but also want him to keep going. Desire coils through me hot and wild.

"So fucking wet, princess."

Oh, fuck. I'm melting against him, ready for the pleasure he'll give me. Someone yells in the background. Suddenly high schoolers are everywhere again, and reason wins out.

"Luke, not here."

"Anywhere I want, princess." He brings his gaze to mine as he continues to thrust his finger in and out of me, stirring up a need I'm not strong enough to resist.

No one can see us back here, anyway. His body blocks me from the rest of the room. My heart throbs as our eyes lock, and the people around us fade back into this low hum of light and noise.

Until it's just him and me.

Wondering how he likes to be fondled in public, I slide my hand down his chest and rub it against his hard cock in his jeans, stroking him firmly and slowly. I raise an eyebrow. Always challenging him.

His eyes twinkle with mischief as he leans in to my ear. "Don't think I won't make you go down on me right here, right now. You on your knees worshipping my cock. I love to entertain my people."

I bite my lip, wondering if he really would. A pulse throbs in my pussy at the thought of everyone watching me take Luke. Shivers slide down my back as I draw my head back, but I keep my hand on his cock. He meets my eyes.

He removes his finger from me and straightens my panties. "Open your mouth."

My chest heaves with denied lust. I part my lips. He slides the finger covered in my wetness in my mouth. The tangy sweet taste of my arousal against my tongue makes my pussy clench.

"Suck it like you'd suck my cock, princess."

My panties grow wetter as I suck my juices off him. I work my tongue around his finger the way I've worked his cock. Need throbs through me. I crave the release he can bring me. Meeting his blazing eyes, I grab his hand to move it in and out of my mouth.

He pulls his finger out of my mouth before crashing his lips brutally against mine. Tasting every inch, claiming it all for himself. I want to grind against him until I get both of us off. I'm tempted to drop to my knees and feel his thick length inside my mouth.

When he releases my lips, they feel swollen. He rests his forehead against mine. "I'm going to take that mouth soon, princess, and then I'm going to fuck your pussy with my tongue until you come so hard you scream. Everyone at this party will know how much you love my cock in your mouth."

That's so fucking hot. My chest heaves with want. If I knew the layout of this house, I would drag him somewhere private to force him to show me. Prove his words to me over and over again.

He smirks as he backs away a little to give me space to breathe. The world rushes back in. The music and the people crowding around us. My cheeks flush hot. Luke is dangerous to my state of mind.

Caden pulls me down onto his lap, but my eyes don't leave Luke's. The promise in them makes me squirm. But I'm completely damned, because I want him. I want him to use me, to hold me, to keep me safe.

My mind is fucked.

"Here, little nympho. Drink. If you want to play with Death tonight, you're going to need this." Caden hands me a cup.

Smelling the Coke, I know there's rum in it. But fuck, with Luke, maybe a little liquid courage would be a good thing.

I lean to say into Caden's ear, "If I drink this, don't leave me alone with Luke."

Caden runs a hand along my thigh under my skirt. "Luke's not the only one you have to worry about, but I'll stay with you."

My eyes have adjusted to the dimness of the room somewhat. I'm wary about drinking alcohol. I know what my body wants and I don't want to give in to it. Not yet. I need more than sexual attraction to give up my V-card. I need a connection, more than just ownership.

I also know if I can't trust them, I'll never be willing to give it up. I take a deep breath and lean in until my lips brush Caden's ear.

"I don't want to lose my virginity tonight. Not here at the party and not at your house later. If I drink this, I'm trusting you to keep that promise and I don't care how much my drunk self begs. I. Don't. Want. It."

Pulling back, I search his eyes. His green eyes seem conflicted, but he nods and leans into my ear.

"I'll hold your boundary for tonight, little nympho, but we will play with you. Drunk or not. I'll stay sober enough to maintain your boundaries, but it will cost you a kiss—"

When I move to kiss him, he stops me with a wicked smile.

"Not now and not there, little nympho."

Heat floods me and suddenly I'm parched. I take a sip of my rum and Coke. Surprisingly not heinous. The crowd moves to the beat of the music while the guys chat around me. I drink and listen and watch all the people.

The Cheermonsters dressed to catch attention tonight as they rub up against some of the senior football players. I've never danced at a party. Studio and competition dancing is different, so I watch how the Cheermonsters move their hips and arms and legs.

Caden keeps adding to my cup. A little soda. A little rum. A little soda. A little more rum.

The dance floor blurs with movement. I'm not sure how much I've had to drink, but I do know I need to use the bathroom. I grab Caden's ear and say, "I need to pee."

"No need to shout, little nympho." He stands me up, and I sway on my feet. Did I shout? Hands grab my hips and I look into Luke's eyes. Warmth floods through me and my panties grow wet. All the earlier lust returns.

As I stumble into him, I giggle a little.

"How much did you let her drink?" Luke asks over my shoulder.

No, that won't do. I reach up and grab his chin, so he's looking at me. Mmm, that's better. Those eyes of his, so cold and hot at the same time. Could he burn as much as I do?

CHAPTER 14

The United Front

CADEN

Luke's waiting for his answer. How much did I give Harper to drink? Fuck. A lot.

"Enough," I answer and stand behind Harper. Her hand reaches behind her to grab my hip. Her touches have kept me hard since the car. "It'll wear off by the time we leave."

Luke raises a skeptical eyebrow. Her hand on his chin lowers to his throat. She curls her fingers like she's going to tighten them, but thinks better of it.

"Let the girl live a little. We've taken most of her high school days away. Let her have fun tonight." Her head leans back against my chest. All that tension that usually fills her is gone.

"I need to pee," Harper yells in Luke's face. I'm sure she thinks she's whispering. It's the funniest shit I've ever seen.

Luke glares before dragging Harper down the hallway. I follow closely behind. I made a promise and I'm going to keep it, even if it breaks me. Luke isn't the only one who wants to fuck our girl. We all do.

Maybe Nico is willing to wait, but he just got his first taste of her last night.

The main bathroom has a line. With the little dance Harper is doing, I don't think she'll make it in that line.

"Take us to Sidney's room," I say in Luke's ear.

He sighs and heads toward a back staircase. Harper stumbles along behind him, glancing back at me every few seconds with a goofy smile on her face. I try to keep my face stern, but then she giggles again.

Fuck, if that isn't the cutest shit I've ever heard. When we reach the stairs, I catch Harper's hips right before she takes a nosedive onto them. Her hands go over mine instead of reaching out to save herself.

"You're no longer in charge of our girl's drinks. She can barely stand." Luke shakes his head. He's disappointed in her current state. I love it.

"Harper likes rum and Coke, don't you, little nympho?"

She stares up at me with her pupils blown. Her fingers reach out to skim over my lips and she nods.

Laughing, I bend and throw her over my shoulder. When she tries to lift herself, I smack her ass.

"Hey," she says.

"Be good, little nympho." I gesture to Luke to carry on, sliding my hand under her skirt to hold her panty-covered ass. I want this pair of panties off her and in my pocket, but she has a valid point.

Our school has its share of creepers who would notice if Harper doesn't have panties on. As drunk as she is, she probably won't be as careful as she would when she's sober.

We make it to Sidney's room, and Luke puts in the code. She keeps her bedroom locked during parties. Of course, she enjoyed the random hookups with Luke and gave him the code. Not sure she'd be pleased we're bringing Harper up here. But fuck her. She should have changed the code.

I set Harper on her feet and turn her toward the bathroom. "You good on your own in there?"

Harper glances over her shoulder, giving me an appalled look. "Of course."

I give her a little nudge, and she closes the bathroom door with Luke and I on the bedroom side. Sidney's room is huge. Almost as big as mine. We sit on the couch while we wait.

"You know she weighs less than half of you," Luke starts, probably on the alcohol again.

"I tried to slow her down, but she's a bit of a handsy drunk." Without her inhibitions, she kept touching me. My face, my chest, my abs. Slipping her hand under my t-shirt. Playing with my hair.

Luke's eyebrow rises in interest as he waits for our girl to be finished. He'll thank me later for loosening her up.

The wrong door opens though. The hallway door crashes into the room, and Sidney stumbles in with Dylan Brewster. They don't even look up as they kiss and shed clothes. She isn't concerned someone might be in her room.

Smirking, Luke leans back to enjoy the show. I pay attention to the bathroom door, ready to jump up in case Harper decides to come out. I didn't like Sidney threatening our girl.

Sidney is hot, leggy, and blond. While I haven't tapped that, she used to be Luke's regular. He usually doesn't like to share, so all of us backed off. After all, there were plenty of cheerleaders to go around.

Brewster is on the football team. He's a cornerback and first string. He's built more like Luke than me. Even has blond hair, but brown eyes. I've seen his dick in the shower after games and practice, and Sidney's in for a disappointment after being with Luke.

By the time they fall back on her bed, they've stripped down to their underwear. Sidney rolls on top of him. She straddles him and rubs her panty-covered pussy over his boxers. He still has on his socks. Pretty sure the dude is going to blow the second she touches him.

He's making way too many noises not to.

Of course, it's this minute Harper walks out of the bathroom. When she sees Sidney on top of someone on the bed, her eyes widen. Her breath catches. Her face falls and her lower lip trembles.

I see what she thinks. To her, that's Luke under Sidney. Harper looks like she's either going to vomit or cry or both.

Apparently I'm not the only one who realizes what Harper thinks. Sidney gives Harper a catty smile as she continues to rub on Brewster.

Luke stands and starts a slow clap. "Thanks for the entertainment, Brewster."

Harper's gaze darts from Luke to Sidney to the guy under Sidney back to Luke. Her mouth drops open. She raises her arm to point, but I get to her first and draw her into my arms.

"We wouldn't cheat on you," I whisper in her ear. She rests her face against my chest as she takes a few breaths to calm down.

"Didn't take you for a creeper, Luke." Sidney cups her bra-covered breasts together and grinds down on poor Brewster. The guy is going to either pass out or blow his wad.

I lean down to whisper in Harper's ear. "I bet he comes in his shorts by the count of ten."

Harper smiles up at me before she rests her cheek against my chest. We watch Sidney moving way too much on poor Brewster.

"If you want to put on a show, we're more than happy to watch." Luke sits back on the couch facing the bed. "We could even give you some helpful critiques."

"You could join in." Sidney pinches her nipples and then drags one of Brewster's hands between her breasts.

Sweat rolls down Brewster's temples. When she shifts, he lets out a loud groan. Harper buries her face into my chest and her silent laughter ripples through me.

"I don't mean to frighten your poor virgin." Sidney gives us a fake pout.

"She's probably wondering if that's it." Luke comes over next to us. "She's used to a hell of a lot more foreplay."

Harper turns her head to look over at Luke.

Sidney glares down at Brewster, before her smile softens. She slides down the bed and drags Brewster's spunk-filled boxers off him. He rises on his elbows to look at his now flaccid dick.

"I can show your little virgin how to take care of a real man."

I snort back a laugh. Yeah, Harper doesn't need any help with that and she's seen better than Brewster.

"Go ahead." Luke takes Harper's hand and weaves his fingers with hers. He waves his other hand. "I'm sure this will be educational for all of us."

"Dude, you guys are going to watch?" Brewster's left eyebrow rises. Poor guy is probably getting performance anxiety and won't be able to get it up. I narrow my eyes at him just to make him even more anxious.

"Oh baby, if you want to play with cheerleaders, you have to know we love to perform." Sidney blows a kiss to Luke before kneeling in front of Brewster's semi-hard dick.

Luke brushes his hand over Harper's hair. Her brown eyes turn to him. "Don't worry, princess, you won't see anything you haven't before. Well, except for a small dick."

Brewster's face reddens, but he knows he can't really say anything. Especially to us. When Sidney draws his dick into her mouth, he looks like he got an electric shock to his junk. He sits upright and pushes his hands into the bed behind him.

As to technique, Sidney has some talent for sucking cock, but she doesn't quite capture the enthusiasm Harper gives. This looks like a chore to her, something she has to do to get to the part where she gets something out of it.

I've touched our girl when she goes down on us. Sucking cock arouses Harper so much she drips with wetness. Making me want to lick every drop until she comes on my tongue. That's a good idea.

Harper must feel me getting hard against her because she lifts a questioning eyebrow to me. I lean down to put my lips against her earlobe.

"Thinking of how good you taste when you go down on us. We need to find a little corner of our own to play in. Somewhere less crowded."

Her breath catches and her brown eyes stare up at mine. Yeah, she's down to play. I glance at Luke. When he realizes I'm looking at him, he turns and looks down at Harper. Our girl obviously wants us. His eyebrows rise slightly before he nods and turns back to watch Sidney.

"Watch, little nympho," I whisper in Harper's ear.

Brewster's mouth is wide open, and he's trying to keep from coming again. I mean, if Sidney's technically correct but mind-numbing blow job gets him there, good for him. If he could see what Harper can do, he'd probably jizz all over himself again. But I won't be cruel enough to show him what he's missing.

Harper is all ours. I won't put her on display to prove a point.

Luke might at some point, but he gets off on that. It won't be tonight though, because he needs Harper fully aware for punishment.

Not tipsy or drunk. Because I'm pretty sure our girl will get off on the humiliation too.

Brewster grunts.

"Dude, at least try to hold back," I say out loud. "Have some fucking self-control."

Brewster groans and comes in Sidney's mouth. She sits back and swallows with a satisfied grin on her face. I'm pretty sure Brewster could come from his pants rubbing his johnson in the right way, so that's not a win in her column.

"Well, if you two are finished." Luke gestures to the door.

Sidney's face scrunches like that girl who wanted more in *Willy Wonka*. Not a good look for either girl. "This is my room, Luke Foster."

"And here I thought this little display was for our benefit." Luke steps forward and glances at Brewster's limp dick and Sidney's scantily clad body. "I suppose if you give it ten minutes, he'll be ready to go again. But I wouldn't put money on it."

I lift Harper up against me. She squeals and puts her hands on my shoulders. Our faces are level and I give her a naughty grin.

"This isn't doing much for me," I say as I look to Luke. "Want to find another room? One a little less crowded? We can see if our little virgin learned what not to do."

Luke gives Harper a wicked grin, and she squirms against me.

Sidney scoffs, but bitch doesn't have any leg to stand on right now. She found a replacement, but that's like replacing a Lamborghini with a Honda Fit. It might get you where you want to go, but the ride won't be as fun or smooth.

The Pincer Movement

LUKE

I lead Caden and Harper down the hall to another bedroom that rarely gets used, because it's a little out of the way and smaller than the others in the house. It's big enough for what Caden and I both have in mind.

"How's your stomach?" I ask Harper as I open the door and turn on the lights. If Caden made her drink so much she gets sick, I will thrash him for it.

"Fine." She hiccups once and covers her mouth.

Laughing, Caden brings her into the room. I lock the door behind us and lean against it. Caden drops Harper on the bed, and she lets out a giggle. That sound shouldn't make my heart beat a little harder.

Her boots thump against the wooden sides of the bed. Her arms stretch out above her, lifting her breasts in that dress that had me hard from the moment she walked in.

"She's still pretty wasted," I remark as I work on my shirt's buttons.

"I'm not drunk." Harper pouts, and looking at those red lips makes me hurry to get undressed. They'll look fantastic around my cock while I watch her take it as deep as she can.

"Good, princess, because we have plans." I hang my shirt on the chair near the door while I kick off my shoes. Her dark eyes roam my chest. She licks her lips like she can't wait to taste me and my cock jerks impatiently in my jeans.

Caden kneels down beside the bed and lifts Harper's skirt to her waist all around. My eyes catch on her red panties and my dick gets harder.

"Fuck," I breathe out.

"Yeah, I've been thinking about getting her out of these since I got under them in the car." Fucking Caden. Of course he touched her in his car. I probably would have done the same.

"I'm not walking around a party with no panties on," she tells the ceiling.

Caden slips them down her legs but leaves them around her ankles because of her boots. "Don't worry, little nympho. I'll leave them on along with your boots, but that means we'll need a different position."

"What?" She squeaks as he rolls her over and pulls her up on her hands and knees on the bed.

Caden dips his finger into her pussy and strokes in and out. Her whimper turns into a moan that has my balls tightening. So innocent but so fucking sexy. I can't wait to fuck her. To feel her come around my cock. To fill her so full and make her mine.

"So fucking wet already. Fuck, little nympho, I've barely touched you. Tell me you didn't get aroused by those two playing in there." Caden smirks my way.

Her head drops, and she follows Caden's finger with her hips. She bites her lip and moans. "Not them. What you said."

After I finish taking off my pants, I nod to Caden and walk around to Harper's head.

Her gaze lifts to my dick, and she licks her lips. Red, wet, and willing. My cock weeps and twitches. Her dark eyes continue up to mine. When I stroke my hand over my cock, her eyes return to it.

"So much bigger," she murmurs.

Caden meets my eyes. "How do you want to do this?"

We could do this in her current position, but I want to have her powerless beneath me. "Put her head on the pillows. Let the princess get comfortable."

He withdraws his finger and sucks it in his mouth. He flips her on her back, dragging her to the edge of the bed, before he grabs a pillow to stuff under her head. She makes little noises as he tosses her about. He ducks under her legs so her boots are on his back, tied together by her panties.

When he blows on her wet, exposed pussy, she cries out. So close already. He cocks an eyebrow at me. "You going to watch or join in?"

Her greedy eyes focus on my cock.

"I want to watch her explode once before she takes my cock." I stroke myself slowly. Control is important.

Caden chuckles before he covers her pussy with his mouth.

Her fingers dig into the bedspread as her dark gaze stays on me, watching my hand on my cock. More precum comes out, and I use it to glide my fist down my cock.

Caden is a noisy fucker when he goes down on our girl, but tonight Harper is almost as vocal. She gives little pants, whimpers, and moans. Her eyes try to shut, but she keeps them locked on me. Like she needs me to be a part of this to get her there.

I tighten my hand around the base of my cock to keep from coming. Fuck, I'm not that weak. She's gorgeous turned on, and when she explodes, I want to be a part of it. I want her to feel every inch of me coming inside her. Any way I can be inside her.

Her lips part as her chest flushes above her neckline. Does that flush cover her breasts too? Her fingers claw into the bedspread, and she arches her back as she cries out her orgasm. Caden doesn't let up, making her whine and twist as he keeps tormenting her sensitive flesh, but I'm done watching.

As I climb on the bed, Harper watches me with those greedy eyes.

I straddle her chest with my knees on either side of her breasts. "Open."

With her eyes on mine, she opens her mouth, and I slip my tip past her lips. When her tongue delves into my slit, licking at the precum gathered there, I groan. She smiles around my cock before she takes it farther into her warm, wet mouth. Her hands grab my ass to help control her and my movement.

Unlike Sidney's blow job, Harper puts a lot into it, enthusiasm and little moans of pleasure. Sure, Caden's got his tongue in her pussy and that's probably a contributor, but even this morning when I fucked her face, she enjoyed every moment.

It's not a chore she wants to finish to get to the good part. It *is* the good part. She puts every piece of her into getting me off. It turns her on. And that's hot as fuck.

One of her hands explores, cradling my balls and teasing my perineum with her fingertips. I put my hand on the headboard for balance. Using my other hand, I grab her hair and wait. Her eyes lift to mine, and I see the moment she surrenders to me.

It ripples through me like an orgasm. The power exchange is potent. Giving in to me. Letting me do what I want to her.

Still touching me, she relaxes her tongue and throat for me. With her under my control, I use her mouth the way I want to. I move slowly in and out, not rough like this morning. I want this to last. She licks and sucks. Now both hands are free to roam over my abs, balls, thighs. And she touches me anywhere she can reach.

I keep my thrusts shallow, not taking her throat, not wanting to hit her gag reflex. She moans as she builds to her own climax. She sucks on me, hollowing out her cheeks until my eyes fucking cross. Her mouth feels so good.

Thrusting a few more times, I come with our eyes locked. She swallows me down. One word reverberates through my head. *Mine.*

I pull out of her mouth and slide down so I can kiss her, needing to be part of her as Caden pushes her over the edge. I catch her scream in my mouth. Her whole body rocks from her orgasm, and I ride through it with her. As she comes down, I kiss her mouth and her nose and her eyes.

She blinks up at me, so connected my heart throbs.

Caden lifts his head. "My turn."

***

HARPER

I'm just catching my breath when Caden lays down on the bed and undoes his belt and pants. Luke helps me up. Our eyes connect again, and that feeling of connection centers me and keys me up at the same time.

I kind of want to take off all my clothes and the shoes that confine me. Press my naked skin against him. But there's something reassuring about not being fully naked, though Luke is. And oh my god, he's the whole package. He just came and his cock is already hardening.

For me.

I meet his eyes. My brain functions a little slower as it swims through the alcohol buzz, but the orgasms are definitely waking it up.

"What next?" I ask.

Luke smirks as he lifts me against his chest. My breasts press into his hard muscles. How easy would it be for him to lift my skirt and pump his cock into my pussy?

My pussy clenches. Part of me wants him to. I get wetter just thinking about it. Part of me wants more. Wants it all. Wants to feel that thickness slide inside me and make me his.

All his.

As if he can read my mind, he smiles. "Those are naughty thoughts, princess."

"You like my naughty thoughts," pops out of my mouth. I don't know what I'm saying or even doing, but it feels so fucking good. I'm so relaxed. My limbs feel loose and my lips buzz. I just want more pleasure and I know I'm going to get it.

Caden spreads his legs wide with his massive cock displayed between. "Come on, little nympho. Time to put your mouth to good use."

I lick my lips as Luke releases his hold on me and turns me. His hands keep my hips steady and up as I bend down to tongue the tip of Caden's cock. Caden groans. I rest my hands on his hairy thighs.

My skirt lifts over my ass again, and I pause and lift my head to meet Caden's eyes.

"Luke's not going to fuck you with his cock," Caden reassures me.

But Luke's naked behind me and kneeling. I can feel the heat of him close between my knees. And then his bare cock slides between my pussy lips. My already sensitive pussy tightens at the sensation, and I press back against him.

"Luke?" Even I can hear the fear in my tone.

"My dick isn't going inside you anywhere but your mouth tonight, princess." Luke's voice is soothing and calms me a little, but his cock is still against my pussy. It's both nerve-racking and insanely arousing as he slides himself up and down through my wetness.

"Focus, little nympho. You'd know the difference between his cock and his fingers. Trust me. I'll hold your line." Caden's green eyes lock on mine. I can see the truth in his eyes and his words.

I whimper as sparks build within me as Luke rocks against my clit. I can almost imagine what it would feel like if he slipped inside me, pushing all the way in, so deep. All mine.

It's enough with Luke pressing against me to push me over the edge.

Clenching Caden's thighs, I come all over Luke's cock. I can feel myself dripping all over him, while my insides spiral with lust and longing, pulsing empty.

Luke's cock leaves me, and I feel the warm press of his tongue against my entrance, cleaning up the wetness he caused.

Leaning down, I take Caden's cock into my mouth, longing to feel the thickness of a cock in my body. The only acceptable place I can handle right now. Moaning at how his cock stretches my lips when I go a little farther down on him.

Luke's tongue thrusts into my dripping wet pussy, and I whimper around Caden's cock. This feels so fucking good. I lick up and down the cock in my mouth as Luke continues to thrust his tongue inside me. My hips rock against him, wanting more, needing more.

I suck on the head of Caden's cock, while my insides tighten and burn with an aching need. His hand comes down to my hair. But instead of grabbing it to take control, he strokes his hand over my head, caressing the side of my face. His look is almost tender.

Luke's tongue leaves my pussy to tease the space between my core and asshole. My pussy gushes as I wonder if he'll do what Eli did to me. Luke strokes his fingers over my clit before one slides inside me, while his thumb continues to tease my clit.

Luke adds another finger in my pussy and the sensation increases. I try to focus on giving Caden pleasure, but then Luke's tongue finds my puckered hole, swirling around it while his fingers keep driving into me.

I can't focus on anything. Everything that touches me sends pleasure spiraling through me.

Caden's fingers weave into my hair.

"Let me take over, little nympho." Caden's voice washes over me, sending shivers down my back.

I release the tension in my neck as he takes over moving me on his cock. Closing my eyes, I focus on what's happening to me. Caden's cock fills my mouth while Luke's fingers thrust in and out of my pussy. I'm on the edge of another orgasm. It's building an inferno inside me, so close to exploding.

Luke presses his tongue into my asshole, and I groan around Caden's cock. It's too much and not enough at the same time. Caden lifts my mouth from his cock and I open my eyes, meeting his.

"Come for us, little nympho."

As if my body was waiting for his permission, the heat spreads through me and I can't take it anymore. The pressure builds until it ruptures, and my release screams out of me. Luke doesn't ease up, and my already spent body is so trigger-happy, flutters of aftershocks rock through me.

Caden brings me back down over him, and a small orgasm shudders through me at the feel of his cock against my tongue. I suck on him as he comes in my mouth with a roar. I greedily swallow every drop.

Luke kisses my ass cheeks and slowly removes his fingers from my pussy. He covers me in kisses, and little aftershocks shake me as I lift off Caden's cock and rest my head on his thigh. His hand brushes over my hair.

"Good girl." Caden's deep voice shatters our heavy breathing as we all come down. My heart flips at those words.

I blow out a breath as Luke eases my panties up my thighs. He gets off the bed and probably goes to put his clothes back on. Caden adjusts his pants to put his cock away and then tugs me up into his arms.

He kisses the top of my head as we lie there for a few minutes. Me warm and content in his embrace.

Luke dresses and sits on the side of the bed. He holds his arms out to me. My heart swells and my pulse skitters along my veins. I kiss

Caden's jawline before moving into Luke's arms. I straddle his lap and wrap my arms around his shoulders as I rest my head against him.

His warmth surrounds me and it feels so fucking right. I release a breath and fall into him. His hand strokes my back. I feel safe and almost loved for a few moments. It will probably pass. I'm sure it's just the post-orgasmic haze, but for a moment, this moment, these guys are mine and I'm theirs.

And I'm right where I want to be.

CHAPTER 16

The Enemy Breach

Nico

Luke, Caden, and Harper disappeared a while ago. Not surprised they aren't back yet. Eli passes me the whiskey bottle. I take a long drag and look out over the room. Ashley, Emma, and Hannah have their eyes on us.

They've moved to dance in front of us, rubbing against each other, probably waiting for an invitation. Hannah and Emma are petite and curvy, while Ashley is tall and lean. The amount of clothing they have on would be more appropriate poolside than at a party, but who am I to judge. There's interest in their eyes when they look at me. Ashley always looked at me with disdain when we were younger.

This entire school changed from when I was here before. What a difference six years make. The five of us made some moves to take leadership when I was still here, but then Dad moved for his job.

My new school was fine. I got exemplary grades and played football, but I didn't develop the kind of friendships I had here. My teammates there weren't my brothers like the horsemen. The girls were all right. I fucked around with more than a few, but they didn't come close to the connection I had with Harper.

My best friend. She should have been my first everything, but that ship has sailed. At least she belongs to me now, even if it's with my brothers.

I barely notice when Hannah slides onto my lap. She smiles as her hand dives into my hair. I've apparently had enough to drink. I pass the bottle to Eli, but Ashley, who is on his lap, grabs it and takes a swig.

Emma bounces on Jack's lap a little. "See, this is the way to party, guys."

Eli scoffs and gives me a cocky smile. No one tries to remove the girls though. Technically that would be touching another girl.

"You're so much hotter than Caden." Hannah smashes her breasts against my chest. "You give off big dick energy."

She licks her lips. A month ago, I would have been down to let her suck me off, but not now. I'm not fucking up my arrangement with Harper for any chick.

"No one is as big as Caden." Emma laughs. "I swear he nearly tore me apart. It took me lots of hot baths to recover from his monster dick."

Ashley meets my eyes. "So Nico, are you as big as Caden? Or are you more in line with Eli?"

She rubs against Eli like she owns him. He acts like she's not even there.

"What my dick looks like doesn't matter." I lean away from Hannah. "It's not like any of you could get it up."

Jack laughs, and Eli smirks. But I might as well have waved a red flag in front of Hannah. She trails her finger down my chest.

"Oh, do you have a problem getting it up?" She gives me a pouty look as her hand reaches my belt. "The little virgin can't be very satisfying, so if you need a real woman." Her hand presses on my cock through my jeans. "You let me know how I can be of service."

She grins as she rubs my flaccid cock. There might have been a time when even a stiff breeze could make me rise to the occasion, but I have more control over my dick now. Enough to thwart this chick.

Her smile fades as she realizes she's not making any progress.

"You done?" I lift an eyebrow.

Her eyes narrow, but she doesn't get off my lap. She does, however, stop fondling me.

"Looks like your plaything is already occupied." Ashley grabs Eli's chin and makes him look at her. "You boys could use company. We've got plenty of pussy to go around."

"Thanks, but we know how your pussy gets around," Eli says with an evil smile.

"Why don't you go out there and find some dicks who want your pussies," Jack says with a nod toward the dance floor. "Plenty of guys don't give a shit where that's been."

"You weren't complaining this summer when I let you and Caden tag team me." Emma lowers her head at him like a bull getting ready to charge. "In fact, you guys hit me up...how many times?"

She holds her hand out as she starts counting on her fingers.

"Just perfecting technique, Emma. Nothing personal, but yeah, go find someone else to bother." Jack makes a shooing motion, which Emma does not appreciate.

"What is wrong with you girls?" Harper leans back against Luke as she stands in front of the couch. She's hot as fuck in that black and red dress with kickass boots. "Don't you have any self-respect? How many times do they have to tell you they don't want you until you get a clue?"

Ashley stands from Eli's lap and looks down at Harper. Ashley definitely has big dick energy. "You need to take our friendly advice. Or better yet, decide who you want to keep and throw back the rest for us."

"I don't have to choose, do I?" Harper's eyes are fierce. "They chose me. I can't exactly throw any of them away."

"You wouldn't be so fierce without Luke standing behind you." Ashley sneers as she looks Harper up and down.

Harper must have drank way too much, as she gives the same look to Ashley. "Tell your skanky friends to get off my men."

Emma laughs, right before she lands on the floor. She glares up at Jack, and he holds his hands up like he didn't do it, but his grin says he did.

I give Hannah a look, and she rises off me.

"Not like I want your broke-ass dick, anyway." She rolls her eyes.

Harper raises an eyebrow at me to ask what that's all about, but I just subtly shake my head.

"You don't have to worry about the horsemen getting aggressive with anyone but you guys if you continue to sit your asses where they don't belong." Harper steps out of the shelter of Luke's arms. "I have all year to keep them satisfied and won't be requiring your help."

She gives the cheerleaders a look of disdain.

"Don't say we didn't warn you." Ashley flicks her hair over her shoulder. "Let's go find some quality dick, girls."

They walk away, and Harper sits in my lap. She frowns. "Did they break your dick?"

The guys laugh as they settle back into their seats. Jack passes the whiskey to Caden, but he hands it to Luke without taking a drink.

"My dick is fine. She just couldn't get a lift out of it." I lean forward and press my lips to her ear as I whisper, "But I've been hard for you since you walked into the room."

I shift her on my lap so she can feel how hard I am. A blush works its way up from her chest. "Oh."

Caden hands her a cup. "Your drink."

Meeting his gaze, she takes a sip and smiles. I take the cup from her and take a drink of it. It's a mix of Coke and rum, but light on the rum.

She stays on my lap while she drinks. The guys and I talk until "Don't Be Shy" by Tiësto & Karol G comes on.

"Oh, I love this song." She passes her cup to Eli and stands. Grabbing my hands, she drags me off the couch and into the crowd of teenagers dancing.

I let her lead me, and Jack follows us. When she settles on a spot, Jack closes in on her back while she dances to the music. She twists her body around and spins in a circle, which lifts her skirt almost all the way up.

Her laughter fills my ears, and all I want is to find someplace private to kiss her until she smiles up at me in that daze she gets. Instead, I pull her hips forward against mine, and her dark eyes pop up, meeting mine. Her hands go to my shoulders, and mine rest on her waist.

Jack's hands sway with her hips until we're all moving to the beat together.

If someone told me I would share my girl with other guys a week ago, I would have told them to fuck off. No way would I share Harper with anyone. She was mine and mine alone.

But these aren't just some guys. We proved ourselves on the football field. Each striving to be the best and recognizing that need in the others. We became more than friends. We became a unit. Leaving the guys and Harper behind was devastating.

Coming home from football camp after spending weeks with my brothers wore on me every year. Sure, I had friends at my school, but I always felt like an outsider.

Returning was an easy decision. I wanted to play football with my team and get the girl. I'm still not sure what this is to Harper. She must be so overwhelmed. Sexually.

I don't know what will happen when the guys finally move to penetrative sex with her. How long can this thing last? Five to one? That type of ratio leaves someone out. Or leaves Harper one exhausted girl.

All I know is, I'll be there on the other side of this. If everyone else leaves, it will still be me and her. I'd swear it to her here and now if I thought it'd make a difference.

The guys and I had a talk after practice. They told me the deal and what the plan is, though a lot of it hinges on Harper. Fortunately, they want her to give her virginity over to them. It's still her choice.

But I wonder if she's already made it. Her body curves into mine as we dance, and I know she can feel my erection pressed against her. Probably Jack's too.

I lift my hand to finger her collar. Her dark eyes meet mine again and her lips part. Unable to resist, I grab the back of her neck and claim her mouth. Kissing her with all the pent-up longing I've felt since I left her.

There's never been another Harper in my life. Someone who gets me on a deep level. When we were young, we used to lie in the grass and talk about everything.

I worried she'd be taken when I returned. That I would have to fight to win her. But then I saw her at the football game and knew I had to have her no matter what it took.

Which meant joining the deal with the horsemen. Things would have gone a lot differently if Luke hadn't accepted me back into the fold. If I can offer her protection from them when she needs it, I will. Right now, everyone seems on the same page, but it's early, and I've only been involved for the past twenty-four hours.

I haven't seen them at school yet. Though football practice was eye-opening. They walk in like they're gods, and the other guys act like it's cast in stone.

She returns my kiss, wrapping her arms tight around my neck, dragging me down until I lift her in my arms so I'm not bent over. Her legs wrap around my waist as we learn each other's mouths. She startles and then moans into my mouth.

Not relinquishing her lips, I open my eyes and see Jack grin at me before his mouth descends on her neck. I slip my hand under her skirt and run into Jack's hand. He has her panties pulled to the side and his finger is driving in and out of her wet pussy.

I slide my finger over her clit, and she tightens her arms around me. Her tongue caresses mine as I add my finger to Jack's pumping in and out of her. Stretching her around our fingers.

Her mouth opens wider as she tries to catch her breath, but I keep mine over hers, ready to suppress any noises she might make. Somewhere in my mind, I remember we're at a party on a crowded dance floor. I should care, but I don't. Fuck, I had too much to drink. All I care about is making my girl shatter in my arms.

I press against her clit with my thumb, and she comes. Her cunt convulses on our fingers as she cries out into my mouth. The music and my mouth muffle her.

We drag our hands from under her skirt, righting her panties. As I lift her finger to my lips, she grabs my hand and sucks my finger like she did my cock yesterday. Her dark eyes hold me prisoner as she takes her time to lick her essence off my finger.

When I pull my finger out of her mouth, I capture her lips. I taste her and want more. The ache deep in my balls craves release. I want to possess her, bury myself deep inside her and fill her with my cum until she never forgets me again.

When I lift my mouth from hers, she gives me that languid smile. She's a little drunk, and we just finger fucked her in front of our classmates. If she didn't have a reputation before this party, this would seal the deal.

She doesn't seem to care now. But when we're all sober, she might be mortified.

We dance for a little while longer. She spins around and kisses Jack. Their kiss pulls at something inside me. It's not jealousy. It's want, desire, need.

Watching her take pleasure from someone else doesn't burn me like I thought it would.

When we head back to the others, Caden curls his finger toward Harper, and she lowers herself onto his lap. He kisses her with a tenderness that surprises me, and she curls up against him like he's a giant teddy bear, not a fucking enforcer on the football field and off.

This girl seems to want all of us. And if it's all of us she wants, I'll give her all of me in return.

CHAPTER 17

Know Your Enemy

HARPER

Yawning, I snuggle on Caden's lap. The music still pounds in the room. His hand rubs down my back soothingly, and I could fall asleep in his arms right here in the middle of a party.

"Time to go, kitten." Eli holds his hands down to me, and Caden helps me up. I stand on my own feet, even though I'd prefer to wrap myself around Eli like a koala. It's hard to remember other people exist when I'm in the horsemen's company.

We work our way out of the party. Each time the guys stop to talk to someone, I lean against Eli. His arm holds me against his side as he strokes his hand up and down my back. I sigh with pleasure.

Being with these guys isn't much of a hardship. Everyone wants to talk to them, and it takes us probably thirty minutes before we actually leave the party. But they all stay with me.

Just like at the party, except when some of them took me off on our own.

I still don't know how this is going to work. I'm ready to sleep and I have at least three guys who haven't come yet. As we walk toward the cars, I don't know what the expectations are.

I texted Mom a while ago saying I wouldn't be home tonight and

112

not to worry. I assured her my purse is filled with condoms. She sent me the emoji face with the straight mouth and a *be safe*.

The party is still going strong, but as we walk down the street, the noise fades. I'm not sure how Sidney doesn't end up with the police at her door.

"Let's stop at a diner. Get some food and energy back into Harper." Jack smacks my ass as he passes me and Eli.

"Hey." I go to cover my ass, but Luke is already there, his hand rubbing at the sting. My eyes go to his, helpless to what he makes me feel. Everything about him draws me in.

"Food sounds good." Caden stops in front of Eli's car and waits for us to catch up. His green eyes twinkle with mischief in the streetlights. "Little nympho and I will be along shortly."

"I'll be riding with you." Nico grabs my hand and pulls me into his arms. He smirks at Caden. "Too many dicks in Eli's car."

Caden raises an eyebrow, as if he's going to fight Nico over this. I leave Nico's arms and hug Caden around the waist as we walk to his car. Nico shoves his hands in his pockets and grins at me as he follows.

"Getting you alone is practically impossible, little nympho," Caden complains in my ear.

My insides burn a little brighter at the thought of all the guys when we get back to Caden's. Not that I don't love being with one or even two of them, but having them all there... My pussy pulses. Maybe I like being overwhelmed.

"Sit in the back," Caden says to Nico as he opens the passenger door for me. "I'm not listening to you two make out while I drive."

"You're no fun." I pout up at him.

He kisses me, dragging me up against him and obliterating my mouth with his. Holy shit, the way this guy kisses me is addictive.

"Get in the car before I ravish you in the street." His green eyes mean business, so I get into the car. Even though a small part of me wants to rebel and see what happens.

He adjusts himself as he walks around to his side.

Maybe I'm going to have to satisfy all my men again. Maybe I'll have some coffee with whatever I eat. I definitely need to work on my stamina and maybe add some jaw exercises into my daily habits.

"What else do you do besides study and horsemen?" Nico asks with a cheeky grin.

"She used to dance competitively," Caden answers for me as he pulls the car out to follow the others. "She's in art. She's good, too."

My mouth drops open.

Caden turns and winks at me. "We got you from the art classroom. It's the advanced class. You're lucky I didn't have space in my schedule, or I would have been in that class too."

"No way." I refuse to think Caden could be in my one class that's all mine.

"You aren't the only one with three years in art. We just weren't in the same classes. I've seen your drawings when I went into my sculpting class. The advanced studio is for anyone with three years' experience no matter what material you use."

"You sculpt?" My mind is blown. Maybe I'm still a little drunk because I can't get over this. "Which ones were yours?"

"Last year, I made the dragon out of wire," Caden says like it's nothing.

My mouth drops open. My favorite piece. I thought about asking Ms. Sullivan whose it was. But the signature was a symbol. "I love that piece."

Caden's lips tip up as he pays attention to the road.

"I signed up for advanced art studio." Nico leans forward between my and Caden's seats. "Third period?"

I smile, honestly excited. "Oh, cool. You'll have to sit with me and Kenz."

Caden scoffs as he parks in the diner's lot. "You're excited for Nico to be in art, but if I'd been in that class..."

His eyes narrow as they meet mine, but he doesn't finish the sentence. Then he opens his door and slips out.

Fuck, is he hurt? Or pissed off?

"Caden," I yell when I get out. That fucker is fast. I catch up and grab his arm. "Wait."

"Why don't you talk to your best friend?" Caden rounds on me, towering over me. A week ago, I would have cowered from him. "He's the only one you talk to."

I step back and my eyebrows cave in. Is that true? "You and I have talked."

"No, little nympho. I told you some stuff, but we haven't talked. Even at lunch, you zone out like we aren't worthy of your attention unless one of us has our hands or mouth on you."

I feel heat gathering inside me as the others join us and stop around me and Caden. "I—"

I don't know what to say. They took charge of my life, and I went along. Eventually, I submitted like the good little girl, but yeah, I don't really talk to them.

"Maybe that's all we are to you. A bunch of cocks." Caden's eyes burn as he looks down at me.

Well, fuck me. Maybe that's what's been missing. I don't really know them. I've been worried about them wanting me for me, but what have I actually shown them of who I am?

I could pick their dicks out in the dark possibly, but I couldn't tell you what any of them want out of life. I couldn't tell you their dreams, their desires, or even something as simple as their favorite color.

But they haven't really tried to get to know me either. Someone has to give a little.

"I'm sorry, Caden." I step forward and put my hand over his heart.

He huffs out a breath but doesn't pull away.

"I really am. I made assumptions about all of you based on what I've been told for years." Swallowing, I take a breath. "I was afraid to talk to you all. Afraid to give you every piece of me. But I also don't know where I fit in. At lunch, you guys talk about football. When we're alone, usually my clothes are off rather quickly."

Caden smirks. "We do like you better without clothes."

Smiling, I shake my head. "How about this? I'll try harder to get to know you guys and be more open about myself."

Caden's green eyes find mine and he softens. "We can probably find something besides football to talk about."

"Can we eat now?" Jack asks. "Because I need some meat."

"Yes, we all know you like meat too, Jack." Caden wraps his arm around my shoulders and drags me into his side as we all walk into the diner.

Besides a slight scuffle to sit beside me in the booth, ordering goes off without a hitch. The server brings out coffees, sodas, and a hot chocolate for me. I'll switch to coffee afterward.

"Okay." I sit up straight, and they all eye me warily. "Plans for the future? College, workforce, occupation choice, military?"

"Can't this just come out organically?" Jack sits directly across from me. He's still sore about not sitting next to me. And probably from the bruise forming on his arm from Caden hitting him for trying to take his spot.

"This is how we get to know each other." I look around. "Hey, you guys kept me from making friends—"

"Not me." Nico raises his hand beside Jack. Jack punches him in the arm. Nico rubs his arm and scowls at Jack.

"As I was saying, I'm not exactly the best at making friends or starting small talk, so if you want to make this a game—" Their eyes perk up. "Then make it a game to break the ice."

"Fine," Luke says next to me. "A game requires rules and prizes."

"What would you suggest?" I take a sip of my hot chocolate and lick the whipped cream from my lips. "What kind of prizes?"

"Alone time with you." Nico clears his throat. "For every answer we give, we get five minutes alone with you."

The guys are all nodding, but Luke looks pensive. "Not until her virginity is gone."

Ah yes, the stumbling block of my virginity. "You don't trust the guys to keep their hands to themselves?"

"No." Luke doesn't even hesitate. "I'm also sure you would prefer to dispose of your virginity without an audience."

I can feel the heat licking my cheeks. "So the time alone would be for after we all..." I end with a wave of my hands.

"Fuck, princess." Luke helpfully supplies the word.

Heat swamps my face. I glance around, but the diner is almost empty and everyone we know is partying at Sidney's. I take in a deep breath and hold it for a moment.

Releasing it, I say, "Is that okay for all of you?"

"Since we're on the topic of your virginity..." Jack smiles and taps his finger. "Any time frame for that?"

I press my lips together and cross my legs under the table. "Obviously I'm not a prude..."

Heads nod around the table. My face heats. This isn't awkward at all.

"I don't know what I'm waiting for." I fold my hands around my mug. "We're going fast, which I know is more a you guys thing than a me thing, but my virginity is definitely a me thing."

"What do you need? Love?" Eli asks. Of everyone, him asking is the most unemotional. He's the logical one. He hides his emotions.

"I'm not a romantic, but I would like something more than I have a vagina and you have a penis, so let's fuck." The whipped cream has begun to melt into my hot chocolate. "I don't know what that something is. Maybe friendship. Maybe connection. Maybe nothing more than sexual frustration. But right now, something is missing and I'm still..." I swallow and admit, "Afraid."

No one says anything right away, and my chest aches with the need to breathe.

"What was Ashley talking about earlier?" Luke asks, and my attention goes to his calculating eyes. I take in a breath.

"What do you mean?" I was still a little high off orgasms and pretty drunk when I confronted them.

Holy shit, I confronted the Cheermonsters. My ass is grass.

"They gave you some friendly advice." Eli leans forward with his elbows on the table.

"Oh, yeah." I fold my hands in my lap and take a deep breath. "Kenz and I were out to breakfast and Sidney, Ashley, and Emma joined us. Not really joined, more like came over to our table and made themselves comfortable."

Luke's hand rests on my thigh, making the butterflies fly around drunk in my stomach. I lift my gaze to his light blue eyes. I should just tell them. I mean, it's not me that's going to get in trouble over what the girls said.

Even the tips of my ears burn when I say, "Sidney told me if I couldn't keep you guys satisfied, they would step in and help."

"The fuck?" Eli shakes his head. "At least they have lady balls if nothing else going for them."

"Did they say why?" Luke's fingers clench into my thigh. I want to say that doesn't affect me, but those butterflies dive bomb my pussy.

Of course, he wouldn't let it go at that, so I continue. "It's some suspicion of theirs that if you don't get sex often, you guys will rage on the school or something weird like that."

Luke presses his lips together and looks thoughtful.

"You wouldn't actually do it though?" Nico asks. "Ask them to step in?"

I shake my head. "No, I don't want them touching any of you."

Caden grabs the back of my neck and kisses the hell out of me. I think I hear low voices in the background talking, but Caden consumes me. His tongue slides against mine and my fingers dig into his hair to hold him there. Luke strokes my inner thigh, winding me tight. When Caden finally releases me, I inhale to fill my starving lungs.

"We'll discuss this later." Luke catches my attention.

The guys are quiet as the server brings the food over. The fevered need inside me dies down a little, and I suspect Caden was a distraction so the guys could talk. I watch them all and wonder.

"I'm applying to college for next year," Jack says after swallowing a bite of food. "Not sure what for yet, but I know I want a job that pays a lot. Mom says I should go pre-med, but I'm not sure. I really enjoy working with computers."

"You hacked my webcam," I realize.

Jack grins proudly. "Guilty."

"I've been on the college track since I was born," Caden says. "My dad wants me to take over the family business, but he travels so much for work, and I'm not sure that's the life I want to lead."

"What about art?" I ask. After all, I'm familiar with what he's capable of, and it's impressive.

"It's a hobby." He shrugs. "My family wouldn't let it be anything more. Business is where the money is. No need to waste an education on crap."

I slide my hand over his on the table and smile. "Your art isn't crap. It's amazing. I'd like to see more of your pieces if you want to show me."

He leans in to peck my lips with a soft kiss. Butterflies burst in my stomach at the simple touch. Huh, that's new.

"I'm going pre-law and then law school." Eli raises an eyebrow at me. "One of us will need to look after these guys once we make it to the real world."

"And that's you?" I give him a teasing look.

"I have the brain. In spring, I'm on the debate team. It's good experience until the mock trials in April."

"My parents want me to go to school to become a doctor," Nico says, rubbing the back of his neck. "But I don't really have the stomach for blood. I haven't really settled on what I want to do, but I know I want to play football in college and figure out my degree while I'm there."

"Mom's a nurse, and I'm not cut out for that. The sight of blood makes me sick." I turn my nose up and shove some hash browns into my mouth. My eyes go to Luke as the only one who hasn't answered.

"My father wants me to follow his footsteps. Harvard Business and then into the family business," Luke says.

"But what do you want to do?" I ask softly.

"It doesn't matter what I want." Those words sound so definitive I almost reach around Luke and give him a hug. Why do I always want to hug Death?

"What about you, sweetheart?"

Everyone's attention is on me when I look up.

"Oh, uh, college for sure, I've started sending my applications and essays for scholarships. I don't have a particular college I really want to go to and I'm applying as undecided. I might want to do something with business or maybe teaching."

"Not art?" Caden takes a piece of bacon and devours it.

"I'm not really talented. I just like art. It helps clear my brain." I shrug and push my almost empty plate away.

We could all end up anywhere. College is a time of growth and finding out who you are. It's not like we're all in a relationship and plan to have a future together, but I will miss them next year and I still hope they get to do what they want. Will they keep in touch with me?

I shake myself mentally and look around the table. My brain is clearly not thinking straight. Keep in touch?

"So what? That's five minutes alone with each of you for me?" I raise my eyebrows at them. "I get the prize too, right?"

Jack laughs. "Can we use our prizes at the same time? So instead of five minutes alone we get ten?" He shifts his attention to Luke.

So I turn to him too.

"I guess that means I get fifteen minutes alone with you, princess."

"Wait a minute," I say over everyone else protesting. I hold my hands up. "Why do you get fifteen?"

"You asked me a follow up question and I answered." Luke wipes his mouth with his napkin. "Caden and Eli also get fifteen."

Jack and Nico look put out.

"It's not my fault Harper is more interested in us," Luke says with an evil glint in his eyes.

"That is not— You didn't—" My mouth falls open and I narrow my eyes on him. "You're diabolical sometimes."

"Only sometimes?" He cocks an eyebrow.

The server stops by with the check. Before anyone else can claim it, Caden hands her a couple hundred-dollar bills and tells her to keep the change.

Caden grins. "Want to ask me another question?"

Smiling, I shake my head.

"Come on, little nympho. You're sleeping in my bed tonight."

"With the rest of us," Luke clarifies.

"Yeah, but you guys don't matter." Caden draws me out of the booth and into his arms. "When this is all over, I'm keeping Harper."

CHAPTER 18

The Coercion

I can't tell if he's joking or just egging on the other guys, but something inside me softens. I think I might like Caden. Like, *like*-like. It's weird as he leads me to his car and helps me in.

I didn't think I could actually like a horseman. Of course, Nico was and is one of my best friends, but he doesn't count. Out of everyone, I didn't figure I'd fall for Caden.

"You look perplexed," Caden says as we pull out of the parking lot.

"You just said you were going to keep her, like Harper is some sort of possession of yours," Nico says from the back seat.

"Yeah, so?"

"You can't just keep a person unless you plan on being more than whatever the fuck we're doing with Harper."

I turn back to look at Nico with an arched look.

He holds up his hands. "I'm not saying we don't have a weird sort of relationship going on, but according to you lot, there is an end date. School ends, this ends."

I rub at the ache in my chest at the thought. Of course, I've always figured it won't make it that long anyway, but it feels wrong to talk about this ending when it hasn't even really begun. But isn't that what I've been doing since the start, worrying about the end?

Isn't that what's really holding me back?

"Of course, Harper could tell me to go fuck myself." Caden talks to Nico like I'm not even here. "But I've got months to sway her to my side and convince her. She'll let me keep her."

"What if I want to keep her too?" Nico leans forward in the seat.

"Well, we can both keep her."

"Wait, what?" My head is spinning.

Caden grins. "Maybe by the end of this, we'll all want to keep her. Do you want your own crew of men, little nympho? You can pick who pleasures you every night. Have fifteen kids. Three each, of course."

"Whoa, I haven't even let you inside me and you're already signing me up for fifteen kids? Are you insane?" Fifteen kids? What the hell is Caden even talking about? When did he have time to figure all this out?

"Not fifteen? That too many?" Caden chews on his lip. "Well, I'm sure we'll be willing to compromise to two apiece then. That's only ten. Totally doable."

"When they aren't coming out of your vagina?" I almost yell. Why are we even talking about this? He can't possibly be serious.

He pulls into the garage at his house. "If I had a vagina, I would carry them for you, but I don't. Though we'll probably need to start working on your Kegel exercises now. Gotta keep that pussy nice and tight."

I close my eyes and count to ten. This conversation did not go the way I thought it would. Of course, I didn't even start the conversation.

"I think she's going to explode, and not in the fun way." Nico chuckles from the back seat. He's not far off. I don't even know what to say.

Caden turns off the car.

"If you can take my cock, a baby won't be that much harder." He smirks.

"Are you fucking kidding me right now?" I throw my hands up in the air and push out of the car. My chest is tight and my breathing comes in bursts. "Ten kids. Like that will fucking happen. What would my mother think of me with five guys? And who knows how we'll keep track of who is whose kid and what if you guys leave me? With ten kids? I am not a breeding cow."

Caden puts his hand on my shoulder and turns me toward the door. "All I'm saying is that at the end of the year, if everyone decides to keep you, I'm okay with it. I don't mind sharing you as long as I get a little alone time with you."

I have nothing to say to the crazy man. I walk out of the garage toward the back of the house, to the door Eli took me in the other day.

"Hey, are you okay?" Nico catches up with me.

"I don't even know. I mean, what the hell?" I jerk to a stop and point back at Caden. "Like this arrangement with the six of us would survive the real world? We haven't even had sex yet. I don't even know if I like some of these guys. I was worried about having a connection for sex, but I wasn't talking love and all the fuckery that comes with that word."

My voice keeps getting progressively higher. "And keeping me? What? Are we going to go to the same college? If we're planning on ten kids, do I need to get knocked up now or am I going to be in my forties and still pushing out kids? Ten?"

I think my brain glitches on that, because I can't even draw in a breath now. What the hell is Caden thinking? It would be different if he had five women and wanted ten kids. "I don't even know if I want kids."

Nico pulls me into his chest and runs his hand over my back. "Like you said, we don't have to worry about any of that. We just need to worry about graduating high school. Before that, we have to worry about winning the championship. Before that, we need to worry about what's going to happen next week during senior week. And before that, we need to worry about tonight, and how you'll keep your five men pleased so you don't have to call in reinforcements."

When I lift my head to glare at him, he smirks.

"And if you end up with ten kids, I'm not going anywhere but by your side." Nico grins. "Just so you know, I'm willing to wait for you as long as you need, sunshine. I'm here for you. Not just sex. If it takes all year or even to the next, I'll still be here."

My eyes meet Nico's deep brown ones, and I feel that connection we had as kids. When we daydreamed about growing up and what it would be like. He's right, all this can wait. Caden isn't serious. I just let myself get caught up in it.

"Next year?!" Caden tugs me from Nico's arms. He shoves Nico back and draws me into him. His arms drape loosely around my waist. "I'm willing to wait too, little nympho. Not a fucking year though. Tomorrow? Is tomorrow good for you?"

I laugh and punch Caden in the gut lightly. He covers his stomach like I hurt him, but smiles and gives me a wink. His green eyes sparkle in the dim light.

"Not today or tomorrow. Maybe never. You guys took me from untouched to a technical virgin in like a week."

"Yeah, but you liked it." Caden grabs my hips and pulls me in against him.

"Like it or not, I need time to adjust to the new status quo." I tug on his dark hair, and he gives me a sly grin.

The rumble of a car makes us turn to see Eli's car coming up the drive. Caden bends his head toward me as he looks at the guys parking.

"I wouldn't mention the kids just yet. Don't want to scare off your crew."

"I'm not going to have a crew or ten kids, Caden." I thwack his chest with the back of my hand.

"You're going to love sex so much, little nympho, that I'll have you knocked up every chance I get." Caden captures my mouth as I try to tell him off.

Instead, I fall into his kiss like I always do and feel that little lift in my stomach at his words. Sure, they're insane words, but the fact he wants to keep me, at least right now, feels awesome. Maybe there is something here we can grow.

"Stop hogging our girl," Eli punches Caden in the arm.

"Little nympho punches harder than you," Caden says.

Eli tugs me into him and kisses me. I realize I haven't played at all with Eli tonight. His kiss is dark and thorough. Everyone tells me he likes it rough, but besides biting my lip, Eli has played fairly nice with me.

Of course, he also ate my ass yesterday. My cheeks burn at the memory. So there is that.

"Let's get inside before you start the orgy." Jack's words make me pull my mouth away from Eli.

Eli's dark eyes are almost black with the low light. "Come on, kitten. It's time I played with you."

A thrill chases down my spine, along with that little touch of fear Eli always inspires in me.

<hr>

ELI

I run my fingers down Harper's nape as we walk into the lower level. Shivers ripple through her. The cleaners have done their job with the basement since the party last night. It's after one o'clock, but fortunately Harper drank some coffee.

She appears sober and awake. Good.

The guys sit on the couch and relax, knowing I want to put on a show. I want to see what our pet can take. Find her limits and push her past them.

I pull out a chair from the gaming table in the corner and set it in front of them.

"Sit here, kitten."

She sits and watches me carefully as I sit on the coffee table in front of her.

"I want to try something with you."

Her breath comes out in a sharp exhale. "Okay?"

She doesn't seem sure now, but she'll get there.

"I want to restrain and blindfold you." I lean forward and rub my hand up her thigh. "Then I'll control who touches you and when you come. If you come before I say to, you'll get spanked."

Her eyes widen and her pupils dilate. Her chest lifts and falls a little quicker. "No fucking though?"

"No dicks in your pussy or ass. Anywhere else is permissible, yes?"

She moves to bite her lip but then straightens and looks at me. "Yes."

I walk into a storage closet and get what I need. Silky ties for her hands and legs and a blindfold for her eyes. I return to sit in front of her.

Her gaze travels over the things I place next to me. She's probably curious why they're accessible, but I've played at Caden's before and having the necessities on hand makes playing easier.

"Stand up."

She stands for me.

One of the guys turns some music on low. A slow, throbbing beat fills the space.

"Turn around."

She turns and doesn't lose her balance. Not drunk still. Good.

I walk over to her and pull her zipper down on her dress slowly. She shivers.

"Cold?"

"No."

A smile tugs at my lips. "Good."

I slip her dress off her, until she's left in her panties and boots. I'm in the mood to let them decide. I move out of the way so the guys on the couch can see our girl.

"Boots or no boots?"

"No boots," Caden says, and the others nod their heads in agreement. "By the way, those panties are mine."

"I didn't know they were your size." I arch an eyebrow at him.

"They fit my dick just fine." Caden smirks.

"Sit, kitten."

She sits in the chair. Her cheeks are red, but she meets my eyes. I lower to sit on the coffee table. There's something so beautiful about how she gives in to us. How she craves our touch, but still holds back. How she meets us head on even when we push her.

"Right foot please."

She lifts her foot up for me. I take my time untying her boot, loosening the laces, and taking it along with her sock off her foot. Meanwhile, she's sitting in her panties on full display for the guys. She clenches the seat of the chair on both sides. Her breasts are just the right size. They rise and fall with every quickened breath. Her nipples are hard and tight, begging for someone's mouth. Soon.

I drop her boot to the side.

"Other foot."

Following orders, she lifts her boot. Fuck, I love a girl who takes orders. My cock twitches with need.

"At least have her touch herself while you do that," Jack says. "You always take too long."

"Hardly. We've never had such a captive audience before." I wink at Harper. "Have we, kitten?"

Her hands clutch the arms of the chair and her eyes track my every movement. I deposit her boot to the side and release her foot.

"Stand." I walk up to her, so close my shirt brushes against her nipples. They tighten even more for me. Her dark eyes meet mine. Her lips part, and I restrain myself from tasting her again. "Caden, come do the honors since they belong to you."

I step back, and Caden comes over to strip the panties off Harper. She puts her hand on his shoulder to lift her feet out of them. I'm surprised he doesn't do anything more to her, but he takes her panties, inhales them, and shoves them in his pocket. Her breath catches a little as she meets Caden's eyes.

I close in on Harper again. "You need a safe word. Something that's not *no* or *stop*. Something so we know you want to end what's happening, or at least pause it."

Her dark eyes lift to mine as she mulls over the word. My shirt brushes against her nipples again, and she sucks in a breath. "Arrow."

"If you say *arrow*, everyone will stop what they're doing to you." I look at the guys, and they all nod. "I need a pillow."

Nico holds one out to me.

Gesturing to the chair, I say, "Sit, kitten."

She sits down stiffly, aware she's naked on someone else's furniture.

"Scoot forward."

When she does, I slide the pillow behind her lower back. I return to the table for the silky ties. She watches, curious, as I tie her wrists to the arms of the chair first. She gives a little tug to see if she can move, but they hold her tight.

"Spread your legs."

"What?" She hesitates with her knees pressed together. Worry lingers in her eyes.

"Trust me to keep you safe." I stroke my hand over her jaw. If this is going to work for the year, she needs to trust us. "If you want something to stop, you have the power. You just say?"

"Arrow."

"And if your mouth is full?"

Her eyes widen, but then she remembers. "I snap my fingers."

"Show me."

She snaps her fingers.

"Spread your legs, kitten." I'm not trying to trick her into fucking us. I just want to play with her on my terms.

She searches my eyes for a moment and must find what she needs to convince her. She moves forward and spreads her legs, showing me her lovely pussy. All pink and wet. Always so wet for us. Like she was created just for our pleasure.

Trust has to be earned. She's still skittish because she doesn't trust us. I'd blame Luke, but we've all pushed in our own ways. I bend to tie her leg to the chair. Then I adjust her position a little to make sure we have access to all the important bits before I tie her other leg. When I stand, I grab the blindfold.

Her dark eyes meet mine, and I can see her trying to trust me. She's willing to try at least. This is a test for all of us, really. She's spread open before us. We could take her, and she might complain but she'd enjoy it. But we'd lose her trust forever. I wrap the blindfold on and make sure it's secure.

I won't let that happen. Not tonight or any other night.

I want her trust almost as much as I want her body. I won't let anyone take advantage of either.

"Remember, don't come and don't talk. If you do, I'll punish you."

"How will you—"

I smack her pussy. Her mouth opens, she curls a little into herself, and her knees flex to close, but my ties are secure.

"Don't speak. Don't come. Or you'll be punished. Nod if you understand."

She nods, and I turn my back on her to talk to the guys.

"I'll be telling you what to do. You also won't speak. I'll indicate who I want to do what to Harper by pointing to you. If you require undressing for what I ask, I leave it up to you how far down you disrobe."

Jack stands and starts taking off his clothes. I shake my head. He's always so eager to be naked.

"Get off as needed. If you come, do so on Harper or in Harper's mouth."

I turn to look at Harper as her mouth opens and closes and then opens again.

"Do you have something to add, kitten? Shake or nod your head."

She frowns, but then she shakes her head.

"Good. Questions?"

"Perhaps some towels?" Luke gestures to the wooden floor. "In case of clean-up, of course."

I nod to Caden, and he walks to the bathroom to grab some towels.

Taking my seat on the coffee table, I study Harper. Her chest and face are flushed red. Her breathing is quick. Poor girl has just started having orgasms, and I'm going to take them away. Caden sets the towels beside me.

I turn and point to Nico. "Put your cock in her mouth."

"Kitten, turn your head to the left and open your mouth."

Let the game begin.

CHAPTER 19

The Encirclement

HARPER

I'm immobile, and the low music masks some of the guys' movements. The anticipation is killing me. As I turn my head and open my mouth, I realize how much trust I'm putting in Eli.

Yes, I have a safe word if something gets to be too much, but I won't know things are too much until they happen. The smell of rain fills my senses as the guy approaches. Nico.

His cock touches my tongue, and I close around him. He rocks his hips to press in and out of my mouth.

"Lick her pussy."

Oh, fuck. Someone settles between my knees, and a breath caresses my pussy before a tongue licks me. I try to figure out who it is.

"Kitten, turn your right palm up."

My brow furrows, but I do what he says.

"Put your cock in her hand." Eli's command makes my pussy clench.

The smooth weight of a cock fits into my hand. I close around it, and it moves within my grasp. My mind is having trouble figuring out who is who as the guy between my legs flicks my clit with his tongue and Nico keeps working my mouth.

I can feel a climax building. The tension inside me tightens.

"Everyone stop," Eli says. They all move away from me.

Fingers tweak my nipple, shooting pleasure straight to my pussy. I press my lips together to keep from crying out.

"Close. So close." He slides a finger inside me, but just holds it still as my pussy flutters around it. I want to rock against his finger and use it to get me off.

He's right, I'm so fucking close.

"Open your mouth," Eli says.

When I open, a cock presses inside my mouth and fills it with cum. The taste is Jack's. I swallow as Jack removes his cock. It's better than having cum drying all over my body. I shudder at the thought and I'm not sure if I like the idea or dislike it.

"Breathe, kitten. Slow it down." Eli's voice is calm and even. His finger is still inside me, motionless.

"I need you to work two cocks. Let the one on the right use your mouth for a count of thirty and then the left for thirty and back and forth until they come. Can you do that, kitten?"

Nodding, I take a breath before turning my head to the right. When I open my mouth, a cock slips inside, pressing deep. Luke? I've had his cock in my mouth more often than the others. I'm more used to his rhythm as I hum around his cock.

Eli's finger moves slowly in and out of me. I want to tell him I need more than that. But I also don't want to come. The smack on my pussy didn't feel great, but it wasn't all bad either. I count to thirty, and Luke withdraws.

Turning, I part my lips. Nico's cock fills my mouth again. I almost smile since I figured both of them out. Eli flicks his tongue against my clit, and suddenly I'm ready to come again. His finger pumps in and out of me, stroking along all my nerves.

It's right there, and he stops. His finger leaves me and so does his tongue.

I groan around Nico's cock, but then he backs out, and I turn to take Luke's again. I lick and suck and hope to hell Eli will let me come at some point. Someone moves to kneel between my legs, and then a mouth closes around my nipple. A tongue flicks the tip, making me moan around Luke's cock.

Heat works its way through me until I feel like I'm dripping on the floor. A finger pushes into me as I'm changing cocks in my mouth. The mouth on my breast changes to the other, winding me up. Nico slips into my mouth, and I know I'm close again. I want to come so bad.

I try to focus on Nico's cock, sucking and licking him. The smoothness of his skin against my tongue. The way he fills my mouth, and not on the finger sliding inside me or the wet suction on my breast. Groaning, Nico comes. I swallow as he removes his cock.

My mouth closes around Luke again. The feel of his cock in my mouth overwhelms me, making tingles rush through me. He takes my mouth, thrusting deep inside in time with the finger between my thighs.

"Don't come, kitten." Eli's in front of me somewhere. His voice is a little distant. "Keep servicing those cocks."

Luke's cock glides between my lips, and I suck on him hard as I fight against my orgasm. He thrusts deep and comes in my mouth. I swallow it all, taking a moment to breathe before I turn to the left. I open, and my mouth stretches to fit Caden's cock.

Whoever is between my knees, Jack probably, kisses my nipple and retreats, taking his finger out of me. Something settles in my chest. This is something I can do. I can have control. I can keep from coming.

My tongue flattens against the underside of Caden's cock. Someone kneels before me, and I tense. Breath bathes my clit, and I can feel myself pulse in response. Other than his breathing, the guy between my knees does nothing more.

Caden withdraws, and I move to accept the right side. The cock that presses between my lips has to be Eli's. A tongue strokes along my thigh from my knee to my groin. I gasp at the flood of sensation rushing through me at the simple touch. I continue to work Eli's cock while I wait for what comes next.

The tongue strokes along my other thigh following the same path, and I try to close my legs. The ties hold me open. My thighs tremble, shaking with need. I don't think I can hold back much more. He slapped me once for talking, but I'm not sure how many I'll get for coming.

"Both hands palm up, kitten." Eli's voice is breathless and in front of my face. A little burst of pride goes through me at recognizing Eli's cock.

Turning, I take Caden into my mouth. My hands both receive a cock. I close around them as they use my grip to stroke them. Jack and Nico, maybe. That means Luke is between my knees.

My pussy gushes at the knowledge of my men surrounding me. All of them finding pleasure in me. Luke's fingers penetrate me, at least two of them. His mouth closes around my nipple and he sucks, bites, and tugs. I moan around Caden's cock.

I can't hold back any longer. Luke slowly drives me insane with the insistent pressure of his fingers working in and out of me. While he keeps attacking my nipple, making my pussy clamp around his fingers.

"Do you want to come now, kitten?"

Caden backs out of my mouth. Yes, so much, yes. I hold back a whimper and nod. All the friction on me makes the need almost impossible to ignore. The ache between my thighs throbs. I won't be able to hold back much longer.

"Do you trust us, kitten?"

Luke lifts his mouth from my breast. Even though I can't see through the blindfold, the heat of his gaze sears me as he waits for my response. All of their gazes. I clamp down on the release trying to shatter through me.

I nod. Luke moves his fingers inside me, and then I feel the slide of his cock against my clit. Parting my lips for Caden, I draw his cock in and suck on it. Shuddering, he comes in my mouth. I swallow as I turn to Eli. Nico and Jack quicken their paces in my hands. Eli thrusts at the same pace in my mouth as Luke's fingers move within me and Luke's cock slides along my clit.

"Let go, kitten."

The fire I've kept banked rips through me as I moan around Eli's cock. Groaning, he floods my mouth with his cum. I swallow while hot wetness spills over my hands and thighs and stomach.

Even as the others back away, Luke keeps on, holding me in a state of orgasm. I hold my breath as the orgasm ripples through me and I shatter again with a cry.

Warmth surges on my stomach as Luke comes on me. His mouth closes over mine and my pussy convulses around his fingers. I thrust my tongue into his mouth, needing that connection to him. We collide together. His hands thread through my hair as he tilts my head and continues to kiss me.

His cock presses against my stomach, and I become aware of the cooling wetness of his release. He moves the blindfold off my eyes, and I blink them open to meet his. Warm pools of summer rain. So different from the cold ice he usually projects.

He breathes me in and shares his air with me as I calm down.

Eli undoes my wrists and legs. He kisses the top of my head as Luke continues to hold me. "You did great, kitten."

A thrill rushes through my insides.

Caden hands Luke a towel, and Luke wipes the cum from my stomach and his. My legs tremble as Luke helps me to stand. Just when I think I'll collapse back into the chair, he sweeps me up in his arms. My arms wrap around his neck.

It feels normal and safe as he carries me into the bathroom and sets me on the counter. The shower isn't as big as Caden's but it's big enough for me and Luke. He gets the water warm before returning to me.

I'm not drunk, but I must still be buzzed, because this isn't setting off the normal alarms. Luke and I are alone and naked.

Alone.

Naked.

I should be reeling with alarm bells.

Lifting me down, he holds me against him as we enter the shower. I drape my arms over his shoulders and rest my head against his chest. His heartbeat is steady in my ear.

As I press into him, he works shampoo and then conditioner into my hair. His cock is firm, but still no alarm bells. He scrubs soap down my back and then turns me to lean my back against him while he takes care of my front. His fingers sweep over my breasts and between my legs. It's a little arousing, but I'm so far gone after all that.

Leading me out of the shower, he wraps a towel around me and then one around his waist before he lifts me in his arms again. My fingers stray to the ends of his damp blond hair, catching the drips as he walks with me down dimly lit halls.

When we reach Caden's bedroom, Caden takes me from Luke's arms and finishes drying me off before pulling a shirt over me. Eli appears in front of me and pulls me into his arms, holding me sweetly, cradling my head in his hand. His heartbeat is strong under my ear.

"How are you?" He runs his fingers over my wrists to make sure I don't have any marks.

"Good. That was—" I stop and look up into his brown eyes. "Amazing. Thank you, Eli."

He brushes his lips over mine. "Anytime, kitten."

A shiver ripples through me at the pleasure in his dark eyes.

"Time for bed, princess." I swear my body lives for Luke's orders.

Nico and Jack both kiss me before pulling me down in bed with them. I snuggle up against Nico and Jack spoons me from behind. I'm sure the others are around me, but I can't keep my eyes open another second.

Jack

It's Sunday morning, and waking with Harper cuddled against me is going into my top favorite ways to wake up. Waking up to morning head being the all-time favorite, of course.

Last night was awesome.

Harper had us all coming so fucking hard, and then when she came... Fuck, that was spectacular. I'm not sure if I prefer her coming multiple times or one massive orgasm. I'm willing to keep trying both until I figure out a winner.

Her shirt rode up over her hips during the night. I slide my fingers between her thighs and dip into her pussy for some wetness before spreading it over her clit. She presses her ass into my cock (we all slept in boxers again last night) and arches a little.

I don't know if anyone else is up yet, so I work her slowly to ease her awake and not wake the others. I want a piece of Harper of my own. Kissing her nape, I lick and suck along her neck. Her breathing gets harder, and she squirms against me.

I peek up at Nico, and he's awake, his gaze fixed on my hand between Harper's thighs. He's on his side facing her. His hand slides up her side, lifting her shirt up as he goes. He cups her breast and draws his thumb in circles around her hardened nipple.

He gives me a conspiratorial smile. I dip my finger into her entrance again. She's wet now, and her breaths come out in pants. I keep working her clit.

What I wouldn't give to lift her leg over mine and slip inside her. I can't wait until she's no longer a virgin. At first, that's what excited me. Someone so untouched we could be her first everything.

Now I just want to fuck our girl and keep fucking her. Last night with her spread on that chair, we each could have taken turns filling her cunt with our cum until it dripped out of her.

Kissing her shoulder, I suck her skin into my mouth. My other hand moves down to thrust inside her from behind while I still torment her clit. She cries out as she comes, alerting everyone else to what I've been doing. Well, what Nico and I were doing.

Nico kisses Harper as I remove my hands from her. She rolls in my arms and kisses me.

"Good morning, Jack," she whispers and cuddles into me.

"Yeah, good morning, Jack," Caden grumbles behind me. He always wakes up sour. But hearing our girl come and not being a part of it probably put him in a worse mood.

Grabbing Harper, I roll her to my other side. Her eyes widen as she lands with her back against Caden. His arms wrap around her and tug her into him. He grins at me over the top of her head.

I claim Harper's lips, pressing her between me and Caden, so she can feel how hard we both are for her this morning. Her hands reach down and one of them rubs on my hard cock while the other slips behind her. When Caden growls low, I know she's stroking him too.

I tease her nipples with my fingers as I devour her mouth.

Our girl is definitely no prude. Thankfully. I keep thinking about

Caden's words from last night. His claim he's going to keep her. Nico seems to want more from her than just her body too.

It has me thinking about what I want for the future. Right now, school, football, and Harper are it for me. I haven't given a lot of thought to the future. When Harper's fingers slip below my waistband and curl around my dick, I stop thinking entirely.

CHAPTER 20

Retreat and Regroup

HARPER

"I really need to go home." I'm pretty sure that's the twentieth time I've said that this morning. Caden's chef made a breakfast spread for us. I'm curious how many females have enjoyed this everything breakfast buffet, but I'm not about to ask.

Fortunately, I slipped an extra pair of panties into my purse last night, knowing the guys' obsession with collecting them. But I'm still in my dress, which is a bit much for first thing in the morning.

"Eat first, little nympho." Caden has me trapped on his lap with a plate full of food in front of us. The others are seated around the huge table.

"It's Sunday. Why the rush, princess?" Luke's gaze lifts to mine, and I blush.

You'd think I'd be done blushing after the past few nights, but this morning in the shower, well... Everyone joined in, and I lost track of who was touching what or who my mouth was on or who I was touching. It was deliciously disorienting.

But Luke has been persistent all morning. I've had his cock in my mouth or in my hands more than the others. And Caden is just as bad, but he wants his mouth between my legs. I squirm in my seat, which happens to be Caden's lap. His chest rumbles behind me, and I swear I'll never be dry again.

"Want me to ease that ache, little nympho?" Caden whispers in my ear, sending a riot of need cascading through my system.

Dammit, I desperately need some distance from these guys.

"Mom expects me home." I pick up some toast and eat a few bites. "I don't usually stay out all night."

"We don't have school tomorrow." Jack looks at me hopefully. "We can play all day, sweetheart."

My insides soften and heat at his words. I'm so screwed when it comes to these guys. Everything they do and say makes me want them.

"I need to go home, change, and check in with my mom, but I might..." I can't believe I'm about to say this. "I might be able to hang out this afternoon."

Nico's smile captures me. We haven't caught up yet. Everything has gone so fast with him being a horseman and joining in their games with me. But his smile is soft. He wants more than my virginity. Even Caden seems to want more.

The others, I'm not so sure of yet.

I'm also not sure how that will work. I mean, relationships with multiple partners exist, but I'm not sure how it works long term. And we're only high school seniors. Our whole lives are spread out before us. How many people actually end up with their high school boyfriend? Especially five of them, and all probably going to separate colleges.

Maybe I should enjoy them while I have them and not get too attached.

My gaze stops on Eli. His dark hair and eyes have held me captive on more than one occasion. I could see him being a lawyer. He'd look good in a suit, and with his commanding presence, he could rule the courtroom. When he notices me noticing him, he winks.

A little spark ignites in my chest.

"By hangout, you mean?" Jack scratches the scruff on his chin.

I turn to Jack. "I mean hangout, not just play sex games all afternoon."

"Maybe we can alternate." Caden's deep voice in my ear makes me want to sink into him. "A movie, some spin the bottle, Monopoly, seven minutes in heaven, a little swimming."

"Monopoly?" I glance over my shoulder at him. I can't imagine these guys sitting down and playing Monopoly.

Caden's grin is sinful as he lifts his hand to cup my breast. "Strip Monopoly with more interesting ways to get out of jail."

I can't help the laugh that comes out of me. "And you'll all play Monopoly?"

I raise my eyebrows as I look around the table. Everyone agrees until my gaze stops on Luke. His eyes burn into me, and my core clenches, knowing that look. He wants to fuck me. And part of me really wants to rip off the Band-Aid and feel him inside me.

Feel them all inside me.

But I also don't want to give in this easily. After all, this wasn't my plan to begin with. They bullied me into being with them. I'm still afraid once they get what they want, they'll leave me. Words are all good, but I don't know if I can trust them yet.

Though they've been building that trust, little by little. They seem determined for me to give them my virginity, and even though they've had opportunities, they haven't taken it.

I can't forget their "punishment." The seven minutes in the closet at school. A shudder rolls through me. When will they decide to punish me again? How far will they take it next time?

"Sure, princess, I'll play Monopoly." Luke's gaze doesn't release mine.

I shake off the feeling. "Who's driving me home?"

I follow Nico to his car, and he opens the door for me. The guys actually played rock, paper, scissors to figure out who got to take me home. I guess alone time with me, even in a car, is precious right now.

When he starts the car, I turn to him. "Tell me about your life."

He grins as he backs out of Caden's driveway. "New York was a trip after growing up here. I went to a really good private school. Made some friends, but no one as close as you guys."

My mouth tightens. "When did you become friends with the horse-men? Seriously, we spent all our time together, so how didn't I know?"

Nico cringes. "I might have wanted to keep you to myself. We were all noticing girls more in fifth grade, and I worried you might like one of them more than me."

I shake my head. "You were my best friend. I would have stayed with you."

The guys weren't as badass back in fifth grade, but they were still popular and cute. I might have had a small crush on Luke once upon a time, but nothing I would have acted on. Especially once they rose to power.

"Besides, being around them was different than being around you." Nico blew out a breath. "You and I still played together. The guys and I were in football camp, and that year we blew everyone else out of the water. We were unstoppable. It felt good to be part of that."

It makes sense. I still don't know how they all became the horsemen, but that story can wait. "Okay, so back to New York. Did you have a girlfriend?"

He glances at me warily. "A couple. They didn't last long. I never fell in love with them."

My chest tightens. Huh? It kind of hurts he had someone special enough to date regularly. The other guys never have and that made me feel special, even if the only reason they're with me is because I am—*was* untouched. I don't know why I assumed Nico would never have had a girlfriend.

"Honestly, those other girls never compared to you. Maybe I put you on a pedestal. This girl who was my best friend. Who was gorgeous, wild, and free. I wanted to recapture that, but those girls weren't the same." Nico glances my way, and I blush at his compliments.

Exhaling, I glance out the window.

"When the horsemen started to take over, I went into lockdown mode. I couldn't go to their parties when we were in middle school, so I kind of snuck by them." Pushing my hair out of my face, I turn to him. "I didn't want to add to their numbers. I didn't want to be one of those girls who was proud the horsemen fucked them. It just seemed like the horsemen used those girls, like those girls were some sort of reward for their hard work."

"And now?" Nico pulls onto my street.

I blow out a breath. "I don't know. At the beginning, it seemed like they were using me to finish their list. But then they wanted to *own* me for the whole year, but how can I trust them to want me all year? Especially after they get what they want from me."

Nico stops in my driveway and puts the car into park. "And what do you think we want from you?"

My breath catches on the *we*. It's so hard to remember he's one of them. But he's also mine. But where does his loyalty stand if he's tested? Will he stay with me or go with them?

"Promise not to tell them?" I hold up my pinkie finger, hoping our bond is stronger.

His face softens, and he holds up his pinkie finger to wrap around mine. "Promise."

I inhale. "They want my virginity, but once they have it, what will keep them with me? I think I'm starting to like them more than I used to, and the thought of them with another girl makes me feel queasy. But once they get the prize, what will be left for them? The novelty of a girl who will let all of them have her at the same time. I know they'll want to continue to have sex with me, but how long will that last?"

Nico takes my hand in his, and his dark eyes hold me. "You've got it all wrong, sunshine. Your virginity isn't the prize. You are."

What? "That doesn't make sense." I start to take my hand away.

"We all want you." His hand refuses to release mine.

"They don't even know me," I spit out. "They know my body, but they don't know me."

"Then stop hiding yourself from them." Nico's other hand tips my chin up. "I think they already suspect you're this amazing girl. You're just afraid to let them in. To let us in. You're afraid if you let us in, even if we see the real you, we might leave you."

I draw in a shuddering breath. "It's not unreasonable to think that."

He smiles, and his thumb traces over my bottom lip. "You're right. You have to trust all of us. And maybe at some point you will. But you can trust me when I say I'm here for you. I want you. The girl with the skinned knees and the potty mouth. The fearless girl who climbed to the top of the tree just to beat me. I want the girl who would call me on my shit."

I smile and roll my eyes. "I'm not that girl anymore—"

"Yes, you are. And even though I hate to say it, I think that's the girl they want too. They want you, Harper. Probably as much as I do. I'm not saying you have to give in to what you feel for us, but consider there may be more to this than just sex."

"It certainly feels like it's about sex." I raise an eyebrow at him to see if he'll try to deny it. Luke and Caden keep asking when I'll give in. Like I can put a date on losing my virginity.

He presses his lips against mine. Gentle and tender. "We want you. Yes. And being guys, our dicks like to lead us sometimes, but there's plenty of other pussy out there. It's not just the challenge we want. Though that's part of who you are. You're fun and spontaneous and willing to try almost anything. You're amazingly brave, and your heart is worth whatever fight I have to deal with to win it."

"This is crazy," I whisper. That I might be enough for them is insanity. That the cravings they stir in me are what they feel for me.

"I know they're all pressuring you to give in, but it's not all part of the game, sunshine. A huge part of it is we all want to enjoy fucking you. A lot." Nico's dark eyes sparkle with mischief as he looks at me. I throb between my legs at the heat in his eyes.

"No one's ever tried to make a play for my virginity. I can't just give in after a little over a week. Where's the fun in that?" Smiling, I tap my finger against his lips. "I need to go get changed. I'll see you later?"

"Count on it."

I get out of his car before I'm tempted to climb on his lap and kiss him the way I want to. As he backs out of the driveway, I wave and head in through the kitchen door. I lock the door behind me and listen to see where Mom might be.

The house is quiet, so I go to the schedule on the fridge. Mom has to work nights starting tonight. Most likely she's sleeping now. I head up to my room and take a quick shower before I change into jeans and a crop top. I grab a bikini I've never been bold enough to wear but was too cute to pass up.

I also throw in a spare set of underwear. These guys will need to buy me more at the rate they're confiscating them. I tie my hair into a ponytail just to get it out of the way, not to give any of them a handle.

My phone dings, and I sit on my bed to check my messages.

TANNER:

How are you holding up?

I bite my lip and look at my closed laptop. Should I even respond to him? Will that get me in trouble or him in more trouble with the horsemen? Do I even want or need his help?

It's hard to remember when the guys act nice to me that they also bullied me into being with them. To remember how they took some of my firsts whether I was ready or not. Fuck it, I might still need a friend if things blow up.

And that friend won't be Nico, even though he claims it will be. They already have their hooks in him. And while I want him to be mine, I can't trust him fully. He kept them from me, not just physically, but he didn't even share they were his friends when we were younger.

ME:

Hanging in there. How's your sister?

TANNER:

She's fitting in well at her new school. I miss her though. What are you up to today?

I'm not sure why he's asking, but I worry about telling him too much or leading him on. I know he wants revenge on the horsemen and right now, I'm not willing to be the conduit he uses to get it.

ME:

Hanging with friends

TANNER:

Nice. Have fun

I don't respond. I don't even know if I like Tanner, but he understands what I'm going through. His sister was a target of the horsemen. Tanner lost all of his status because of them. He wants revenge, which is why I'm not sure I should talk to him.

Suddenly I remember Kenz was supposed to tell me about him. I text her.

ME:

Can I call you?

KENZ:

Busy now. Later?

ME:

Maybe

Later, I might be occupied with horsemen. I put together my bag and head downstairs. No sign of Mom. She won't wake until late this afternoon. I grab a notepad and pen and tell her I'm going to hang out with the guys and Nico today. I also text her the same info.

I need to stay honest with her about what I'm doing. She trusts me, and I don't want to abuse that trust. She knows about the guys, just not about what they hope to accomplish.

The house is so quiet. Tonight, I'll be here all by myself unless the guys convince me to stay with them again. It wouldn't be hard to convince me, but tomorrow I'll need to work on my homework or I might fall behind. But that doesn't mean I can't stay the night. My body heats at the memory of them sleeping with me. It's weird sleeping with all of them, but also comforting.

Maybe I'll ask for the night off so I can consider how I want to lose my virginity. Luke said it's up to me. But does that mean I pick who goes first or how it happens? Every other first they've controlled, or chance did.

Do I want to leave it to chance again? It's not like I won't end up fucking them all. I could roll a die to see who gets to fuck me first. I shake my head. This is ridiculous.

I shouldn't be managing how to lose my virginity. It should just happen.

My phone dings.

PENNY:

Hey girl. Got plans for today? Haven't heard
if there's a party yet

Shit, what do I say? I know these girls are the hanger-on types who want to be close to the horsemen. If I wanted to make sure today doesn't turn into another orgy, I could see about inviting more people to Caden's pool.

Maybe Penny's trying to find out where the party will be tonight and figures I'll know or will find out.

I've never had so many complicated relationships to muddle through when it was just me and Kenz. Today I would have spent binge watching some new series and talking with Mom when she woke up.

I wouldn't have had to worry about plans or parties later.

ME:

Don't know about a party but will let you
know if I find out anything

PENNY:

Sweet! We're going shopping if you want to
come with

ME:

Thanks for the invite but I'm already spoken
for today

PENNY:

Okay talk to you later *heart emoji*

I shake my head as I walk out to my car. Having my car at Caden's will be a new novelty. I can leave whenever I want. I check out the new tire we got yesterday and make sure no one has tampered with anything before sliding into the front seat.

Taking a deep breath, I hold the steering wheel. I'm willingly going to Caden's for the day. No one is forcing me to go, but Nico is right. I should get to know these guys better. Maybe it will help me decide whether to go through with whatever this is or keep fighting it.

CHAPTER 21

Gathering the Defenses

LUKE

While Harper is at her house, I figure it's a good time to go home and get a change of clothes. Caden has extra swim trunks, and we all have a set there in case we get in the pool, but it's probably a good time to check in on my house.

Dad's BMW is the first thing I notice when I pull into the garage. My chest tightens, knowing he's here. But I breathe out and release the tension. I'm in control. He has nothing to hang over my head right now.

I head in through the kitchen, but have to walk past his office to get to the stairs.

"Luke." Dad's voice is stern and commanding as I start past his door.

I turn and face him. Thankfully, I take mostly after my mother. My dad has light brown hair and hazel eyes. Though his physique is similar to mine and he keeps it toned, I'd hate to look in the mirror and see that bastard staring back at me every day.

"Yes?" I stand perfectly still in his doorway, waiting to see if he'll call me in or just wants my attention.

"Come. Sit." He gestures to the chair in front of his desk without standing.

I do what I'm told. I have one more year in this house before I'll be

148

away from him at college. Fortunately he isn't around much, so I don't have to see him very often. These talks happen rarely.

"Did you get your application in for early decision at Harvard?" He folds his hands on the desk.

"Of course." I cross my ankle over my knee. He only cares about one college, so I don't mention the others I applied to. I'm not sure I can break away from his plans for me.

"Good. How is football going this year?"

"Undefeated."

"Any recruitment yet?" My father could not care less if I play football, but he wants me to be the best at everything, so that means being recruited by universities even if I don't intend to play there. When I showed interest in the sport, Dad enrolled me in football camps and hired personal coaches to help me train.

"Not recently." I take a deep breath and wonder how much parenting I'll have to put up with today. Dad leaves me alone more than he's here, which means I don't have to answer to anyone usually. But now and then he remembers he needs to control my life.

"Hmph." Dad reads something on his phone before returning his gaze to mine. "The Lees are back in town. You were close to their boy, right?"

I nod. Nico is one of us. And another guy I have to share Harper with. If Dad doesn't wrap this up soon, I might miss out on time with our girl.

"You should put in some hours working at the company this year. It will give you experience and look good on your college application." Dad leans in. "You can get a leg up and understand what's necessary to run our business."

This isn't the first time Dad has tried to get me to work for him. The problem is, there is a legit side of his business, and a questionable side as well. I've tried to keep my nose out of it, so when his empire falls, it won't take me out with it. But I don't know how much longer I can avoid his company.

"I'll see what time I can make. It will have to wait until the end of football season." I keep my voice calm and don't tense up. As long as my arguments are rational, he'll hear them. I can't make them emotional. I don't dare mention Harper as a reason I don't have time. "I can't let my grades drop now that Nico is back. He always had a high ranking, and I'm sure he'll be up there with me, Eli, and Jack."

Caden isn't far behind us either, but mentioning Caden is like a red flag to my father. Our fathers used to be partners until they fell out a few years ago. Dad wants me to stay close to Caden to find out what he knows about their business.

"You need to learn to balance your time better." Dad motions to the door. "We'll have dinner tonight. Be here at seven. Don't be late."

Fuck. Family dinners are the worst with my dad. Nothing like Harper's birthday dinner, where her mother tried to make us all feel welcome. It was warm and inviting. This will be cold and sterile.

"Can I bring someone?" My mind flashes to having Harper beside me.

Dad narrows his eyes. "The guys? It would be good to see how they're doing. They may make formidable business partners in the future."

Nodding, I stand. "I'd like to bring Harper as well."

"Harper?" Dad's interest is piqued. I've never asked to bring a girl to dinner before.

"Harper Davidson. Her mom is a nurse." She doesn't have an influential family, so I'm not sure how this will play out.

Dad sits back and studies me. He's always looking for weaknesses. If he thinks Harper might be a weakness, he'll use her against me. "Girlfriend?"

As much as I want to say yes, I know it will be better for everyone if I say no. "A friend of ours."

"Fine." Dad waves his hand, already dismissing Harper in his mind.

I turn to leave.

"Don't be late and bring Nico Lee with you."

I nod before I escape to my room and get ready to head back out. When Dad's home, I try to spend as little time here as possible. My father has plans for my future. I'm not sure I can get around them, but I'm still searching for my way out.

ME:

Dinner with dad tonight. 7. We'll all be there

HARPER:

You want me to have dinner with your dad?

ME:

I've had dinner with your mom

NICO:

Do we need to bring anything?

ME:

Just need backup

CADEN:

We'll be there

HARPER:

I may need to check in with mom before she
goes to work tonight but I'll try

I haven't forgotten about the night Harper was alone and frightened. And if her mother is working, there's no way she's staying there alone.

ME:

Talk at Caden's. Be there soon

***

HARPER

I park where I've seen the others park, but it looks like I'm the first one back. Should I stay in my car and wait for someone else or just go into the basement? They've always brought me places with them.

I don't usually show up willingly.

My door jerks open, and I startle.

"Come on, little nympho. I'm not sure how long I'll have you alone." Caden reaches his hand down to me.

Butterflies go rampant in my stomach at the thought of being alone with him. When I don't immediately take his hand, he squats down next to my car. His green eyes smile up at me.

"Don't tell me you're afraid to be alone with me." He doesn't reach out and touch me, but even this close I can feel the heat of his body calling to mine. His dark hair is ruffled like he didn't bother doing anything with it this morning.

Grabbing my things, I take a breath before climbing out of my car. He stands and hovers over me.

"How's the car?"

I blink at his question like my brain just doesn't compute. Then I remember. "Oh, the tire is new. No other damage. The shop said it could have been a pothole."

Caden nods and grabs my hand to lead me around his house. He doesn't seem convinced.

"Why do we always go in through the back?" I glance at the front of the colonial-style house, which has two columns with a two-story roof over them for a porch. It looks intimidating.

"Everything we want is down here. But if you want the tour, it'll cost you." He turns and walks backward in front of me with a sly grin.

I raise an eyebrow. "What's the price? My panties?"

"Far from it." He winks. "Every room has a different cost, but nothing too high for you to pay."

Okay, I'm worried now, but I'm also very curious. We walk into the basement. Caden takes my bag from me and sets it near the couch.

"So what do you think, little nympho? Want the tour?"

I glance over my shoulder at the door. I don't know how long it will be until anyone else gets here. It's not like we set a time.

"Promise I won't have to walk around your house naked?" I give him a stern look.

He rubs the corner of his lips with his finger. "You won't have to walk around the house naked, but there may be partial nudity involved in some rooms."

He closes the distance between us and grabs the belt loops on my pants to drag me in close to him. "No boundaries will be moved."

Not that there are many boundaries left. Shrugging, I place my hands on his chest. Fuck, his chest is firm. His muscles twitch beneath my fingertips.

"Fine. Show me your house."

Caden's grin should have warned me, but he lifts me over his shoulder.

"Put me down." I laugh and smack his back.

"Sorry, this tour comes with a free ride, and since those boundaries are still in place, I had to compromise." He smacks my ass.

Thankfully, I wore jeans and not a skirt. Not that it seems to matter with these guys.

He spins around in a circle, and I cling to his shirt. "This is the basement, but you've been here before so no cost."

"Great. Can I walk yet?"

"Not yet, little nympho." He walks into the corridor he took us into Friday night. It's just as dark. "This is the main house. You're in luck. Sunday is everyone's day off. Otherwise, we might have gotten interrupted on our tour."

"But your cook was here earlier."

"Just for breakfast. I'm on my own for the rest of the meals." He carries me to the first door and opens it.

"Where are your parents?" I have to ask. They travel, but I've been at their house more than they have. Whether the guys will be enemies or friends, it's still a good idea to know them.

"Europe. On some grand tour." Caden lowers me to my feet and turns on the light in the room.

"When do they get home?" I look around the room that has floor-to-ceiling bookshelves filled to the brim. It's impressive. A table and some comfy chairs fill the floor space.

"A few weeks to a month." Caden shrugs. He pulls me over to the library table and his fingers go to the fastenings on my jeans.

I grab his hands to stop him, feeling a rush of desire flowing through me. "What are you doing?"

"The cost for the library is a taste." Caden lowers his head beside mine and whispers in my ear, "And not of your sweet mouth."

He pulls my jeans and panties down over my hips and turns me to face the table. "Bend over. Hands on the table."

I'm used to following orders now, so without a thought, I do as he asks. No one is here to stop him if he goes too far, but if I don't trust them, I can't be with them. So I have to trust I'll stay a virgin through this tour.

He strokes a hand down my back and over my bared ass. "I love it when you obey."

When he smacks my ass, I yelp. His chuckle fills the room. It's so quiet with just the two of us.

Kneeling behind me, he closes his mouth over my pussy and licks the wetness that gathers there for him. Every one of them goes down on me differently, but when Caden does, he's ravenous.

I clench my fists as he sucks and nibbles and licks me. He thrusts his tongue inside me until I'm pushing back into him for more. I'm so close to the edge. He stops suddenly and stands. My breath shudders in and out of me as I try to figure out what's happening. He lifts me from the table and straightens my pants.

I'm turned on and slowly ebbing away from completion. When I turn around, he wipes his mouth with his t-shirt, giving me a huge grin.

"And that's the library."

I glare at him. The fucker.

"Next room." He leads me out of the library like nothing happened. Like I wasn't about to come all over his face. Asshole.

CHAPTER 22

Asymmetric Cost

Harper

We walk down the hall and enter a glass-enclosed room filled with plants, with a view of the pool in the back. It's a little warmer in here than in the hallway.

"The solarium. Mom pays a gardener to come in daily to take care of the plants so they look good when she's home." He walks down the aisle of plants to a small fountain that has a tipped jar flowing water over a stack of stones and into the pool below. "On your knees."

I meet his green eyes and drop to my knees in front of him. He's wearing athletic pants that barely conceal his erection. I doubt he's even wearing boxers.

"Take my dick out and suck it, little nympho." He raises an eyebrow like he dares me to.

I grab the waistband of his pants and pull them down. No boxers in sight. Just Caden's huge hard cock. I take ahold of it with my hand and stroke once up and down before I lean in and suck on the tip.

I'm not feeling very generous after his library trick, so I stay shallow. Licking the tip and sucking gently while stroking the base of his cock. When he groans, I back away entirely and lift his pants.

Standing, I smirk. "And that's the solarium."

Caden reaches for me, but I dance backward until I'm hurrying out the door and into the hallway.

"Next room please," I say sweetly when he catches up.

He takes my hand and drags me into the next room. There have to be three washers and three dryers in this laundry room.

Caden grabs my pants and panties and drags them all the way down before lifting me and setting my bare ass on the edge of a dryer.

"Hey," I say, mostly in surprise.

He pulls my pants off the rest of the way and spreads my legs wide.

"Laundry room." He cocks an eyebrow before his mouth covers my pussy. I cling to the edge of the dryer as he tongue fucks me and drags his nose over my clit. Going down on him made me even more wet and ready for him. I'm already on the edge.

After a few seconds, I scream out his name when I shatter all around him. He doesn't let up. I'm already sensitive and cry out when another orgasm slams through me. Panting, I push at his head to make him stop.

Caden straightens while I'm trying to catch my breath and kisses me. I can taste myself on his lips, and his fingers explore me, rubbing my clit before he thrusts two of his thick fingers inside me, pulsing them in and out of me while his thumb rubs my clit. His tongue sweeps through my mouth to tangle with mine. He curls his fingers inside of me. I come again with my fingers digging into his hair.

"Just imagine, little nympho." With his mouth pressed against mine, he thrusts his fingers inside me again, causing ripples of aftershocks. "My cock buried deep inside you while you come and come and come until you can't stand anymore."

I can't breathe as my pussy convulses around his fingers. It's too much. He lifts me against him from the dryer. My legs wrap around his waist as he thrusts his fingers within me, keeping me high.

"Fuck, Harper. You and I will be epic together." He takes my mouth again as he slips his fingers out and trails them to press at my asshole. I make a small noise to protest before he pushes deep inside and thrusts in and out.

I bite his lip as I moan. My insides are a riot of need and want. He presses me back against the wall and his other hand slips to his waistband. The edge of his bare cock slides against my clit.

"Caden?" I clutch his hair and pull his head back to look into his darkened green eyes. It feels so fucking good, but fear ripples through me. They promised not to take my virginity, but no one is here to stop him. No one is here to stop me.

"Just a tease, little nympho." He grins.

I'm so wet his cock slides between my folds and nestles against my clit as he continues to finger fuck my ass. My pussy throbs empty as our eyes stay connected.

He shifts his hips to slide his cock against my clit, like Luke's done before. My head falls back against the wall as he moves against me. My insides feel like they could explode as the pressure within keeps building with every thrust.

"We could just be done with your virginity right now," he whispers against my lips. "Then we can all take turns pounding into your perfect pussy until you're all of ours."

I whimper, but shake my head. "Not like this."

A growl rumbles through his chest against me, and I tip over the edge again. He keeps sliding against me until he curses and comes on our stomachs. His mouth devours mine as he removes his fingers from my ass and holds me against his still hard cock.

"Giving her the tour?"

We turn to see Jack leaning against the doorjamb. Our chests rise and fall like we've run a marathon. Fuck, it feels like I've run a marathon.

"Of course. What kind of host would I be if I didn't give her the tour?" Caden grins and lowers me to my feet. He grabs a towel from a stack behind him and wipes us both down.

"Exactly how many girls have gotten this *tour*?" My cheeks heat as I pull back on my jeans. I don't like the thought of other girls with the guys. It's part of their history, but I like the idea of being special. Even if I'm not really.

I do up my zipper and button. A skirt definitely would have been easier if this is how I'll spend my day.

"You're the first, little nympho." Caden gathers me against him and kisses me.

Jack reaches out for my hand. "I'll join you. Some of my favorite rooms are coming up."

Caden grabs my hips as he follows behind us. The next room they lead me into is the kitchen. It's huge with marble countertops and multiple islands spread out the length of my living room at home.

"This is a full nudity room," Caden says as he lifts off my shirt.

Jack turns, and suddenly I'm in a Caden/Jack sandwich. Jack undoes my jeans and lowers them and my panties. I step out of them while Caden takes off my bra.

Caden lifts me onto an island and pushes me back to lie down. The marble is cool against my heated flesh as Caden circles to the other side of the island, where my head is. Jack steps next to my knees.

"What's the price?" I ask, breathlessly. My legs dangle over the edge of the island.

"It's a tasting menu." Caden chuckles as he lowers his mouth to hover over mine, upside down. "We'll get a taste of all of you."

Heat flushes through me as Jack lifts my foot to rest on his shoulder. He kisses and licks his way up my leg, while Caden takes advantage of my mouth. It feels odd kissing him upside down, but then Caden's hands slip to my breasts and he pinches my nipples, right as Jack bites the inside of my thigh. I jerk in their hold.

My breath catches as Caden trails kisses and nips down my jawline to my neck, while Jack kisses my other leg, bringing them both up, my feet on his shoulders. He leans in, spreading them wide. He licks all the way to my groin and stops. I ache for his mouth on me, but he doesn't go to where I need him the most.

Caden chuckles as he kisses down my neck and over the tops of my breasts. He kisses circles around my breast, getting closer and closer to my nipple, while Jack teases the insides of my thighs, biting, sucking, licking. Winding me up. Making me ache.

I pant, waiting for more. Waiting for them to *really* touch me.

As if they are one, Caden takes my nipple into his mouth at the same time Jack licks my pussy. I arch and cry out as heat rolls through me. My hands clench uselessly on the countertop, needing something to hold on to as they drive me crazy.

Jack uses his tongue as a weapon as he flicks my clit and dives into my pussy, making me rock against his face while my legs remain bent and spread wide. Caden sucks as much of my breast as he can into his mouth while his tongue acts like my nipple is his favorite candy, licking around and around.

They both pull away and move around the island. Jack trails kisses up my stomach while Caden trails down the other side of my stomach. Jack's lips close around my nipple. Caden presses my legs up into my stomach and he licks my puckered hole before driving his tongue inside.

"Fuck." I breathe out.

"Is that a request, sweetheart?" Jack's blue eyes dance down at me.

I shake my head and bite my lip. Still not ready for that.

Jack slides his fingers over my clit to press inside me and returns his mouth to my nipple. The fire engulfs me as I come. Caden chuckles against my ass as he bites one of my cheeks and fingers my ass again.

I don't think I can come again. But they're relentless.

Their fingers move inside me in rhythm with each other until I fall back over the edge. A sharp cry escapes my mouth as my body clamps around them. Jack lifts his mouth from my breast and kisses me while slowing everything down.

Caden steps away and grabs a kitchen towel to wipe me as I lie prone on the stone, staring at the ceiling trying to come down. Holy shit, they're trying to kill me by orgasm.

Jack kisses me softly. His fingers drift over my nipples and I shudder.

"Do you like the kitchen, kitten?" I turn my head to find Eli standing there. His dark eyes trail over my naked body. I don't know how much more I have left in me.

"The tour is about half over." Caden lifts me and he and Jack dress me again like I'm a doll. I can barely hold myself up as I lean back against Jack and stare up at Caden.

Reaching up, I grab the back of Caden's neck to drag him down into a kiss. I swear this is his whole purpose. Drive me so crazy I can't think of anything but sex and coming. He lifts me against him and matches me with his tongue and lips.

When we part, he doesn't set me down, but carries me with his arms under my ass to the stairs with Eli and Jack following. We head back into the basement.

"What about the tour?" I ask when Caden sets me down.

He lowers his face until we're eye level. "Cost is too high. Soon though."

CHAPTER 23

The Exhaustion

HARPER

Caden's green eyes lock on mine. My body softens and heat fills me. What this man can do to me. Fuck, between all of them, I'm lucky I haven't already given in.

Eli spins me around and tugs my ponytail back before claiming my mouth as his. His tongue strokes against mine, lighting up my insides again. He tastes of mint. His hands draw my hips against his, pressing his hard cock into my stomach. One hand delves under my shirt and bra until his fingers pluck at my nipple.

I gasp into his mouth at the tug from my breast all the way to my pussy.

"You've got your work cut out for you, kitten," Eli says against my lips. He pulls me toward the couch. Jack and Caden are already sitting next to each other. Eli sits next to them. "Down on your knees."

I lower myself to my knees because I want to, not because they demand it of me. My mouth salivates at the thought of them between my lips. They shift their pants out of the way to release their cocks. I move on my knees between Jack's and meet his eyes before I lower my mouth over his cock.

His blue eyes meet mine as he caresses my neck gently. I take him as deep as I can while stroking the base of his cock. The buzz of my arousal makes me hum around him.

Caden grabs my ponytail and lifts me off Jack's cock. "My turn."

I lick the tip of Jack's cock, taking his precum into my mouth, while he takes over stroking it. Jack groans when I smile his way.

I shuffle on my knees to Caden and meet his gaze. He grins as he tightens his hand in my hair. He won't let me tease him this time. This time he wants to be in control.

But when I put my lips on his cock, he lets me tease the tip with my tongue for a few seconds before he takes over. He bobs my head up and down over him while I try to lick and suck when I can. To balance myself, I rest my hands on his thighs. He pushes as deep as he can go inside my throat.

Breathing through my nose, I swallow around him. His groan ripples through me, making me soak my panties. All I can think about is the feel of his cock against my clit, rubbing me until I exploded all over him.

He doesn't completely fit in my mouth, and I can't help but wonder how his cock would feel inside me. How much deeper he would go than his fingers. How much more I would stretch to take him. I moan, needing a little friction. Knowing if I touch myself right now, I will come.

Caden pulls my head up a little, so he's not so deep. I lift my gaze to his and suck on him as hard as I can. Biting his lip, he groans as he comes in my mouth.

As I finish swallowing, Eli takes hold of my hair and lifts me off Caden's cock. I meet Caden's darkened eyes, and there's a promise in there that makes my lady bits tremble. I'm so fucking close right now. He could breathe on my bare pussy, and I think I would come.

Moving on my knees to Eli, I focus on his dark eyes. When I open my mouth how he likes, he grins and lowers me onto his cock. He holds my hair tighter and pushes me farther with each motion. I drag my nails over his balls, and he shudders.

"Play nice, kitten." He shoves me all the way down on him until my nose touches his abs. Just as I'm about to tap out, he pulls me off and moves me up and down over his cock like his fist strokes him when he gets off to me. I suck and lick when I can.

The tension keeps winding up in me, and I can't even squirm my way to release.

Eli pulls me off him and gestures with his head to Jack. I shift to kneel before Jack and stroke his cock along with him, our fingers entwined. My jeans rub against my swollen pussy, but not enough to get me there.

"Suck Jack's cock, little nympho." Caden strokes himself again. I'm not sure I can keep doing this. Not without a release of my own.

But I can try. Leaning forward, I take Jack's cock back in my mouth and hum around it. The hairs rise on the back of my neck before I feel heat engulf me. My insides buzz at the feel of Luke's body pressed against mine.

He opens the fastenings on my pants and slides his hand inside against my clit. I shudder at his touch.

"So fucking wet, princess." His lips brush over my ear as he talks. I try to focus on Jack as Luke thrusts a finger inside me. "You like sucking cock, don't you?"

I whimper as he presses his thumb against my clit. It throbs beneath his touch.

"If you like the way we feel in your mouth, imagine us in your pussy."

Luke teases me, going slow and pressing against my throbbing clit instead of caressing. His words are like strokes of their own. He doesn't build a rhythm, but thrusts in and then drags his finger out along every nerve.

"We could just fuck you all afternoon. Make you come until you're hoarse. Until you can't stand anymore."

I groan around Jack's cock as Luke teases my clit. Luke's hard cock presses against my ass. Just a little more and I could—

"Fuck." Jack comes in my throat. His hand brushes over my cheek as he slides out from under me and Eli takes his place.

"Take him deep, princess."

Fuck, yes. I spread my legs wider for Luke.

My insides tremble so close to the edge as Luke plays me like a fucking instrument, keeping me from falling over. I suck on Eli's tip for a second before taking him deep like Luke wants. Luke adds another finger as he thrusts them into me, stretching me.

I moan and wetness floods over Luke's fingers, but I'm still not coming.

"Let Eli show you how he wants to fuck you." Luke's words make me look at Eli.

He smiles at my attention and takes hold of my hair. "How do you make it stop?"

My mouth is full of his cock as I suck. I snap my finger.

"Good, kitten."

Eli thrusts into my mouth as he holds my head. Luke kisses me behind my ear and then trails kisses and nips down the back of my neck while his fingers thrust inside me at the same pace as Eli fucks my mouth.

Sitting next to Eli's leg, Caden reaches up my shirt and tugs on my nipple.

I shatter. My moan rips through me with my release. Eli comes with a roar as my pussy convulses around Luke's fingers. I swallow on instinct because right now my body is so not my own.

My pussy keeps squeezing on Luke's fingers as he lifts me off Eli's cock.

I collapse back against Luke as he eases me down, stroking gently in and out of my core. My breathing is chaotic and my heart is racing a million beats a minute. He sucks gently on my shoulder before he bites me.

When I jerk in his arms, he chuckles. He removes his fingers from my pants, leaving a wave of aftershocks in his wake. He sucks his fingers into his mouth, and I watch him over my shoulder.

These boys and their games are dangerous and leave me wanting so much more. So much more.

Nico

Never would I have imagined coming back to our town and walking in on Harper sucking Luke's dick while Caden eats her out. Luke and Caden are on the floor with her. She still has on her shirt, but is bare from the waist down.

Sitting behind Caden on the couch, Jack's fingers circle her asshole while Eli is stroking himself slowly, watching the whole thing play out.

Luke holds Harper's ponytail while he thrusts up into her mouth. She moans around his cock as Caden makes obscene noises while eating her out. Jack rubs lube on his fingers before he slides two inside Harper's ass.

She moans again and jerks against Caden's face as she comes. It's the most beautiful thing I've ever seen.

Luke groans as she swallows down his cum. He lifts her lips to his as he claims her mouth. Caden licks her from clit to ass, making her jump while Jack keeps thrusting his fingers in her ass.

She whimpers as her hips follow his motion.

This should be messed up, but watching my friends with Harper only makes me want her more. The way her body strains against theirs as they pluck notes from her vocal cords. She gives in so beautifully and keeps coming back for more.

I never imagined she would accept what I want from her. I figured I would have to go slow and kiss her sweetly, nicely, and entice her to want more. Every other girl I've been with needed me to go slow.

But not Harper.

She wants my darkness. Our darkness. She wants that little twinge of pain with pleasure. She needs it, and I want to give it to her. Slam my cock into her cunt and have her come all over it.

She pulls her mouth from Luke's, her hands wrapped in his shirt, as her eyes squeeze shut and she moans again. Caden sucks on her clit, and she stops breathing, frozen in her climax. Her forehead rests against Luke's chest as Jack and Caden pull away. Her body twitches as Luke rubs her back.

As much as I want her, right now she needs some care.

I kneel beside her and hold out my arms. "Come on, sunshine. Let's get you cleaned up."

Lifting her head, her eyes meet Luke's. At his nod, she falls into my arms and wraps herself around me. It doesn't escape me how much she looks to him to lead her. It plucks at the jealous cord in my heart.

But then she rests her head on my shoulder and clings to me, and something settles deep inside.

I nod to the guys, lifting her and carrying her to the bathroom. Setting her on the counter, I brush some strands of hair back that fell out of her ponytail.

"Wait here."

She nods and leans against the mirror. When I turn to go get her clothes, Jack stands in the doorway with her jeans and a bag.

"Mind if I help?" Jack meets my eyes. He's giving me the option to either let him in or not. I can care for her on my own or I can realize I'm not the only one who cares.

When I give him a nod, he steps in and closes the door.

"How are you, sweetheart?" Jack goes to the shower and starts the warm water.

"Exhausted." She laughs. "I'm going to have to take up running or something to get my endurance back up. I never should have quit dance."

"You're perfect the way you are." I cup her cheek. She's always been perfect to me.

Her eyes narrow on me like it's a line. It's not, but we're still getting to know each other again. I help her take off her shirt and bra.

"You want to shower alone or with company?" I raise an eyebrow.

She bites her lip, and her cheeks flush as she looks at me and Jack. "Company is nice."

Both Jack and I strip down. I hold out my arms to her again. She wraps herself around me like a koala, and I step into the shower. Jack takes her ponytail holder out and runs his fingers through her hair as she rests her cheek on my shoulder.

I hold her while Jack washes her hair and conditions it. I release her so we can wash her. She leans back against Jack as I run my hands over her gorgeous body. She reaches out to stroke my hard-on, but I push her hand away.

Her brows furrow as she looks up, but I smile. "Later. Right now is about you. Not me and not Jack."

He kisses her shoulder. "We've played enough, sweetheart."

A little shiver ripples through her, and she nods. I don't know how long they've had her here or what all they did to her while I was gone. I have to trust my brothers to keep her safe.

"Where did you learn to hack computers?" Harper asks Jack as she leans against me so he can wash her back.

"I kind of picked it up as I went along." His fingers linger between her legs, and she lets out a sigh. "It was little things at first, like checking out a teacher's email account or looking up grades. Then I realized how many people don't secure their computers. We've got some videos that could potentially ruin people if we need to."

Her brow furrows as Harper looks over her shoulder at him. "Did you record me?"

He grabs her chin. "Never. Though if you wanted to, we could make some quality home movies."

He winks and she chuckles. I rinse her off, turn off the shower, and grab a towel. We both dry Harper. I give her a kiss before we leave her to get dressed.

The rest of the guys are lounging on the couch.

"She good?" Caden asks.

I nod. "Probably needs a quiet activity and some lunch."

Eli snorts. "She'll be fine."

"A movie sounds good." Jack steps next to me, and it feels like we're on the same page. "We haven't even shown Harper the theater room."

Caden's eyes light up and his grin is wicked. "Hmm, the theater room."

"No more tour." Harper's voice rings through the room.

"But little nympho, that's the fun part." Caden crosses the room and lifts her up. "I'm pretty sure the movie theater is topless."

She puts her hands on his jaw and leans in to kiss him. "Of course it is."

"We'll be topless too, so it's fair." Caden's eyes sparkle with mischief.

Her laughter fills the room. Even Luke has a touch of a smile on his lips. Yeah, we're all goners for this girl.

CHAPTER 24

The Knowledge

HARPER

After I refused to abide by Caden's topless policy, we watched a movie sitting in heavenly recliners with surround sound. I picked *Zombieland* since it would be the least likely to make the guys hornier.

A girl needs a break. Though I did snuggle with the guys during the movie.

Afterward, Caden takes us to the kitchen and pulls out the makings for sandwiches. I make him a peanut butter and jelly. He wolfs it down in three bites before kissing me.

I pick at my sandwich while we sit at the kitchen table. "Swimming?"

"Nude swimming," Jack suggests.

"I have a bikini I've never worn." I eat a bite of sandwich while five sets of eyes roam over my body. If I don't want to be on my knees all afternoon, I should at least suggest... "Should we invite others?"

"You have someone in mind, kitten?"

I shrug. The more the merrier. "Kenz and Brandon. Maybe some of your teammates, and there's this group of girls who—"

"Are only kissing up to you for an invitation like this," Eli says, shaking his head.

"You aren't wrong, but seriously what can it hurt." I could use more girlfriends.

The guys exchange looks around me.

"What am I missing?" I put my sandwich down and drink some of my soda.

"Those people will want something from you, and right now, we don't want to share you, little nympho." Caden tugs on my braid.

"Fine, but can we maybe not do sex stuff in the pool?" I glance at their feral smiles. My body warms and softens. They really have ruined me.

"What counts as sex stuff, princess?" Luke reclines and gives me a smoldering look that melts my insides further and makes me want to put all the sex stuff on the table.

Technically, we're in the kitchen, and that island is sitting there without me naked on it. I shake my head and concentrate on answering Luke.

I have to think about this carefully. They'll take advantage of any loopholes I leave. "Touching or kissing beneath bathing suits."

"And if you aren't wearing one?" Nico asks with his eyebrows raised.

Okay, he hasn't gotten off since we got back, so I could see him wanting to do a little something to ease the ache. But I've been through the wringer already and need a break.

"No taking off my swimsuit or yours." I stand and take my plate to the sink, saying over my shoulder, "Everyone stays covered, and we just enjoy the sunshine and each other's company."

"I always enjoy your company, little nympho." Caden cages me in from behind. His erection presses against my ass.

"Maybe enjoy it a little less, War." I arch my brow at him over my shoulder.

He chuckles as he backs off. "Fine. We'll play it your way. Boring as fuck."

I smile, and we all head downstairs to change into our swimsuits. I close myself in the bathroom to change even though they've seen and touched everything I have. If I get naked in front of them, I have a feeling they won't let me put my swimsuit on, and we'll spend the after-noon fucking around without actually fucking.

I do enjoy orgasms, but Nico is right. I need to get to know these guys with their clothes on. Spend time with them when they aren't actively seducing me.

As I leave the bathroom, I hear splashing through the open patio doors. The guys are outside already. I pause in the doorway to watch them for a moment. Luke and Eli have their arms crossed over their bare chests as they watch Nico and Jack wrestle over a beach ball.

I take a breath. While this bikini offers more coverage than most, it still bares a lot. It's red polka dot with strings holding the bottoms together, and the top is a glorified bra, basically, and barely qualifies. But it covers all the important parts.

"You coming, little nympho?" Caden closes in from behind me. His skin is warm against mine. "Because I'll be coming picturing you in this bikini later."

I glance at him over my shoulder. "Want to rub sunscreen on me?"

When I hold up the bottle of lotion, he grins and takes it. His hand lands on my lower back as he guides me outside into the sunshine and over to a lounge chair with a beach towel already spread over it.

He pours some lotion in his hand and caps the sunscreen. I glance over and see Luke heading this way. My breath catches as Caden rubs lotion slowly onto my neck.

"Need some help?" Luke picks up the sunscreen and goes behind me. Soon both men have their hands rubbing sunscreen into my skin, and I can barely breathe. Tingles race below my skin at every touch. Caden's fingers dip beneath the cups of my bikini top, while Luke's hands slide beneath the back.

"Sure you want tan lines, princess?" Luke whispers in my ear, while his hands trace down my sides. He tugs on the sides of my bikini bottoms. My breath catches as his hard chest rubs against my back.

"Tan lines are fine." I swallow the desire welling within me. I'm the one who wants a non-sexual activity. But I also know they'll do whatever it takes to make me want sex. The problem is, it takes less and less.

I'm not sure if they'll all want sunscreen too, but I can imagine running my hands over their chests and down their backs.

Luke's hands slip over my ass beneath my bikini. Caden is doing the same in the front over my hips.

"This would be easier if you took off the suit, little nympho."

I glare up at Caden. "I don't need sunscreen on my lady bits, Caden."

I grab the bottle. "I can get my legs and arms, guys. Your services are no longer required."

Caden leans in. His lips hover dangerously close to mine. The heat of him overwhelms me. "Fine."

His lips capture mine, and Luke presses in on me from the back, his hard cock obvious against my ass. I pulse empty.

"We don't want you to burn, princess." Luke dips his fingers beneath my top and strokes over my hardened nipples, cupping my breasts.

I whimper into Caden's mouth. These boys don't play fair.

They release me as one and back away with smirks. I glare at them for keying me up before I sit on the lounge chair. Ignoring them, I squeeze the sunscreen into my hand. While I work on spreading lotion up my legs, the guys go back to the pool and jump in.

Eli sits next to me.

"Need any help, kitten?" He gestures to the bottle.

"I think the others got me covered." I blush a little. No sex, find out more about the guys. "Do you know where you're going to school next year?"

Eli leans back on his hands as he watches me. "I have a few different options. I'm waiting to see where the others land. All of us will get into the right schools. I'd like to stick with my friends if I can."

Eli trails his fingertip down my back along the string tying my bikini top in place. "How about you?"

"I'm in a good position to get into my first-choice school, but I want to keep my options open." As his finger trails along the back of my bikini, I swallow. "I waver between wanting to stay close by my mom and getting as far away from here as possible."

"Away from us?" Eli's voice is soft and not accusatory.

I straighten and look into his golden-brown eyes. "Honestly, that was one of my primary motivations, but now—" I look at the pool and the guys playing in it. "I don't know. I don't know what the future looks like anymore."

"Do you have an inkling of what you want to be?" Eli takes his hand from me.

"Career wise? Not medical. Maybe engineering or business. I like to be creative, but I also don't want to sit at a desk for fifty to sixty hours a week." I smile when my gaze catches Caden's. "Of course, if Caden gets his way, I won't have time for a career because I'll always be knocked up my entire adult life."

Eli sits up, and our shoulders rub against each other. "Do you see a future with us in it, kitten?"

Surprised, I turn to him. "Do you?" I look down at my hands and then up at the sky. "This isn't even really a relationship. It's fun, but how long can it last? I mean, outside this bubble of our world, there's judgement and censure waiting to knock us down. Even within this bubble, girls are already calling me a slut, even though if they had the chance they would line up for you guys."

The corner of Eli's lips quirks up. "The great thing about being us is we don't care what other people think. The only ones who matter are us. So what do you think, kitten? Could you imagine a future with us in it?"

I glance at him before I take in Jack, Caden, Nico, and Luke. Could I imagine being with them beyond this arrangement? What would that look like?

Eli slips his hand under mine and threads our fingers together. It's gentle and almost caring. My eyes raise to his, and he brushes some hair off my forehead.

"You belong to us, kitten. We don't take that lightly. We care about you and want to keep you safe, but we also want to fill you with so much pleasure." Eli raises my hand to his lips and presses a soft, delicate kiss to my knuckles. He turns my wrist and drags the edge of his teeth against the sensitive skin.

Tingles shiver through me.

"I don't really have a choice in any of this, and because I was the only one left, neither did you guys." I squeeze his hand. "The only reason you're after me is for my virginity, which is slowly being chiseled away."

"Ah, the virgin sacrifice." Eli smirks. "You honestly think we give a crap you're a virgin?"

My eyes go wide. "Uh, yeah, that's the whole purpose to this. I'm the last virgin in the senior class, therefore I belong to you."

Eli stands and pulls me to my feet, but he leans down and throws me over his shoulder before I can stop him. His hand grabs my ass to stabilize me.

"What are you doing, Eli?" I smack my hand in the center of his back. "Put me down."

"Nah, you need a lesson, kitten." He walks to the edge of the pool. "Guys!"

Oh, what new hell am I in for now?

Eli plants me in front of him and turns me to face the guys. His arm wraps around my waist, holding me against him. The guys move toward us in the pool and look up.

"Who's only interested in Harper's virginity?" Eli calls out, loud enough if Caden had neighbors they definitely would have heard.

Heat creeps up my neck and cheeks. I wait while all of them look at me. No one lifts their hands.

"If Harper wasn't a virgin, who would still want her?"

All of them lift their hand. Something in my heart feels lighter. But what does that even mean?

"Do we want to be the first?" Luke lifts himself onto the edge of the pool at my feet. Water streaks down his cut muscles, and I swallow. Fuck they're all gorgeous. He pushes to stand directly in front of me. Water drips from his hair onto my nose, but I hold his eyes.

"Isn't the whole point I'm the last?" I keep my expression neutral.

"The whole point is you're ours." Luke cups the side of my face. "Every bit of you. But if you weren't a virgin, we'd still want you. You aren't like other girls."

"What's that supposed to mean?" I back into Eli as Luke presses in on me. Even with swimsuits on, so much of our skin touches and stokes the fire burning within.

"Part of what we like about you is your innocence, but not because you're a virgin. You aren't jaded by other guys. You aren't worried about what we'll think if you make noise." His hands lower to my hips and draw me against him. "You're loud and wonderful and soft and so fucking sexy."

"You also care about us when you should have been running away." Caden trails his wet fingers along my arm, and I look up at him. "You don't always cave to us. You didn't jump at your chance to be with the horsemen. You fought against us. Pretended to get grounded to fuck with us. You give in so fucking sweetly, but you make us work for it too."

Jack and Nico join the circle around me.

I don't even know what to think. They want me now. But I can't get rid of the voice that says when they get what they want, they won't want me anymore.

"You guys punish me." I turn so I can meet all their eyes. "You've taken pleasure from me when I didn't want you to. I never asked you to choose me."

"But we did, kitten." Eli brushes his lips on the nape of my neck. "You're ours to do with what we please, and if it pleases us to keep you, we will."

Those words should terrify me. They aren't asking for permission or consent. If they want me, they'll have me. But the want doesn't go one way. It's been building in me, but I enjoy being theirs. I want them to touch me, kiss me, pleasure me, and I want to do the same to them. I want them to want to keep me, because I want to be kept.

My gaze lifts to Luke's. His pale blue eyes are beautiful in the sunlight. The same color as the sky. He's a bright god surrounded by dark demons, but he's the darkest of them all.

"Keep your virginity as long as you like, princess. We'll still be here. Waiting. Wanting." He leans in and kisses me before jumping into the pool.

Jack draws my face his way and kisses me. Then Caden. Then Nico. They all return to the pool. Eli turns me in his arms, and I furrow my brow. This definitely isn't how I thought they felt.

His fingers smooth the wrinkles on my forehead before his eyes lower to mine.

"Do I want to see you spread out naked before me while I pound into your sweet pussy?" Eli cups my cheek and traces his finger along my lower lip. "Do I want to tie you up and stuff you so full of cocks you scream in pleasure? Do I want to take you until you come so hard you forget your own name?"

Holy shit, he's making me so wet. I want that. I want him to do those things to me.

Eli drops his mouth to hover over mine. "Do I want to make you mine?"

I almost whisper *yes.*

His lips capture mine and he sweeps me up into his arms. He tastes me delicately and fights with my tongue for dominance. When he lifts his mouth from mine, I can't separate him from me.

"Fuck yes, kitten. I want all of you," he whispers. "Take your time, but know once you let us in, we'll still want you just as much, if not more."

CHAPTER 25

The Considering

HARPER

"Mom?" I walk into my house after spending the afternoon playing in the pool with the guys. It didn't take much to break the tension. Jack grabbed me and jumped into the pool with me in his arms. Then we all acted like children with the beach ball.

Of course, they put me on their shoulders a lot. There was plenty of kissing and touching, but nothing overtly sexual.

"In here," Mom calls from the family room. She smiles when I enter the room. The TV is paused in the middle of an episode of *Love is Blind*.

"What have you been up to all day?" she asks.

I sit in the chair across from the couch, twisting the ring on my finger. "Movies and swimming mostly."

"Have you picked one guy or still playing the field?" Raising a quizzical brow, she sets the pillow on her lap to the side.

"I guess playing the field." I shrug and take off my shoes to put my feet up on the chair. They don't seem to want me to choose, and I don't want just one of them. I want them all. "I don't see a reason right now to hang out with just one of them, and they don't mind hanging out with me all together."

Mom nods thoughtfully. "How very mature of you all."

"I don't think playing keep away with a beach ball is very mature." I smile, remembering Caden stalking me through the pool until I could get rid of the damned thing. Of course, it turned out he wasn't stalking the ball and pressed me against the corner of the pool to kiss me until I damn near forgot what we were doing.

"I'm glad you're getting out of the house more." Mom turns off the TV.

"Kenz is busy with her boyfriend. I'm actually making new friends at school, but I'm afraid their intentions might not be on the up and up." I fold my hands together in my lap. Both the girls and Tanner have ulterior motives to want to get close to me.

"Trying to hang out with the only cool kid in school?" Mom grins.

"Trying to hang out with the kid the cool guys hang out with is more like it." I sigh. "It's not an issue, and I'll deal with it if it becomes one. And I always have Kenz... and you."

"Nice save there." Mom folds the blanket and puts it on the back of the couch. "I've got to leave for work soon. You sure you don't want to stay at a friend's house?"

I bite my lip. I know the guys are hoping I'll stay with them tonight, but honestly I could use some me time. A little time to myself to think about what I want and to process all that's happened. "I think I'll be fine here, but if I end up going somewhere, I'll let you know. The guys and I are going to have dinner with Luke's dad. I'm not sure how long that will last."

Mom grabs the pendant around her neck and rubs it. Something she does when she's nervous or agitated. "William Foster?"

"Yeah." I shrug, not really looking forward to sitting at the table with Luke's dad. If Luke is bad, he had to get that from his father. After all, that's the only influence in his life.

"Be on your best behavior. He's got a lot of influence around town and serves on the board of directors at the hospital." Mom blows out a breath.

"I wasn't planning on making a nuisance of myself." I raise an eyebrow at her behavior. What is going on with her? "Is there some-thing I should know?"

"No," Mom says too quickly. "I need to get ready for work." Mom walks toward the stairs. "Maybe you should stay with a friend tonight or have someone stay with you?"

"Maybe. I'll let you know."

She nods and disappears upstairs.

The more she harps on me being alone, the more nervous I am. I remember the last time she worked nights all too well. The fear and terror when someone pranked our house. But if I'm with the guys, I'll feel safe and probably have multiple orgasms. The orgasms must be turning my brain to mush and making me crave them.

I'm beginning to really want to experience that next step. Their fingers and tongues are amazing, but there's this fire inside they can't seem to put out. I love the way their cocks fill my mouth. I'm definitely curious how it will feel to have them inside me.

But I can't shake the worry.

I head to my room and change into a nice respectable dress, cream with little blue and green flowers on it. Curl my hair. A pair of strappy sandals on my feet. I even put on some light makeup. My hand shakes a little while I apply it.

I'm actually nervous about meeting Luke's dad. My hands feel clammy.

Mom stops in my doorway. "You look pretty tonight."

"Thanks." I take in her scrubs. "Good luck at work."

"I'm not looking forward to night shifts, and this week is a full moon too so all the crazies will be out." Mom leans against the door-jamb. "Call if you need anything. Bob and Fran have your number and know you'll be here on your own. So if you decide to have someone over, let them know so they don't call the police."

"Bob will bring his bat, but I still have my piñata stick." I reach beside my bed and grab my purple and pink ribboned weapon. "I'm zombie apocalypse ready."

"Let's hope neither of you have to use them." Mom holds out her arms for a hug. I step into them, taking in the smell of her coconut shampoo. "You stay safe. I love you."

"Love you too, Mom." I squeeze her back.

She releases me and shakes her head. "I'm going to kill whoever is in charge of scheduling."

"If you kill them, at least I'm eighteen and won't have to go into foster care." I wink.

"There is that. See you later."

I listen as Mom leaves and then grab my purse and head downstairs to wait for my ride. They insisted someone bring me tonight.

A knock at the door sets my heart to racing. I've basically spent all weekend with them. I shouldn't get excited to see them after only an hour of being away from them.

When I open the door, Eli stands on my steps. He looks good in a dark blue shirt and black slacks. I search beyond him, but it's only Eli.

"They trust you to pick me up alone." I give him a doubtful smile.

"We're on a tight schedule, so there's not much I can do." He backs me into the house. "Is your mom home?"

Not much he can do? I raise an eyebrow. "She left for work about fifteen minutes ago."

He closes the door behind him.

"That dress is very pretty." Eli's gaze sweeps over me as he closes in on me.

"Thanks." I hold it out to the side. "I've had it for years and thought it would be appropriate for a parent dinner."

He backs me up more until I'm pressed against the island. His dark eyes burn with a fire that lights me up. "Show me your panties, kitten."

Rolling my eyes, I lift my skirt. "I'm keeping my panties. I'm going to run out if you all keep taking them."

These are my favorite. White and lacy.

Eli turns me to face the island and grabs the sides of my panties to lower them, but only down to my thighs. I'm already wet. My body can't help but respond to his closeness.

"Eli, what are you doing?"

"Keep your dress up, kitten. I'd hate to stain it." The sound of his zipper is loud in the quiet house. "Don't worry, we'll be quick."

I look over my shoulder at him stroking his cock. A surge of lust races through me. Along with a tinge of fear. They all said they'll wait for me to be ready, but he's here alone.

"Palms on the island." Eli closes in on me, and I feel his cock against my bare ass. Heat boils within me rapidly. With me turned this way, it means he's not going for a blow job. Butterflies flutter through my stomach.

"We should—" I begin to turn, but he holds my hips. His thumbs dig in a little rough, forcing a gasp from my lips.

"My cock won't penetrate you, kitten. Promise. But I want to play."

Inhaling, I put my hands on the island. He trails his hand over my hip, wrapping around to slip between my thighs. He sweeps his fingers over my clit and presses inside. Sparks flood my system. My head hangs as the now familiar rush of arousal flows over me.

"So fucking wet, kitten. I could fuck you right now. Fill you with my cum. All during dinner, you could feel my cum dampening your panties."

Wetness flows out of me to coat his fingers.

"You like being a naughty kitten, don't you?" He removes his fingers from me, and his cock slides between my thighs and presses between my pussy lips, rubbing against my clit. "Hold still, kitten. I don't want to accidentally take what you'll give us willingly."

I press my hands into the counter as he slowly slides his cock back and forth between my thighs, rubbing my clit with every stroke, building the fire within me. My panties around my thighs keep me from spreading my legs wider to feel it more.

Eli slides his hand between us and slips his fingers inside my pussy. He doesn't move them, just holds them there as he thrusts his cock back and forth over my clit. Our breathing comes out heavy. My head hangs between my arms.

"Eli?" I whisper as I get close.

"Let go, kitten. I want to feel you come all over my cock." Eli quickens his pace and with his fingers still in my pussy, I explode.

He grabs a napkin from the counter and holds it in front of his cock as he comes, careful not to get any cum on my dress. Sliding out from between my thighs, he kisses the nape of my neck.

"Bend over."

Using a chair to balance on, I bend over. He lowers himself onto one knee and licks all the wetness from my pussy. My breathing is still chaotic, and I can feel the edge shifting closer again.

When he thrusts his finger inside me, I cry out and push back against his hand, aching for release.

"Shh. Don't come again until later tonight." He curls his finger, hitting that spot inside me that lights me up.

Closing my legs around his hand, I moan to keep from coming again.

"Good kitten." He straightens and withdraws his finger. When he licks his finger, a pulse ripples through my pussy. "Pull up your panties and drop your skirt."

I do as he says, and he walks to the sink to wash his hands.

My pussy throbs empty. Fuck, I won't make it long as a virgin around these guys. I'm questioning why I'm holding out. We've pretty much done everything except the act. It's just one more way to come.

Butterflies rush through me.

Eli draws me into his arms and kisses me, winding me up until I squirm against him. He lifts his mouth from mine and stares down into my eyes. "You need it, don't you, kitten?"

I whimper, wondering if he'll make me come if I ask.

"Good." He holds my chin in his hand and meets my eyes. "Waiting for it will make it even better later when I fuck your mouth with my cock while Luke sucks your pretty pussy into his mouth and Caden thrusts his fingers into your needy cunt. Nico and Jack can suck on your pert breasts until you come so hard you see stars."

I clench my thighs against the pulse of need that flows through me.

He traces my lips with his finger one last time and then leads me outside to get into his car. The ride to Luke's house isn't very far. I take a few deep breaths to calm myself down.

"What would be different if I weren't a virgin?" I know his words will just turn me on more, but I want to hear it.

At the stop sign, he glances at me. His smile is pure evil. "Your cunt would be full of our cum all the time. I would have taken your pussy against the counter while my fingers rode your clit instead of my cock pressed against it."

I cross my legs against the ache. I want to know. I need to hear it. "What about later?"

"Are you trying to rile me up, kitten? Because if you want, I can pull over and take your virginity so later we can fully play with you."

My eyes widen. That would definitely lead to me being punished. Luke wouldn't like that. "No. I'm just curious."

"Curious kitten," he murmurs as he turns the car.

"You guys seem satisfied with taking my mouth, so what will change?" I clasp my hands in my lap and wait.

Eli sighs. "Instead of servicing one of us or three if you use your hands, you can get us all off while we get you off. It's not a time saver really so much as more satisfying to fill you with our cum and then do it all over again and again."

I take a huge breath in. "What if I'm not good at it?"

Eli chuckles darkly. "Practice makes perfect, kitten. And we intend to practice a lot until you get it just right."

CHAPTER 26

The Interrogation

LUKE

Harper's cheeks are flushed when Eli brings her into my house. We agreed to meet in the basement and walk up together for dinner. With her hair down and a nice floral dress on, Harper looks beautiful and innocent.

But that wildness in her lurks just beneath the surface and it's all ours.

I walk up to her before anyone else can claim her and tilt her chin up to look over her makeup. She waits patiently for me to settle my gaze on her. Her lips are a little swollen and the pulse in her neck races against my thumb.

"Excited, princess?" I brush my thumb against her lower lip, and her lips part. Her eyes darken with the lust I incite in her. My cock twitches.

"Eli and I had a conversation in the car." Her gaze drops to my lips.

I don't look away from her. When she returns her gaze to mine, I lower my lips to kiss her, soft and subtle. She leans into me and opens beneath my kiss. I meant to keep it simple, but when she offers me more, I take it.

Kissing Harper is unlike any other girl I've kissed before. Nothing is fake or artificial about her. She wants to kiss me. She's not shy about it. When she wants me to deepen the kiss, she opens for me.

When my tongue strokes hers, she shivers in my arms and clutches at the sleeves of my shirt. My insides burn for her.

I need to fuck her. I cup her ass in my hands as I devour her mouth. She whimpers a needy little sound that makes me even harder. What I wouldn't give to back her against the wall and drive my cock into her dripping wet pussy.

I'd find release in her mouth, but I'm not about to have her on her knees before meeting my father. So I break off the kiss before my mind gives in to my body's desire. Her eyes are even darker, her lips swollen and parted.

"Later, princess." I press a quick kiss to the corner of her mouth before stepping away.

The room comes back into focus, and it isn't just Harper and me. I meet each of their eyes. Eli, Jack, and Caden know the drill, but Nico and Harper don't.

"My father is a hard man. Stay alert and answer what you can. Only answer what he asks."

Harper slides her hand into mine and squeezes. When she smiles at me, suddenly I want to hide her away from my father. I regret asking to include her. It was selfish of me. I want her close, but I'm putting her in the line of fire.

I'm showing him my weakness, my obsession. The object of my desire.

She's too soft to handle my father, but as long as he doesn't suspect there's more between me and her, he should behave. If he figures out how much I want her, he'll use my desire and her against me.

"As far as my father is concerned, you're our friend." Sweeping my thumb along her jaw, I cup Harper's cheek as her brow furrows. I wish it were different. "Trust me. It's better this way."

"Okay." She nods and steps away from me. I let her and her warmth slip away.

Fuck. "Let's go."

I lead them up the stairs and into the dining room. The table is set, but my father isn't here yet. Of course, it's five minutes before seven. He would never be early.

When Harper goes to sit next to Nico on the end, I capture her hand and lead her to sit next to me. Again, it's selfish, but I want her close to me. I want to feel her heat warming my insides as I stare into my father's cold eyes.

She squeezes my hand and gives me a reassuring smile. So fucking innocent. I should let her out of our deal, but I can't. I won't.

Releasing her hand, I take a minute to return the shield I raise when dealing with my father. No one says anything as we sit and wait. After a minute, my father walks in.

"Gentlemen," he says boisterously. His focus falls on Harper. "And lady."

His speculative gaze lingers on Harper as he sits at the head of the table. I should have let her sit next to Nico, instead of between me and Jack. Have I shown my cards already to my father?

"How are you all this evening?" Dad takes his napkin and lays it in his lap. That's the signal for the staff he hired for tonight to start service. The first course is a salad with a vinaigrette dressing.

"Very good, sir," Caden replies. He's accustomed to my father and knows what he expects. Knows what my father wants to hear. He's played this game almost as much as I have. Our fathers are very similar.

"How's your father's business?" Dad arches an eyebrow at Caden.

"As well as can be expected." Caden's non-answer gives my father pause.

But Dad nods and lifts his fork, indicating everyone can eat. "How's football this year? You planning on playing, Nico?"

The guys fill the space with football talk while we eat salad. As each of us finishes, the staff comes and removes our plate. Once my father is done, dinner is served. Plates filled with coq au vin are set in front of us.

Dad lifts his fork, but then his gaze settles on Harper. I tense, wanting to hide her from him. I'm careful to not show any emotion or regard for her.

"Luke tells me your mother works at the hospital?"

Harper nods. "Yes, sir, she works in the labor and delivery ward."

"And what does your father do?" Dad takes a bite, intent on his food instead of Harper.

"I wouldn't know. He left us when I was five." Harper takes a small bite of food.

"You don't hear from him at all?" My father is an asshole. He glances up at her and watches her carefully.

I want to interject, but I can't let him know I want to protect her. She has to stand on her own.

"No, sir. My mother is enough for me." She takes a sip of her drink and her eyes dart to me for a brief second.

"Of course she is." Dad takes another bite. "How are your grades?"

Harper blushes. "It's only been two weeks since school started, but I'm ranked in the top five percent of our class."

"Given that the boys at this table make up the top five overall, I'm not surprised." Dad glances around like he might shift to one of the others, but then his focus returns to Harper. "You're what? Eighteen?"

"My birthday was this past week." She takes another small bite. I'm proud of her acting like this isn't painful. For keeping her answers succinct.

"Plans for college?"

The others shift uncomfortably, wanting to step in, but they can't any more than I could. It would make her appear weak to my father. She either holds her own or she fails in his eyes.

"Of course. I've applied to a variety of schools, including some Ivy League. I'm still working on my essays for some scholarships, but even if I don't get in everywhere I apply, I will get my degree."

"How did you fall in with this group?" Dad leans back in his chair, abandoning the pretense of eating, and steeples his fingers against his lips as he waits for her answer. No longer trying to pretend like this isn't the interrogation it is. His dark gaze sweeps over her, making my fist clench under the table.

She swallows and sets down her fork. "Nico and I were best friends in grade school before he left. I've known the guys all my life, but we only became friends this year."

She doesn't hesitate on the word friends. Relief slices through me.

"Planning to lock down one of these young men for the future?" Dad asks with an arched brow.

She glances around the table at us. "No. I'll go to the school that's best for me. If they happen to be there, I'm sure we'll be friendly, but

I'm not looking to *lock down* a guy in high school. I have my whole life to find someone to spend it with. If that's what I decide to do."

My dad makes a thoughtful noise. He studies her in a way I've never seen before. I hold my breath. Bringing her was a misstep on my part. I feel it in my soul.

Harper takes another small bite of food, probably waiting for the next bomb to fall.

His gaze narrows on her for another second before he shifts to Nico. "Your family is back in town. I'm surprised you transferred here for your senior year."

I release my breath. She did well, and I almost smile with pride, but that would make my father even more interested in her.

"The football team here is better." Nico explains about his academics and the friendships he wanted to rekindle.

I reach my hand under the table to Harper's and brush her knuckles with mine. She doesn't glance at me, but her lips tip into a small smile as she looks down at her plate. I hadn't been lying at the pool. I'm willing to wait, but I don't want to.

If we only have a year with Harper, I don't want to waste one minute of it.

Harper

Next to his father, Luke is warm and loving. Even though Mr. Foster's eyes are a warm hazel, they're cold and calculating. Every question seems to have a purpose. His interest in me makes me feel like I've done something unforgivable.

When he changes topic to Nico and football, I relax and eat as much as my churning stomach can handle. Luke is stiff next to me. He's been that way the whole dinner. The urge to slide my hand into his and just hold it to support him almost overwhelms me.

These boys mess with my brain. It's one of the reasons I want to take tonight off. Get a little space to actually figure out what all this means. But I also know the minute we're alone, I won't be strong enough to walk away.

Because I *want* to be around them.

I like when they make me feel good. It's too easy to forget the way things began. Especially when they pluck the cords of my desire like strings on an instrument only they know how to play.

A cell phone vibrates. Mr. Foster gets his phone out and looks at the screen.

"Sorry, boys. And girl. I need to take this." He stands with his finger hovering over the Accept Call. "Enjoy dessert without me."

His eyes go from Luke to me with a knowing smile before he leaves the room.

No one says a word as the wait staff take away the dinner plates and bring out plates of chocolate cake with raspberries on it.

"Dude—" Caden starts in a voice that says he's about to complain. Maybe about Luke's father?

"Not here." Luke's tone is curt as he glances around the room. "Enjoy your dessert and then we can leave."

Jack's hand finds mine under the table and squeezes it. I release my breath and pick up my fork. When I lift my eyes, Nico's meet mine. His smile is gentle, and he gives me a wink before shoveling a bite of chocolate cake into his mouth.

The chocolate is decadent, but I'm not hungry enough to eat it all. I just want to relax in a guy's arms while we chill and watch movies. Seriously, I love all the sex stuff, but there's something magical about being held.

"Come on, sweetheart. I've got dibs on taking you home," Jack says.

Everyone stands, and so do I. A little confused. "I'm going home?"

My gaze finds Eli's. Mostly because he promised more later, but if they're taking me home...

Luke steps close. Not close enough to touch, but close enough to speak quietly so only I can hear him. "We're coming to your house, princess. Eli, Jack, and Nico have to go home later because their parents actually care sometimes. But Caden and I are staying with you tonight."

My mouth opens but nothing comes out.

Jack tugs me into his arms. "Come on. If we beat them there, I get a little alone time with you."

CHAPTER 27

The Trojan Horse

HARPER

Jack and I are the first out the door. His car is the first out of the driveway. I text Mom and Fran from the car, needing to warn them so Bob doesn't show up with his bat.

ME:

> Just a warning the guys are coming over to hang with me for a bit. Mom knows about them. They've been at the house before

> Just some homework and TV to keep me company

> Then they'll go home

Most of them. I'm not about to tell my Mom two of the guys are staying the night. Likely in my bed. I chew on my nail lightly as I wait for Mom's reply. I don't know how this is going to work. My bed doesn't come close in size to Caden's massive bed.

Luke and Caden were in it for an hour on my birthday. The last time Mom worked nights, Luke and I snuggled in it. But it's not exactly large enough for three. Not to sleep.

"You shouldn't chew on your nails." Jack drives almost as carefree as

189

his personality. One hand on the steering wheel and the other on his thigh. Some alt rock station plays softly in the background.

"Mom has the neighbors watching the house. So I had to tell them you guys are coming over." I drop my hand on my lap, but my foot taps while I wait for her reply. What if she says no? It's not like the guys actually care what parents say. They've snuck into my house before. But if Bob or Fran notices, they might think someone is breaking in and call the police.

"Your mom is cool, Harper. You've got nothing to worry about." Jack focuses on driving. I almost laugh at that statement.

My mom is *not* as cool as she wants to be with all this. But I've never really tested her before. This is the first year she's had issues with anything I do.

Even if she gives the go ahead, it wouldn't surprise me if Fran shows up at the door with cookies and stays until the last guy leaves. All because Mom asks her to watch over me. That would be so embarrassing.

My phone buzzes in my hand.

MOM:

Okay, don't let them stay too late. It's a school night.

ME:

Not a school night. Tomorrow's Labor Day

FRAN:

If you need anything, just call or text.

If anyone gets fresh, Bob has his bat ready.

I snort a laugh and cover my mouth. Bob facing off with any of the horsemen would be like David and Goliath. Bob is only a little taller than me.

A smile quirks the corner of Jack's lips as he glances my way. "What was that?"

"A laugh?" I drop my hands in my lap again. Still smiling at the image.

"What was it for?" Jack turns and his blue eyes sparkle in the dashboard light. He's got this smile and lightness to him that makes it easy to forget he can be just as dark as the others.

"My neighbor offered to send her husband over with a bat if you guys got fresh." I smile and lift my phone. That's when I notice a bunch of messages I received during dinner.

"Fresh? Damn, sweetheart, we plan to get more than fresh. I'm sure I could talk him down." Jack turns onto my street, but I'm only half listening to him.

On my phone, there are the usual chat messages from Penny and the girls about their shopping trip and a party. But there are a bunch of texts from Tanner. Why would Tanner be texting me?

Jack pulls the car into the driveway before I can look at them. When he stops the car, I put my phone down. Nerves scatter through me. It can wait until later. I don't want to get caught looking at another guy's texts. Who knows what sort of punishment the horsemen would inflict.

I squirm in my seat as heat floods me.

"First ones here. Yes! Hurry, sweetheart." Jack climbs out of the car. "I never get you alone."

Glancing behind us, I don't see any of the others' cars. Not even headlights. How fast did Jack drive? I grin at his eagerness.

He opens my door, and I get out. As I'm digging for my keys in my purse, Jack wraps his arm around my shoulders, drawing me tight into his side.

"Any cake left?" Jack tugs me toward the door.

"We *just* ate." I laugh softly and pull out my keys. When something moves in the shadows near the door, I startle. Jack's arm tightens around me.

"I guess you're fine after all." Tanner steps forward with his hands in his pockets. His shoulders are hunched like he's trying to appear harmless, but he's still a tall, built guy. Nothing about his expression says harmless to me.

Jack stiffens next to me. "What the fuck are you doing here?"

"I was checking on my *friend* to make sure she's safe. My dad works at the hospital and said her mom was working tonight. I'd hate for anyone to take advantage of that."

Cold runs through me. That didn't sound pleasant. It almost sounded like a threat. I lean closer to Jack.

Tanner rubs the corner of his lips. "She's got four assholes who don't take no for an answer."

"Like you have room to talk." Jack subtly shifts us around so he's standing between me and Tanner, protecting me? Hiding me? Getting me out of the way in case he wants to throw a punch?

Tanner's eyes narrow. "Fuck you, Jack. You don't know shit about what went down."

Jack takes a menacing step forward. "I know everything you did."

"And what about what you and Caden did to Mia?" Tanner puffs up his chest like he's preparing to fight. This isn't the guy who I met in art or at lunch. That guy seemed sweet, almost caring. Was that all an act? Because this guy actually freaks me out. There's something not right about his eyes.

"We didn't do a thing she wasn't one hundred percent on board with. Unlike you."

While I only know the basics of the story, what they're saying isn't making much sense. I touch Jack's back and feel the tension in him. I don't have any experience with boys and fighting, but I have a feeling unless I find a way to diffuse this, I'm going to find out real quick.

"Guys." I try to move to Jack's side, but he puts a firm hand on my hip and keeps me behind him. I glance down at where his touch burns into me like always, but he's also controlling me, handling me. Making the situation worse instead of deescalating this confrontation.

"I'm trying to be a friend to Harper. She needs someone willing to stand up to you." Tanner brushes a hand through his hair and seems to take a relaxed stance, but his muscles are still coiled, still ready to react.

Jack laughs. Not the light, brilliant laugh he usually has, but dark and ominous. "I'm sure you just happen to be friends with the girl we claimed for the year. Tell me exactly how that happened?"

"If anyone understands what she's going through, it's me." Tanner puffs up again. "We both know you're going to drop her as soon as you get what you want."

A car door slams behind me. I'm not sure how many are in that car. Fuck. I spin around. This is going to get out of hand. Especially if

Tanner keeps popping off. He's lost his damn mind. There are five horsemen and only one of him. This won't end well for him.

"Leave, Tanner." I return my gaze to him, knowing we only have seconds before the others realize there's someone else here. No one needs to get hurt. "I'm fine. I'll text you later, but you need to go."

Jack looks down at me with confusion. "No, you won't."

Tanner chuckles, but an edge cuts through it. "Yeah, Harper. You can't have your own mind. Not when the horsemen own you."

This is just a pissing match so far. "Just go before—"

"Tanner Lewis." Eli's voice is smooth as molasses as he comes to my other side.

My eyes close. Too fucking late.

Eli's hand finds my hip and tugs me back behind him and Jack, closing the gap between them, shutting me out again.

Is this some macho thing? I roll my eyes. I'm surprised they don't just hump my leg in front of him to prove I'm theirs.

"Tanner was just leaving." Maybe I can still make this go away before anyone else gets here. I move toward the door to unlock it. "Come on. Let's go inside before my neighbors come over to see what's happening. You guys can measure dicks some other time."

I push open the door and cross my arms over my chest. On the step, I'm at least closer to chin level on the guys.

"She's right, you should leave." Jack finally is being reasonable. More car doors slam.

My heart pounds harder. Even two against one aren't the best odds when they're the horsemen. But five against one... I know how overwhelming all of them can be.

Jack chuckles darkly. "I'm guessing you have ten. Nine. Eight."

I turn to see Caden and Luke walking toward me, with Nico behind them.

"Seven, six."

"What happens if I don't leave? What else could you possibly take from me?" Tanner holds his arms out to the sides before dropping them and the fake smile. He steps forward into Jack's space. His voice is quiet, but I hear him loud and clear. "Be careful, Hill, or I'll take something of yours."

Tanner's gaze meets mine. *What the actual fuck?*

"She'd never choose you over us." Jack shakes his head and steps back in front of me, crowding me against the door. "One. Should have left when you had a chance, asshole."

"What are you going to do? Beat me up? Four on one? How fucking original."

"Not me." Jack's arm cages me behind him as Caden roars past us.

"You motherfucker." Caden's fist slams into Tanner's face.

I let out a small shriek and jolt forward to do... what I'm not sure. Jack holds me firm. Nico and Luke are quick to pull Caden back before he can get in another swing. Were they surprised by the first one or did they let it happen?

Caden tugs to get free. His lips are curled and his eyes focused on Tanner. Tanner is bent over, but he straightens.

"Leave, Lewis." Luke almost shouts the words as he strains to hold Caden back.

Tanner rubs his jaw. His hand comes away with some blood, but he laughs bitterly. "Or what, Luke? Seriously. I have nothing left for you to take. You all want to get in a shot? We're eighteen, fuckers. I could go to the police station right now and file charges. Put your beast in jail."

I gasp and cover my mouth.

Eli slow claps. "Great idea, Tanner. Here's another great idea. Leave before we let Caden loose on you. He never reported what you did, but I guarantee the statute of limitations hasn't run out. Go ahead to the police. We'd love to talk to them. I'm sure they'd love to look through the videos on your cloud account."

All of their words confuse me. What happened between these guys? Jack has me pressed against the door while Caden is still struggling to get at Tanner. Eli is so calm, like none of this fazes him.

"Cool down, Caden," Nico says softly. "He's not worth it."

I shove past Jack, who clearly wasn't expecting me to do that. I step between Caden and Tanner. "Please leave, Tanner. Or I'll call the police myself."

Tanner turns his blue eyes on me and he gives me that winning smile of his, but it doesn't reach his eyes, shooting chills through me. "I'm trying to protect you from your keepers. I promised to be your hero and save you from them." He licks his lips, dropping his gaze down my body. "After all, we all know how good you taste."

My mouth drops open. The heat of the guys' eyes burn into me. My face heats and my stomach sinks. I don't even think before my hand flies, aiming for his face. He catches my wrist and tugs me toward him. As I stumble, an arm wraps around me, drawing me back into a hot body with a low growl.

"Leave." Caden's voice is hushed and terrifying in my ear. His arm is steel around my center. I want to sink into him and let him protect me, but what if they believe Tanner's lie?

Tanner smirks and drops my wrist. "Another time, Harper. You've got my number."

He steps back into the shadows and fades away, leaving me to deal with the fallout.

CHAPTER 28

The Blind Spot

CADEN

The red clears from my vision when Tanner leaves and Harper relaxes into me. Her vanilla scent floods my senses, easing anger. Tanner Lewis at Harper's house might as well be a red flag in front of a bull.

The guys work to keep him out of my path, knowing I can't see reason around him. And fearing I'll take it too far. They aren't wrong. I'd like nothing better than to wrap my hands around his neck and squeeze until that knowing, taunting light dies in his eyes.

Harper runs a smooth hand along my arm. She gasps when she feels my knuckles. They're already swelling a little, but I can't feel it with all the rage and adrenaline pumping through me.

I look at Jack, needing clarity. "What was he doing here?"

Jack frowns and glances at Harper. "Checking on Harper."

Her attention is on my hand. She's either really focused or avoiding talking about it. This is a pile of shit we can't ignore though.

"You need ice," she whispers, looking up at me with those soft brown eyes. That fucking caring tone in her voice will always be my undoing.

I sigh and look around at Luke, Eli, and Nico. Luke is fuming. I'm not sure what Tanner said, I didn't catch any of it. My blood thundered through my ears and my vision narrowed to only Tanner.

Nothing else mattered. But whatever it was, it pissed off Luke. Eli watches Harper with suspicion in his dark eyes. Nico? Nico looks confused as fuck.

"Come on, little nympho. Fix me up then." I turn with Harper toward the door and guide her into the kitchen. I'm no longer amped up, but it's slowly morphing into a need our girl isn't ready to fill.

Nervously, she moves away from me with a glance back before she opens a drawer and gets out a kitchen towel. The others file in and take seats, while she digs in the freezer for some ice. Luke stands like the asshole he is, slightly in her way, making her go around him. I lower into a chair at the table and watch her.

This is the first time I've seen Tanner all year. The guys are careful to keep him out of my sight. Especially after I threatened to kill the fucker after what he did.

But Tanner was here. For Harper.

That burns me deep inside. The betrayal sits uneasy because she may not know. If she knows though... if she knows and still let him close to her. Some small part of me would want to hurt her for that. I don't know how to feel about that part, because the majority of me only wants to protect her.

She brings over the towel filled with ice and sits in the chair beside me. Our knees brush. She takes my hand in hers and holds the ice against my knuckles, wincing when she touches them like she's the one with the injury and not me.

Her brown eyes flick up to mine. Uneasiness is in her eyes, like she's not sure where we stand. No one says anything.

I draw in a breath and blow it out. "What did he say?"

Harper flinches and her gaze falls to my hand. Luke straightens from leaning against the counter. Harper shivers but doesn't move away from me. He takes in every inch of her, as if he's weighing her.

"He said he tasted her." The words are clipped and damning from Luke.

She winces. Her hand tightens on mine slightly.

"And then she tried to slap him," Jack offers.

When Tanner grabbed her, everything in me stilled, and instead of being the aggressor, I became the protector. For her.

Her gaze lifts to mine. Unshed tears shimmer in the light. They beg me to listen even though she's not saying a word.

"It's not like Tanner Lewis is an honest guy." Eli taps his finger on the island where he sits. "We all know he's after one thing."

Nico shakes his head. "Not all of us know. Who the fuck is Tanner Lewis?"

Fuck, it's my story to tell. "He's a liar and a cheat."

Harper's startled gaze meets mine. So fucking innocent. If he'd ever had the chance to taste Harper, he never would have left her the way she is. She would be broken, because he doesn't leave innocents whole.

"How do you know Tanner?" I ask Harper.

"He's in my art class. He needed to sit close to the board and Kenz was gone, so he sat next to me for a class." She licks her lips, and a little of that mutinous side of her sparks. "He said you guys did the same thing to his sister, and that's why he missed the first week. He helped her settle into her new school."

Jack scoffs. "Mia Lewis begged us to plow her, and she most definitely was not a virgin when it happened."

Harper turns to Jack. "He said you all—"

"Nah, little nympho. Last year, she wanted to see what it was like with two guys. There was no coercion at all. She came to us."

She returns her gaze to mine, more confused than before. "But then why did she transfer?"

"She got into a fancy art high school." I lift my hand and brush a strand of hair behind her ear. A shiver works over her.

"He said you guys got him kicked off the football team and made him a social pariah." She rubs her thumb over my hand. Is she even aware she's doing it?

"Did you let him touch you, princess?" Luke steps closer. His energy is darker than usual. "Did you let him taste you?"

"No." She straightens and looks offended. "I barely know him. Fuck, he offered to be my boyfriend, and even I know he'd only be doing it to get revenge on you guys. I'm sorry, but I value myself more than being someone's revenge plot."

Luke studies her like he can see into her, but it's not him she needs to hear about. A rock settles in my stomach.

"Tanner targeted my little sister." I take the ice off my hand and hold hers.

"What?" Harper's brows draw together.

Standing, I pull her up and lead her into the living room. I sit in a large chair and draw her down onto my lap. "If I'm doing story time, I'm getting comfortable."

She curls into my side as the others come into the room and find seats. When she leans her head against my shoulder, something settles deep inside me. Some missing piece I might never have known was gone if I hadn't met her.

"Ava was fourteen, just before her first year in high school, when we were rising juniors." I clear my throat. The memories weigh on me like lead, dragging me underwater. "She was here for the summer before her first year of high school. Mom insisted she go away to a boarding school."

That house used to feel alive with her in it. Mom and Dad were home more often as well. It was almost like we were a family. Even with as cold as Dad is, it still felt better than the empty halls.

Harper takes my hand and her fingers massage it. I inhale. "She had a group of friends over, and the football team were all hanging out at my house."

I never should have had them over, but the girls were all kids. I didn't figure anyone would mess with them.

"My little sister was a kid to me. Fuck, all freshmen look like kids. It's one of the reasons we made them off limits. It was different when we were the same age and fucking around. But once we were older, there were plenty of other more acceptable women to go after."

Her dark eyes lift to mine, and all I see is forever in them. A lifetime of this girl, and children running around, filling the house with noise and love. That's what I see in Harper's eyes. Something few of us have. The capacity to love. A future bright and filled with laughter. Even for dark boys like us.

"What happened?" she asks softly, like she's almost afraid to know.

"Tanner brought his sister. Other girls were there too. Cheerleaders and some popular girls. Mia flirted all day with each of us. She wanted us to take her inside, which at that point we didn't. It seemed pretty fucked up to fuck a girl when her brother was a few feet away, so we passed."

She raises an eyebrow.

"We do have standards and rules, sweetheart." Jack draws her attention to him. "It doesn't mean we wouldn't fuck her. We were being respectful because her brother was there. Mia Lewis is hot just like her brother. That's a sandwich I would totally be the meat in, if he wasn't such a douchebag."

"Seriously?" Luke shakes his head.

I ignore Jack. "It didn't matter that we were respectful. I didn't know it, but Tanner started flirting with Ava. A secret flirtation that went on all summer, until Ava came crying to me."

Harper takes my hand and squeezes it, trying to give me strength maybe. Comfort possibly. But right now, my insides are numb. The events play out before me as I describe them to her.

"Ava was shattered. Tanner slept with her and then dumped her. Worse than that, she found him with another girl, and they both laughed at her for thinking Ava and him had something special." My fingers dig into the arm of the chair remembering her tears. She was crushed.

"They hadn't used protection, but she was afraid to talk to anyone about it. I wanted to take her to a doctor, but she refused, saying Mom would find out. I got her the morning after pill, but they aren't that effective, especially since she didn't tell me until a few days after." I wanted to kill Tanner. Hunt him down and gut him like he gutted my sister. The guys talked me down, saying it was consensual. Ava made that decision.

"She begged me not to go after him. Even after all that, she still thought she loved him." I can't imagine being that ignorant.

"But you went after him?" Her words are tentative.

"It's not the end of the story, princess." Luke breathes out.

"Fuck." Nico pushes his hand through his hair.

"It's not that easy. Life never is." I close my eyes as I tell the next bit. "Ava found out she was pregnant. She tried to tell Tanner it was his. He called her a lying whore and gave her a thousand dollars to get rid of it. Not only had she loved him, but she thought he might still want her if she was having his baby. She refused to tell our parents. She was fourteen years old and pregnant, and the only one she trusted was me."

I draw in a breath and open my eyes, letting Harper see my pain. She wraps her arms around me and squeezes me tight, like she can hold me together.

"I took her to the doctor, and then she left for boarding school, heartbroken." My voice cracks. I don't know if I can continue the story. Ava is still at the boarding school this year. Over the summer, she traveled with our parents, so she hasn't really been home with me except on the holidays.

"Mia came to us," Jack fills in. "She wanted to take two guys. We fucked her and thought everything was fine until she dressed to leave."

Finding my voice, I say the rest, "She told us her brother saw her flirting with us and went after my sister as payback. She laughed about it. Said how stupid her brother was when we hadn't even fucked her. Yet."

Luke leans in. "That's when we made their lives hell, princess."

CHAPTER 29

The Yield

HARPER

My chest aches for Caden and his sister. I don't know where to put everything I'm feeling. Anger. Hate. Sadness. I straddle his lap and hug him to me like I can fix this. Except the damage is long done.

His hands rub my back as if he's comforting me, and that's when I realize my tears soak his shirt.

Sitting back, I swipe at the tears, angry they're falling. Caden helps me wipe them away.

"He needs to pay." The words come out of me from deep inside. Tanner can't get away with what he did. It's disgusting and so much worse than anything these guys have done. He led on a girl who definitely wasn't old enough to make that decision.

Caden's lips curl into a smile. "I knew I liked you, little nympho."

"I'm serious. It's not enough. Whatever you've done isn't enough." A tear slips out, and Caden captures it with his thumb and brings it to his lips, kissing it away. My heart aches a little harder.

"We took away his social status. He got kicked out of football on his own." Caden smiles deviously. "Well, after someone let Coach know he had drugs in his locker. That got him a month of suspension. He would have been expelled, but he passed a drug test."

"Even we have limits, princess." Luke stands and paces to the door.

"We have dirt that could ruin him, but it would also ruin the lives of the girls in the videos with him. He has a collection."

My chest burns. He has a collection of videos?!

Luke turns, and his eyes burn with hatred for Tanner. The fire inside me answers his, wanting vengeance. Needing it.

Caden tips my chin back his way. The fire burns softer as I lose myself in his green eyes, so open and unguarded in this moment. "I know he lied about tasting you, Harper. Because if he'd had a taste, there's no way he wouldn't have made you his. You're addictive."

Awareness shivers through me, pushing away the darker thoughts, making me notice the hardness pressing between my legs. But also realizing now isn't the time.

Not after that story.

"Thank you for believing me." I cup his jaw and kiss him softly.

"Is there anyone else I need to know about before school Tuesday?" Nico sounds pissed. Maybe he knew Caden's sister. I'm not familiar with her, but I never went to his parties growing up.

I glance over my shoulder at Nico. "Don't ask me. I've been hiding under a rock apparently."

"That's why we couldn't find you." Eli smirks.

Turning back to Caden, I press my forehead to his and draw in his cinnamon scent. "Thank you for telling me. I'm sorry I didn't know."

"Few do."

Kenz might. She warned me about Tanner, but I thought the enemy of my enemy is my friend. Except the horsemen aren't really my enemy anymore. At least not really.

I release Caden and stand, holding my hand out to him. A peace offering. "I think there's some cake and ice cream left if anyone is hungry."

THE EVENING WAS QUIETLY SUBDUED. WE WATCHED SOME TV and ate cake and ice cream. While I brush my teeth getting ready for bed, I remember all the passing touches. The occasional kiss. And snuggles on the couch. But between Luke's father's interrogation and Caden's sister's story, my heart feels sick.

I also texted Mom to remind her tomorrow is Labor Day, not a school day, therefore I could sleep in and intend to. I don't need her banging on my door at 6 a.m. Especially not with two guys in my bed.

After I finish, I open my bathroom door and look at the demons waiting on my bed. One dark and intimidating. The other light and twisted. Both relaxed on opposite sides of the bed in only their boxers. I pause and lean in the doorway, dressed in a camisole and pajama shorts set.

They both tempt me beyond reason. Being alone with them is dangerous.

"What are you waiting for, little nympho?" Caden's green eyes hold me. His smile is devilish.

"Have you guys ever gotten someone pregnant?" I swallow around the lump in my throat. The question wasn't even on the tip of my tongue. I'm not sure where it came from, but I need to know.

"No." Luke draws my attention. "And if we had, we would have taken care of what's ours, princess. Now come to bed."

I still hesitate, my toes freezing on the tile. Of all my horsemen, these two have more power over me. My lust for Luke magnifies when he touches me. And Caden... Fuck, I'm lucky I'm not soaking wet every time he's near. What he can do to me... My blood boils with the need for it. For them. Do I worry I won't be able to control myself when I'm caught between the heat of them?

Hell yes.

"Harper?" Caden's tone is gentle, drawing my gaze back to him. "Come to bed."

He holds his hand out, and I step forward without another thought. Craving his touch. His story still resonates in my chest. His sister's story. I crawl onto the bed between them and join them under the covers.

My pulse picks up. I've slept in Caden's bed for the past two nights. Now it's just me, Luke, and Caden. Earlier, Eli keyed me up with promises of later, but this night ended so differently from how it started. The others all hugged and kissed me before leaving, promising we'd spend time together tomorrow.

Luke leans over to the nightstand and opens my laptop. The video turns on, and the live feed shows Jack working on his computer. Eli sits in bed with a book. Caden's and Luke's rooms are empty and dark.

"There." Jack finishes with a flourish, and a new feed pops up. Nico walks by the camera in only a towel, with water dripping down his abs. My mouth goes dry. They're all amazing athletes, and their bodies tell that story. Hard with rippling muscles, lean and firm. A teenage girl's wet dream brought to life.

Jack whistles. "Damn. You sure you don't go for guys? I'd be more than willing to help you experiment."

Apparently not just a teenage girl's dream.

Nico turns and notices the light on his computer for his video, I imagine. His eyes narrow and he sits at his desk. "How the fuck did you get into my computer, Jack?"

"Trade secret." Jack winks. "I'll let you in on it for a kiss."

"Just kiss him to shut him up." Caden laughs. "That's what I had to do."

I tuck that knowledge away for another time, my attention on Nico.

Nico's cheeks redden as he shakes his head. His gaze goes from screen to screen before he finds what he's looking for. He grins as he spots me. "Sunshine."

"Welcome to my life in a fishbowl." I return his smile and hold my arms out like I'm presenting some kind of award.

His longish black hair falls over his eyes. "I would have worn something special if I'd known I was going to be on pay-per-view."

"Fuck, Nico, you missed all the good shows." Jack's mischievous smile should have warned me. "We should catch you up to where we are."

"What exactly does that mean?" I'm not sure what he's missed. After all, I've had his cock in my mouth and his fingers in my ass. We've showered together multiple times. I think we're pretty well caught up.

"He needs to do never have I ever." Jack stretches. "Don't worry I remember the order and everything. If you've done something, you take off an article of clothing. When we played, Harper had to give us something she'd never done, and we had to give her something we've done."

"I'm only wearing a towel, Jack." Nico flicks a hand at the screen. "I wasn't exactly expecting you to pop into my room."

"Good. This won't take long to get to the good part." Jack rubs his hands together, and I can't help but laugh. Jack turns his gaze to my screen. "Don't get cocky, sweetheart. You have to play again. It's only fair. If something's changed since we played, you remove something."

"Yeah, little nympho." Caden drags me back against him, sitting me between his legs. "You want to put on a show for your new horseman, don't you?"

Caden's fingers slip under my camisole to tease the skin at my waist. My gaze lifts to find Nico's. He watches Caden's hand, almost mesmerized by it. Sparks flood my system.

Luke moves the camera until it's mostly on me.

"Never have I ever sent someone a naked pic." Jack sits back in his chair.

"Sorry." Nico runs his hand through his hair, slicking the wet strands back. "What about you, sunshine?"

I shake my head. "Still a no on that one."

"Never have I ever kissed four guys in one day. That one was mine." Jack winked. I'm not sure if he's winking at me or Nico. Maybe both. I've never really thought about what being bi means to Jack. It's something I should ask him about.

Caden lifts my shirt off me before I even think of taking it off, leaving me completely topless. "Little nympho's probably done it more days than you have by now, Jack."

His large hands cover my breasts, massaging them. I suck in a breath. When he traces my hardened nipples with his fingers, I sink into him, needing his warm, hard chest against my naked back. His touch makes me warm all over.

Nico's eyes darken as he licks his lips. Luke strokes a hand over his erection in his boxers, and our eyes collide. Wetness gathers between my thighs. My insides burst into flames at the banked desire in his blue eyes.

"I'd work on that, but I don't want to make Harper mad." Jack strokes his cock, pulling it free from his boxers. "Never have I ever had a threesome."

Caden's hands slide down to my shorts. I grab hold of his hands to stop him. "Wait a minute. I haven't had a threesome."

Luke cocks an eyebrow at me. "Yes you have, princess. In fact, so have I now."

"But we didn't have sex," I protest. My breath catches as Caden's thumbs dip below my waistband to stroke my skin along my hipbone.

"A threesome is three people engaged in sexual activity." Luke stands next to the bed and takes off his boxers. His cock stands tall and proud. Every inch of him is aroused for me. My lips part and my pussy throbs with aching need.

"I guess that means I've also had a threesome." Nico stands and drops his towel. You'd think I'd be immune to seeing their cocks by now, but damn... The ache amplifies. Being surrounded by beautiful boys isn't exactly a hardship.

Caden arches my back, lifting my hips from the bed. "A little help, if you don't mind."

Luke climbs on the bed and straddles my legs. Our gazes lock as he draws my shorts down my legs and off. My panties are wet and the only thing left on me. Caden lowers my hips back onto the bed, and Luke moves beside my legs, stroking his hand up and down my thighs.

My gaze keeps bouncing between Luke's cut body and Nico's. *Fuck, I'm a lucky girl.*

The thought startles me, but before I can get lost in my thoughts, Caden slips his hand over the front of my panties to rest between my thighs against my pussy. I inhale sharply as I wait for his touch.

Jack smirks. "Never have I ever watched porn."

Nico stands and strokes his hand down his cock. "What about you, sunshine?"

I nod, trying not to grind my pussy against Caden's waiting hand. "It's not really my thing though."

Nico sprawls back on his chair. "Prefer the real thing?"

Helplessly, I watch as Nico strokes his hand over his cock, rubbing over the head before thrusting up into his fist. Butterflies burst inside me.

Caden's finger twitches against my pussy, and I bite back my moan. Nico's eyes are knowing as he holds mine.

"Never have I ever had a one-night stand."

"Still no on that one." I watch Nico carefully. It's not important. Not really, but I want to know. He's had girlfriends. Hell, all but Luke have had one-night stands.

"Sorry, not my thing." Nico gives me a cocky smile.

"Never have I ever had a sex dream about someone in this room." Jack laughs. "After the last two nights, if you say you haven't, I'll know it's a lie. In fact..." Jack stands and takes off his boxers. "I had a dream about Nico the other night."

Nico stands. "I've dreamt of Harper every night this weekend."

Caden taps my pussy with his finger again, and I gasp at the burst of pleasure coursing through me.

"What about you, little nympho? Any new dreams?" His voice is rich and deep in my ear, sending goosebumps over my flesh. He hooks his thumbs into my panties.

Putting my hands over Caden's, I hold them still. When I find Nico on the screen, I give him a reluctant smile. "I haven't really had any dreams the past few nights, and while I've dreamed of Nico in the past, they weren't sex dreams."

Nico winks and smiles cockily. "We'll have to change that."

My cheeks flush hot. It's only a matter of time. If I weren't so exhausted by the time we fell asleep, I'm sure they all would have haunted my dreams.

"Never have I ever watched someone else have sex while I was in the room."

Luke straddles my legs, and Caden lifts my hips again. Luke leans over me and kisses my trembling stomach as he takes the sides of my panties and pulls them down.

"Wait a minute." Jack sits back. "What did we miss?"

Eli straightens from his spot on his bed. "Kitten, have you been naughty?"

Luke's heated gaze focuses on my pussy as he draws my panties down. "Sidney gave us a show in her bedroom with Brewster."

He drops my panties off the side of the bed and lifts my knees. I let them fall out to the side, opening myself to him. To all of them.

"Honestly not that good of a show." My voice is breathy as Luke slowly comes closer between my legs. His fingers lightly trail up my inner thigh, almost tickling me. His touch burns me.

"No, it wasn't a good show." Caden draws his hands back up to my breasts.

Luke's hand reaches my pussy and he spreads it apart, staring with fierce eyes at all of me, showing all of me to them. "A uninspiring blow job and an early ejaculation. Not exactly thrilling."

"Except for Brewster." Caden chuckles and squeezes my nipple, making me moan.

Luke slides his finger inside me and holds it there. My pussy flutters around his finger. I squirm slightly, needing friction. With a raised eyebrow, he turns to look at the camera. "Continue, Jack."

CHAPTER 30

The Resurgence

HARPER

"Never have I ever watched a guy jerk off." Jack's eyes roam around his screen as he strokes his cock. "Give me a few minutes and I'll show you if you haven't already seen it."

Nico chuckles darkly, his hand stroking his own cock while staring at the screen. The video of us in bed fascinates me. I'm reclined against Caden with his large hands caressing my breasts. My legs are parted and Luke holds me open while his finger is buried inside me. My pussy tightens around his finger, and his gaze lifts to mine.

Luke reaches down and squeezes his cock. A wave of lust crashes over me. His heated gaze holds mine enthralled, waiting for him to do more than this. Needing more. His eyes flare with heat.

"Our game got interrupted at that point." Jack's voice sounds strained.

My gaze jerks back to his feed, watching his cock shuttle in and out of his hand. My hips buck with his motion. His jaw tightens as he groans his release, covering his hand in cum. I lick my lips as if I could catch a taste of him there.

"Fuck, sunshine." Nico groans as he comes.

Eli watches it all like he's above us. His cock is hard in his shorts, but he hasn't put down his book. "Fuck her with your finger."

Luke's finger glides in and out of me. My lips part, and I fight the urge to close my legs around his hand.

Eli smiles. "Better, kitten?"

Nodding, I tip my head back against Caden's chest as every stroke brings me closer and closer to the edge. My hips follow Luke's fingers.

"What do you think, little nympho?" Caden's rich voice is dark in my ear, making shivers course through me. "What have you never done that you want to do right now?"

When I open my eyes, I meet Luke's. Light blue pools of warmth scorch me. They burn for me. Set me on fire.

I can barely focus, but Caden's words haunt me. There's not a lot left I haven't done. They've thoroughly taken me from untouched to practically not a virgin anymore.

"What do you want, princess?" Luke's voice is so damned tempting as his finger pulses inside me, making me need more. He leans in until his breath caresses my breast Caden holds for him. Luke's gaze flicks to mine. "What do you need?"

He surges forward and takes my nipple into his mouth, drawing hard on it until a responding ache forms in my pussy.

My head falls back onto Caden's shoulder. I shudder, so close to tipping over. "More."

Luke draws his finger out of me. I whimper and shudder as he drags it up to circle my clit. "More what?"

"More, please." Fuck, what does he want from me?

He slides his finger back down and pushes two inside me.

"Oh, fuck." I watch his fingers move in and out of me on the screen. The others watch me with lust in their eyes. He sucks on my nipple while Caden holds my breast for him, caressing the other nipple with his fingers. Rolling it, pinching it, tugging it.

Luke's cock weeps with need. I reach for him, taking his cock into my hand and sliding my hand down it. The soft skin stretches over his hard length as he presses his fingers deep inside me, making me gasp. He thrusts into my hand, sending heat through my veins.

The thought of him covering me with his body. Our skin sliding against each other's. Him thrusting his cock into my pussy. Filling me full. Coming around his hard length. It makes me whimper.

Releasing my breast Luke draws on, Caden's fingers brush over my lips. "Suck on them, little nympho. Get them nice and wet for me."

I part my lips, and he slides his fingers inside. I suck on them, tasting his salty skin, feeling his roughened skin with my tongue, sliding it along his fingers like I would his cock. His hard and unrelenting cock currently digging into my back.

I stroke my hand down over Luke's cock. My hand follows Luke's rhythm as he thrusts his fingers deep inside me, stretching me, filling me. His tongue flicks my nipple, and I cry out around Caden's fingers. Luke twists his fingers as he draws them out and pushes them back in deep.

It's too much stimulation and not enough at the same time. Caden pulls his fingers out of my mouth. His breath is harsh in my ear.

"Fuck, little nympho. Are you ready to fly?" His fingers slide between my ass cheeks until he finds my puckered hole.

"Caden," I gasp as he presses his fingers inside my ass. The world spins around me as I'm caught up in a tsunami of sensations. Their fingers thrust deep together, making me whimper with need, knowing they'll get me there. Luke's thumb taps on my clit.

"I've got you, little nympho." Caden's deep voice guides me through the darkness. "Let go."

Luke twists his fingers inside me, and I lose all grip on reality. My moan fills the room as everything tightens and releases and tightens again. Both of them thrust in and out of me through my orgasm, keeping me high and bringing me down.

I float down to myself, tucked safely in Caden's arms. Luke's lips find mine. His chest presses against my breasts as he takes my mouth, claiming every inch of mine as his. His fingers slide from me, leaving me empty.

His kiss moves across my cheek back to my ear.

"Harper." My name on his lips is a plea filled with need. He pulls back and rests his forehead against mine.

He wants me, needs me. I hold all the power right now. I want to give him everything he's given me.

It would be so easy to give in. To line his cock up with my entrance and give him permission. His blue eyes burn with that fire that calls to everything within me. Makes me ache just as much as he aches for me.

Caden's hand slips down my stomach and covers my pussy, pressing a finger inside me. "Not tonight."

Luke looks over my shoulder, and I look at the computer to see Caden's face.

"Luke." Caden's eyes narrow. His voice is firm. "Not tonight."

I stroke Luke's cock firmly. His eyes lock with mine. He squeezes his eyes shut for a moment as I continue to stroke.

"Give me your mouth, princess," he whispers.

I shift onto my knees, never losing his gaze. Caden's hands shift with me, and his thick finger pushes inside my pussy, pressing deep, filling me.

Lowering my head, I open my mouth and dart my tongue out to taste the precum on Luke's cock. He wraps his hand in my hair and tugs it slightly before I can take him in between my lips.

I glance up at him, waiting. Caden pulls his finger out of my pussy before pressing back in. His other fingers remain buried in my ass, not moving. When Luke traces his finger over my lower lip, I taste myself on it.

My hips rock with the motion of Caden's finger, pushing me closer and closer to the edge. Luke never takes his gaze from mine.

"Open, princess."

When I part my lips, he guides me down over his length, pushing in deep. Breathing through my nose, I swallow around his tip, feeling a corresponding pulse in my pussy.

Luke lifts me and lowers me over his cock. Taking my mouth achingly slow. Making me take him so deep, tears well and roll down my cheeks. "Soon, Harper. I'll bury my cock in your sweet pussy."

The words are ominous. They resonate in my soul. Caden stopped him this time from taking what belongs to him, but Caden might not stop us forever. When Caden's mouth closes over my pussy and he sucks on my clit, I jerk as I come all over his hands and face.

Luke pushes in deep, holding my nose almost against his abs as he groans and fills my throat with his release. I swallow around him while Caden keeps my climax going.

Luke pulls me off his cock and lifts my mouth to his, still holding my hair and keeping me in place as his tongue thrusts between my lips.

With his other hand, he tugs on my nipple, sending a shockwave rippling down to my pussy. Caden's tongue flicks my clit, and I'm over the edge again.

Caden draws his fingers out of me and trails kisses over my ass cheek to my lower back. Hot, wet kisses work their way up my spine, until he reaches my nape and sucks on the skin there, sending shudders of pleasure through me.

When Luke lifts his mouth from mine, I gasp in a breath. Caden hasn't gotten any attention. His hard, thick cock strains against the fabric of his boxers. Luke's eyes search mine before he releases my hair and falls back on the bed, one hand behind his head, the other on his flat stomach.

He arches an eyebrow, as if to ask me what I'm going to do. Caden's kisses move to my shoulder. As I turn his way, he lifts his head. His green eyes are so dark with lust. Wetness gathers between my thighs.

Cupping his jaw with my hands, I lean in to kiss him. He draws me down on top of him as he falls back on the bed. I straddle his stomach to keep kissing him. To keep that connection unbroken. I'm not only feeling tingles in my pussy for Caden, but full-blown butterflies race through me. His hands smooth over my back to rest on my ass.

My hair falls around our faces, closing us into our own little world. Air is inconsequential as our mouths melt into one. Even though I'm the one on top, he dominates my lips, my tongue, my being.

When my lungs feel like they'll burst, I lift my mouth, gasping in a breath. He opens his darkened eyes and holds my gaze as his thumb rubs my ass cheek. He's not pushing for more. Not right now. But I want to give him more.

Something I haven't done yet.

I kiss along his jaw, sucking, nibbling, licking until I slide down his body and kiss his throat. I'm aware of Luke sitting there watching, his hardening cock in his hand. As much as I'm aware of Nico, Jack, and Eli. Their eyes glued to the video feed. All of them fill me with this raging need for more. For everything.

As I move lower on Caden's neck, he squeezes my ass. I smile against his throat and suck on his skin, drawing hard, hoping it will leave a mark. Something everyone will see to prove he's mine.

"Fuck, little nympho. You're going to make me blow in my shorts."

I press on his chest to sit upright, straddling his abs, my pussy wet against his hard muscles. Glancing over my shoulder at his cock straining against his boxers, I raise an eyebrow when I turn back to him. "Then you better take off your shorts."

He grins wickedly. "Nah, little nympho. I wouldn't want to ruin your fun."

Putting his hands behind his head, he smirks. I look him over, every inch of him mine to do with what I please, at least for now. He's already said not tonight. But that doesn't mean I can't play with him the way they play with me.

I glance at Luke, but he doesn't move, just watches me. The others are all patiently watching, waiting to see what I'll do with this opportunity. An opportunity where they aren't directing me, manhandling me. Instead, letting me do whatever I want.

If I want, I could stop right now, lie down on the bed, and end our night. I curl my fingernails into Caden's chest, scratching him lightly on his pecs, paying close attention to his expression.

His eyes darken, and his tongue darts out to wet his lips. His gaze drops to my breasts, and they tighten under his attention. I lean down and kiss the marks I left on his pecs, dragging my tongue over his flat nipple. The transition from his skin to his smooth nipple fascinates me, and I take my time exploring it with my tongue and teeth.

He hisses, and my gaze jerks up to his face.

"You're fine, little nympho. It feels really good." His expression encourages me.

I kiss a path to his other nipple and explore to my heart's content, grinding my pussy against his abs with little thought. It just feels good.

My tongue follows the lines of his muscles down. I shift lower so I can continue to explore. The cotton of his boxers rubs against my thighs. When I lower my hips, my pussy settles on his hard cock, and I hiss at the feel of him pressed there.

His hips thrust up, and my gaze meets his. "Take me for a ride, little nympho."

I bite my lip and sit up. So many ideas flood my head, but I can't seem to settle on one. "How?"

"Take off his boxers, kitten." Eli's dark eyes take me all in. "I'll help, but just chase your own pleasure. He'll love whatever you choose to do."

My pulse races as I move a little farther down on Caden's legs so I can get his boxers off. He lifts his hips. Standing, I tug them off. His cock is huge and red, demanding all my attention.

Without a thought, I straddle him again. This time when I lower my pussy down over his cock, it slots perfectly against my clit. I press my hands down on his hard abs.

"Slide back and forth. Rock your hips." Eli's voice is a dark consciousness in my ears. "Cover him in your slick."

My gaze locks with Caden's. His arms are tense behind his head, as if he's struggling to hold himself back from touching me. When I rock my hips, his cock twitches beneath me. They've done this to me before.

Luke, Eli, and Caden have all rubbed their cocks against my clit, using me to get us both off. I'm the one chasing my pleasure now. I experiment with the angle and pressing down until I find the rhythm that keys me up and makes me pant.

"Good girl," Eli practically purrs.

I keep my gaze on Caden's. On those muscles in his arms straining so hard. I trace my fingers through the ridges of his abs until I brush my thigh. I suck in a breath at the feel of my own skin and the rush of excitement my touch brings.

Remembering the day they led me through my first self-administered orgasm, I draw my fingertips up my thighs. Caden's eyes burn with need as I drag my fingers up my trembling stomach. I stop short of my breasts, and he groans.

"Fuck, love. You know you want to touch them." Caden bucks beneath me, making me gasp as pleasure spirals through me. "Cup them, show me what you want me to do to you."

I bite my lip and cup my breasts, dragging my fingers over my tightened nipples. I moan as I slide along his cock. My pussy pulses, empty.

"That's it, kitten. Use him." Eli's voice weaves its spell around me.

I'm so focused on Caden and me, I barely register the groan over the laptop speakers. The pressure builds until I can't take anymore. My hands land on his abs as I moan through my release. His cock pulses and throbs against my clit. His groan is the only warning I have as I'm rolled onto my back with Caden on top of me.

His mouth claims mine, and his warm cum presses against our stomachs. I give myself to the kiss, falling into it and not caring about anything else but this warm glow inside me and the taste of this man on my tongue.

His lips trail to my ear, and he says in a low voice only I can hear, "I want to fuck you so hard." He growls and I shiver with need. "We'll be epic, little nympho. When you're ready."

He kisses beside my ear and takes his heat from me. I inhale deeply as I stare up at the ceiling. The water runs in the bathroom. My eyelids are heavy.

When Luke shifts on the bed next to me, his arms engulf me, dragging me into his heat. Sighing, I snuggle back into him. A warm, wet towel swipes at my stomach, and Caden focuses on his task.

He smiles as he moves away, and then darkness swallows the room. The bed dips, and another warm body presses against mine. For a second, I worry about putting something on, but I'm too tired to move.

CHAPTER 31

The Evasion

Smooth, warm skin presses against mine. I reach for it and drag it into me. Soft curves fit perfectly against my hard muscles. My hand flows over her, and she snuggles deep into me. Her leg goes over my leg and brushes against my already hard cock.

I wake up enough to know I can't just roll Harper onto her back and thrust into her perfect, tight cunt. I blow out a breath. Last night was hot. I'd prefer to be buried inside her, but she definitely took care of me. Gotta hand it to the girl. She tries to keep up without giving it up.

The bed shifts as Luke rolls and presses against her back. She releases a low whimper, and I slide my hand between her legs to find her already wet. Luke's finger thrusts in and out of her pussy. Her hips buck against my leg.

I open my eyes and glance at the computer screen. The feeds are still live, but no one else is up. The sun isn't even up yet. She buries her face into my chest and her hand clutches at my waist.

Circling my finger over her clit, I wait for her to wake up. Wait for those dark eyes to lift to mine and acknowledge I'm the one who makes her feel this way. It's my touch she craves.

Luke kisses her shoulder and lifts his gaze to mine. Her body is captured between the two of us. It would be so easy to slide inside her and feel her pulse around my cock.

Of everyone to be a cockblock, I had to last night. It wasn't the right time, and now when she's half awake isn't a good time either. When I take her, I want her one hundred percent on board with it.

I want her to want it so badly she can't go another minute without. I take her breast into my hand and tease the nipple into a hard peak. Her hips rock against my finger, seeking release.

She cries out softly as she comes. Her fingers dig into my skin, and her leg tightens around me.

"Harper?" a woman's voice calls out.

Fuck. Luke and I take our hands off her like we weren't just making her come, but Harper hasn't exactly woken up.

A soft knock sounds on the door, and Harper lifts her head from my chest. She doesn't even open her eyes. "What?"

"You okay? I thought I heard something." The knob rattles like her mother closed her hand over it, but she hasn't turned it. It's locked. We made sure of that last night. Not that bedroom locks aren't easy to unlock.

Harper's room is small, and there's a bathroom attached we might hide in, but that would require us getting out of bed and across the room before her mom opens the door. Not to mention our clothes on the floor.

"I'm sleeping, Mom." Harper drops her head on my chest and curls around me. I guess if her mom comes in, we brazen it out. So much for her mother liking me best.

"Okay. Text me what you're up to today. I assume you'll be hanging out with the guys again." The statement comes out with a little question to it.

"Mmm. Probably." She rubs her nose against my pec like it itches.

"Be careful, baby." The words are soft before she walks away from the door.

Luke strokes his hand down Harper's side, and she clings to me. Neither Luke nor I have parents who give a shit about us outside of what we do in the future. Mine barely noticed when Ava didn't eat for a week. They definitely didn't know about her nightmares when she was little.

She's always been my responsibility.

"Caden?" Harper's voice is barely above a whisper. Her breath is warm against my skin.

"Yeah?" I smooth the hair out of her face. Her eyes are still closed.

"You're thinking really loud."

"What?" I chuckle, wondering what she's talking about.

She turns and kisses my chest before resettling into her spot on me. "You're tense all over. Whatever's spinning through your brain is stressing you out. Do you want to talk about it?"

She yawns. Luke is curled around her and already back to sleep.

"I was thinking about my parents and Ava." The words slip out before I can think twice about them. "Go back to sleep."

She raises her head and rests her chin on her hand on my chest. Her sleepy brown eyes open. "You don't have to do that."

"Do what?" I brush the hair from her face and cup her jaw. How did we miss her? I didn't lie to her when I said I noticed her. The others might have overlooked her for the hotter girls in our class. The more eager ones. The ones who wanted to be noticed.

But there is this quiet strength Harper emits that draws me. Always has.

"You don't have to shut me out." She shrugs like it isn't a big thing. "I'm here. I'm yours. At least for the year."

I hate that she qualifies that. She knows I want to keep her, but she doesn't believe me. I have time to make her believe and I will.

"I know they aren't the holes that interest you the most, but I have two ears and I'm a great listener." Her smile is cheesy as her large, brown eyes watch me.

"You're lucky, little nympho. You have a mother who will do anything for you. Who cares about you so much that the littlest whimper brings her running." I thread my fingers into her hair. "Ava and I don't have that. I'm the one she came to when she had nightmares. I'm the one who bandaged her scraped knees. I'm the one who should have castrated Tanner the minute I found out he touched her."

"You said she asked you not to. That matters, Caden. You didn't go off on him because she trusted you not to." She leans into my hand as I rub her scalp. "You may not have had parents, but she at least had you."

"And look where that got her. Fourteen and pregnant." It still makes my insides burn. I should have known. I should have been more vigilant.

"And you were what sixteen? Seventeen?" She kisses my chest. "You can't blame yourself for wanting a life or not guarding hers. I don't know what your life was like growing up, but I'm sure you made hers better just by being you."

I can't help the smile that tugs at my lips. "You see me as something I'm not. You know that, right?"

"I see the man you could be. I see the kind heart you bury deep inside." She tips her head to the side. "Part of me wants to believe what you show me is real. The other part is terrified you're only pretending to get what you want. But the more time I spend with you, the more I want to believe you're real."

I *tsk* her and shake my head. "Never trust a horseman, little nympho."

She leans into my hand again and smiles sleepily. "Probably shouldn't sleep with them either."

"Go to sleep, Harper. Maybe today I'll let Luke fuck you." I draw my hand out of her hair.

"Not up to you," Luke murmurs, and his arm tightens around Harper, eliciting a squeak from her. "Princess will let us know when the time is right."

"Go to sleep, Death," she murmurs as she rests her head back on my chest. "Be glad my mom trusts me, or she would have lectured us for hours this morning."

As much as I distrust the adults in my life, somehow I think I might have liked that. To have a parent care so much that she tries to parent me too.

CHAPTER 32

The New Tactic

HARPER

For a Monday morning, the diner is full of students. I feel self-conscious sitting between Luke and Caden while we look at menus, waiting for the others to get here. The booth is one of those curved ones, so we're on display to the whole restaurant. Whenever I glance over the menu, I accidentally meet someone's gaze as they watch our table.

It's unnerving.

Almost as bad as the school cafeteria. Caden's hand rests on my thigh, and I jump at the touch. He chuckles and squeezes me.

"Relax, Harper."

I cover my mouth with the menu when I say, "Easy for you to say. I've never been the center of anyone's attention."

"I love it when you're the center of our attention." His green eyes grow mischievous as his hand trails up my thigh higher. Heat floods me, but I clamp down on his hand before he gets too high. I hope my look communicates how not appropriate that is.

I slept naked between two horsemen and didn't lose my virginity last night. The way they played with me though... My cheeks heat. It's like everyone in this restaurant can tell what they've done to me.

Caden smirks and puts his arm around my shoulders, tugging me close until our thighs touch. "Chill, little nympho. No one's coming near you with us here."

Luke glances at me with a dark heat in his eyes that makes me squirm with need. Fuck.

"What's the plan for today?" I clear my throat and set the menu on the table.

"I vote we play a game." Nico slides in beside Luke. His smiling eyes meet mine, and a pulse of awareness shoots through me. Nico and I haven't had much time to talk since he returned, but it also feels like he never left. We have this huge gap in our history, and I want to fill in the details.

"I'm game to play." Jack slides into the booth next to Caden. He gives me a smile. "Last night was awesome, sweetheart. Best show yet."

My cheeks flush hotter. It's different when it's just us, but right now it feels like the entire student body studies our every move. Leaning in to hear whatever we say.

"If it involves getting Harper naked, I'm game." Caden squeezes my shoulder. He isn't exactly quiet, and more than a few heads turn our way. I didn't realize my face could feel this hot.

Luke takes my hand under the table and squeezes it slightly. My gaze finds his light blue eyes. He leans in to my ear. Our cheeks brush, sending sparks rushing through me.

"Ignore the others, princess. They just want to find out why we're all fascinated with you." He places a soft kiss beneath my ear, and a shiver works through me. When he draws back, there's this softness on his face I haven't seen since the night he spent alone with me.

I lift my hand and cup his jaw to check to see if he's real. He leans into my hand and closes his eyes for a second, as if savoring my touch. Everything in me freezes as I take in the beautiful boy before me.

This is what draws me like a moth to the flame when it comes to Luke Foster. The little pieces of vulnerability he shows me, and then just as quickly they're gone.

When he opens his eyes, he's once again the king of the school. Cold, heartless Death. "Don't let them have any of you, princess."

He draws away, and part of me longs to draw him back in. His hand still holds mine below the table, and his thumb rubs over my wrist, sending sparks through me.

Eli joins the table. His dark eyes focus on me. He's been sweet to me. Most girls claim he's rough. That makes me pause. How much of what these guys have shown me is only to get into my pants?

Everyone knows they're bullies. They rule the school with iron fists. They basically trapped me in this thing we're doing.

But as I look around at my guys, I'm pretty sure it's time to test my theory. I want them all, and it's time I let them in a little further. And hope what they claim is true. That I'll be theirs and they'll be mine.

Worst that will happen is I lose my virginity in a spectacular way, and then they leave me. But I'm not sure I believe that will happen anymore.

"I hope you brought the jerseys." Sidney and her posse of Cheermonsters, Emma, Hannah, and Ashley, stand in front of the table like a gang ready to do battle. Fists on cocked hips. All of them in perfectly sexy outfits, designed to show off their assets.

Sidney lets her eyes rest on each of the horsemen, but her gaze skips over me like I don't exist. After my drunken call out, it could have been much worse. I snuggle into Caden's side and cling to Luke's hand.

Nodding, Eli holds out a stack of four jerseys. "Nico got his on Saturday, so you can use his as well."

"That makes this easier." Sidney takes the jerseys and shifts through them, reading the names on the backs. "So, Caden gets your whore first then?"

Luke tightens his hand around mine. Sidney lifts her calculating eyes to him with a smirk and glances my way. I don't react. Maybe she was hoping for it, but I know exactly what these girls think of me. It doesn't matter what they think. The guys are mine, and I've already told the Cheermonsters I won't be needing them to help me out.

"If you'd rather find someone else's jerseys to wear, that could be arranged." Luke's voice is calm, but there's a sharp edge to it.

Sidney laughs like Luke said something funny. Her friends join in. "I could easily get other guys' jerseys—"

"Worried about your jaw hurting?" Caden traces circles on my shoulder while his smile to Sidney doesn't reach his eyes. I keep my expression flat, trying not to remember her giving Brewster a blow job in front of us. "Gotta admit you have some decent technique, but the quality of the show was definitely lacking."

Sidney doesn't even flinch. "We just love supporting the best of our team as cheerleaders."

"I'm sure you do." Caden leans back and smirks.

"But..." Ashley steps forward and gives Eli a look "After your pet's little outburst, don't come crawling back thinking we'll be waiting for you."

If the guys gave the Cheermonsters even a hint they might want them again, these girls would be all over them. I'm beginning to get it. Their attention is addictive.

Eli chuckles darkly. "Your services are no longer required."

A flash of hurt crosses Ashley's face before she turns her furious gaze to me. I'm so fucked.

"We agreed on the jerseys for next week. We'll make sure to trade off with Harper. But keep your little pet on her leash. Make sure she knows her place, and we'll make sure her life doesn't turn to hell." Sidney steps back with a cocky smile. "Otherwise, you'll have to be careful about letting her stray."

Luke tenses again, but I squeeze his hand. If he says something, it will only make it worse for me. The threat is out there. I don't need to be any more visible than I already am. The Cheermonsters want to continue to rule the school. Their fear is I'll somehow rise to the top because of the guys, but that won't happen.

I'm not meant to be popular and I'm good with that. But I'm not giving up my guys.

When Luke doesn't say anything, Sidney spins on her heel.

"Ticktock, little virgin," Hannah says as they walk away.

Crossing my legs, I look down at the menu. A weight settles in my gut. Those girls will make my life hell. Sure, they won't beat me up or bully me, but they'll paint a target on my back and let the other girls take their chunks out of me until there's nothing left.

"Want me to do something about that?" Jack's words make me glance at him. His expression is fierce and protective. I look around at the others, and they all have similar looks. My heart beats a little quicker at the realization they all would step up for me.

"If you did something, it would only make things worse," I admit. "As long as they stay on top, I'll be safe."

I think.

"I don't like it." Luke threads his fingers through mine like he's never going to let go, and a small part of me doesn't want him to. "Too much power has gone to their heads."

"We could take them down a notch." Eli rubs his fingers over his lips. "Just enough to remind them who's on top."

I tense. I can't help it. The guys can't protect me every second of every school day. Even I, with my head in a hole, know how powerful those girls are. The retaliation won't be at the guys. They'll aim for the weakest link. Me.

"Not today." Caden strokes his hand down my arm. "Today we should head back to my place. We can decide later if the girls are worth the trouble."

I release the breath I didn't realize I was holding and give Caden a small *thank you* smile. He leans down and brushes my hair away from my ear, sending shivers through me.

"I want to play with you, little nympho. So fucking badly."

When he pulls back, his green eyes have darkened. A pulse of awareness races through me. Last night comes back into my mind. The feel of his cock between my legs. I tighten my legs against the ache building. Fuck it. I'm ready for more.

"You guys ready to order?" The server is in her late twenties, and her eyes flit from guy to guy. Admiration shines in her eyes, and she winks at me when she notices me watching her.

After taking our orders, she leaves. The guys chat about random stuff, some new video games, and I lean my head against Caden's shoulder. Something settles inside me.

Surprisingly, I'm not nervous about my decision, but I'm not sure how I'm going to pick. Even the who is difficult. Nico would have been my first if he'd stayed. I have no doubt we would have been together. The connection we felt as kids would have developed into more as naturally as a flower blooms.

But as much as I want him, he still feels new. We've done a lot this weekend, but I still don't know teenage Nico the way I knew elementary school Nico. I want to know him better. Not to mention he might think it means more if I choose him.

Jack is fun and obviously the right size for the job. Though he's still pretty big. I smile to myself. He's been kind and caring. He's not as aggressive as some of the others. Even our first kiss, he let me lead.

I don't really want to lead with my first time.

Eli makes me feel alive. He's considerate and he can turn on the charm like no one else. I can't help but want his aggression, but maybe not for the first. I'm already worried about how it will feel.

If it will hurt. It can, but it doesn't always. At least that's what I've read.

I want to enjoy my first time. While I may enjoy the way Eli fucks me, maybe even crave it, I don't want my first time to be rough. A little shiver ripples through me.

The server returns with our food, and Luke lifts my hand and kisses my knuckles. Our eyes meet, and that tension flows between us. That longing and craving for each other. He kisses my knuckles again before releasing my hand to eat.

Luke Foster. The pale horseman. There's something magnetic about him that keeps drawing me in, even if he's the most problematic of the group. He's jealous and possessive, but when he touches me, I crave him. I want him to fuck me.

But he doubts me. He thought I let Tanner touch me. If I let him possess me first, who's to say he would let the others have me? Claim me as just his? Last night, I was tempted. I could have let him take me.

I want Luke. There's no denying it. The chemistry between us is intense. But he wants to own me, and giving him that piece of me might make him think he does own me. I can't give him that leverage, because I'm not sure I'll be strong enough to deny his claim.

Caden's leg shifts next to mine. When I look up into his green eyes, he smiles before tearing into a piece of bacon. A breath escapes me as butterflies race through my veins. If Nico had been here, he would have been the one, but now...

Caden cocks an eyebrow, questioning me silently. Everything

Caden's done has wrapped me closer and closer to him. Even when he's been an ass. He wants me in his life, and like an insane person, I like him even more for that.

He's soft and hard, loving and fierce. He pushes me, but then he holds me back. He's a monster and a teddy bear. And yet, he also has a really huge cock, which is terrifying. But we were made to fit together. My pussy throbs thinking about how he fills my mouth and feels sliding against me.

"Dirty thoughts, little nympho?" he asks in my ear. "Any way I can help with those?"

I search his eyes, making sure this is the right answer.

He was my first kiss. When my car had a flat, he championed me even when they were punishing me. He believed me with Tanner. My refusal to get to know the horsemen made him angry.

He wants to keep me.

And part of me wants to keep him, even if it's ridiculous and we're only eighteen. And there's no way I'm having ten kids.

I reach up and rub my hand over the scruff on his jaw. He smiles and pretends to nip at my hand. My heart thumps against my chest.

This is easier than I thought it would be.

I'll get to be with all of them, but for my first time, I want it to be Caden.

CHAPTER 33

The Acceptable Loss

CADEN

The drive to my house is short. Luke and I are in Harper's little car. Last night, Nico drove us to her house so our cars wouldn't be in the driveway. That would have been pushing it with Harper's mother.

Harper's been quiet since the Cheermonsters tried to assert their dominance again. Fuck those chicks. They need to be knocked down a peg.

"I don't see why I couldn't drive my own car." Harper sits with her arms crossed in the backseat.

I chuckle and glance at her in the rearview mirror. "I'm being chivalrous. Luke's being an ass since he called shotgun."

"Fuck off." He's been a little pissed since last night when I cockblocked him. But he had to know it wasn't the right time. Fuck, after hearing my sister's story and his father's interrogation, our girl was traumatized. She wasn't in the right place to lose it.

She's definitely getting there though.

I want her writhing in pleasure, which she was, but there was a sad edge to last night that seems to have cleared this morning. Not going to get my hopes up, but the way she looked at me in the restaurant, like she was really *seeing* me, made my chest puff up a little more.

When I pull into the driveway, three other cars pull in behind me.

229

Eager little bastards all of them. Not that I blame them. They didn't get a taste of our girl last night. I could use another taste of our girl.

Opening my door, I get out and open Harper's. She steps out and stands in front of me. A thoughtful look of determination on her face as she looks at me. She doesn't say a word, but her lips part and that flush works its way up her neck.

She's gorgeous when she gets turned on. Even more so when it's me who turns her on.

I press her up against the side of the car, grab the back of her neck, and claim her mouth. She arches into me and opens beneath my lips. I'm fighting a losing battle when it comes to her. I know we should wait, give her space and time to adjust to us. But when she's in my arms, my brain isn't the thing that's working hardest to get my attention.

Dipping down, I grab under her knees to lift her up against me, pressing my cock against her pussy. She's wearing jeans again. If I had my way, she'd wear nothing but skirts, so I could just thrust deep into her whenever the mood struck.

The way she clenches around my fingers when I'm buried deep in her pussy... Fuck, I need to feel her around my cock. Her mouth is divine, but I'd prefer to fuck her cunt.

Her fingers dig into my hair and tug lightly. I'm going to need her to suck me off or to take a cold shower. But I don't want to relinquish her mouth quite yet.

We all stole a mint on the way out of the diner. So she tastes fresh and sweet. Last night, it damn near killed me to let her chase her pleasure on me. Her pussy hot and wet dragging over my cock. It took all my willpower not to flip her under me and give her exactly what she needs.

Fuck me. I need her.

"Caden?" she whispers as she pulls away and presses her forehead against mine. She opens her dark brown eyes, and my heartbeat stops for a second. Passion dilates her eyes, making them look like deep abysses. I want nothing more than to dive in and drown in her.

"Yeah, little nympho?" I rub my nose against hers as I grind my cock between her legs. So much better without the jeans in the way.

"Can we continue this inside?" She leans in and kisses me, running her tongue along my bottom lip. Her eyes open and meet mine. "In your bedroom."

Hell yes. I hold her tight against me, refusing to put her down. She wraps her legs and arms around me as I walk to the back of the house with four shadows following close behind. If my little nympho wants to play games, I'm all for it.

We walk through the lower level and the dark hallway. We don't pass anyone on the way to my bedroom, but I know they're there. The household staff my parents pay to watch over me.

My parents don't assert their will on me very often, but they keep track of all the comings and goings. By now my father knows a girl has been present and four of my friends have stayed at my house with me and the girl.

I don't give a fuck what my parents think. They can think whatever they want. They don't matter, but as I push in the door to my room, the only thing that does matter is the girl currently clinging to my body.

And how I'm going to get her off this time.

HARPER

Caden sets me down, and I step away, needing to catch my breath. That kiss only solidified my decision. My panties are damp, and this buzzing sensation lives under my skin, needing more.

Jack flops down on the bed behind me. Eli leans against the couch. Nico sits on the arm of a chair. Luke crosses his arms and leans against the closed door. They're all hot and so focused on me.

"Umm." I twist my hands in front of me, suddenly nervous about what I want to tell them. Worried about their reactions. What if they decide they don't want to do this all together? What if they're upset I didn't choose them? What if Luke gets angry and leaves?

It wouldn't be the same without him. It wouldn't be the same without all of them.

Luke must sense my drowning. He drops his arms and strides over to me. Cupping my cheek, he tilts my face up to his.

"What do you want, princess? Anything you want, we'll give it to you." His thumb brushes over my lower lip, and my lips part on an exhale. This hum of energy vibrates beneath my skin, so in tune with these guys.

This seemed so easy in my head. I glance at the others, watching me with curiosity. I don't want to tell them my reasons for choosing Caden over them, but maybe I can make them understand how much I want them all.

I swallow. "I don't want to be a virgin anymore."

"If this is because of what those girls said—" Nico stands, ready to fight for my honor. My heart thumps a little harder for him.

Shaking my head, I smile. "It's not about them. It's about us. All of us."

I hope Luke can see what I need in my eyes, like he always does.

His face softens. "You've made a choice?"

I nod and swallow at the thickening in my throat. "All my firsts are gone except two. I'm sure we'll get to the other one, but I'm ready to give the first one."

Luke steps in closer, and I put a hand against his chest, not to stop him but to finish what I have to say. If he puts his hands on me more, I'll succumb to my desire.

"I want to have all of you, but someone has to go first." A lump forms in my throat as I meet Luke's eyes. I don't want him to be mad at me, but I have to go with my heart on this one.

I feel a connection to each of them, but there's one connection that's been stronger than the others. One that's growing into something I never expected.

"Who did you choose, princess?" Luke brushes my hair behind my ear, sending pleasure spiraling through me.

"Caden." My gaze finds those green eyes wide and shocked. He looks shell-shocked, like he can't believe I chose him, which makes me glad I did. I give him a smile.

"I'm honored, little nympho, but fuck..." Caden's hand digs through his hair as he steps toward me, closing in on me and Luke. "I know what I said the other day, but I knew you weren't ready. What if I hurt you?"

I shrug. "It might hurt with anyone. It might not. You've had other virgins—"

He shakes his head. "No, I've aided Jack in devirginizing women, but I've never taken anyone's."

Okay, that surprises me. My mouth drops open, but Luke tips my chin up, capturing my eyes. He searches them for several seconds before he nods slightly.

"We're all here for it." He strokes his thumb across my cheek.

I glance at Caden, who still looks worried. I admit, "I want you all. All of you to be a part of it, like everything we do."

Eli moves to join us. His hand claps on Caden's shoulder. "If we get her ready, it will be easier."

"Especially if she has a few orgasms first." Nico gives me a nod as he joins us, like he understands my thinking. His words make me burn. They've all made me climax, and the anticipation of more orgasms makes me squirm.

Jack steps behind me. The crisp scent of apple joining the combination of scents from the guys. His hands curl around my hips as he draws me back against him. "We could spend all day getting her ready to be fucked."

Leaning into Jack, I glance back at him, but his eyes are on Caden.

"We won't let you hurt her," Jack promises.

Someone has to take charge, and I know it won't be me. My gaze returns to Luke, and I give him a pleading look.

He steps into me, trapping me against Jack's body. "Once he's done, we'll all claim you, princess."

My breath catches, and an ache starts low in my gut. This is it. This is what they've wanted from me. At least in the beginning. They all have admitted they don't care about my actual virginity, but they want to fuck me.

"We should play spin the bottle." Caden steps back and finds the bottle we've used before. "It seems fitting we let the bottle help get you ready."

I wet my lips and gaze up into Luke's eyes, waiting for him to give us rules. Leaning on him probably more than I should in this moment, when I've basically said I want another man to fuck me first. But we're all a part of this.

Like Luke said in the beginning, only one of them can fuck me first, but they can all be there. That terrified me at first, but now, I wouldn't want it any other way. He searches my eyes and traces my cheekbone lightly with his thumb. He kisses me softly, briefly, before stepping away, taking my hand, and leading me to the couch.

Sitting in the center of the couch, he tugs me down onto his lap. "New rules. Anything goes. Except for the grand finale. The coin chooses who gives and who receives. Harper chooses where. She'll sit on our laps, and whoever the bottle lands on will come to us. Disrobing Harper will be the responsibility of whose lap she's on. Timer will be for two minutes. She changes laps with every spin of the bottle. Questions?"

I squirm on his lap, already wishing I hadn't worn jeans and a t-shirt today. The rules are a lot less complicated, but he's leaving all the choice up to me.

"I'd like to propose a rule change." I raise my hand and then lower it self-consciously.

Caden smirks as he sits next to Luke. He places the bottle on the coffee table.

"Turn around and tell me, princess." Luke's voice is dark in my ear, and shivers skitter down my spine.

Standing, I turn and straddle his lap. I put my hands on his shoulders. His hard cock presses against my pussy. The urge to bite my lip is strong, but I resist. I don't want a sore mouth today, and Eli will punish me for it.

"What do you want, sweetheart?" Jack sits in the chair, and Nico takes the other one. Eli settles in on the other side of Luke.

I meet Luke's eyes. "I want the horseman to choose the where, and for the person whose lap I sit on to take part."

Luke's eyes smolder with banked heat. "Anything else, princess?"

I look up like I'm thinking, but then shake my head.

He grabs my hair and tilts my head back as he hovers over me. "Next time we play spin the bottle, my cock will be buried in your cunt while you sit on my lap."

My breath catches as heat rages through me. He captures my lips, claiming my mouth the way I'm sure he wants to claim me. I want to get beyond this first time, so I can have them all. But I appreciate they want to make sure it's as painless as possible.

Luke tugs my head back, and our eyes lock. "Time to play, princess."

I rise off his lap on shaky legs before lowering back down, facing the coffee table. He holds my hips while I lean forward to spin the bottle. It slows to point at Nico.

Jack flips a coin. "Heads."

Nico stands and moves in front of me and Luke.

"Choose what you want her to do to you, and I'll be doing that to her." Luke's voice tickles my ear and sends a wave of lust through me.

Nico sits on the coffee table before me. "Kiss my neck, sunshine."

Luke lifts me, and I drop to my knees between Nico's legs. Luke follows me down and his body presses against my back. He lifts my hair to drop over my shoulder. Shivers tickle down my spine. "Whenever you're ready, princess."

Luke takes my hands as I lean in and kiss Nico's neck, inhaling his fresh rain scent. Luke's lips land on the nape of my neck. Sparks trickle through my veins. Heart pounding, I trail kisses down Nico's neck to suck on the spot where his neck and shoulder meet.

Nico's breath teases my hair to dance across my skin, making shivers flow through me.

My pulse throbs as Luke closes on the spot that seems to have a direct line to my pussy. When he sucks hard, I groan and press into Nico. Nico's hands lock on the edge of the coffee table. His breathing is heavy in my ear.

I want it all.

Now that I've made my decision, I don't hold back anything. I explore his neck, kissing, sucking, and drowning in the feel of his skin beneath my lips, his taste on my tongue, while Luke's mouth fills me with sparks, tingles, and aching need. I'm wet and eager to move beyond the neck.

"Time," Eli says.

My clothes feel tight on my body.

When I pull back, Nico captures my neck to hold me still while he takes my lips. I press into him as much as I can with Luke holding my hands. He tastes me with a gentleness that makes my heart skip a beat.

When he releases me, he gives me a smile and returns to his seat. For a second, I regret not choosing Nico to be first. But in the end, I'll have all of them. Luke's hands squeeze mine.

Eli holds out his hand. "Come here, kitten."

He helps me sit on his lap. I lean forward to spin the bottle. When I fall back against Eli, he wraps his arm around my waist. His fingers caress between my jeans and shirt, riding the edge and tormenting my skin. The bottle stops on Jack. He flips the coin and holds it out showing it landed on heads.

"Chest, sweetheart." Jack takes off his shirt and tosses it to the side.

Eli lifts the hem of my shirt, and I raise my arms for him, never taking my gaze from Jack's brilliant blue eyes. My hair falls around my bare shoulders as my shirt disappears. Eli's fingers work the hooks of my bra with ease.

When he removes it, hungry eyes devour my breasts. My nipples tighten and my breasts grow heavy, needing to be touched, anticipating the feel of Eli's mouth on them. I glance over my shoulder at Eli.

"How do we do this?"

Eli grins and lifts me to my feet. Jack sits on the coffee table with his legs spread, with Eli sitting on the floor between them. Once he's settled, he reaches for me, and I let him pull me down to straddle him while kneeling. His hands on my ass hold me steady.

Jack puts his hands on the edge of the coffee table and gives me a smile that makes me wet. When I press my lips to Jack's chest, Eli takes my nipple into his mouth and sucks. I moan as the pulling sensation travels all the way down to my pussy.

I kiss my way to Jack's nipple and explore the texture change from his smooth nipple to his skin, sucking and dragging my teeth over it. Eli switches to my other breast. He flicks his tongue over my nipple until I can't think anymore. My hips rock against his chest.

"Time, little nympho."

Before I can lean back, Jack captures my face in his hands. He lowers his lips to claim mine. Eli keeps sucking my breast, making my insides churn with heat. My pussy throbs with the need to be touched. Needing more, I whimper into Jack's mouth.

Chuckling against my lips, he caresses my other breast, teasing the nipple with his fingers. He draws away, and Eli pops off my nipple. Eli's hand threads through my hair and tugs my mouth down to his, taking everything I have to give. I lower my hips down until we grind against each other.

He thrusts his hard cock up against me while he dominates my mouth. I moan, so keyed up it wouldn't take much to push me over the edge.

I need more. I crave their touch. I don't want to be confined to the game. I want to explore each of them until I figure out what makes them moan. What makes them beg for more. I want to take my beautiful boys to the next level.

CHAPTER 34

Conquering War

HARPER

Eli smiles. "Go to Nico, kitten."

The game will give me what I want. It gives me a chance to be with each of them before Caden fucks me. My gaze lifts to Caden. His eyes blaze with heat and need that echo deep inside me. My pussy throbs empty.

Eli helps me stand. My knees barely hold me as I cross to Nico. Nico, the boy who came back for me. His dark eyes hold so many secrets we've shared. I want to share more with him. He takes my hips to lower me to his lap. There's something here between us the others can't touch. His hands touch my warm skin. I hiss as each brush of his shirt against my naked back keys me up.

"Spin the bottle, Harper." Luke leans forward with his elbows on his knees, watching me intently. My panties are so wet. I long to be touched more.

Leaning forward, I spin the bottle. It spins around and around as I lean back against Nico. He explores my sides, fingers tickling my ribs, but he doesn't touch my breasts.

This feels so different from the times before. This is my choice. I want to be here. I want to give in to them and the way they make me feel.

The bottle stops on Caden. When I meet his eyes, he gives me a feral grin that heats my blood.

"Tails." Jack raises an eyebrow at both of us.

"You know I'm going straight for your pussy, right little nympho?"

My pussy throbs. That man and his mouth. He'll have me coming in less than a minute. It takes all I have not to stand and strip as quickly as possible.

Chuckling, Caden stands and gestures to my pants.

Nico helps me stand and undoes my jeans, sliding them down over my hips. His hands touch every inch of me, leaving a blazing trail of desire in his wake. I toe off my shoes and socks and step out of my jeans. Nico hooks his fingers in my panties and draws them off, leaving me naked in a room full of beautiful boys who are still fully clothed. Except Jack is missing his shirt.

A couple weeks ago, I would have been mortified, but now, I can't wait for them to get naked with me.

Caden lies down on the floor and gestures for me to come to him. "Sit on my face, little nympho."

The urge to bite my lip makes me glance at Eli. His hand strokes the outside of his jeans over his hard cock. The sound of a zipper makes me jerk my gaze in Nico's direction. He's already stripped his shirt off, and yanks down his pants and boxers, leaving him as naked as I am.

Precum pools on the slit of his hard cock. I lick my lips as heat floods me.

Taking Caden's hand, I lower myself over him. Nico kneels before me. As I move into a better position to take Nico's cock into my mouth, Caden inhales obscenely and blows out his warm breath over my pussy.

I curl in on myself at the sensation pouring through me. My need is almost overwhelming.

"You smell good enough to eat, little nympho." Caden grabs my hips and pulls me down onto his face. He devours me in a way that makes me gasp.

"Oh, fuck," I whisper as he uses his tongue and teeth and lips to drive me insane. He lashes my clit with his tongue, and I moan.

Nico takes my hair and guides my mouth to his cock. "I've got you, sunshine."

Opening my mouth, I take him in. I'm engulfed in flames, on the verge of explosion as Nico fucks my mouth and Caden eats my pussy. I place my hands on the floor to steady myself and feel my breasts sway with every move. They work in tandem. Nico slides in deep until my throat swallows around his cock, just as Caden thrusts his tongue up into me, over and over, until I can't hold back any longer and moan my release.

Caden doesn't let up, making my release endless. Nico pulls out and pushes deep again. His cum fills my throat as I swallow him down. Lifting off him, I inhale deeply. Our eyes meet for a second before Caden rolls me onto my back.

The world spins and Caden hovers above me, wiping his mouth on his sleeve before he leans down and claims my lips. Our kisses are always a battle of wills as he gathers my naked body against his fully clothed one. I cling to him as we kiss, tasting myself on his lips.

Wrapping my legs around his hips, I arch up into his hard body.

"Anyone have a firehose we can turn on those two?" Jack chuckles darkly.

Caden lowers me back to the ground. His kiss slows as he explores my mouth. I clutch at his shirt, feeling vulnerable to him. Like I've shown him too much.

"Epic," he whispers against my lips.

I open my eyes to his smiling green eyes.

"Keep playing the game, little nympho." He lifts me to sitting. "Jack?"

Jack draws me up and onto his lap. His naked chest presses against my bare skin, and I hum in pleasure. My skin buzzes wherever it touches his.

"Spin the bottle, sweetheart." His low voice sends shivers over me.

It stops on Luke. Jack flips the coin in front of me, and it lands on heads. My gaze lifts to Luke's, wondering what he'll want to do.

He stands and takes off his shirt. Then reaches for his pants. Kind of a predictable move for Death.

I climb off Jack and lower to my knees in front of Luke, waiting for him to strip. Jack kneels behind me and rubs his hand over my ass. I lean back into his warmth as Luke kicks off his jeans.

He strokes his hard cock, and a bead of precum forms on the tip. I lick my lips and look up at Luke, already wet and ready for his cock.

"Tell me what you want," that defiant part of me says to Luke.

"Suck my cock, princess."

I rise onto my knees and take him into my mouth. Jack rises with me and strokes his hand down over my stomach, until he slides his finger over my clit. His other hand thrusts two fingers into my pussy.

I swallow around Luke in surprise. Luke smiles down at me.

"We didn't say anything about mouths this time, princess." His hand threads into my hair and presses me forward to take his cock deeper. I relax my throat for him.

Luke begins a slow pace. The soft skin of his cock rubs against my tongue. My hands go to his muscular ass to hold on as he thrusts deep into my throat and pulls almost all the way out. Jack follows the pace, fucking his fingers into my pussy while rubbing my clit with his other hand.

I'm caught between them on the edge again. So close to falling over. Luke reaches down and tweaks my nipple, pinching, pulling it as he thrusts into my mouth. Jack's lips trail over my nape before latching onto the place where my shoulder and neck meet. He sucks there, and my mind scatters.

I burst into a thousand pieces as I shatter all over Jack's fingers. I moan around Luke's cock as my pussy convulses. My thighs are wet from my own slick. With one final thrust deep into my throat, Luke groans and comes. I swallow every last drop.

As I come down from my high, I'm aware no one's timing this anymore.

Jack sucks on his fingers as I sag against him. Caden lifts me from the floor onto his lap and thrusts two of his thick fingers into my pussy, sending an aftershock through me.

Moaning, I barely resist the urge to ride his fingers to chase after another orgasm.

"Good girl." His deep voice makes another pulse ripple through me, tightening around his fingers. He settles me on his lap, holding me there with his fingers buried inside.

He slides them slowly in and out of me, stretching me a little with each stroke. He draws me down to lie back on him, spreading my legs to either side of his.

"How do you feel, little nympho?" He thrusts a little deeper as his other hand caresses my breast. I lean my head back against him as my hips follow his lead. It's slow, unlike the rush to orgasm before.

"Good," I whisper as the pressure builds again.

Jack kneels between Caden's legs. His hands stroke the inside of my thighs before he leans in and sucks on my clit. My breath shudders in and out of my lungs. Caden relentlessly pumps his fingers in and out of my pussy. Each stroke fanning the flames even higher.

My eyes lock with Nico's and drop to his hand stroking his cock. Luke trails kisses down my shoulder, kissing over the rise of my breast until he sucks my nipple into his mouth.

"Oh, fuck." My fingers dig into Caden's shirt beneath me as they overwhelm me. I cry out as a wave of orgasm crashes over me, dragging me under. Someone's finger joins Caden's inside me. I can't breathe as they stretch me and wind me up again.

I topple over the edge. Luke releases my breast to capture my moans with his mouth. He gathers me against him, pulling me to straddle his lap as he sits back against the couch. His skin is hot against mine. When his hard cock presses against my stomach, a flurry of butterflies flutter through me.

Eli strokes his fingers down my side, sending sparks through my veins. I lift my head to meet Luke's eyes. The heat in them captures and holds me, lighting me up.

When Nico crowds in on my back, his bare skin brushes against mine. My eyes close at the sensation. His hand slips between my legs and he thrusts three fingers inside me. So fucking full.

Luke captures my gasp in his mouth as he strokes his fingers over my clit. I can barely breathe as Eli finds my nipple and teases the tip with his fingers.

I writhe between them as Nico kisses my shoulder and neck. He thrusts his fingers in and out of me. My hips follow his rhythm. Luke pinches my clit, and I cry out into his mouth as I climax again.

Before I can come down, Caden lifts me against his naked body. I twist in his arms to hold on to him as my body comes down from the high. Rubbing his hand down my back, he sits on the edge of his bed with me still wrapped around him.

"Still good, little nympho?" He strokes my hair away from my face.

His green eyes are blown like I'm sure mine are. Reaching for his cock between us, I rub my thumb over the tip. Fuck, he's big, and soon he's going to be inside me. Fucking in and out of me like their fingers do. My pussy clenches. He presses his forehead against mine as our breath mingles.

I lift my eyes to his and draw in his breath.

"It can wait." His hand threads into my hair, holding the back of my neck. "We can wait."

His eyes assure me he'll hold back anyone who can't.

"I don't want to wait," I whisper and lean in to take his lips.

The bed dips around us, and I know the others are here. Turning with me, he lays me back on the bed and stands above me.

"Come for me one more time, little nympho." Caden grins before he drops to his knees between my legs and drags my pussy to his mouth. I'm already super sensitive as he devours me again.

Sparking me into flames. My body arches as the heat engulfs me.

Hands stroke over my skin before the guys fall on me with their mouths. Nico claims my mouth. Kissing me possessively like Caden kisses my pussy. His tongue thrusting deep into my mouth.

Luke and Eli engulf my breasts, sucking and flicking my nipples. Jack dips his tongue into my belly button before trailing kisses across to suck on my hip bones.

Caden's tongue and mouth make my blood sing. I can't think. All I can do is feel their mouths on me. My fingers dig into soft hair as I'm lifted higher and higher. I arch into them as they press me down. Pleasure drowns out everything, and for a second I'm weightless and falling.

But they don't stop. Caden's mouth leaves my pussy a throbbing mess. Something presses against my entrance, bigger than a finger. A finger swirls around my clit as the others lift from me. Their hands take the place of their mouths. I can now see Caden, standing between my thighs. His green eyes hold mine as he presses just the tip of his cock into me.

"Fuck," he whispers and scoots me onto the bed more before

coming down over me. "You feel fucking amazing." He searches my eyes, hovering over me so it's only us. "Are you sure, little nympho?"

The guys are close and they still touch me, but right now, it's just me and Caden. I thread my fingers through his hair and lift my hips toward him in offering. I'm so fucking ready. I need him inside me.

"Yes, Caden. I'm sure. Please."

For a moment, I worry he's changed his mind. He watches my face as he presses in and stretches me more than before. My breath catches. Jack's fingers work my clit, distracting me from the feeling of fullness, while Eli and Luke pluck at my nipples, sending bursts of need down.

Caden draws back, and I suck in a breath at the feel of him moving. He presses in deeper this time. Oh, fuck, it feels so good. Eli tugs on my nipple, and I jolt forward, lifting my hips and taking Caden even deeper.

"How does it feel?" Caden asks, his voice strained as he hovers above me.

"Different?" I gasp as he sinks in a little more, stretching me out, filling me so full. I'm not sure I can take anymore, but I want all of him. I pant as they work me over. "Caden? Please."

He pulls out again, but then presses in steadily. I feel a slight burn, but it fades as his hips press against mine. He's inside me so deep, and my pussy flutters around the intrusion. I feel so full of him and so connected.

I want to stay like this forever.

"Fuck, little nympho. I'm not sure I'm ever going to want to leave this pussy." He brings his mouth down on mine and lifts my body up against him. Every inch of our skin touches, and I let out a sigh. I wrap my legs around him as I slip into his kiss.

He rocks his hips a little against me, and a different kind of burn fills me. I gasp at the feel of him. Slowly he works his cock out a little more each time before sinking back into me. Our foreheads meet as we both look down at where we're connected, as he pulls almost all the way out before thrusting back in.

My breathing shudders in and out of me. The fire blazes inside me as he continues to thrust deep into my pussy until it's too much. The flames consume me. Crying out, I arch up against him as my pussy convulses around his cock.

"That's it, little nympho. Come for me." Caden's finger finds my clit and keeps my orgasm going while he thrusts deep inside me. He pushes in deep and groans, taking my mouth with his as his cock jerks inside me, filling me with his warm cum.

When I collapse onto the bed, he crashes down over me, bracing himself on his arms. Leaning over me, he kisses me softly.

"Fuck, little nympho. We're going to wear each other out."

I catch his face in my hands, still finding my breath. "Not possible."

I touch my forehead to his and just breathe for a moment.

He pulls out a little before thrusting deep into me again. "Epic."

"Epic," I whisper with a smile.

As he pulls out and collapses on the bed next to me, dragging me into his arms, I let out a shuddering breath. I snuggle against him, laying my head over his heart and loving the steady rhythm of it.

It would be so easy to slip into sleep, but the day is just beginning, and I'm far from being done. Caden strokes his hand down my back and gives me a wink as I sit up.

Nico offers me a hand. I take it and let him lead me into the bathroom.

"Do you want to be alone?" He rubs the back of his neck, like he's not sure what to do.

"Maybe for a minute to use..." I gesture to the toilet, feeling the wetness between my thighs cooling.

He grins and steps out. I clean up the best I can. There's a little tinge of blood on the toilet paper, but nothing major. That was it. That was my virginity gone. Such a fuss over something so minor.

My pulse races as I look at the door. I have four more firsts to get through today. Each of the guys will be different, feel different. I don't know if everyone gets a turn or what.

I didn't think we'd get this far honestly. But I can't wait to find out.

CHAPTER 35

The Lit Fuse

LUKE

Caden stands and heads for the bathroom. I follow him. My mind still can't wrap around what happened. She chose Caden to be her first. Not me.

Does she only want Caden, and she's tolerating the rest of us?

Fuck that.

Caden knocks on the bathroom door. "You okay?"

Harper opens the door with her cheeks stained pink. She nods and looks at me. Her dark eyes flash with heat. My body responds with a primal need to claim her, but I hold myself back.

"What do you need?" Caden cups her cheek, tipping her head to meet his eyes. "It's up to you how we go from here."

Her eyes widen, and her gaze darts back to me. Her face softens when she turns back to Caden and puts her hand over his. "I'm good. We can explore more or do something else."

"Why don't we put on a movie and relax for a little while?" Nico suggests.

My jaw clenches, but I can see their point. Just because I want to fuck her, doesn't mean they don't want to fuck her too. But she might be sore. Caden is a huge motherfucker.

I grab my boxers and my t-shirt. Before anyone else can, I step forward and put my t-shirt on over her head and help her get her arms through. Needing to claim her in whatever way I can.

"Thank you." She looks up at me shyly and brushes her hair behind her ear. This uncertain, shy thing she's got going is new. I'm not sure I like it.

The others go to find their boxers, and I step into mine. She bites her lip as I put away my hard cock. Stepping into her, I feel her warmth against me and draw her into my arms. She wraps her arms around my waist and rests her head over my heart.

Can she tell how hard it pounds for her?

"We'll go as slow as you want, princess." I press my lips to the top of her dark hair, even as I want to rip out my own vocal cords. Every time I imagined Harper losing her virginity, I was the one taking it.

Now, Caden's cum is the first our girl has tasted and had in her tight little cunt. Sure, I took her first orgasm, the first taste of her pussy, and the first to sleep with her, but fuck, I wanted them all.

Harper squeezes me tight and looks up at me. The others have moved to the TV and are scrolling to find something. Her dark eyes fascinate me.

"I don't know how to do this," she whispers. Her eyes search mine.

"Do what?" I glance over at the guys, who focus on the TV. Well, mostly focus. They glance over at Harper.

She swallows and drops her gaze to my throat. "I don't want to be done."

My cock throbs at what I hope she's saying. I tip her chin to force her eyes to meet mine. "You want to play more, princess?"

Her tongue darts out to wet her lips. She nods.

The opening credits of a movie play in the background.

I can't stop the smile that forms on my lips as I take her hand and lead her to a chair. I sit down and draw her down onto my lap, straddling me.

Sliding my hand between her legs, I stroke her pussy gently. She makes this little needy noise that makes my balls tighten and ache with need. Eli glances over at us from his chair and lifts an eyebrow at me.

I part her pussy lips and slip a finger inside her wet cunt, watching her eyes closely. "Sore?"

Her eyes lock on mine as she shakes her head. Her hips roll against my hand and finger.

I draw her down so I can speak in her ear. "Do you want to be passed around, princess?"

Her pussy clamps around my finger. "Yes."

I grin. "You want my cock inside you? Do you want me to fuck you?"

Her fingers dig into my shoulders. "Yes, please, Luke."

She lifts her head and meets my eyes as her fingers trail down my bare chest. My muscles twitch beneath her. I thrust my finger deeper into her before slowly sinking it in and out.

Her breathing gets rough, and her dark eyes seem endless as she reaches for the waistband of my boxers and lowers them, drawing out my cock. Her hand strokes me, and I bite back a curse.

"I need to feel you inside me," she whispers. My cock twitches in her hand.

Drawing my finger out, I tease her clit. Her lips part and she gasps.

"I thought about this last night." Her words are barely loud enough for me to hear, but they make my insides burn. She lifts her hips and rubs the head of my cock against her pussy before positioning it at her entrance. Our eyes lock and my breath catches. "How easy it would be to just guide you and take you."

She lowers her pussy down over my cock. Slowly taking me all the way inside her. Her wet cunt surrounding my cock.

"Fuck." I rest my forehead against hers as I fill her completely. She blows her breath out. I grab her hair and crash our lips together. Tentatively she rolls her hips against mine, and I almost lose it.

Never have I felt something as intense as this. Her movements are shy and unsure, but I don't take over, letting her find her way because being inside her is enough. Knowing she trusts me enough to let me inside is enough.

I thrust my tongue into her mouth as she rides me. Tasting every inch of her mouth, rediscovering her. She's slick and wet, and I never want this to end, but I want her to come on my cock. My free hand slides up under my t-shirt to palm her breast. So soft and supple. She groans into my mouth, pressing down harder, grinding her clit against me.

Reaching between us, I release her mouth and hold her. "Open your eyes, princess."

She opens her darkened eyes. For a second, it's just me and her and this chemical reaction between us that feels on the verge of exploding. Her hands slide around the back of my neck and dig into my hair.

"Luke. Ah, fuck." Her lips part as she moves faster.

It takes all my strength to not thrust up into her, to let her find her pleasure.

I slide my finger against her clit. She tips her head back as she falls apart around me. Her pussy convulses, drawing me deeper. It's so fucking intense, and I'm so fucking close. I thrust up into her. Her eyes come back to me. Her hands dig into my hair as I work her faster and harder.

I thrust deep inside her. Her eyes widen as she shatters around me again with a throaty moan, dragging me into my release. Groaning, I come inside her. Collapsing on top of me, she wraps her arms around my neck and buries her face into my shoulder.

Catching my breath, I rub my hand down her back. My gaze lifts and meets Caden's. He smirks and arches a brow. I almost flick him off, but she's in my arms. Fuck, this girl makes me feel something. I inhale her vanilla scent with the musk of our sex, loving the way she's still wrapped around me.

I don't want to let her go. I want to stay in this moment as long as I can. This moment of perfection. I also want to keep fucking her all day and into the night.

"Thank you, Luke," she whispers in my ear. Her breath caressing it and making a shiver flow through me.

She lifts her head, and we look into each other's eyes. In this moment, I would burn the whole world down for her if she asked. That kind of power over me should make me want to fight. But that's part of the wonder of Harper, she wouldn't ask that of me.

"Should I...?" She gestures to the bathroom.

"Come over here and give a repeat performance?" Jack says, drawing our attention. His hand strokes his cock as he raises an eyebrow. "I mean, when you're ready, sweetheart. I don't care if you're overflowing with cum. As long as I get to add to it."

Her dark eyes return to mine, and she kisses me, pressing her hips down over me, and her pussy flutters all around my cock. When she tries to pull away from the kiss, I grab her hair and wait for her eyes to meet mine.

"Next time, *I'm* fucking *you*, princess."

She shivers against me, and I capture her lips, taking everything I can from her. My cock is still hard inside her, and I thrust up into her sweet fucking pussy. She gasps against my lips and grinds down on me.

I'm never going to get enough of this girl. I tear her mouth away from mine. She's not just mine, as much as I want her to be. I smack her ass, and she tightens around me again.

"Go help Jack, princess."

Her fingers trail over my jaw before she rises from me and makes her way over to Jack. My chest fills, knowing she's wearing my shirt and filled with my cum. It's enough for now.

JACK

Watching Harper get fucked is a whole new stage of arousal. I'm always game to watch each of us play with her, but watching Caden fill her with his cock was some next-level shit I'm going to need to see a lot of.

And her and Luke. I could sell tickets to that and make a mint if I wanted to share her with more than this group, which I don't. I'm not sure Luke would let me, because that possessive look on his face... It was enough to almost make me cum.

She walks over to me almost shyly. This girl took all of our cocks in her mouth, and now she's got a shy bone in her body. I'll have to fuck that right out of her.

I stand as she reaches me. Her eyes lift to mine. I drop my boxers and take off her shirt, leaving us both naked. The TV plays in the background, but I'm sure no one is actually watching it right now.

She steps into the space dividing us. "Jack."

I cup her cheek and lean down to claim her lips. She meets me like she always does. Our tongues collide, and she presses against me. Her hands rest on my chest.

When she's nearly breathless, I lift my mouth. "Are you feeling sore, sweetheart?"

She meets my eyes and shakes her head.

"Want to try something different?"

Her eyes widen as her cheeks flush with heat. "What do you have in mind?"

I bend down so my lips are against her ear. My fingers go between her thighs and shove inside her, gathering the cum leaking out and shoving it in deeper. She gasps in my ear.

"You suck Caden's cock while I fuck your pussy from behind."

Her cunt squeezes around my fingers, and she releases a breath in my ear.

I grin. "You like the thought of that?"

When I lean back to see her answer, she nods. I draw my fingers out of her and bring them to my lips before taking them in. Her eyes widen. Cum doesn't bother me. I enjoy going down on guys, so I'm not sure why she's surprised.

I draw them out with a pop. "Did you want some?"

I slide them back inside her, and she grabs my arm. Her eyes darken as I fuck her with my fingers. When I pull them out, I hold my fingers in front of her lips. She takes them into her mouth, sucking and licking off the combination of her, Luke, and Caden. A heady mixture.

"Good, right?" I draw my fingers out and capture her mouth with mine. Tasting her. She moans into my mouth. This girl is everything I hoped she'd be. My cock twitches between us.

I shift us as I kiss her, until we're in front of Caden. I lift my mouth from hers and turn her in my arms, holding her tight against my body, my cock resting against her ass. Nico sucks in a breath as he looks at her.

"Caden, be a good guy and get out your cock for your little nympho." I slide one hand up to cup Harper's breast and my other hand down to tease her clit. She squirms against me, making those needy little noises from earlier that almost made me come.

Caden draws his cock out of his shorts and strokes it.

"Damn, girl. That was inside you." I lick my lips. "Even I haven't taken anything that big. Yet."

"Do you prefer guys?" she asks. I squeeze her nipple and rub her clit.

"My only preference is still breathing, sweetheart." I kiss her jaw. "Trust me, I want to fuck you so badly. On your knees."

We lower together in front of Caden, my hands still caressing her body.

"Take him in your mouth, and I'll fuck your sweet pussy." I dip my fingers inside her, and she gasps and widens her stance. Removing my hands, I press her to bend over Caden's cock.

She glances up at Caden. With a smirk, he tucks his hands behind his head.

"This is your show, little nympho."

She takes hold of his cock and pumps a few times before she opens her mouth and takes him inside. I rub the head of my cock against her slit. From the front all the way to her entrance and back forward.

She moans around Caden's cock. Fuck, this girl was untouched two weeks ago, and now she wants all of us to fuck her. I wanted her from that first day, but I didn't think we'd get here. Not really.

She takes his cock deeper, and I breach her entrance, pushing into her slick cunt easily. It's tight all around me as I bury my cock into her. Wet and tight and everything I imagined it would be. She moans around Caden's cock and presses back into me.

I grab her hips and spread her ass cheeks, staring at her little puckered hole as I pull out and thrust back into her. I pull out completely and shove my fingers inside to get them nice and wet, fucking her cunt with them a few times until she's pushing back on me.

Drawing out my fingers, I thrust my cock deep into her pussy, and she pulls off Caden's cock to groan. I slide my wet fingers around her asshole while I thrust into her pussy over and over again.

When she takes Caden into her mouth, I slip my finger into her asshole as I thrust forward. She cries out as she comes all over my cock.

"Suck his tip while I fuck you good, sweetheart."

She backs off to just sucking Caden's head in her mouth. I thrust deep and slide my finger deeper into her asshole. I add a second finger into her tight ass before I fuck her sweet pussy, holding my fingers deep inside her.

She makes the sweetest noises as I fuck her and she sucks on Caden's cock. Her pussy tightens around me again as she comes, drawing me into my release. I slam into her as my cum fills her pussy. I fuck her ass with my fingers and feel her tighten again.

Caden groans his release as he fills her mouth with his cum. She swallows and convulses around me. Breathing heavily, she rests her head on Caden's thigh. With gentle hands, he brushes her hair out of her face.

I ease out of her, and she sighs. Using my other hand, I push the cum back up inside her, sliding my finger in and out of her until she stiffens with an aftershock. I kiss her shoulder.

"You feel as good as I imagined you would, sweetheart."

She snuggles back against me. "You too."

CHAPTER 36

The Overwatch

ELI

The few times Jack and I took a girl together were hot, but nothing like watching my friends fuck Harper. She lifts her head from Caden's lap, and our eyes meet. Fuck, this girl is dangerous. Even though she's been thoroughly fucked, she looks like she needs more.

Like she wants more. I'm almost glad I wasn't the one to take her virginity. I'm not sure I can control how I want to take her. I definitely wouldn't have told her we could wait.

She stands and walks over to me, completely naked and completely fucked. I wait until she stops before me.

"Kneel, kitten."

She drops to her knees and looks up. I take her chin in my hand.

"I'm not used to being gentle with girls." I smooth my thumb over her lower lip. "If you want to wait, we can, but you need to remember your safe word if we're going to fuck."

Her eyes darken, and her tongue darts out to trace my thumb. "Arrow. I don't want to stop."

I lift my gaze to Luke. "I need assistance with my kitten."

Luke stands with his boxers once again in place. He comes up behind Harper, drops to kneel behind her, and kisses her shoulder. Her eyes flutter shut, and a shudder works all the way down her body. So fucking responsive.

His hands grab her hips, but his eyes meet mine. Waiting to do whatever I say.

Focusing on Harper, I lean back. "I want you spread out before me. Luke will hold your hands down, and you'll be mine to play with until I relinquish control of you. Do you want that, kitten?"

She swallows and nods. "Yes, Eli."

"We'll play other games later, but for now, I just want to fuck you."

Her dark eyes never stray from mine as I stand and lower my boxers to the ground. While not as big as Caden, I'm large enough to be careful with my cock. But I can't wait to tie Harper to the chair again, when nothing is off limits.

Dropping to my knees, I capture her lips with mine, palming her breast and pinching her nipple. She gasps into my mouth as I take from her. My cock brushes her stomach, and her nipples rub against my chest. I'm determined to last, but she tries my patience.

She reaches for my shoulders, but Luke takes her hands and holds them behind her. Sliding my hand down her belly, I lift my mouth from hers and watch her face.

"Open your eyes, kitten."

She meets my eyes as I slip my hand between her thighs. I slide three fingers inside her. She moans, but I don't see a flinch of pain. Good. I thrust them deep a few times, making sure, because I want to ride our girl hard. But I don't want to hurt her. A little pain later won't be an issue.

But the guys will throttle me if I hurt her while she's getting used to us. I'll be curious how far I can push her once I'm able to play with her on my own. But right now, she's soaking wet with her slick and their cum, which should make this easier on her.

I grip her chin with my other hand and thrust my fingers in deep. "You don't come until I tell you to, kitten. Or you'll be punished."

"Yes, Eli." Her lips part, and her pupils are dilated. Her cunt flutters around my fingers. It won't take much to get her to come. My cock twitches at the thought of punishing her.

Speaking to Luke, I say, "Lay her down. I want her arms stretched out over her head."

Nodding, he whispers something in her ear before helping her down. I position her legs with her knees bent and out to the sides, opening up her pussy for me. She's wet, pink, and a little swollen.

I slide two fingers back inside her. Her cunt clutches at my fingers as she holds my gaze. I curl my fingers inside her in a come here motion and brush her front wall, pressing on the spot that should make her come.

"Fuck," she hisses as she tries to curl into herself.

I apply pressure, and she closes her eyes. Raising her hips, I slide a pillow beneath them before bending down to suck on her clit.

She squirms. Her breathing comes out in quick bursts. "Eli?"

I pull away. "Yes, kitten?"

Her dazed eyes meet mine. "If you keep that up, I'm going to come."

"That's the point, kitten." I spread her thighs and lick her clit before latching on again. I press harder on her G-spot.

"Oh, fuck," she cries out before she gushes all around me.

"That's my girl." I lift up and thrust my cock deep into her cunt with one stroke.

"Fuck," she breathes out again. Her walls convulse around me, drawing me in.

Pushing her legs wide, I thrust deep into her over and over as she tries to hold herself back.

"I can't. I'm going to..." She whimpers. Luke grabs both of her hands with one of his. He reaches down and plucks at her nipple. She cries out as she comes again.

"That's two, kitten." I keep thrusting hard and deep inside her. She moans as she can't seem to come down. I fuck her harder, and she takes it beautifully. "You remember your word, right?"

"Mmhmm."

"Do you want to use it?"

She shakes her head. Her dark eyes focus on me.

"Good." My thrusts push her toward Luke.

Luke holds her hands down as he strokes his cock over his boxers.

"Now, Harper, one more." I reach for her clit, sliding my finger over it in circles until she screams out. Her cunt gushes and tightens around me, trying to squeeze the life out of my cock.

Her body arches as I thrust in deep and find my release, coming deep inside her. Leaning back, I take in her flushed body before me. Her chest rises and falls as if she's run a marathon. Her eyes are closed and her lips parted.

She's gorgeous. I pull out and thrust my still hard cock back into her, sending her into another orgasm.

She cries out.

I pull out and turn her on her side, spanking her ass three times. Slowing down, I take my time, rubbing the pink skin as she huffs out her breath.

"Good kitty." I can't wait to do that again.

Lifting her head, she opens her eyes and meets mine. Luke still has her hands over her head, and she drops her head down onto the floor. "No words."

"Think you could take more, kitten?" I slide my hand up her thigh, and she shivers beneath my touch.

"With a little practice." She smiles and draws in a deep breath.

Nico

I figured this would be the part that would be too hard to watch. My friends all fucking my girl. The one girl I've longed for over the years. But damn, the way she takes them. The pleasure she receives.

Who am I to deny my girl that?

Eli strokes his hand down her side, and she sighs. His eyes lift to meet mine. She's mine to take if I want. Luke helps her sit up, and she turns to me.

"Come here, sunshine." I stand and give her my hands.

She grabs hold, and I hoist her up to stand with me.

"How about a shower?"

Her eyes widen, but she nods. I keep ahold of her hand and pull her toward the bathroom. Luke follows us. Not sure if he doesn't want me to be alone with Harper or if he wants to join in. Either way, this is my turn.

I reach in and start the shower as Luke closes the door on the others.

"How are you doing, princess?" Luke threads his fingers through her hair, cradling the back of her head. Their bodies move in close to each other. He still wears boxers, but she's completely naked.

"I'm good." She reaches for his boxers and pushes them down. She kisses his cheek.

When he releases her, she moves over to me and grabs my boxers to help me out of them. Her dark eyes meet mine.

"Are you sore?" I ask as she rises to stand before me.

"A little, but it's not going to stop me." Her eyes are determined. She wants all of us. She said it before.

I make a noise in the back of my throat before ushering her into the shower. Caden's shower is big enough for all six of us, so the three of us have plenty of space to move around.

She steps under the showerhead, and water flows over her curves. She pushes her hair back over her shoulder. Every inch of her is divine. From her full breasts to her narrow waist to her solid ass, she's a teenage boy's wet dream.

Luke stands beside me. She grabs the shampoo and eyes the two of us while she washes her hair.

"She wants all of us." Luke's voice is low, but she can hear him. "You're the last."

She steps under the spray again and rinses her hair. Her arms are up, elongating her form. Tempting me with that gorgeous body. The girl I knew had banged up knees and taught me how to catch fireflies.

This girl... I can still see some of my best friend in her, but she's different. Not in a bad way. Just different. Luke steps in when I stay still. He grabs the conditioner and puts some in his hand before stepping behind her and massaging it into her hair.

She closes her eyes and moans softly. The sound is like a jolt of energy to my being. I close in on her front, grab her face in my hands, and kiss her, dragging her body against mine. Her arms circle my neck, and she presses every inch of that divine body against me.

All the other things fall away as I lay claim to her mouth. We have always been each other's. It doesn't matter that I've been with other women and she's just been with my four friends.

She's mine and I'm hers.

When I break off the kiss, I press my forehead against hers.

"Hi, sunshine."

She smiles. "Hi, Nico."

"Let's get you clean. So we can dirty you up more." I reach around her for a pouf and some soap. But then I think better of it and toss the pouf, putting the soap directly in my hands.

As I rub my hands together, her eyes darken. She leans back against Luke. He kisses her shoulder before biting down on her skin. She gasps. His chuckle fills the shower before he gently sucks the spot.

My hands glide over her breasts and down her stomach, making sure I cover every inch in bubbles. When I slide my fingers between her legs, she parts them for me. I lift my gaze to hers as I rub her clit.

"We have so much to teach you, sunshine." I close in on her. Luke slides to the side when I back her up against the wall. "So many new things we can do, and when we get to your last first, it will open up even more possibilities."

She strokes my cock while her wide eyes search mine. "But right now, are you going to fuck me?"

My mouth crashes down over hers as I lift her up against the wall. My cock slides deep into her pussy as her legs wrap around my hips.

"Like that, Harper?" I murmur against her lips. She tightens around my cock, making me want to just stay right here buried inside her wet, tight cunt. "Is this what you want?"

"Yes, Nico. Please fuck me." She claims my lips as she wraps her arms around my neck.

If I had a choice for our first time, it would have been on a bed after a nice dinner out. But now I grab her hands and hold them up against the wall while I fuck into her. I pull back to meet her eyes.

"I like the way you feel inside me," she whispers, like we're sharing secrets.

"I like the way you tighten around me." I thrust harder and deeper, until her head tips back and she lets out a guttural moan. Her cunt spasms around my cock as she topples over the edge.

I pick up the pace and join her, slipping over the edge into oblivion deep inside her for the first time. Gathering her against me, I walk us under the shower stream and kiss her again. Her hands dive into my hair and hold me there, like I'm going anywhere. Not a chance in hell of that. I'm in this relationship or whatever the fuck we're doing.

For me, this is it. After I pull out, I lower her to her feet.

She's a little unsteady, but Luke comes up behind her to support her.

"I think it's time for a nap, princess." He takes the pouf and gently washes her as she clings to him. I help rinse her off and grab a towel to wrap her in when she steps out of the shower.

I kiss her nose as I dry her.

She blinks up at me. "What was that for?"

"For finally having my dream girl." I draw her into my arms and hug her. My eyes meet Luke's, and I see that touch of jealousy he always has with her. He'll get over it eventually. Because jealousy can't be a part of this equation.

Harper is more than willing to be shared at this point. And as long as she's happy, I'll be happy. And I'll take on anyone who makes her unhappy, even if that means taking on one of my brothers.

CHAPTER 37

Bang-Bang

HARPER

A nap is the right thing. My body feels weird, like I've exercised too much. Luke pulls his shirt over my head. That soft, seductive scent of his cologne mixes with something undeniably Luke. It makes me warm all over.

Not that I would ever tell him that. He doesn't need any more ammunition to use against me. He already has plenty.

Nico opens the door to the bedroom, and Luke scoops me into his arms.

"Hey!" I cry out, surprised, wrapping my arms around his neck.

Luke smirks. "If I'm taking you to bed, princess, I'm doing it in style."

I tug on his blond hair, and the smile he gives me makes my heart melt. Fuck, that's dangerous. Luke wouldn't know love if it smacked him upside his head. I'm not the one who's going to show him and live happily ever after.

I'm only eighteen years old. We're not even in a regular relationship. I'm *owned* by the horsemen for the year. Like everyone hoped, I gave it up quickly, but that doesn't mean they get to stray.

Luke lowers me to the bed, and Caden makes his way over to us.

He grabs me and lifts me into the middle of the bed before crashing down beside me. "Did you have a good morning, little nympho?"

He plucks at the hem of Luke's shirt. Luke lies down beside me. Suddenly I'm aware of the fact I'm not wearing panties. I pull down the hem of the shirt to cover me. After all, I'm technically open for business now.

I gave them what they wanted, but I wanted them too. I want them. But maybe a break would be nice.

"Maybe someone should get my panties?" I glance at Jack as he climbs on the bed.

He chuckles darkly. "If you're looking for a savior, sweetheart, you're looking at the wrong man. I like that you're all soft and naked under Luke's shirt. Easy access."

He strokes his hand down my leg, sending sparks through me. Yeah, that's what I'm afraid of.

"Easy, princess." Luke draws me back down into his arms. "You've just gone round one with the horsemen. You need some time to adjust. So sleep. You won't wake with a cock buried in you."

Luke whispers next to my ear, "Yet."

My eyes widen at the possibility. Fuck, that could happen. What would that be like?

I press my thighs together at the need throbbing there. How could I be horny already? Seriously, I just got fucked by five guys. My skin feels tight as Luke draws me in closer to him.

In front of me, Caden opens one eye. "What's wrong, little nympho?"

I'm forcing myself not to squirm back against Luke, but there's this restlessness beneath my skin I can't seem to calm down. Caden smiles like a predator who's found his favorite prey.

Grabbing my leg, he drapes it over his hips, opening me up as he slides closer. The guys are all back in their boxers, but it wouldn't take much to pull them down. I groan thinking about going another round with Caden.

I'm tempted to roll onto my back and just let them have their way with me.

"Shh, let me take care of you." Caden's finger trails up my inner thigh, and I suck in a breath. His fingers slide between my folds, making liquid heat flood me. Oh god, that feels good. His green eyes remain locked with mine.

Luke's hand slides over my ass cheek, and I forget to breathe as tingles course through me. Their fingers meet in the middle and push into my pussy. My lips part and my eyes close as my senses go into overload.

"When I can't get to sleep, sometimes I have to jack off to ease the tension, so I'm not so tightly wound." Caden brushes his nose against mine. He presses featherlight kisses over my eyes and nose.

I gasp as he caresses my clit, while his and Luke's fingers gently work in and out of my pussy.

"Just let go, princess." Luke's voice makes me arch into Caden as they take me higher and higher. "Come one more time and you'll go right to sleep."

Caden captures my lips, teasing them with his lips and tongue. I can't breathe as they quicken their pace. The climb is steep, and when I get to the edge, I fall over it. Moaning into Caden's mouth as they work me through my orgasm.

As I come down, sleep rises up and draws me down into its depths.

I WAKE TO THE SOUNDS OF ACTUAL BATTLE. MACHINE GUNS, guys yelling, explosions. I blink the sleep from my eyes and sit up in Caden's bed. A blanket falls to my lap. For once, I'm all alone on the bed. The guys are sitting around the TV with controllers in their hands.

All except Caden. I look around the room, but he doesn't seem to be hiding anywhere. Not that someone his size could hide.

I stretch and yawn before scooting to the edge of the bed. Walking behind the guys, I pad barefoot to the bathroom, so they don't notice over the noise from the game. After I use the bathroom, I find the toothbrush Caden let me use over the weekend. He put it in the space next to his in the toothbrush holder. He even found me a hairbrush, said it was his sister's and she wouldn't mind.

Falling asleep with wet hair gave me weird kinks, so I braid it and tie off the end. I'm still in Luke's shirt. All my clothes are out there. I should check my phone to make sure Mom didn't try to get ahold of me.

Today was a fun escape, but reality waits for us. Before I walk out, I look at myself in the mirror, trying to see if I can tell the difference, but it's just me staring back.

It's weird. I feel different but don't look different. Shaking my head, I return to the bedroom. Someone folded my clothes and put them in a pile. I pull on my panties and jeans, but I leave on Luke's shirt. It's warm and smells so fucking good.

I'm not going to dwell on that.

Caden comes into the room with a tray of food. "Good, you're awake."

Someone pauses the game, and they all turn to look at me.

"Hi." I raise my hand and wave like an idiot.

Seriously, someone should just put me in a place for special losers who don't know how to interact with society properly. That acronym would be a nightmare. Maybe they could just make it SL for special losers.

"I brought food." Caden sets the tray on the coffee table.

The game is paused with four little screens of soldiers holding weapons.

The guys all grab a sandwich and sit back where they were before. Their gazes never leave me. I step around and through them to the tray and grab a bag of chips. Settling into the corner of the couch with my feet up on the edge, I open the bag.

I look up and arch an eyebrow. I gesture to all of them with my bag of chips. "Is this going to be a new thing? The staring thing?"

Eli smiles. "Nah, kitten. We're just wondering what version of you we're going to get."

A blush heats my cheeks. Yeah, I felt very self-conscious after sex for the first time. And then with all of them. The flames inside stir. But I've rested, and though I'm a little tender between my legs, I'm just famished.

I shrug and put a chip in my mouth.

Chuckling, Caden sits down next to me with his sandwich. He tears off half and holds it out to me. When I don't immediately take it, he shakes it in front of me. That's weird.

"Thanks." I take it to get him to stop.

A grin crosses his face. "You need more than chips."

I must look super confused, because Caden takes food, he doesn't give it. But when I bite into my sandwich and chew it, he seems pleased with himself. Go figure.

"What are we planning to do with the rest of today?" I glance around at the guys, who are busy eating. I add, "Because I need to get some homework done this afternoon."

"Did you become a nerd, sunshine?" Nico gives me this fake wide-eyed look.

I shake my head. "Don't tell me you get jock grades now?"

"I take fluff classes to keep my 4.0." He wiggles his eyebrows.

"Yeah, fluff." Jack snorts. "How many AP classes are you signed up for again?"

Nico shrugs and gives me a wink. "Easy A's."

I take another bite of sandwich. "I don't know what we're supposed to talk about now."

"The same thing we talked about before, princess." Luke's eyes linger on my breasts, but maybe he's just checking out his shirt. My breasts don't get the memo and grow heavy under his gaze. I should have put on my bra.

"Do we get our alone time with Harper now?" Nico glances around at the others.

Luke's jaw muscle ticks. If I'm alone with any of them, he won't get to control the situation.

"I think that's fair." Caden leans back on the couch. "As long as we all agree her ass is off limits for dicks until we decide she's ready."

I choke on a chip, and Caden grabs me a bottle of water. Oh god, I'm going to die. I cough and sputter before taking a swallow of water. Grinning, Caden winks.

"While you might want to wait for us to tap that, we need to do some prep work." Caden draws his finger down my arm, and a shiver ripples through me.

"Prep?" I thought losing my virginity was going to be the hard part.

"We can work on that when we're all together." Jack takes a drink. "We'll get you nice and ready before any of us takes that ass."

My toes curl into the couch as I take in the guys surrounding me. "Do we really need to do... that?"

I gesture vaguely in the air. Because seriously, while a finger might feel good, I'm not confident about any of these guys burying their dicks in my ass at this moment. It was a lot to take them in my pussy, and that's where they're supposed to fit.

"There's a lot more we can do together if you're open to anal, kitten." Eli leans back on his hands. His arm muscles bulge with the movement. I never forget how ripped these guys are. "You'll love it. But Caden is right, we need the right prep. We won't do anything that might make you not like something."

"Thanks?" I squirm in my seat. Still not one hundred percent on board with the notion.

"I'm definitely up for some one-on-one time with Harper," Jack says. His blue eyes meet mine. "There's all sorts of things we can get up to on our own, or maybe with a friend."

His eyes trail to Caden, and an ache throbs through me, remembering taking them both. I'd be more than willing to do that again. But my brain sticks on something.

What if that's what they did with Parker Ford? She lost her virginity to both of them. So did she take one in her mouth and one in her pussy, or did she do anal and pussy? I want to ask, but I don't know the boundaries of our arrangement.

Do I really want to bring up other girls? What if they bring up other girls because I did it first? Yeah, not the best idea.

"If we're going to do homework, I'll need to go home and grab my books." Eli stands and brushes his hands off. "Do we want to work here or somewhere else?"

"You mean like the library?" I finish the last bite of my sandwich. The library is my go-to study place. It always feels like it's abandoned. All the nooks and crannies I can get lost in for hours.

Luke chuckles. "No, princess. We don't go to the library, but we could go to a coffee shop to work."

I've never been able to go to a coffee shop to work. Too easy for the horsemen to find me there. But I'm not hiding anymore. I get to be a semi-normal teenager with five guys breathing down my neck.

"Yes to coffee. Always yes to coffee." Leaning back, I look at them. "I'm also up to spending time with just one or two of you. I'd like to get to know you guys better."

Even if this thing is only for a year. The year's just starting.

CHAPTER 38

The Fugazi

We all go our separate ways. Well, Caden sticks with me, but he actually lets me drive my car back to my house. He follows in his Mustang, parking behind my car, insisting I ride with him to the coffee shop.

When I step on the first stair, I turn and put a hand on his chest.

"Mom's asleep. That means be quiet. Don't talk unless you need to. Or stay out here and wait for me." I narrow my eyes to show I'm serious.

Caden's eyes twinkle with mischief as his hands grab my hips. "Nah, little nympho, I'm not letting you out of my sight."

"Fine, but behave." When I turn to unlock the door, his hand curves around my waist, sliding under my shirt to tease my skin.

"I love when you're loud." His voice is dark in my ear. "I want to find out how quiet you can be."

"I'm serious, Caden. Mom needs her sleep." I push open the door and turn to him, holding my finger over my lips.

He smirks and follows me into the house. Most of my books are upstairs. The house is quiet, like it needs to be when Mom works nights. We move silently up the stairs and into my bedroom.

Caden closes the door quietly before sitting on the edge of my bed. He says softly, "What about in here?"

"As long as you keep it down, we should be fine." I give him my best stink eye while I gather up my books and laptop.

"Are you good, Harper?" His use of my name instead of his nickname gets my attention. I finish shoving my stuff in my backpack.

"What do you mean?" I arch an eyebrow as I sit in my desk chair.

He rubs a hand over the back of his neck and looks up. "You slept quite a while. Did we hurt you?"

His brows furrow as he looks me over. I don't think, I just stand and walk over to him. Lowering myself onto his lap, I run my fingers through his hair before I focus on his green eyes. His large hands cradle my ass.

"I'm good, Caden." I tip his chin up so we're eye to eye. "Am I a little sore? Yes, but did I do anything I didn't want to do? No."

Smiling, Caden pulls me in tight against him. His hard cock presses against my pussy through our jeans. My breath catches and my pulse quickens. These guys intoxicate me.

"I'm supposed to let you rest." His nose trails over my jawline before he kisses me right by my ear. "I've never been good at being good."

Heat scorches through my veins, but reason wins out. I tug on his hair. "My mom is sleeping, Caden. She's not at work. Maybe we'll play later."

He blows out his hot breath over my neck, and a full body shiver works through me. "You should get your things then, little nympho."

He slaps my ass. Glaring, I move off him. I grab my backpack and pull open the door. Giving him the signal to keep it quiet, I head toward the stairs with him following close behind.

Honestly, I'm surprised Mom didn't wake up. We weren't that quiet, but she might have had a rough night. I should come home for dinner and make her food before her shift. Breakfast for dinner for me, and breakfast for breakfast for her.

I lock the door behind us and follow Caden to his car. He holds open the passenger side for me, and I slip in. Glancing back at the house, I don't see anything out of the ordinary. My childhood home hasn't changed now I'm no longer a virgin.

It's weird. I didn't expect bells and whistles or a cake or anything, but maybe I thought something about me would change. Maybe I wanted something to change.

Caden puts the car in gear, backs out of the driveway, and heads to the coffee shop. He turns toward me. "What's on your mind?"

I shrug. "I just thought it would be different. After."

Caden chuckles. "Trust me, little nympho. It's going to be different. We're still in our bubble. People will notice something's changed but won't know what."

"Maybe." I pick at the hem of Luke's shirt. I probably should have changed so Mom wouldn't see me in a guy's shirt and ask questions. But Luke didn't ask for it back. And I didn't offer. He left in one of Caden's shirts after pressing a kiss to my lips. I touch my lips, remembering the tingling and butterflies that leapt to attention. I like wearing his shirt.

I'm so screwed.

"How do you keep sex and love separate?" I twist in my seat to watch Caden.

He cocks an eyebrow. "Um, sex is a base need. It's physical. Love is something you feel for your family and friends. Those closest to you. Not physically, but emotionally."

I chew that over. Maybe.

"Why, little nympho? Afraid to catch feelings for your horsemen?" He pulls into a parking space for the local coffee shop. The smell of coffee permeates the car.

"Maybe." I lean my head back against the seat and turn to face him. "Maybe I worry I won't be able to separate the two, since you guys are mine for the school year."

His fingers chuck me under my chin. "Would that be such a bad thing?"

I smile and shake my head. "It would be awful. We may all end up going to different colleges. Barely see each other. It wouldn't be long until one of us cheats and the others find out. Then we break up because long distance is hard."

"Hmm, that sucks. Why wouldn't we go to college together? Fuck long distance." He pushes open his door, but waits until I grab my backpack and slide out my side. He takes his backpack from the backseat and puts it over one shoulder.

"Six people all at the same college?" Laughing, I join him on the sidewalk. "First, you guys can afford any college you want. Unless I get an amazing scholarship, I'm going to be lucky to afford state with scholarships. Second, what college would work for all of us? It's not like we all want to be business majors."

"True." He throws his arm around my shoulders and leads me toward the door. "But it could happen."

"Sure." I give up. Caden doesn't really work on reason. "It could happen. Just like you keeping me will happen."

He pushes me against the brick building before the door and lowers his face to my level. His green eyes search mine. "If you didn't want me to keep you, you shouldn't have given me your virginity, little nympho. You're mine now."

My cheeks flush hot, and I glance around to see if anyone heard him. "Caden, I—"

His lips claim mine before I have a chance to finish my thought. I don't even pretend I don't want his kiss as he presses into me. I'm not sure what I would have said. Even if I gave him my reasoning, he'd still have the same reaction, so fuck it.

I open my mouth to his questing tongue, and he gives a low growl of approval that makes me want to climb up on him.

"Seriously, you two." Jack's voice penetrates the haze. "We won't be able to leave you two alone."

Caden lifts his head from me and pushes Jack in the center of his chest. "Quit your whining."

Caden wraps his arm around my shoulders and draws me into his side. When he opens the door, I step inside. The aroma fills my lungs, and for a second, I forget about my entourage. That scent of coffee and baked goods always makes my mouth water.

Caden drapes his arm around my shoulders again and draws me to the counter. "Get whatever you like. On me."

I give him a skeptical look, but then remember his life. Yeah, he can afford my seven-dollar coffee and a scone. We finish ordering, and Caden pays.

Jack grabs my hand before Caden can reclaim me and tugs me deeper into the coffee house. We pass by some tables of other guys who

ME:

Studying. Got a ton of homework

IZZY:

Cool. We were going to study today too

VICKY:

I'll text you the address in case you want to
join *heart emoji*

I set my phone down as Luke stands behind me. Looking over my shoulder, I spout off, "Can I help you?"

His grin should have warned me. "You're in my seat, princess."

I glance at Jack and Caden, who both shrug. What the fuck. When I go to close my book so I can move to a different seat, Luke lifts me into the air and sits with me on his lap.

My legs fall open around his as I lean back against him. "Is this necessary?"

His lips brush my ear. "Just be glad I don't ask for my shirt back."

I grab the hem of the fabric, as if to hold it down. "You could have asked for it back at Caden's."

"I didn't want it then." He captures my earlobe in his mouth and sucks on it.

My heartbeat races, and my panties are definitely wet at this point.

"I need to study, Death." My voice is breathless as I melt into him.

"I work better with an incentive." Luke's hands tighten on my hips. "What will you do to tempt me, princess?"

"There's really no pressing urgency to make me want to help you work harder." I lean forward to open my book back up.

He leans with me, covering my body with his. Every inch of me sparks with awareness. "Tempt me, princess."

Tingles dance down my spine. I seriously need a break from these guys. My previously non-existent libido is on overdrive. Which is why that horny bitch inside me speaks for me.

"What do you want?" I turn my head to meet his gaze.

"How much homework do you have?" He looks at my books on the table.

"A paper in English that needs to be proofread. Statistics problem set. Reading for History." I think through if there's anything else. Pretty sure that's it.

"I still have to write the paper for English. My Calc 2 problem set. And the reading for History." His lips graze my ear again, causing goosebumps to cover me. "Turn around, princess."

I glance around the table, but everyone but Jack is actually working. Jack's watching us in fascination. He waves his hand. "Don't mind me."

Sighing, I stand and turn around to straddle Luke's lap. He brushes a strand of hair behind my ear as our eyes lock. "Yes, Death?"

He grabs the back of my neck and captures my mouth. Aware of our audience, I try to keep from falling too deep into the kiss. But when Luke growls against my lips, I part them and let him in. My fingers dig into his hair as he plunders my mouth.

His cock hardens between my legs, and the last thing I want to do is study. He breaks off and we're both breathing heavily as he rests his forehead against mine. The surrounding noise and chatter fill my ears, and my face gets hot.

I tug slightly on his hair. "That wasn't very nice."

"It was very wicked though." He presses a quick kiss to my lips. "What will you give me if I finish before you?"

I don't know how much time his problem set will take, but he hasn't even written his paper yet, so I'm starting out with an advantage. But I don't really trust Luke to not find a way around so he can win.

"A kiss?" I offer.

He smirks and leans into my ear, pressing his chest against mine. "The bathrooms here are hookup spots."

I glance over at the bathrooms with my mouth gaping open. Seriously, the bathrooms? *Ew.*

"Focus, princess. If you beat me, I'll go down on you in the bathroom. If I win, you go down on me." He leans back to gauge my reaction.

"How about... no." That doesn't sound very sanitary, and all these people will know exactly what we're doing in there. Not that I'm really worried about my reputation at this point. At least I have a reputation now.

His blue eyes burn with that fire that draws me every time. "If I check right now, I'll find you wet and ready for it, won't I?"

His fingers go to my jeans, but my hands grab his to stop him.

"What's it going to be, Harper? You going to help motivate me, or am I going to finger fuck you at this table?"

CHAPTER 39

The Ally Invasion

HARPER

Why am I not surprised by Luke's ultimatum? His eyes are triumphant, knowing he's backed me into a corner. And to avoid the punishment, I'll take the deal. He makes it damn hard to like him. But I catch glimpses of the other him, those small moments of kindness or caring, and it makes me want to do whatever it takes for him to be like that with me.

He unbuttons my jeans. I gasp and, making sure no one else noticed, refasten them. "Fine. You have a deal."

His face transforms into a wicked smile. "Then we better get to work, princess."

I roll my eyes as I stand and look for another chair. Luke pats his lap. Knowing there's no alternative if I don't want another punishment, I take a deep breath before lowering back to sit on his lap. At least it should slow him down with me in his way.

Nico gives me a smile before he goes back to whatever he's working on. Wait...

"How do you have homework?" I gesture to his laptop. "You don't start school until tomorrow."

"I got the work sent to me last week, so I'd be able to catch up with classes. I figured I'd have the weekend to work on it." He gives me a heated look. "I didn't realize I'd be preoccupied most of the weekend."

My cheeks flush with warmth. Luke shifts below me.

"It's not her job to make sure you graduate on time," Luke says as he leans around me to set up his laptop. This seriously won't work well.

I want to point out Luke just made a deal with me to help incentivize him to work, but I don't really want any punishment.

I pull up my paper and start proofing it. I'm almost to the end when a group of giggling girls comes in.

"Hey, Harper."

I glance over and see Penny and her gang at the counter buying their coffee. "Hi."

Her eyes sweep the guys at my table before Penny grins and turns to talk to the others.

"Kitten, what did I say about clingers?" Eli sets his book down, and his dark eyes focus on me.

"Look, you guys have each other. I have Kenz, but she's got Brandon." I lean in and say softly, "So what if they're clingers. I could use some more friends."

Luke grunts behind me. "You have us, princess. Ditch the excess baggage."

Well, if that's the way Luke feels about it, it makes me want to be better friends with them. I rest my back against his chest and tilt my head to look up at him.

His fingers stop on his keyboard, and he finally acknowledges me. "What?"

"What if I want excess baggage? Wouldn't it be good to have a group to be in when I'm at the games? When you're too busy to watch me?" Sure, the Cheermonsters are occupied, but I can't forget the slashed tire. As soon as the rest of the high school realizes the horsemen are monogamous, I'll have a target pinned to my back for all the girls. Like that table over there.

The girl who struck out glares at me on Luke's lap. An involuntary shudder runs down my spine. I don't know what tomorrow at school will be like. Probably a lot like that. I may have a week or two before they truly figure out the guys won't stray. Or maybe they will stray?

I glance around at the guys studying. Nico's dark hair falls into his eyes as he concentrates on his laptop. Jack does some work before looking around, like he has to know what's going on around him. Caden hovers over his paper. Eli still looks at me with a displeased look on his face. I don't bother looking at Luke.

"If you want to sit with them at games, that's fine." Eli leans forward. His dark eyes capture mine. "But the minute they draw your attention from us or they use you to gain our attention, you'll accept the punishment I give you. Enthusiastically."

I swallow even as tingles race through me. I don't know what kind of punishment Eli has in mind, but if it's private, I might be more inclined to press my luck.

Eli's lips tip into a knowing smile. "Back to work, kitten."

I squirm on Luke's lap a little, and his harsh inhale against my ear makes my insides flare hot. He grasps my hip to keep me still, but his erection presses into my ass, making me even hotter. How I'm supposed to get any work done on Luke's lap is anyone's guess.

My gaze lifts to Jack's. He grins before giving me a head gesture to come over to him.

Raising my eyebrow, I give him a questioning look, knowing better than to say anything Luke could contradict.

"I could use your help on Statistics, sweetheart." Jack grabs a chair from the table behind him and pulls it between him and Eli. "We'll get done faster if we work together."

Luke holds me tight for a moment before he releases me.

When I stand and he doesn't drag me back down, I gather my things and move around the table to sit next to Jack. I almost let out a sigh of relief, but that would only make Luke force me back on his lap.

Once I have everything settled, I lean over and whisper, "Thanks."

Jack grins and nods across the table. "You might not thank me when Luke can fully concentrate on finishing his work."

Shit, I didn't think about that. I really don't want to kneel on the bathroom floor. Jack chuckles low, making a ripple of awareness shoot through me. His laugh makes me want to lean into him.

We're just getting into our homework assignment when a female voice says, "Hey, Harper."

The guys don't acknowledge Penny's existence, each deep into their work. Turning, I smile at Penny.

"Hey, what's up?"

She twirls a finger through a strand of her hair as she looks at the guys. Her shoulders droop a little when they don't appear to give her the time of day.

"Did you want to come over and hang out with us a little?" Penny straightens her shoulders and smiles.

Eli's hand locks on my knee under the table. I jump, not expecting him to touch me. The rush of heat between my thighs is also unexpected. I glance at him, but he appears focused on his work. His hand squeezes my knee though.

"I..." Don't want to be rude, but I also don't want to be punished. "I need to finish up my homework." I smile to lighten the blow.

"Oh, yeah, of course." Penny brightens. "Maybe after a little bit? We're all working too."

She gestures to Nat, Vicky, and Izzy. When I look over at them, they all smile and wave. I smile and wave back. Eli's hand creeps a little higher on my thigh and squeezes again.

"Maybe." I squeeze my thighs together so Eli's hand can't go any higher.

Penny dips her head and then heads back to her table. The other table of girls watch this interaction with calculating eyes. When they look at me, I turn back to my paper.

I hope they don't all want to be my friend suddenly.

"Kitten." Eli's voice is a low rumble that crawls under my skin and creates sparks.

Taking a bracing breath, I turn to face Eli. "Yes, Eli?"

"Bathroom, now." His dark eyes flash with heat.

"What?" My voice is too loud, and the guys all look up. So do a few tables. Oh, fuck.

"Unless you want your punishment now." His voice is loud enough for me to hear, but too soft for the surrounding tables.

Fuck, fuck, fuck.

Eli stands and holds out his hand to me. My gaze flicks to Luke, wondering if he might stop this (whatever this is), but he just smiles. Caden leans back in his chair and watches me rise.

I take Eli's hand, and he leads me through the tables to the bathrooms. Great, the bathrooms where the high school gets busy apparently. There are two in the hallway. They aren't labeled specifically to gender. Eli opens the door to the first one and pulls me in.

It's a normal bathroom with a toilet and sink. The door lock clicks behind me, and my breath catches. I'm alone with Eli.

I can't help but think of what he did in my kitchen the last time we were alone together. Eli is behind me again, and I'm almost afraid to turn around.

My panties are already wet. I should not be thinking about sexy times in a coffee house bathroom.

"What did I do wrong?" I keep my voice from trembling.

"They came over to use you to get to us." He slides his fingers along my nape, making tingles cascade down my spine.

"What's my punishment?"

"You asked me how things would be different after you gave us your virginity, kitten." Eli's dark gaze meets mine in the mirror. His hand drops away from my neck.

"I did." My breath catches in my throat. He can do whatever he wants to me, and it won't break any rules. There's barely a boundary left.

He closes in on my back and grasps my hips, but he doesn't press against me. Desire pools hot and heavy inside me.

"Me being able to do what I want with you is a perk. You belong to me now, kitten. More than you did before." He slips his thumbs into the back of my jeans' waistband and slides them around to the front.

I suck in a breath at the sparks trailing under his touch.

"Hands on the sink, kitten." He undoes the button on my jeans.

"What are you going to do?" My voice comes out breathless as I keep my focus on his eyes. I grip the edge of the white sink.

He *tsks* me as he lowers the zipper on my jeans. "Those girls are using you to get to us. You're fully aware of that fact, and yet you want to encourage them."

He skims his hands over my ass beneath my panties as he drags my jeans and panties down. He rubs my ass cheeks, making me forget my own name, let alone keep track of the conversation.

"Eli?" My voice trembles. My entire world is focused down to this moment, his touch.

"Shh, kitten. I know your pussy is still tender. I'm not going to fuck you." He rubs his thumb over my puckered hole.

I inhale sharply as I grow wetter. My gaze locks on his in the mirror.

"Count your punishment. Five." Eli's only warning before his hand comes down on my ass, hard.

I jolt forward, but he holds my hips steady.

"Count."

"One," I force out of my lips.

He rubs the sore cheek, causing those conflicting pleasure/pain signals to my brain. "Don't encourage them to come to you when you're with us, kitten. That's our time. Even when we're in public."

He brings his hand down again on the same cheek.

"Two," I groan. He's not gentle, but I didn't expect him to be.

He skims my puckered hole again as he rubs my ass cheek. I bite my lip to keep from moaning at the lust pouring through me.

Eli smirks and shakes his head. "Kitten. Kitten. Kitten."

Oh, fuck. I release my lip and meet his eyes again.

"Don't hold back your moans from me." He smacks my ass.

"Three."

"They're mine. So are those lips."

He smacks my ass again without any rubbing between.

"Four," I whimper as the sting gets to be too much.

"The only one who can hurt you is me or the others. And only when we say so." His hand comes down hard on the same cheek.

I cry out at the explosion of pain. "Five."

He presses kisses to the hot, throbbing flesh of my ass. I whimper at the pain, but then his mouth dips lower, and his tongue thrusts into my wet pussy. He holds my hips, spreading my ass apart as he licks and fucks my pussy with his tongue.

My fingers turn white as I hold onto the sink for support, while he pushes me higher and higher. I cry out again, this time as a wave of pleasure overtakes me, dragging me under. Eli licks higher and tongues my puckered hole, keeping that wave crashing over me.

I whimper as he squeezes my sore ass cheek. He thrusts two fingers into my pussy while his tongue presses into my ass. My hips buck against his fingers, seeking relief. My pussy convulses around them. He draws them out and thrusts them into my ass, using my slick as lube.

"Eli, I can't..." Another wave crashes over me as he fucks my ass with his fingers.

"You can, kitten."

I hear his zipper come down. The head of his cock presses against my pussy. He eases in the tip and holds there. Just the tip.

"Fuck, kitten." His dark eyes meet mine in the mirror, and I know he's trying to control himself. He said he wouldn't fuck me.

But I want it. I need it. I push my hips back to take him inside me. Thick and full. So fucking good. I cry out as the next wave takes me under.

"Such a sweet cunt you have." He draws back and thrusts into my pussy while his fingers thrust into my ass.

I can't tell which way is up anymore as he takes me slowly. I beg softly, not even knowing what I'm begging for. "Eli."

"One more, kitten." He smacks my ass as he surges deep inside me.

I'm sure everyone in the coffee shop can hear the noise I make, but I couldn't stop it if I tried. My body shakes as the release rips through me. Eli catches me against him as his cock jerks inside me, filling me with his hot cum.

His breath echoes in the room with mine. "Fuck, kitten."

When he pulls out of me, I suck in a breath. I can't move. My fingers are glued to the sink. His arms wrap around me to wash his hands. His still hard cock presses against my ass. Little aftershocks keep taking me under, drowning me in pleasure.

He steps away for a moment and then cleans us both up. Raising my jeans over my hips, he fastens them. My breathing is almost normal, and the sting of my ass cheek finally penetrates the fog surrounding my brain.

Eli lifts me against him. "You were so dripping wet, kitten. I hadn't planned to fuck you."

I lean into his warmth. We're in the bathroom at a coffee shop, and we have to go back out there. There's no way anyone missed the sounds coming from this bathroom.

Groaning, I turn into his arms and bury my face against his chest. I'm sure this will be all around the school tomorrow. "Can we sneak out the back door?"

Eli wraps his arms around me and chuckles. "Nah, kitten." He tips my chin up. "It was bound to happen. I'm just surprised I was the first to drag you in here."

"That's not very reassuring," I grumble.

He claims my mouth. It's different from his normal kisses. Almost gentle in comparison.

"We'll play more this week. Did I hurt your pussy, kitten?" His dark eyes search mine.

I shake my head. "Still a little tender."

He presses his lips to mine again and takes my hand. "Keep your attention on us. You belong to us."

My cheeks burn red as he leads me out of the bathroom and back to our table. I sit down gingerly, trying to avoid the others' eyes. I need to focus on homework. But when I lift my gaze, it locks on Luke's, and I see that possessive look in his eyes. It grabs and tugs at something deep inside me.

I'd like to say it's my survival instinct, but it's not. It's something far more primal.

CHAPTER 40

Fog Friction Chance

JACK

Eli fucked Harper in the bathroom. No one could mistake those sounds coming from our girl as anything else. The tentative way she's sitting, I'm confident he spanked her too.

It's a dangerous precedent to set if Luke's eyes on Harper are any indication. While we didn't say anything specific about not fucking Harper, the girl just lost her virginity to five guys. She could use a little time before we descend on her.

But I can see how Eli got carried away. She's so fucking responsive. Damn near addictive.

The door to the coffee shop opens, and I glance that way and wish I didn't. *He* walks in like he owns the place. The Greek God.

"Hey." Patrick stands from the table of football players and walks over to my Greek God. "Coach Turner, how's it going?"

Assistant Coach Darius Turner. Yet another reason I shouldn't have fucked around with him. Of course, at the time, he didn't work for our school.

He's tall and built, only a couple years out of college. His t-shirt molds to his chest muscles. He's got on gray sweatpants that do little to disguise the cock he's packing. His cock isn't as big as Caden's, but he's a close second.

"Just getting some coffee, Patrick. You keeping your grades up?" He moves forward in line. He runs a hand over his tight curls, and his dark brown eyes flick my way.

I don't drop my gaze. Never have, never will. He started coaching at Sherman High this year. I didn't lie to him when I told him I was eighteen. He just didn't ask if I was still in high school. Made for one hell of an awkward first practice.

His eyes narrow on me for a hot second. Was he disappointed I didn't come over this weekend? It's his job he put on the line contacting me. I give him a brief nod of acknowledgment before turning back to our table.

Caden's lips are tight. He saw the exchange. There's not a lot I keep from Caden. We've always been tight. He knows about me and the coach. He also knows it's over.

"Did you get the answer to the second problem yet?" Harper's dark eyes meet mine. Girl's still focused on homework, while I'm trying not to look at my ex-hookup. A fallen eyelash clings to her cheek.

Using my knuckle, I lift the eyelash away. Her eyes darken, and the only person I can see is Harper. I wish I could have been in there with her and Eli as he took her. Just watching is enough to get me off.

"Blow, sweetheart." I hold my knuckle up in front of her lips.

She purses her lips and blows the eyelash away. I slide my hand around the back of her neck. Her breath catches as her gaze drops to my lips. Fucking addictive.

A throat clears behind us. "How's homework going, guys?"

"Good, Coach Turner." Caden leans back as he emphasizes the word *coach*.

I rub my thumb along Harper's jaw, and her lips part a little. I give her a look that promises this will be continued before drawing my hand back to my paper.

"You guys excited for senior night?" Darius keeps his gaze moving around the table to the other guys.

I slide my hand over Harper's thigh. Darius's gaze drops to my hand, and his jaw ticks before he moves on. It's not like we were in love. We hooked up a few times.

"We plan on winning, Coach." Luke doesn't miss the nuances of my or Darius's behaviors. He heard me telling Caden it was over between me and a guy. Luke's intelligent enough to figure it out.

He'll also keep it to himself.

Harper shifts under my hand. She looks uncomfortable with me touching her in front of the coach, or maybe any adult. She's not used to any of this yet. I squeeze her thigh.

Her gaze darts to me. She'll get used to it.

"Keep it clean, guys." Darius's hand comes down on my shoulder and squeezes it. "We need you all in peak condition to go to state this year."

His hand slips away. A rush of sparks flows through me. The attraction is still there, but I can't be with someone who can't and won't acknowledge me. Plus, while the attraction might be there, what I feel for Harper is intense.

Her hand falls on top of mine.

"Always." Luke's gaze locks on my and Harper's hands.

"See you tomorrow for practice." Darius heads toward the door. Thank fuck he's not sticking around.

As soon as the door closes, Luke's cold eyes search mine. His scowl is fierce, but I just smile like nothing fazes me. That always pisses him off.

Harper's gaze bounces between mine and Luke's. I grab her chin and tip her head my way before claiming her mouth. If I were a dick like Luke, I'd drag her into the bathroom and fuck her senseless, but this will have to do for now.

She falls into the kiss, opening for me and tasting me. I grab her hips and guide her onto my lap so she's straddling me. Her hands slip into my hair and tug on the strands as we devour each other.

Fuck, maybe I will take her to the bathroom. We could both get off without me fucking her. I drag her against my hardened cock, and she whimpers into my mouth. For a second, I forget we're in the coffee shop.

It's just me and Harper, which I definitely want to happen. Just the two of us.

"And I'm the one who needs to be hosed down." Caden's sarcastic words penetrate the lust fog in my brain.

Harper breaks away from the kiss. Her cheeks are red. Her eyes are wide as they search mine and she realizes where we are.

"Sorry, sweetheart, got a little carried away." I tuck her hair behind her ear.

She clears her throat. "Problem set two?"

Chuckling, I help her back into her chair and scoot up under the table to hide my raging erection. "Yeah, we can focus on homework."

Her gaze flicks to Luke's before she goes back to the textbook. Maybe we should give her some time off from us. Or maybe we need time away from her to get ourselves under control.

I focus on the problem, and we work through the set, which gives me time to calm my libido. Harper glances at me shyly occasionally. How long will it take for us to work those nerves and embarrassment out of her?

"Done." Luke closes his laptop and sits back in his chair like a king. His hot gaze tracks Harper.

"Not possible." Her lips pinch together as she shuffles her papers. "I haven't even started the reading yet."

Luke strokes his finger beside his lip. "I didn't spend time in the bathroom."

Eli chuckles softly, even when she throws him a glare.

"Time to pay up, princess." Luke leans forward on the table.

Harper presses her lips together. I can see the wheels turning in her head, trying to find a way out of going down on Luke in a public restroom. Nico lifts his head from his computer and pulls out his headphones.

"What's going on?" Nico glances around the table.

"Harper lost." Luke stands. "And now she needs to pay up."

She leans across the table and whispers, "I'm not kneeling on that bathroom floor."

"You agreed to our deal, princess." Luke leans over the table, hovering above her. "Obviously you're not shy about public spaces."

Her eyes dart to Eli, but her cheeks flush red. "That was a punishment."

"So is this." Luke straightens. "Unless you want to go back to me finger fucking you at this table."

A guy at the table next to us snickers. This isn't like our private games, but she had to know this was coming. She's lucky Luke doesn't have her get on her knees right here.

He leans in again. "Maybe I'll be a gentleman and let you use my shirt to kneel on."

His gaze drops to the shirt she's wearing.

Her dark eyes narrow. Her fingers dig into her shirt. "Whatever."

Standing, she stomps to the bathroom, calling over her shoulder. "Let's get it over with."

The table of guys makes a long, drawn out *ooh* like Luke's in for it.

Pretty sure Luke isn't the one in for it as he presses his lips into a thin line and follows her.

Yeah, this could be bad. I hurry after them. Before Luke can close the door, I sneak past him. Luke raises an eyebrow as the door closes. I step closer to Harper, whose chest rises and falls with each angry breath.

Leaving angry Luke and angry Harper together is a recipe for disaster.

"You gonna lock it, or do you want an audience?" I jerk my head toward the door. "Well, except for me, but I'm the good kind of audience. I'm all for audience participation."

"You want to watch? Watch." Luke closes the distance between him and Harper.

Her chin tips up defiantly. "I'm not taking off this shirt."

"No?" He takes ahold of the back of her neck and draws her against him. She sucks in her breath as her hands come up to rest on his chest. He lowers his mouth to hover over hers. "What did Eli do?"

"Uh…" She glances toward me before swallowing.

He pops her jeans button and pulls down the zipper. She tries to back away, but he holds her fast. His hand slides into the front of her jeans, and she gasps as her hands grab his shoulders.

"He fucked you, princess." Luke's eyes burn as his hand shifts in her pants.

I lean back against the wall, watching him finger fuck her. Her lips part as a low moan works its way out of her.

"Luke," she bites out. Maybe she's trying to hold off the inevitable.

"Did you come for him, princess?" Luke's gaze flicks to me. "Pull her pants down, Jack. So you can see better."

"Wait," she tries to back away from Luke, but I catch her hips in my hands.

"Shh, sweetheart." I kiss her nape while I ease her pants over her hips.

Her breath shudders in and out. Teasing her shoulder with my teeth, I take hold of her panties and draw them down, letting them fall to her jeans at her knees. I drag my hands back up her thighs, lifting Luke's shirt.

When my hands slide over her ass, she hisses, and I pull away. One cheek is still pink from Eli's punishment.

I caress it. "Still sore, sweetheart?"

"Tender." Her voice hitches as Luke's finger continues to pump into her.

"How many times did he spank you, princess?" Luke steps back to watch his finger work her. I draw her back against me, holding her shirt up so we can both watch.

"Five."

I slip my finger lower until it meets Luke's wet finger. I slide my finger in deep with his.

"I—" Her voice cuts off as she gasps. Her cunt tightens around our fingers. Her entire body tenses as her release finds her.

Luke buries his finger inside her and tips up her chin. "You don't want to kneel?"

She shakes her head. Her eyes are dark, and her pussy still convulses around my finger. Fuck, she's tight and wet and so fucking responsive.

"What about you?" Luke lifts his gaze to me. "Will you kneel?"

I smirk, knowing he's talking about kneeling for her. "Always."

She tries to look over her shoulder at me. Luke drags his finger out of her and over her clit. A little aftershock clutches at my finger, and she sucks in a breath.

"Open, princess." He holds his wet finger against her lower lip, tracing it with her wetness.

I slide a second finger inside her. She gasps, and Luke presses his finger between her lips.

"Suck it."

When she sucks on it, I thrust my fingers inside her, rubbing my thumb over her clit. She moans around his finger.

"Taste good, sweetheart?" I drop to my knees behind her. "I'll find out for myself."

Luke pulls his finger from her mouth and opens his pants, freeing his cock. She licks her lips as she looks at his cock. Her cunt gets wetter around my finger. My hot breath bathes her pussy, making a shiver flow over her.

"You ready, princess?" His hand wraps around her hair as he backs up a few steps.

"For?"

My tongue licks around my fingers, sliding in and out of her. Her pussy quivers around me. I press her legs open as Luke tugs her hair to make her bend over, giving me more access.

"Open," Luke rasps out.

She takes his cock into her mouth. Leaning in, I suck on her clit, flicking my tongue over it while fucking her cunt with my fingers. Filling my mouth with her delicious taste.

She moans around his cock, and I'm sure he's fucking her mouth. Luke hates giving up control. That he let her take control her first time with him meant something. Maybe he's caught up in her already. Maybe he doesn't even realize he's hers.

With my free hand, I reach into my pants and drag my hand down my hard cock. Her cunt is tight and wet. I want to slide inside her, but I'm not going to be that dick. I bring my free hand up to her cunt and slide more fingers into her, curling them toward the front of her.

She makes a guttural noise in the back of her throat and gushes her release on my fingers.

"Good girl." I lick her clit before removing one of my hands and using her slick to stroke my cock faster. I suck her clit again as she pushes back against my fingers thrusting into her.

Luke groans as he comes down her throat. He pulls his cock out, still stroking the hard length.

"Finish in her mouth, Jack."

She moans as I suck a little harder before rising to my feet. I draw my fingers out of her as Luke steps behind her and thrusts his fingers inside her.

"Fuck," she breathes, bracing her hands on my thighs as he pushes her forward.

"Open, sweetheart." I take her hair and press my cock against her lips, smearing my precum on them. She parts her lips, letting me into her wet, sweet mouth.

She licks and sucks my cock, tasting her wetness on me. I'm busy watching my cock disappear in her mouth when she jolts forward, almost gagging herself on my cock.

Luke stands behind her with his cock buried in her pussy. I arch an eyebrow at him, but I'm not worried about Harper. She was dripping wet. Luke won't take her rough because he wants to continue to play with her. Backing off my cock a little, she sucks harder as he thrusts slowly into her, holding her hips still.

"So fucking tight and wet, princess." Luke watches his cock as it strokes in and out of her. "My pussy."

She whimpers when he picks up speed. I lift her off my cock.

"You good, sweetheart?"

Her dark eyes lift to mine. Her hands are braced on my thighs as he rocks his hips into hers. "Oh, fuck."

"Can you take me too?" I rub the head of my cock against her soft lips again.

She opens her mouth and takes in the tip, hollowing her cheeks out as she sucks me. My hips buck, involuntarily pushing a little deeper.

Luke reaches between her legs as he thrusts deep inside her. "Come for me, Harper."

She moans around my cock, long and drawn out as she gives into her release. The vibrations tip me over the edge, and my cock jerks in her mouth as I come down her throat. Luke groans as he thrusts deep inside her and holds still. His face contorts with his orgasm.

When I draw my cock out of her mouth, she pants. I lift her upright with Luke's cock still buried deep inside her and take her mouth with mine. As my tongue tangles with hers, I reach down and lightly caress her clit.

"Ah," she cries out into my mouth as she comes again.

"Fuck." Luke thrusts into her, and she trembles between us.

"I think it's time to go home." I make sure Luke is on the same page.

He draws her hair over her shoulder and kisses the side of her neck. Another shudder goes through her as she blows out a breath.

"Good, princess?"

"Yeah, I'm good." She shivers, and her dark eyes lift to mine. "Let's go."

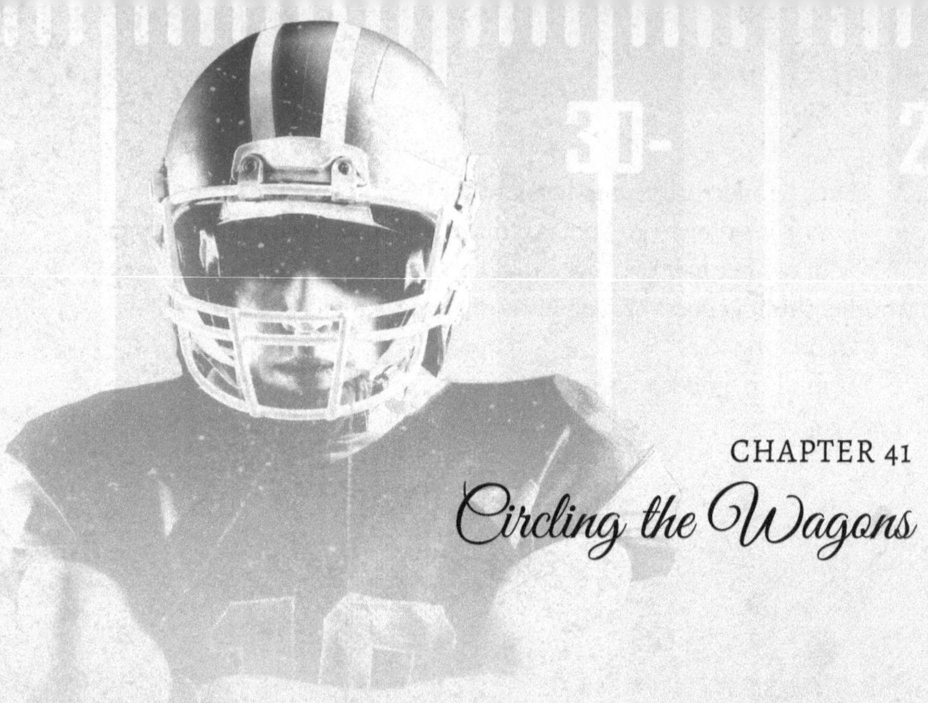

CHAPTER 41

Circling the Wagons

HARPER

I need to put a *closed for repairs* sign around my neck for these guys. I'm definitely sore now. Jack holds my hand as we leave the bathroom. Luke leads the way, giving me a little buffer. I don't want to meet anyone's eyes so I stare at the floor.

I can't handle the knowing looks. The whispered words behind hands. The interested looks from guys.

My face is probably bright red as we walk back to our table and gather our things.

Seriously, how do other girls do this?

Do they come out of the bathroom to some victory music with their fists in the air, taking bows? No one else seems to have used the bathrooms for hookups since we got here. At least I don't think they have.

Maybe by the next time we come here, I'll care less about what people think of me. Maybe I'll hold my hand up for high fives. After all, I just got laid. Snickering, I put my laptop into my bag.

If anyone thought after this weekend's parties I'd given in, this little study trip definitely provides more gossip fodder. Fuck, I'm one of those girls Kenz and I always talked about on Monday mornings. How long before someone whispers to their friend I lost my virginity to all the horsemen?

Nico slides my bag off my shoulder and throws it over his. His arm wraps around my waist, tugging me into his warmth. I lean my head against his side, grateful to have somewhere to hide as we walk outside.

I can't even look at Penny's table and I don't hear them saying goodbye.

They know this is the deal, right? That I'm nothing more than a pet to the horsemen? To be used whenever they see fit? That's what it feels like right now. But earlier I was in control, and fuck did it feel good.

Maybe I need some time to figure out what I want from this situation and how I can get it on my terms.

"Where to next?" Nico asks as we head to the back of the lot where we parked. He tosses my bag in the backseat of his car. No one complains about him claiming me for the ride home.

"I need to go home for a while. Have dinner with my mom." I need time to decompress, to think through everything that's happened. I've spent the whole weekend with them. Fucked all of them. A couple of them twice.

I need a break and time to think.

Caden nods and steps forward. "Come here, little nympho."

I step toward him hesitantly, but he draws me into his arms and presses my cheek to his chest as he hugs me. His heartbeat is steady under my ear. After a second, I relax into his hug. He really gives the best hugs.

"Behave." He kisses the top of my head and releases me.

When Caden steps back, Jack takes me into his arms. He rubs his hand down my back before letting me go with a smile. Eli kisses the side of my head before wrapping his arms around me.

"Rest up, kitten." His voice is low next to my ear and sends a shiver of desire through me.

When Eli walks to his car, I glance at Luke. His light blue eyes search mine. I definitely should have expected him to fuck me. It was almost a challenge after Eli did. Luke wasn't as rough as I thought he might be.

"Your mom works tonight?" He tips up my chin, forcing me to look him in the eyes. They aren't icy anymore when he looks at me. They're like the inner flame on a candle. Intensely hot enough to melt through anything.

"Yes." It's also a school night, which means I'll be sleeping alone.

"Do you want us to come over?" His thumb sweeps over my jaw, sending tiny butterflies soaring through me. My insides soften.

Do I want them? Yes. Do I need a break? Also yes. "I can call Kenz and see if she can stay tonight."

He nods before pulling me into him. I wrap my arms around his waist and give him a squeeze. He's still awkward as hell about hugs, but he'll get better with time. When he releases me, he heads to his car.

Sighing, I watch them all get into their cars. Nico grabs my hand and reels me into his side. I smile up at him. Punishment isn't really a thing with Nico yet. I mean, yes, he's taken part in my punishment, but I kind of liked that kind of punishment.

"Come on, sunshine, let's get you home."

As soon as I'm in his car, I get my phone out and text Kenz.

ME:

Can you hang out?

KENZ:

OMG yes! I need to hear updates lady

ME:

Be home in fifteen

KENZ:

See you soon

I set my phone on my lap and glance out the window at the houses rushing by.

"Your friend?" Nico asks.

I look at my phone screen and smile. "Yeah."

I lean my head back on the headrest and study Nico's features. I can still see the little boy I used to know, but the softness is gone. Masculinity and sharp angles define his features. He's really fucking gorgeous.

"Do I have something on my face?" He rubs his chin before he glances my way.

I shake my head. "No, just trying to reconcile my best friend growing up to you."

This weekend has been so different than I thought it would be. Nico surprised me. First by being here. Second by being a horseman. Third...

Fuck, the way he held me against the shower wall and fucked me. I squeeze my thighs together as the memory brings back the aching need. It seems impossible I want more.

"Are you okay with everything that happened?" Nico turns his car onto my block.

"I don't know yet." I look down at my phone. "Basically I opened the door and let the horsemen take over my life. They allowed me to hold back my virginity until I was ready. Do you think I gave in too soon? Made the wrong move?"

I lift my gaze as he pulls into my driveway and parks the car.

He leans back against the headrest, and his gaze locks on mine. "This isn't a chess match, Harper. There are no wrong *moves*. Only what feels right to you in the moment."

He reaches over and takes my hand in his, threading our fingers together. Warmth spreads through me like a warm cup of hot cocoa. A rush of sparks dance from his hand to mine.

"Do you regret it?" His dark eyes search mine.

"No." The word comes out of me without even having to think about it. I don't regret a moment, but I can't help but worry... My insides twist a little. "You aren't mad I didn't choose you first, are you?"

He smiles as he traces patterns on the back of my hand. "I could never be mad at you, sunshine. You have your reasons I'm sure and you don't have to tell them to me if you don't want to. Honestly I worried I'd be jealous of the others taking you."

"Are you?" I straighten. I didn't even think of that. He said he came back for me. He didn't know who I'd be when he got here. Probably didn't expect me to be a virgin. Definitely didn't expect me to fuck other guys in front of him.

"Watching them fuck you was hot." His darkened eyes lift to mine. "You took your pleasure from each of them. You took your pleasure from me."

My heartbeat cranks up a notch, and I wish we weren't sitting outside my house. Somewhere a little more private would be nice. I can't believe I want more after today.

"I think I understand your reasoning for choosing Caden." He slides his seat back and undoes my seatbelt and his own. My pulse throbs a little harder as he tugs on my hand.

"You do?" I climb over the console and straddle his lap.

He cups my jaw and brings my forehead down to rest against his. "You like Caden. The others all have their merits, and so do I, but there's something genuine about the way Caden watches you. I'm just glad you didn't choose Luke. He's a possessive fucker."

"Yeah, I like Caden," I admit. I rub my nose against Nico's as I brush my lips over his. Tingles float through me. "But I like you too."

His hand cradles the back of my head, and he smiles softly. "I like you too, sunshine. As long as they take care of you, I'm all in. Watching Jack fuck you while you sucked Caden's cock almost made me come right there."

I arch an eyebrow and grind down on his growing erection. "Yeah? You enjoy watching me fuck other guys?"

"I can't wait to take you with someone." His thumb pulls down on my lip, and I flick my tongue out to lick it. He groans. "Watching you take someone's cock into your mouth, while I fuck your tight pussy..." He shifts his cock in his pants. "Fuck, sunshine, you're getting me all worked up."

He's not the only one getting worked up. I capture his lips, tasting the caramel coffee he drank, sliding my tongue against his. I grind down on his hard length, rubbing it against my pussy, flooding my body with heat.

His hand tugs me back by my hair. Our eyes lock as we catch our breath.

"When we get you used to anal..." His hand slides up my leg, and he presses his thumb against my clit through my jeans, rubbing against me.

"Tell me, Nico." Resting my forehead against his, I roll my hips against his hand, chasing the sparks and pleasure. It feels so fucking good.

"Eli can fuck your pussy while I fuck your ass, filling you so full of our cocks you can't help but come all over us." Nico's eyes lock with mine. He unbuttons my pants and draws done the zipper. "You could even take a third in your mouth."

I glance toward the house. It's still early. Mom shouldn't be up for another hour.

His hand slides beneath my panties and over my pussy. "So fucking warm and wet."

I reach between us for his athletic pants, sliding beneath the elastic waistband and into his boxers, finding his hot, hard cock. When he slips his fingers inside my pussy, my lips part on a breath.

Stroking his cock, I glance around quickly again to make sure no one can see us before I claim his mouth. He fucks his finger in and out of my pussy, rubbing his thumb over my clit. Winding me up as our tongues slide against each other.

He pulls away to watch our hands. "I get why Eli and Luke fucked you at the coffee shop."

I bite down on my lip as I glance at the house. His tinted windows make it difficult for anyone to see us from the street. His fingers feel good, but now I know his cock feels better. My jeans make this so awkward.

"I definitely need to wear more skirts," I whisper against his lips as we pant together.

"If you wear more skirts, you won't get any breaks, sunshine." He curls his fingers inside me and presses down on my clit.

"Nico," I cry out and ride his hand through my climax. I tremble when he draws his fingers out of me and holds them against my lips.

"Suck them like you want to suck my cock, sunshine."

Holding his gaze, I take his fingers into my mouth as far as they'll go, licking and sucking. My hand works his cock between our legs. He groans low, and his cock jerks in my grip as he spills his cum over my hand.

Pulling his fingers from my mouth, I bring my hand with his cum up to lick it clean. His eyes flare hot.

"Fuck, Harper." He grabs my neck and crashes our mouths together. His tongue sweeps through my mouth, tasting me and him mixed.

When we come up for air, he smiles. "I can't wait to get you alone more often."

"I thought you wanted to watch the others fuck me?" I raise an eyebrow as I fix my pants.

He grabs some tissues and finishes cleaning himself. He opens the door to let me climb out. Following me, he backs me against the car and claims another kiss, stirring the lust all over again.

I break away and laugh. "This is going to be bad if I'm as insatiable as a guy."

He rubs my lower lip and smirks. "That might come in handy, since you have to keep five guys happy."

Groaning, I rest my forehead against his chest. "I'm so going to end up knocked up."

"No, you won't." Nico kisses my head and steps away to grab my backpack. "Need me to walk you in?"

I bite my lip. His eyes darken and fall to my mouth. I could bring him up to my room and have his cock buried deep inside me again. My pussy throbs. "That would definitely be a bad idea."

He catches the back of my neck and draws me in for another lingering kiss. I press against him as I give him everything I have to give in that kiss. When he lifts his head, he brushes my hair behind my ear.

"You need me, I'm here, sunshine." He kisses my forehead and then smacks my ass.

"Hey!"

He smirks. "Just keeping it real, Harper. See you soon."

I stand there with a dopey smile on my face and my backpack over my shoulder. His engine roars to life, and he pulls out of the driveway. Fuck, I could feel something real for Nico. This year could be dangerous.

I take a deep breath. I could end up in love.

CHAPTER 42

The Deployment

HARPER

"At the coffee shop?" Kenz sits on my bed with her back against the headboard. "In the bathroom?"

I press my hands against my hot cheeks. I'm sitting in my desk chair. "Yes. I should just write *whore* on my own locker at this point, right?"

"Fuck that." Kenz sits up and throws a pillow at me. "Own that shit. You fucked all the horsemen in one day. You're a fucking legend." She stops and giggles. "Like literally."

I throw the pillow back at her. "I'm a sore fucking legend."

"I can't believe you took Caden first. Holy shit, H. That's the definition of go big or go home." She grins. "Like real big."

My blush this time has little to do with being embarrassed. "He was so patient."

Yes, my heart flutters remembering. No, I'm not telling Kenz that. But when he kissed me outside the coffee shop, oof, my heart leapt in my chest. He makes it so easy to want to be with him.

Kenz leans back. "Now I'm jealous I'm only getting one dick. It's a good dick, but you get five."

"Sore. That's what I am." I've showered and drank a glass of cranberry juice as a precaution. Pretty sure that's my new go-to morning juice this year.

"Girl, I'm lucky to get a couple orgasms, but you get a couple from each guy. I understand why the girls will riot when they realize the only pussy the guys want is yours." Kenz gives me a kissy face.

I crash on the bed next to her. "How long were you sore after the first time?"

Kenz laughs. "Oh, honey, I took one cock, one time, and then we waited a few days before going at it again. I don't know what your situation would be like. But damn, seven times, H."

She puts her hands next to her head and makes a mind-blown gesture.

I sigh. Yeah, I was afraid of that. I'm just not sure how much time I'll get to recuperate. "How are you and Brandon?"

"Apparently I've got to get him up to certain standards. I thought three times was a lot." She shakes her head. "But we're good. He's been sweet lately, and getting to spend the night with him on Friday was awesome."

I move closer to Kenz and whisper, "Caden and Luke slept here last night."

"For real?" Kenz glances at my door. "What about your mom?"

"She works nights this week." I shrug but then remember. "Think you could spend the night?"

"I'm not sure. I can ask Mom. You could always stay at my place. I'm sure she wouldn't mind." Kenz picks at the bedspread like she knows what I'm going to say.

Spending the night at Kenz's means sleeping in a sleeping bag on her floor, surrounded by dirty clothes. "It's okay if you can't stay here. I'll be good on my own."

I've been fine here on my own many nights before the horsemen noticed me.

"I'll check, but she doesn't really believe I spent the night here on Friday." Kenz tugs at her hair and grins. "It's like she's got a sixth sense for shenanigans."

A knock sounds on my door before it opens. Mom stops in the doorway.

"Hey, girls." Mom smiles. "Catching up?"

"Yeah." I roll to sit on the edge of the bed.

Mom steps into the room and brushes my hair off my face. She tips up my chin and looks confused for a moment. Can she tell what I've been doing all day? What they did to me all weekend?

"I'm making breakfast for dinner tonight." I give her a smile, hoping to distract her. Releasing me, she brushes it off.

"Are you staying for dinner, MacKenzie?" Mom's dark eyes leave me, and I breathe a little easier.

"No, Mom's on a rampage about family dinners." Kenz shrugs. "But your breakfast sounds better than meatloaf any day."

"What about the guys?" Mom's questioning gaze falls on me. Heat floods my face. Yeah, I don't think seeing the guys with me will be a good thing right now. Mom will definitely figure out something happened.

"Yeah, Harper, what about the guys?" Kenz makes eyes from behind my mom.

"I'm not sure what their plans are for tonight." And I honestly don't. I'm a little curious, but not enough to text and get lured in again. Am I supposed to turn on my webcam? "I could use a night off."

"Sounds like hanging out with them is a job." Mom searches my eyes.

She's not far from the truth. It might as well be a job. They're a lot to keep up with, but I've had fun too. It's nice to have people to hang out with. And they aren't all bad.

"They have big personalities, and I'm used to being on my own or just with you two." I smile. "I'm going to enjoy the silence."

Kenz snickers, and I smack her leg.

"Well, I look forward to dinner with my number one bestie." Mom squeezes my shoulder before she heads out the door.

I close the door after her.

"What really needs a break is your vajayjay." Kenz falls over snickering into the pillow.

I shake my head, but she's not wrong. I'm curious enough to ask, "Do you want it all the time?"

Kenz grins and nods. "That first week we did it so many times."

"I'm so screwed." Times five. Five guys who want in my pants all the time. I fall back on the bed again.

She leans over me. "Yes, you are."

"Is Kenz coming back and spending the night?" Mom asks before eating a bite of waffle dripping in butter and syrup.

"No, her mom said not tonight. Apparently she was gone most of the weekend." I eat some of my waffle. Kind of like I was.

"You did okay last night on your own?" Mom's eyes search mine.

"Mmhmm." I continue to chew my waffle, glad my mouth is full. The guys have been radio silent for the past few hours. I don't know whether to be worried or grateful they've given me this time without the constant communication.

"I'll be fine. Bob and Fran are a call away. It's a school night, so kids won't be running around pranking the neighborhood." I lick the syrup off my fork and pierce a sausage link. "I'll watch something nice and wholesome before bed. No zombies."

Mom grunts around a mouthful of food before swallowing. "That's a good plan. I had zombie dreams all day today. All that moaning..."

I swallow hard.

Shaking her head, she cuts her food slowly. Her full attention is on her plate when she asks, "The guys aren't planning on hanging out with you?"

"We studied earlier, and it's a school night." I shrug. If I asked them to, they would. But they think Kenz is spending the night, which may be why they haven't asked to webcam. But they would have to communicate with me to find out if anything changed, and right now, they've basically dropped me.

"You could have them over, if you want." Mom glances over at me. "They definitely would scare off anyone stupid enough to mess with you."

I smile a little. "They do strike fear in the hearts of others."

I never found out why Tanner was over here the other day. What did he hope to accomplish? He said he was worried about me, but then basically threatened to take me from the horsemen. I'm definitely avoiding him in the future, and I blocked his number.

After what Caden told me about his sister, I want nothing to do with Tanner Lewis. I knew he wanted to use me to get revenge, but I didn't understand the lengths he'd go to. A shiver runs down my spine.

"Still not settled on just one of them?" Mom hedges. "Maybe Nico? You two were inseparable as kids."

"Not dating exclusively this year, Mom. You'll just have to deal with me hanging out with a group of guys." I lift my fork and point it at her. "I'm going to college next year and don't need to do the long-distance thing. Besides it's kind of nice having all of their attention."

I shove a bite in my mouth to keep from thinking about all of their attention.

"As long as everyone is on the same page. You don't want to end up with hurt feelings because someone didn't get the memo. Guys can be emotional too." Mom pushes her plate away.

"Not these guys, but yes, we're all on the same page."

Except maybe Caden, who wants to *keep* me. And maybe Nico. Who knows what Luke is thinking? Maybe Eli. Possibly Jack. Fuck, that would be weird.

I shake my head and grab my plate and hers.

"I need to get ready for work. Do you need help with the dishes?" Mom stands and stretches.

"No, I've got them."

After the pans are in the drying rack and the dishwasher is running, I take my books out of my backpack to make sure I have all my homework done. When I get to my statistics homework, I have two worksheets.

Jack's name is in bold at the top of the extra sheet. Oops.

I grab my phone and pull up my texts.

ME:

I accidentally grabbed your statistics homework

FAMINE (JACK):

Should I come get it?

ME:

I'll see you tomorrow morning right?

FAMINE (JACK):

Maybe I want to see you tonight

"I'm heading out, sweetie." Mom stops and kisses the top of my head. "Stay safe."

"I will. You too."

She grabs her keys, and I blow her a kiss she catches before heading out the door.

ME:

I'll give it to you first thing in the morning

FAMINE (JACK):

Is Kenz there?

I lean back in my chair and stare at the text. Do I lie and say she is? Mom's gone, and I'm all alone tonight, but seriously, I could use some time off.

ME:

Not yet

FAMINE (JACK):

Come play with me online then

My laptop is still closed on the table. I have to open it to finish some of my homework. It's not like I can lock Jack out of my computer. If I could even find a way, he'd find a way back in.

I open my laptop, and the video streams come up as my camera turns on. Jack grins, and something settles inside me. Luke walks by his camera with no shirt on, dripping sweat. He has AirPods in his ears, and his hands are wrapped in white tape.

Sweet mother of mercy, that man is hot.

"No drooling, sweetheart." Jack makes my gaze return to him.

"You guys aren't hanging out tonight?" The other rooms are dark and empty.

"Finishing up homework. My parents wanted to have dinner as a family. Luke's home alone, but Caden's family is in town tonight, so they're pretending to be normal. Not sure what Eli and Nico are up to."

"Oh." So maybe no one would be able to spend the night with me after all. Guess I didn't need to worry. "I just had dinner with my mom."

"Yeah?" Jack leans back in his chair. "She off to work?"

I nod. Luke walks by his camera again. His blond hair falls around his face as he tugs at the tape on his hand with his teeth. His muscles are all in sharp relief, and sweat rolls down the valleys between them.

"He's got a gorgeous body." Jack runs his fingers over his lips, his eyes locked on the screen.

"Yes, he does." I sigh, remembering his bare chest rubbing against mine in that dark car. I press my thighs together.

"He can hear you two." Luke's eyes shift to look at us without turning his head. I didn't notice his headphones weren't in anymore. Oops.

"Whatever." Jack waves a hand at the screen. "You're hot and you know it. If you bent even a little in my direction, I'd be all over you."

Luke shakes his head as he drops the wad of tape in the trash. "What are you doing on?"

I'm not sure if he's asking me or Jack.

Jack answers before I can. "Harper stole my homework so she'd have an excuse to text me."

He winks, but I shake my head.

"Where's MacKenzie?" Luke leans his hands against the edge of his desk, and his face fills the screen.

Fuck, he's gorgeous. Even hot and sweaty. Maybe even more so hot and sweaty.

"Uh..." Yeah, my brain has left the building as all the blood in my body focuses between my legs.

Luke's eyebrow lifts, and the corner of his mouth tips up. "You all alone, princess?"

Jack isn't being helpful anymore. Instead, he looks curious.

"My mom just left for work." Stick as close to the truth as possible.

Luke uses his teeth to rip up the end of the tape on his other hand. A whimper slips out of me before I can stop it.

My eyes widen. Oh, fuck. I grab my book. "I have homework I have to get done."

"Feeling needy, princess?"

I glance at Luke's knowing expression. Yes, my body hasn't gotten the memo it's not getting any tonight. "Nope. Just need to work on homework, then go to sleep."

He makes a knowing noise before he throws the tape in the trash. "I need a shower."

"Have fun in your shower." I wave a hand in his general direction. He stretches up, and my helpless gaze flutters to his abs and that V that leads to his D.

Luke chuckles before moving out of frame. I drag in a breath and blow it out.

"Fuck, sweetheart. I swear I feel the heat rolling off him all the way over here." Jack takes a drink of his water. His look turns naughty. "Want to flick the bean? Take the edge off?"

"I still have homework to do." I glance around my kitchen at the windows, like someone could peer in.

"It doesn't take long, sweetheart." Jack leans forward. His dark hair falls over his blue eyes. "I bet you could get off faster than I can."

I've only masturbated the one time, with Luke guiding me through it. My pussy throbs with need. It's got to be better than having one of them come over and take care of it. Then again, they're really good at getting me off.

"Take me up to your bedroom, sweetheart. We'll strip down and get off to each other." Jack's voice is like a siren song luring me to do forbidden things. "You can't get in trouble if I'm doing it to you."

I'd forgotten I'm prohibited from touching myself without permission. Would I just be making myself even more needy? How many times have I already come today? When will it be enough?

"I should do my homework." I bite the end of my pen as I pull over my history textbook.

"Fuck, sweetheart. Suck on the pen." Jack's hand works his cock below the line of the camera, but it's obvious what he's doing.

My pussy pulses in time with his strokes. I pull the pen out of my mouth. "What?"

"Your mouth is fucking divine. When I slip my cock between your lips and you suck—"

"Jack! What if someone comes into one of the other guys' rooms while you're doing that?"

"Hmm, you're right. Fuck it." He stands. His cock, red and swollen, fills the screen before he pulls his sweats up. "Be right there."

His computer clicks off.

"Wait. What? Jack? Oh, fuck." I grab my phone and text.

ME:

What do you mean?

Answer me

Walking over to the door, I make sure it's locked. I return to sit in front of the computer, but his screen is still down. I don't know what to do to bring it back up. He's not coming over here. Right?

Fuck, what if he's coming over here? They'll find out Kenz isn't coming over.

What if he wants to fuck me? Ugh, I should not be getting wet thinking of him fucking me.

ME:

You shouldn't come over

How far away is Jack's house to mine? The way he drives, he could probably be here in a few minutes. What am I going to do?

"What's wrong?" Luke appears in a towel and fuck, he looks even better damp and freshly showered.

"Jack said he'd be right here. Does that mean he's coming over?" I glance toward the door like he's going to magically appear in front of it.

Luke sits in his desk chair in only his towel. "What exactly were you two doing, princess?"

CHAPTER 43

The Interruption

JACK

"I'm going out," I yell and grab my car keys off the rack.

"Jack." My dad's voice stops me.

"Yeah?" Fuck, I have Harper all to myself for minutes and I want to get there before Luke thinks to head over. Not sure where the others are, but they can miss out. I'm not planning on fucking her, but we can definitely get each other off a few times.

My dad walks across the kitchen toward me. It's obvious where my genes come from. His dark hair has flecks of gray in it now, and he wears glasses over his blue eyes. He usually has an easy smile on his lips, but his lips are pressed thin today.

"Something wrong?" I clutch my keys tight. He's been good about letting me do my own thing lately, but I know he worries.

"Are you going somewhere?" His gaze drops to my hand holding the keys. Dad is a stay-at-home dad. He takes care of me and my eight-year-old *oops* sister, while Mom works long hours as a doctor. "You've been out almost all weekend."

Before I can answer, the little terror races into the room at full tilt.

"Jacky!" Lucy runs into the kitchen dressed in a princess gown. A crown sits lopsided on her dark curls. She slides across the floor on her socks. "Catch me!"

I drop my keys on the counter and catch her before she careens into my legs. Smiling, I lift her and toss her slightly in the air. This was easier when she was a few years younger, but she's still a little thing.

She giggles the whole time. When I set her on her feet, she puts her fists on her non-existent hips and pouts up at me. "Are you going to be my prince? Or what?"

Dad shakes his head. "She's been waiting for you to play with her all weekend."

Well, fuck. I rub the back of my neck, thinking of the other girl I planned to play with. But Lucy's been having a tough time in school. Some girls are picking on her, and I can't do a damn thing about it.

Her big blue eyes blink up at me. I give Lucy a smile, knowing I'll be caving to her demands. "Of course, but you need to find my horse first. I can't be a prince if I don't have my horse."

Her eyes twinkle when she smiles. She rises up on her tiptoes and squeals. "I know where he is."

She takes off to find her stuffed horse. She'll be a heartbreaker when she's grown. I need to make sure the little shits in her grade know I'll tear them to pieces if they try anything with her.

"Thank you." Dad sits at the kitchen table. "I know you've got places you'd rather be—"

"It's okay, Dad. Lucy is important." I pull out my phone and see the texts Harper sent in a panic. Dammit. I blow out a breath.

ME:

> Sorry sweetheart, something came up. Rain check?

"You've been busy lately," Dad hedges. "You seeing someone new?"

I lower into the chair across from him. "Kind of."

My situation has never been a typical one. When I came out to my parents as bi, they were supportive. But Dad always seems confused. Like he thought Caden and I were a couple for a while which, while hilarious, makes me wonder if he'll ever get it.

There's this assumption that because I'm attracted to both sexes, if I date one I'll be unfulfilled or something. Pretty sure when I find the right person, they'll be it for me. Even if I have to share her. I glance at my phone to see if Harper texted back.

"That's good." He blows out a breath. "We'd appreciate it if you let us know when you won't be home at night. Just so Lucy won't expect her good night kiss."

Ouch, that was a punch to the heart. "I usually text when I'm out."

"And we appreciate that." Dad struggles to find something to say.

"I found him! I found him!" Lucy comes racing into the kitchen waving a stuffed horse. "Come be my prince, Jacky! We need to save the dragon."

I grin. "Don't you mean slay the dragon?"

"Why would we kill the dragon? He's a nice guy. He has a cold and when he sneezes, fire goes everywhere. So the villagers are ready to hurt him, but we'll save him."

I shake my head and glance at Dad. "We good?"

"Yeah, go play with your sister."

HARPER

Luke raises an eyebrow when my mouth opens and closes like a fish.

"Harper." My name on his lips does something I can't quite describe to the piece of me that's so fucking attracted to Luke.

My phone finally dings.

At Jack's text, I breathe out a sigh. Luke still watches me.

"He's not coming over." I wave my hand at Luke. "You can go back to whatever you were doing. I've got to read my history assignment still."

"Me too."

What? My mouth drops open, and I narrow my eyes at Luke. "You said you finished."

That bastard. He smirks.

"It's mostly done." He shrugs and leans back in his chair. "I got the gist of it."

A drip falls from his hair onto his shoulder and trails down his chest. My mouth goes dry. I rub my hands on my thighs.

"You cheated." I sit back in my chair and shake my head. "You owe me."

"What do I owe you, princess?" Luke's dark voice flows down my spine.

I arch my eyebrow as I consider. I'm not about to spank Luke Foster like he would me. No need to encourage that behavior.

If I had won, he would have had to go down on me in the bathroom, not the other way around. I would have preferred to not do anything in the bathroom. Heat flushes through me at what we did in there, and Jack did go down on me at the same time.

"Come on, Harper." He licks his lips. "You know what you should ask for. Just say it. Tell me what you want me to do to you."

I narrow my eyes before I shake my head. "I need to think it over."

"Coward," he mutters and stands. His towel stays around his hips as he walks off screen. Now all the screens are empty. I stare at those empty rooms.

What happens now? Do I let them use me whenever they say so, or do I take control of what I want? I want them, so it doesn't make sense to deny what I want. But I don't know what will happen at school.

Will I have a choice, or will they drag me to a closet and fuck me? A shiver goes through me. Maybe I'll be the one doing the dragging.

I open my history book and stare at the words on the page. This whole weekend plays on repeat in my mind. Spin the bottle. The parties. This morning. Taking my pleasure from them.

I have to go to school with all this new baggage like it doesn't matter. Like two guys didn't finger fuck me in the middle of a dance floor at the party. Like I didn't disappear with two other guys. Like I didn't take all of them inside me.

Am I supposed to like it? Am I supposed to be coy and pretend it didn't happen?

What if one of them loses interest? It's not like I can be equal about everything. I'd never have time to myself.

There are plenty of girls willing to pick up my slack. And what happens if the guys stray? Is it over? Just with that guy or with all of them?

"You okay, kitten?" Eli's voice makes me jump.

"I forgot that was on." I hold my hand over my thundering heart.

He smiles. "You get this wrinkle between your eyebrows when you process things."

"I do not." I rub between my eyebrows and frown.

Eli chuckles. "You do, kitten. So what's on your mind?"

"The unknown." I sigh. I can try to plan for any number of things, but in reality, I just have to take things as they come.

"Deep." Eli nods. "Not that I don't enjoy finding you in my bedroom, but why are you on?"

Heat fills my cheeks. "I accidentally took Jack's homework, and he asked me to get on webcam. Then it seemed like he was going to come over, but he didn't. And Luke said he lied about finishing his homework so he should have gone down on me and not the other way around. And I don't know why I'm still talking."

I snap my lips closed and shake my head.

"Where are Luke and Jack?" Eli glances at the other empty screens.

I shrug. "Jack said something came up. Luke just finished a shower and went off some direction."

Eli gives an acknowledgment of my statement and picks up his pen.

"How are you after today?" Eli slides his pen through his fingers.

"Honestly a little sore, but fine." I touch my warm cheeks. The sun has set outside, and darkness presses against my windows. I haven't been alone all that much since the horsemen took ownership of me. "Can I ask you a question, Eli?"

"Sure, but I can always refuse to answer it." He tips back a little in his chair. His dark eyes are focused on me.

"That's fair." I almost bite my lip, but stop myself. "What are the expectations now?"

Eli leans his elbows on the desk and cocks an eyebrow. "Expectations?"

"We've done what you guys set out to do." I gesture vaguely in the air. Heat swamps my cheeks. "So now what?"

Eli grins. "We didn't just want a taste. We own you, kitten. As to expectations, I'm sure we all have different needs."

I cross my legs, thinking about their needs. About my needs.

"We'll get more time with you alone, but still do things together."

Eli draws his fingers across his lips. "I won't lie. We're going to want to fuck you. A lot. We all have different desires."

"What do you like?" My mind goes to the chair, being restrained and used for their desire. What he said to me about needing to remember my safe word with him. Right before Luke held me down for Eli to fuck.

"We'll always talk before we play, but you've experienced some of how I like to play. Tying you down. Using you. Punishing you. We'll get a little rough occasionally." Eli leans in. "We'll start slow, kitten."

I cross my legs against the ache Jack promised to ease. It's back with a vengeance.

"You curious, kitten?"

"A little," I breathe out.

A knock sounds on my door.

Eli straightens. "Expecting someone?"

"No." I hesitate, and the knock comes again. I glance at the other screens, but no one else is in their room. Luke didn't say he was coming over, and if he did, he probably wouldn't knock. He'd just appear.

"Kitten?" Eli says as I stand.

"Yeah?" I brush my hair behind my ear.

"Point me at the door."

For a second, I watch him, trying to decipher his meaning, but then I turn the laptop so the camera faces the door.

Taking a deep breath in, I cross the room. This isn't the frantic knocks from that night. I turn on the porch light and glance out the window. My breath releases.

Caden stands there.

I open the door. "What are you doing here?"

He smiles and backs me into the house before shutting the door behind him. "I forgot to give you my jersey to wear tomorrow."

He holds out a folded football jersey.

"Oh." I take it and hold it up. The number thirty-four is on both sides, and Ross is on the back across the shoulders. "I guess I'm yours tomorrow."

"You're always mine, little nympho." Caden grins and looks around the room before grabbing my hips. His green eyes focus on me. Sparks race along my skin. He nods at the laptop. "I didn't know we were supposed to meet tonight."

"We weren't planning on it," Eli says.

"Where's your mom, little nympho?" Caden draws my hips against his. I gasp at his hard cock against my stomach. My insides soften and heat as my panties grow wetter.

"Work." My voice comes out a little breathless, and Caden's smile widens.

He crowds me back to the table. "And MacKenzie?"

I shake my head. "How did you decide whose jersey I wore first?"

"We let fate decide." He leans over me and shuts the laptop on Eli.

"Whoops." His hand goes to the back of my neck. "So you're saying we're all alone?"

"Caden." I put my hand against his chest, I think to stop him. Instead, I curl it into his shirt.

His smile widens as he lowers his head. Hovering over my lips, his lips brush mine, making fire pour through my veins. His breath is hot against my lips. I can almost taste the cinnamon.

Fuck it.

I surrender. I push up on my toes and pull him down by his shirt until our lips collide.

CADEN

I had solid intentions. I was going to bring my girl my jersey and then head home to my empty house. Turns out my parents came in for dinner before they flew right back out for parts unknown.

Harper wasn't supposed to be alone tonight. MacKenzie was supposed to be here, and we were all willing to give Harper space. After all, she gave us so much today.

But MacKenzie isn't here, and fuck if Harper isn't giving me *fuck me* eyes. A guy is only so strong. And when she pulls me down and kisses me, I'm lost.

When I sweep her up in my arms, she wraps her legs around my waist. My brain takes real quick inventory of all the places I could fuck her down here, but my girl just lost it today. I probably shouldn't fuck her, but I can make her feel good. Carrying her upstairs to her bedroom, I kick the door closed behind me.

"Caden." She breaks away from my lips. "I..."

"You what, little nympho?" I brush my lips over hers, and she gives this needy little noise as her legs tighten around me. I lower her to the bed and hover over her while I work on taking her shirt off.

"I'm a little—" She blushes as I kiss her neck and slide my hands under her to undo her bra.

"Sore?" Peeling her bra off her, I drop it beside the bed. Fuck, I love her breasts. They're a good size for my hands and mouth.

She nods. When I cup her breast, she arches into my hand. My cock throbs with the need to slide deep inside her. I take her other nipple into my mouth and suck. Her fingers dig into my hair, holding me tight against her as I draw on her. Her breathing quickens.

I drop my hands to her jeans and undo the button and zipper while she tugs at my shirt. I pop off her breast and let her drag my shirt off over my head. She grabs hold of my face and draws me down over her, taking my lips in a carnal kiss. All lips, tongue, and teeth. Our chests brush, and heat pours through me.

Fuck. We unleashed something in this girl that makes me crave her.

I tug her jeans down and slide my hand into her panties. Her pussy is hot and wet. She groans into my mouth. Jerking back, I yank her jeans and panties all the way off before falling to my knees beside the bed.

I want the taste of her on my tongue. Want to feel her shatter on my face.

Dragging her legs over my shoulders, I dive in to feast on her perfect pussy. Her fingers tug on my hair as she writhes under my tongue and mouth. While I explore her, I put a hand on her hip to stop her from bucking me off.

"Caden, oh fuck." Music to my fucking ears.

I suck on her clit and flick it with my tongue. When I thrust two fingers deep into her tight cunt, she cries out. Not in pain, but in ecstasy as she shatters all over my fingers and tongue.

But I don't let up. Fuck no. I want my girl completely and utterly spent. I curl my fingers to hit her G-spot and use my tongue to force her back into another climax. Her pussy soaks me as she comes, and I love every second of it.

I slide my wet finger back to her puckered hole and tease the opening.

"Caden." Her darkened eyes meet mine, and I slide my finger deep into her ass. Her lips part and she moans as I slowly fuck her ass with my finger. Licking my way to her entrance, I thrust my tongue into her perfect cunt.

I could spend forever going down on her. Capture every hitched breath. Every jerk of her limbs. Every clutch of her around me. So fucking responsive.

Her whole body jerks as she cries out, convulsing around my finger and tongue. My name slips from her lips over and over. That's fucking right. My name on her lips.

I drag my finger out of her and kiss up her stomach, moving her up on the bed. When I reach her breasts, I take my time to worship her nipples properly, drawing them deep into my mouth as she trembles beneath me.

When I kiss up her neck, her breasts drag against my chest, and her breath catches. I suck on a spot on her neck, wanting to mark her. So everyone knows she's mine, because that's what she is. Mine.

Her legs part around me as I rest one knee on the bed between them.

Kissing her jaw, I make my way over to her mouth, claiming it. She undoes my pants, and I register her moving beneath me, dragging my jeans down, pushing them down my legs with her feet. She arches her body so her pussy rubs against my cock.

Her breath rushes out into my mouth. I swallow her air as she wraps a hand around my cock and slides it along her wet clit before notching it against her entrance. She whimpers this needy little sound that makes my cock ache.

"Harper." I have to find some control, because everything in me wants to thrust into my girl and make her mine all over again. I roll to my back beside her on the bed.

But she follows me, straddling me and guiding my cock back to her sweet cunt.

I thrust my hands into her hair. "You don't have to do this."

She grins and licks my lips. "I want to."

Sliding down over me, she takes me in deep, moaning with every inch, matching my groans.

"Fuck, you feel so good, little nympho." I claim her mouth as she slides up my cock and back down.

She rears up, pressing her hands against my stomach as she chases her pleasure on my cock. I run my hand up to cup her breast, tugging on her nipple as she pants over me.

Our bodies slap together as she rides me. I'm in awe of her. Her beautiful body arches above me as she shatters all around me. Growling, I roll her under me and lift her leg to bury myself even deeper inside her.

Her hands slide into my hair. "Caden."

I can't get enough of her.

I thrust deep before dragging out and sliding all the way back into her. My finger rubs her clit.

"Open your eyes, Harper. I want to watch you shatter for me."

Her dark eyes are blown as she meets mine. I drop my forehead against hers as I fuck her faster. Needing to fill her. Needing to watch her come.

"Almost there. Come for me one more time, little nympho. Come on my thick cock buried in your tight cunt."

Her eyes widen as her lips part on a moan. When her cunt clamps down on my cock, I can't hold back.

"Fuck." Shouting, I come deep inside her, my cock straining to empty inside her, giving her every ounce of me. Spent, I catch myself on my forearms to hold my weight off her.

Her skin glistens with sweat as her hands rub over my shoulders to thread into my hair.

"Still sore?" I don't pull out. I never want to leave her pussy.

She shakes her head and takes a deep breath. Her legs tighten around my hips like she doesn't want to let me go. She gives me a shy smile. "I feel a little sticky."

Keeping her against me and my cock buried inside her, I lift her and walk to her bathroom. She leans over and starts the shower before wrapping her arms around my neck and resting her head against my shoulder.

I rub her back, enjoying all her naked skin wrapped around mine. Needing to hold her as close as possible.

"Aren't your parents in town?" She nuzzles her nose into my neck.

"Dinner and then a late flight out." When I kiss her shoulder, she shivers against me. "Cold?"

"Not at all." She sighs and squeezes me with her arms and legs.

I check the water temp. When I walk us under the showerhead, she clings to me as the water pours over us. I lift her higher as my cock softens, pulling out of her, but she doesn't release me.

"Everything okay, little nympho?" I fill my hands with her soap and stroke it down her back, cupping her ass and sliding my hands between her cheeks. Her breath catches in my ear.

"Yeah." Her arms tighten around me.

I lower her down to stand on her own feet and tip her chin up to look at me. Her dark eyes meet mine, but that little line is between her eyebrows.

"What's on your mind?" I stroke my soapy hands down her arms before lathering up her breasts.

"We just had sex." She sighs.

I smirk as I pay a little too much attention to her nipples, but fuck, her breasts are awesome. "Yeah."

"That makes eight times today." She bites her lip as she glances down. Her startled eyes pop up to mine, and her cheeks deepen in color.

"I'm feeling you up, little nympho. My cock gets hard all the time around you. I'm not planning on doing anything about it. Right now." I slide my soapy hand between her legs, and she grabs onto my arms. Her mouth opens as I rub her pussy.

"How can I want more?" she whispers, more to herself than me.

Carefully I rinse away all the soap before I crowd her against the wall. "Sex can be addictive, little nympho. Coming is a high unlike any other. It's okay to crave it. To want it."

I slide my fingers between her legs again. She presses her head back against the shower wall and gazes up at me with hooded eyes as I stroke her pussy.

"You don't have to be ashamed to want this, Harper." I brush my cheek against hers.

Her breath catches, and I lower my mouth to her neck, kissing her gently along her pulse while exploring her pussy with my fingers.

"It's one of our core needs." I slide my finger inside her tight, warm cunt, and my cock jerks. I want to fuck her again, but not tonight.

Her hands trail down my chest. I lift my head to meet her eyes. She takes hold of my cock and tentatively explores it with her fingers. Her eyes never leave mine as she strokes down over me.

I release a breath. "That feels good."

We're in our own little cocoon here. The shower runs behind us, hitting my back. No one else is here to tell me to slow down or stop. No one except Harper.

She licks her lips as her gaze falls to my cock. Precum flows out onto the tip, and she runs her thumb over it. She wraps her hand almost all the way around it and strokes me.

I press my hand on the shower tile next to her head as I watch her explore. When she cups my balls, I groan.

"Too much?" she whispers. Her breath comes out in little pants as I slowly fuck her with my finger.

"Never, little nympho." I could never get enough of her. My intentions might have been pure coming here, but there was a part of me that hoped to get another piece of my girl. To feel her tight cunt squeeze around my cock.

She's not like any other girl I've known. I don't just want to get off in her. I want that connection. To watch her dark eyes as I break her into pieces and put her back together again.

Fuck, this girl is everything.

Her pussy convulses around my finger.

"You feel that. Don't deny yourself that pleasure, little nympho." I take my finger out and suck it. Her eyes watch me.

My cock aches, but this isn't about me. This girl is going to kill me.

I rinse both of us off in the shower quickly, before turning it off and drying her.

"What's the rush?" She makes a squeaking noise when I lift her naked body against mine and carry her into her bedroom.

I toss her on the bed and come down over her. "I'm hungry, little nympho."

HARPER

My whole body buzzes with desire.

Caden trails kisses down my neck and pauses at my breasts. My breath catches as his mouth closes over my nipple. Licking, sucking, tugging, while my fingers dig into his hair, holding him against me. My breath comes out in quick pants. Each stroke of his tongue makes me wetter.

We should stop. Fuck, I don't want to, but we should stop.

"I should finish my homework." I squirm under him. "Caden?"

He kisses along my stomach before drawing my knees up and spreading me wide. Licking his lips, he stares at my pussy. "Don't worry, little nympho. I'll get you off, and then you can do all the homework you want."

My face burns, but he doesn't stop looking at my pussy. When he dips down, I hold my breath as he licks me from my clit to my ass.

I release a jagged breath before he consumes me. The noises he makes and what he does to me make me squirm until needy noises pour out of me. My hips follow his tongue, riding it until I shatter. Arching, I try to slow down my breathing.

Before I can come down, he pushes me back up, thrusting his finger into my pussy, making me explode again. I can't breathe. I can't come down.

It's too much.

"Oh, fuck," I breathe out as I arch like a woman possessed. My pussy gushes on Caden as I come again.

When he slides his finger out of me, I take a shaky breath in and out as he slowly licks and kisses my pussy. All I can do is twitch and breathe beneath him. My hands cover my racing heart.

Crawling up my body, he hovers over me. "Good, little nympho?"

"Can't. Breathe. War." My hands clasp his jaw and bring his mouth down to mine. I taste myself on his tongue and strain my body up against his, feeling his hard cock against my stomach.

"You're beautiful, little nympho." He kisses me again before he eases away to the bathroom. If I had an ounce of energy left, I'd follow him in and do something about his erection.

But fuck.

I could fall asleep like this. Spread-eagle on my bed, without a care in the fucking world. My body is mush. I'm definitely not telling Kenz about that. Poor Brandon would never measure up.

"Come on, little nympho. You've got homework and you need to feed this beast." His t-shirt lands on my chest.

Drawing in a breath, I sit up and tug on his t-shirt. His warmth and scent cover me. He draws his boxers over his erection. I raise an eyebrow as I consider how I could help.

Tipping my chin up, he shakes his head. "Not this time, little nympho. Keep your dirty thoughts to yourself."

He kisses me briefly before dragging me to my feet. I grab a pair of panties from my dresser to put on.

"Hmm, I might have to talk you out of those later." Caden steps in closer, and I swear a little spark tries to light inside me, but damn am I tired. He chuckles before steering me out of my room and downstairs.

At the refrigerator, I pull out some sandwich makings and put them on the island. After washing my hands, I make us each a sandwich, since my stomach growls loudly. I've had a lot of physical activity today.

Caden grabs our plates and sets them on the table as he takes a chair. I bring over some water for us and pull over my history textbook.

"You said MacKenzie would spend the night." His eyebrows arch as he inhales his sandwich. It's getting late, and she hasn't shown up. I exhale.

"No, I said she *might*." A little thrill goes through me at the thought of punishment. What the hell is wrong with me? They've thoroughly warped my mind. "Her mom said no."

He tips back on the chair legs as his eyes never leave me. "Were you going to tell us, little nympho?"

"I've stayed here many times on my own with no issues." I don't lift my gaze from the textbook. "You all have beds of your own you can keep warm."

"Not going to happen." Caden downs his water. Tension radiates off him.

"What's not going to happen?" I finally lift my gaze to meet his possessive green eyes. Fuck. I ignore my body's arousal at his mere presence.

His fingers grip my chin so I can't look away. "You belong to us. We can't protect you if we don't know you need it."

"I don't need protection." Pulling away, I close my book. I'm sure I can find time to read it tomorrow. "This isn't new to my life. Mom's work has rotating shifts. It's been a while, but she works nights. News-flash, I sleep at home alone when that happens. And I'm fine."

I pick up his plate and mine and take them to the sink, rinsing them before putting them in the dishwasher. His chair scrapes the floor, and his heat closes in on me from behind.

Tingles dance down my spine, anticipating his touch.

"You weren't claimed then." His fingers curl around my hips. "You didn't have weird shit happening around you then."

His lips press against the nape of my neck, and my knees weaken. I grab onto the counter to help support myself.

"Let me take care of you, little nympho." His voice is enticing. The tip of his nose presses against my neck, drawing a trail up to my ear. "You like when I take care of you, baby."

Oh fuck, he's fucking potent. I crave him and what he does to me. He's right, it's like an addiction, a need.

"What would the others think about you sleeping here?" I don't say *on your own*, but it's implied in my words. We're in (excuse the phrase) virgin territory here. Caden and I just had sex without everyone else being nearby or present. They definitely aren't aware.

Maybe Eli will figure it out since I didn't come back to the webcam.

"We agreed we could spend time alone with you." He draws me back against him and runs his hand under the t-shirt, across my belly. When he strokes his thumb over my bare skin, he sends those butterflies racing. "I didn't fuck your ass, so we should be fine."

I squeeze my thighs together. "You want to spend the night with me?"

His dark chuckle flows through me, lighting me on fire. He turns me and lifts me onto the counter before stepping between my legs. He tips my head back with his hand cupping my cheek.

"You tempt me to misbehave, but I need to let the others know." He dips his head down and claims my lips, tasting me, conquering me. I moan into his mouth as his cock presses against my pussy. A twinge of soreness accompanies my pussy's throb.

My hands trace the muscles on his chest. I mean, I'm already going to be sore tomorrow. I might as well enjoy myself tonight. My legs tighten on his hips.

"More?" He caresses the back of my neck.

"No." Heat rushes to my face. Fuck, I'm addicted. "Yes. I don't know."

He helps me off the counter and urges me back to my homework. He gets his phone, and notifications buzz back and forth while I try to focus on my history reading. When I open my laptop to figure out if I'm missing anything, the others are all at their computers.

Well, except Caden. He sits next to me in only his boxers.

"Hi." I lift my hand and wave like a complete idiot.

Jack smirks. Eli raises an eyebrow. Nico smiles. Luke... he's definitely not happy. And when Luke's not happy, I usually get punished. I swallow.

Caden caresses my thigh under the table. Not sure if it's to give me support or to steady me for whatever is about to happen.

"Stand up, princess."

It's pretty obvious I'm wearing Caden's shirt. I practically swim in it.

Sighing, I stand in front of the camera. I could be wearing booty shorts with this t-shirt and they wouldn't know. "Is this really necessary?"

"Lift it." Luke's eyes have that icy edge to them tonight.

I pull up the shirt to show my panties. Thankfully I put them on. Not that they all haven't seen me naked, but I'm pretty sure things would be worse if I'm sitting here with no panties on.

"Do I get to see your boxers next?" Fuck, that imp inside me who likes to poke at Luke has no sense of self-preservation.

Caden chuckles and runs his hand up the back of my thigh. "Seems only fair."

"Fair?" Luke leans back.

"I don't see what the problem is." I lower my shirt and sit back in my chair. "Caden brought me his jersey to wear tomorrow to school."

"And what, princess?" Luke's voice is clipped. "What happened next?"

"Afraid you missed the show?" Caden's words are like ice to my overheated body. "Do you need a play by play? Or blow by blow?"

This is a game I'm not qualified to play.

"This is ridiculous. Harper can do what she wants with her body." Nico leans forward. "It's not like he took something she wasn't willing to give."

"Any of us could have gone over there tonight." Jack smirks. "Fuck, I know I planned to go help her relieve some tension, but got side-tracked."

"This isn't a fucking free for all." Luke clenches his fist on the desk. A muscle ticks in his jaw. My heart races like a trapped rabbit.

"Isn't it though? She belongs to all of us." Eli isn't smug or smirking. He's completely calm. "Or do you want to control our access to her?"

All eyes go to Luke. That's exactly what he wants. I know it. They know it. The question is will he be honest about it.

His eyes lock on me. It should be hard to tell on video chat, but it's not just seeing him. It's feeling him. The way he slips beneath my skin to rile me up.

The wheels spin behind his eyes as he figures out how to make this work best for him. It's infuriating. He wants complete and utter control of me. While I don't mind sometimes, he needs to understand I'm still me.

"Are you going to need to fuck me every time one of them does?" The words spill off my tongue. "Do you need to come fuck me now to prove you have control over me? That you own me? That I belong to you?"

I stand, feeling caged. "Or do you just need to hear what happened? Is it every time someone's been alone with me? Like when you slept with me? Or how about the time you *punished* me by getting me and yourself off in your car on the way home?"

Laughter, tight and hot, pours out of me. "Or is it just the ones you don't know about? Like tonight? Yes, Caden and I fucked. It was my choice, and I probably would have fucked him again, but he thought he should tell you—his friend—he's staying here tonight because I would have been alone otherwise."

"You said MacKenzie was staying." The words are bitter. But of course, out of everything I said, that's what he would focus on.

"I asked. Her mom said no." I straighten. I'm not nearly as tall as them and probably look smaller in Caden's t-shirt. "I can be by myself. I've spent years perfecting it while hiding from you."

"You want to be alone, princess?" Luke holds me pinned there while he looks me over.

My heart stops. No, I don't. That day they were all cold to me. I don't want that. Not after this weekend. Not after giving in. Fuck, they could drop me and go back to their lives. Go back to other girls. They got what they wanted. They got what they claimed me for.

My legs shake, and I collapse into the chair. I can't help poking at Luke, but I poke too hard. He's going to end it all. I'll go back to being invisible, and they'll go back to the other girls.

Everyone will be happy. And I'll be alone. Again.

"Enough."

CHAPTER 46

Conceding

"You want to be alone, princess?" Rage courses through me.

She wants Caden. She can fucking have him.

I wait for her answer. Her face goes pale, and she sinks into her chair. Her eyes never leave me, but there's a distant look in them, like she's already retreating into herself.

Fuck. That dull look comes over her like she's already gone, and something inside me cracks.

"Enough." Eli leans forward. "You two need a few hours alone in a closet together. You'll either fuck it out or yell at each other to spite yourselves."

I keep my eyes trained on her as I lean back in my chair and fold my hands in front of my lips. He's not wrong. She drives me insane. I'm not built like the others. I normally don't share. Never was good at it. Not toys. Not women.

Everything in me wants to claim Harper as mine. Only mine.

We agreed to share her, but fuck it's hard. I can share her, but on my terms.

"This works if Harper belongs to us all equally." Eli taps his pen on his desk. "We all have healthy sexual appetites. We have one woman to share for the duration of the year."

I'm going to be a problem. But we might all be a powder keg waiting to explode. This is the deal we agreed to. What we agreed to put Harper through. She just gave us her virginity and she's had sex eight times today.

Most women wouldn't put up with that.

"No more punishing her by ostracizing her." Caden draws her onto his lap and holds her against him, rubbing her arms like she's cold. "We banished her from living her life for years. It's cruel."

"She decides." Jack leans forward. "Yes, we all get her, but she gets to decide when she needs a break."

Her dark eyes meet mine. She usually seems so strong, but on Caden's lap she seems small. Do I do that to her? Do I make her feel small? Why the fuck does my chest ache?

"Your mom works nights all week?" Nico asks.

"Yes." Even her voice is small.

I swallow my fucking pride.

"Caden and I have the most flexibility to stay with her." As long as I stick to facts, I should be fine. But I know I have to be more open with them. More open with her. Because I'm not giving her up. Not without a fight, even if I have to fight her. "What about you guys?"

Jack shakes his head. "Lucy would riot if I'm not home for bedtime kisses. And Dad doesn't want me out on school nights."

"Lucy?" Curiosity heightens Harper's voice.

"My eight-year-old sister." Jack grins. As far as big brothers go, Lucy hit the lottery with Jack. "You should meet her. She's a character."

She smiles a little. "I'd like that."

"My parents are making a habit of family dinners." Eli pushes his hand through his hair. "Their new tactic is to get involved with me. Senior night is going to be a fucking tug of war."

Harper's eyes go soft with concern when she looks at Eli. He needs to let loose on someone, and that someone will be Harper this year. Holding her down while he fucks her is only the beginning. Tying her up and controlling who fucks her was just a hint of what he wants. What he needs.

"My parents are going to be all over me this week." Nico looks disappointed. "Sorry, sunshine, I'd love to stay with you, but they want to make sure I transition smoothly."

I breathe out. Harper's eyes flick to me. She's still on Caden's lap. Part of me wants to rage while another part of me is glad he's there to comfort her.

"Harper?" Eli sighs as his eyes flick back and forth between us. He knows I want to dictate this, but she's a part of us now. I need to learn to trust her to include me. "How do you want to do this?"

"What?" She's startled, probably thinking we would make the decision for her.

"We'll all see you after practice most nights, but someone needs to stay with you, kitten. You can be an independent woman who can stand on her own next year at college." Eli rubs the back of his neck. "We have enemies."

"Like Tanner. Guys who would do anything to get back at us," Jack fills in. "You being alone at night is an opening most won't resist."

"You're our weak link, princess. We've never claimed a girl before. The knocking and the tire are just the beginning." I hope I'm wrong, but we've never had a vulnerability. "We can't let someone use you to hurt us. We can't let someone hurt you."

She sinks into Caden's embrace as she taps her lip. Her eyes never leave me. I'm not the easiest horseman, but there's something real between us. I know she feels it too.

She leans forward. "You're by yourself in your house?"

I almost laugh. This softness in her is her vulnerability, but it also works to all of our benefit. She can think we're her broken little toys for the year if that's what it takes for her to let me in. "Yeah, princess. Just me."

She glances at Caden. Her two strays she can't help but claim. Neither of us are really loved. We're obligations to our parents. They hope one day we'll fill the role of taking over their businesses, but right now, we're still being molded and shaped into what they want.

Caden runs his hand over her arm, and a little shiver works through her.

"My bed isn't that big," she leads with, but when her eyes find me, that softness is in them. "But—"

"Sunshine, you can't keep every stray you find." Nico gives her a knowing smile. "When we were young, she would bring home kittens and dogs and hurt things for her mom to fix. How many scratches and bite marks did you get trying to help?"

I raise an eyebrow. Does Nico think I'm some feral animal? Maybe with Harper I am. Is this his way of protecting her from me? Fuck that.

"If you don't mind sharing, I'm okay with anyone staying." She doesn't look me in the eyes, and she doesn't say she wants me to stay. She left it open on purpose. I don't need to be her fucking charity case.

Technically she would be fine with Caden there. Probably fit better in her bed too. I narrow my eyes on her. I'll be damned if I cave first.

HARPER

Luke can go fuck himself if he thinks I'm going to invite him to come sleep with me after he went possessive caveman on me. But I also know how lonely it can be in a house by yourself. My heart is torn.

Nico's right. I have this thing about strays. Especially the ones that are all snarly on the outside like Luke. And like Caden.

I rest my head back on Caden's shoulder. He's being possessive but not snarly.

"Looks like you're all set for tonight then." Luke's a feral animal that would bite off his own paw to escape. "Are we staying logged in?"

Jack talks briefly about staying logged in and finding a way to disable the cameras in case someone else is in the room for the future. It would probably be easier to set up a separate chat.

My phone buzzes with a notification. I lean forward and pick it up.

PESTILENCE (ELI):

Kitten you know he won't cave

ME:

Why should I care?

PESTILENCE (ELI):

Because you do

He's not wrong. That muscle ticks in Luke's jaw as he listens. Everything is so fucking easy for him. He decides to claim me for all of them and then wants to monopolize me. He can't have it both ways.

PESTILENCE (ELI):

You've met his dad

I release a breath, and my eyes return to Luke. Yes, I met his dad. If I thought Luke was cold, his father is frigid. Luke is prideful and stubborn. He'll never admit a weakness.

He helped me explore my desires. He spoke for me when I couldn't. Instead of taking control, he let me control my first time with him. My pussy clenches remembering how good he felt inside me.

Fuck.

Fuck, fuck, fuck.

I shouldn't be rewarding his bad temper. I shouldn't care he's all alone in that big house every fucking night. He should be used to it. He deserves it.

His gaze lands on mine. For a second, I see the guy who dragged me back into his arms in the center of my bed and held me when I was afraid. The guy who shared me with his four friends, but helped me through the process without making me feel bad. Giving in to my desire on my terms.

Fuck.

"Luke, would you come stay with me?" The words are easier to say than I thought they would be.

His eyes widen for just a second before he masks his emotions. "Caden's already there."

Caden squeezes my hip. The others have fallen silent.

I'd roll my eyes if it wouldn't make him even more stubborn. "I like sleeping between two of you."

It's not a lie. There's something about having hard, warm walls of man on either side of me that makes me sleep easier. I know Caden will do anything to protect me, but so would Luke. Neither of them have to be alone while they have me. Just like I don't have to be alone since I have them.

"If I wouldn't get in trouble, I'd go." Eli scoffs. "Don't be an ass."

Luke stands and walks off the screen. Did I make him angry? What new nightmare level of punishment will be waiting for me at school tomorrow?

He comes back on screen with his backpack on his shoulder. He meets my eyes before he shuts his computer. Awareness makes the hairs on my arms stand on end.

Luke is coming here.

"Do we need to talk about him?" Nico runs a hand through his hair. "I get not wanting to share Harper, but is he going to be a problem?"

"He never participated when we played with the same girl." Caden draws me against his warm chest. "It always turned into a competition to him. His number is low for a reason."

Twelve, was it? While the others are in the twenties. It surprised me when he said it. Honestly their numbers are all lower than I thought they would be. As much as everyone claims to have fucked a horseman, I would think their numbers would be in the triple digits by now.

"He's fine using girls' mouths though," Jack points out helpfully. I don't want to think about them with other girls. "He wants girls who keep themselves for him. Like Sidney always did."

Heat churns in my gut thinking of Sidney and Luke.

Caden gives a little shudder. "Fuck, if he's used to Sidney, no wonder he's possessive of Harper. Sid gives a technically great blow job, but it's a fucking job to her."

"Most girls only do it because they know we like it." Jack rubs the back of his head and winks. Just thinking about giving them head makes me a little wet.

"Luke will figure it out." Eli stretches. "Don't worry, kitten, I'm sure he won't take it out on you."

I scoff. "Sure."

Caden rubs my thigh. "I need to run home and grab things for tomorrow."

I tip my chin up to look back at him. "You're leaving?"

He smiles. "Not until Luke gets here."

"Wait, you're leaving me alone with Luke?" I straighten. He's in a dark mood. Who knows what he'll do?

"He won't hurt you, Harper." Caden kisses my head. "The good thing about Luke is while he's possessive as fuck about them, he doesn't break his toys."

I arch an eyebrow. That doesn't sound too reassuring.

"We'll be here with you, kitten." Eli stands with his laptop and moves to his bed.

"We never finished what we started earlier." Jack wiggles his eyebrows.

"I think I'm tapped out for the night." I glance up at Caden, who gives me a wicked smile. Sparks race through my bloodstream. Yeah, my body is way too interested in them. "Maybe I should make up the guest bed for you and Luke."

I go to stand, but he holds me fast to him.

"You're good, little nympho. I'm not the horseman you need to worry about tonight." He nuzzles into my neck, scraping my neck with his scruff, making me squeal a little.

"We should plan for a round of seven minutes in heaven at Caden's tomorrow night." Jack rubs his cock below the screen. "I'm sure it will be even more exciting now."

I squeeze my thighs together. "I think I'm going to need a longer break than that."

"Hmm." Eli contemplates me. "Maybe we can play a different game."

I'm not sure I like the little smile on his lips. My insides burn though, craving whatever he'll give me.

"Wear your collar tomorrow, kitten." Eli takes his shirt off and slides off his jeans, leaving his boxers on. Fuck, his body distracts me. He climbs onto his bed and picks up the tattered book from his nightstand.

Tugging my laptop over, I make sure I got all my homework turned in, while Caden's fingers skate down my back. I shiver a little, loving the warm feeling flooding me.

A knock sounds at my door, and my entire body tenses, preparing for Luke's arrival. Caden chuckles as he sets me on my chair and goes to the door. He glances out the window before unlocking it.

The hairs on the back of my neck stand on end as Luke steps in. I keep my face turned to my computer, finishing one last thing.

"I have to grab a change of clothes for the morning." Caden's tone seems calm, but there's an underlying tension. Is he checking to see what Luke plans to do to me before he leaves?

Caden disappears upstairs to grab his pants. Hopefully he doesn't need his shirt back yet.

Luke's heat and soft, seductive scent wash over me. My insides grow warm as need swells inside me. Fuck, does this thing have an off switch?

"Princess." His hand slides over my hair, practically petting me.

I turn in my chair and meet his gaze. I gave in this time, inviting him over. How many more times will I give in to him? "Death."

CHAPTER 47

Fit to Receive

Caden comes down the stairs. "I'll be back in fifteen."

He stops next to us and looks from Luke to me and back. "I'll try for ten."

"We'll be fine, Caden. Won't we, princess?"

I purse my lips. If I were the betting kind, I'd bet Luke plans to have me on my knees before him as soon as the door closes behind Caden. I wish my panties didn't grow damp thinking of his cock thrusting into my mouth.

"Yes, fine." What could possibly go wrong leaving me here alone with Death? I swallow but smile at Caden.

He rolls his eyes. "Work it out, you two. Fuck or fight."

He punches Luke in the arm. Luke doesn't even flinch. Caden goes out the door, disappearing into the night. Luke goes over to lock it, giving me a little breathing space.

I almost close my laptop, but remember the guys are still on it. They may not be in the room to tell Luke to back off, but at least they'll be here if I need them. Kind of.

Luke lifts the chair Caden was sitting on and spins it around, straddling it with his arms resting on the back. "You never answered me, princess."

"Answered you about what?" I cross my legs and tug at the hem of Caden's shirt, suddenly feeling vulnerable and mostly naked.

Luke's gaze flicks to the webcam. "What you and Jack were doing before he disappeared?"

Jack chuckles darkly. "I wanted to help her masturbate, but she was worried someone would come into the other rooms and hear, so I said I'd be right over."

Luke's fiery gaze meets mine, and I inhale sharply at the heat.

"That shouldn't be a problem now, right princess?" Luke doesn't move toward me, but his presence still overwhelms me.

"Yeah, sweetheart, the rooms are all filled. No one else but us here." Jack lowers his camera and slides his sweats down, revealing his hard cock. "We can talk about whatever we want."

My pussy throbs with need already. I press my legs together, trying to get the restless ache to go away. For fuck's sake, I've had enough orgasms for the day. I should not need or want another one.

Luke's fingertip slides down my neck, startling me. My breath catches as his finger dips inside my collar. My pulse increases as I meet Luke's gaze. He watches his finger and wets his lips.

When he draws his hand back to the chair, his gaze lifts to mine. My breasts feel heavy, and need throbs between my thighs. I'm so going to lose this battle.

"Lose the panties, sweetheart. I want to watch you flick the bean." Jack's voice draws me to watch his hand stroke his cock. Arousal swells inside me.

"Need help, princess?"

Luke smirks when I glare at him. My breasts rise and fall with the pace of my breathing. Fuck it. I don't care who gets me off. My body wants it. This restless energy isn't going away.

I stand and slip my panties off, setting them on the table.

"Take off the shirt too, kitten."

My gaze falls on Eli. He rubs his cock through his boxers. I grip the hem of my shirt and take it off. My hair falls down around my breasts, tickling my sensitive skin.

When I go to sit in the chair, Eli makes a tsking noise.

"Kitten, you need to be elevated a little." Eli smiles indulgently. "Luke can help with that."

I swallow. I'm naked standing in front of Luke. If he doesn't touch me, I'll be fine, but the second he does, I swear we'll burn together.

Luke stands and moves his chair out of the way to close in on me. My lips part as his shirt brushes my tightened nipples. His hands grip my hips, and I gasp at the heat of them. I don't dare look in his eyes.

If I do, I'll be lost.

He backs me up and then lowers into my chair. He centers me in front of him and then looks up with an evil grin.

"Spread or bent over?" he asks.

My brow furrows. "What?"

"Spread," Eli says.

"Bent over," Jack says.

"Hmm, could we have a demonstration of both?" Nico's voice makes me look over my shoulder as he slides his hand over his thick, hard cock. My pussy pulses, remembering how his cock felt buried deep inside me.

"Of course." Luke scoots the chair back and draws my head down to his lap. I make a little surprised sound. "Legs apart, princess."

The blood flowing to my face isn't the only reason my face is red. I do as he asks because fuck it. This is my life now. Standing in my kitchen, giving a naked webcam show to three of my five boyfriends. If you can call them that.

Owners more like.

"Bent over," Luke slides his hand over my hip and pulls my ass cheek open. Fuck.

The sultry cologne he wears messes with my brain. I brace my hands on his legs as wetness drips out of me. His muscles tighten beneath my touch.

"Very nice," Nico says.

Luke pushes my shoulders up to standing. I feel like a freaking doll. He takes my hips and turns me in front of him before drawing me back to sit on his lap. His hands draw my legs to the outside of his. Every touch makes me more needy.

With his hand on my breast and the other on my waist, he slouches a little and spreads his legs, forcing mine open obscenely wide. His hard cock rests against my ass.

Fuck, I'm ready to get off.

"Spread," Luke says matter-of-factly. His dark voice in my ear makes me shiver.

I lean back on his shoulder, trying to ignore his hand on my breast and all the other arousing triggers of him being so close to me.

"Definitely spread." Nico strokes his fingers over his lip before gripping his cock.

"Tell us what Caden did to you, princess." Luke's fingers squeeze my breast softly. Fuck my life. "Don't leave any part out."

Is this his method of punishment? My skin is hot and tight all over. His shirt and jeans are soft beneath me. His body is hard and unyielding.

I swallow the desire raging inside. "He took me upstairs and went down on me."

"You said he fucked you." Luke slides his fingers down my stomach, over my clit to press inside. "He came inside you, princess, so he must not have just gone down on you."

My breath catches in my throat as Luke's fingers squeeze my breast, while his other fingers remain inside me, holding my pussy. I clench around him, and his breath releases next to my ear.

I lick my lips as I watch the others stroking their cocks onscreen. "He made me come with his mouth and fingers three times before he lifted over me."

Luke rewards me by teasing my clit and rocking his finger in and out. His other fingers pinch my nipple, and I press back against him. "What next, princess?"

Focusing on Jack's blue eyes, I say, "I pushed down his jeans and grabbed his cock. I brought it to my pussy, but he rolled onto his back."

Luke draws his hand out of me, and I let out a little whimper of need. He takes my hand and curls his fingers around mine, holding them in position. "What next?"

He brings our hands between my legs, and I stroke my clit.

"Mmm." I close my eyes as I linger on the spot that feels the best.

"He told me I didn't have to, so I straddled him and took his cock inside my pussy."

I slide my and Luke's fingers back to my entrance and press inside. I gasp at the thickness of both of us penetrating me.

"I rode him until we both came." I roll my head on Luke's shoulder as my insides burn with the need to come.

"Then we took a shower." Caden's voice comes from my computer. I open my eyes and meet his. "I fucked her with my finger."

He sits in his chair and watches my finger and Luke's moving in and out of me.

"I fucked her until she came all over my hand again."

My eyes dart to the others, who are stroking their cocks in time with my and Luke's strokes. A moan wells up from inside and escapes as I rock my hips, feeling Luke's restless breath on my temple. His hand massages my breast and teases my nipple with his fingertips.

I wet my lips. Caden leans back in his chair and watches me with hooded eyes.

"I took her back to her bed and sucked her little clit. Thrust my tongue into her tight pussy. And fucked her with my fingers."

Tipping over the edge with a moan, I arch my body. Luke works my clit to keep me right there in the moment. Groans fill my speakers, and I open my eyes to see them coming for me.

Caden stands, his hard cock visible in his jeans. He shifts it and winks. "Be there in five."

He walks out of the room and shuts the light off. The guys give me smiles before they head to clean themselves. For a moment, I'm naked and alone on Luke's lap.

His finger holds mine buried inside me as he nuzzles my neck. "I didn't mean it."

His words are so quiet, I almost didn't hear him. "Mean what?"

"I wouldn't have left you alone, princess." He slides his finger out of me and holds it in front of my mouth.

Taking it into my mouth, I suck and lick off my wetness.

"I'm not easy to be with. I know that." He draws his finger out of my mouth and closes his legs, so I'm no longer spread wide. He tips my face up to the side, and his light blue eyes draw me in. "I'll figure out how to share you, but I won't leave you."

His lips press against mine. Soft and questioning. A promise in them.

I twist on his lap until my legs are to one side of his. My hand cups his jaw as I part my lips and touch his with the tip of my tongue. He parts his lips for me, and I feel powerful. I'm naked on his lap, but in this moment, he's the one who seems vulnerable.

His hands hold me to him as we explore each other's mouths. I shiver as the cool air touches my heated skin. He pulls back and takes his shirt off. Our skin touches, and sparks ignite within me, making me burn hotter.

Instead of drawing me back in, he pulls his shirt over my head and down on my body.

I'm sure I have questions in my eyes as he cups my cheek.

"It's time for bed, princess. No more playtime tonight." He leans into me and grabs my panties from the table, pressing them into my hand. "We have a whole year to play."

I rub my thumb over his jaw before standing and putting my panties on. The fire raging inside me fills me with heat, but Luke's right. I need to go to sleep.

We have school in the morning.

A knock sounds on the door. Luke stands and heads to open it for Caden. They grip hands in that odd handshake before closing and locking the door.

Caden's steps eat away at the distance between us until he lifts me in his arms and kisses me. "Time for bed, little nympho."

Luke grabs my laptop and his backpack. We turn everything off and make sure there are no signs of them in the house before climbing the stairs.

I slip into my bathroom and get ready for bed. It's been a long day, and I'm almost wiped out. When I step into my bedroom, I pause seeing Caden and Luke in my bed, waiting for me.

I don't change out of Luke's shirt. I can let him claim me this way for tonight. This won't be the last time we'll have issues. And I really worry the others will lock us in a room at some point and just leave us there until we work them out on each other.

Taking a deep breath, I crawl between them on the bed. Caden tugs my leg over his, and I snuggle into his side. Luke curls up around me from behind. They're mine and I'm theirs, and for now, I'm willing to accept that.

CHAPTER 48

The Bugle Call

HARPER

When my alarm goes off, I reach out to snooze it, but I'm stuck between two hard bodies. I'm getting used to waking up like this. Though lately, I've woken halfway to coming... Caden hands me my phone, and I turn off the alarm.

My new life is so fucking weird.

I stretch between them, feeling their erections against my stomach and ass. My insides light up, but I shut that down quickly, especially with the aching soreness between my legs.

Maybe I should've been content with one time. I don't want to open my eyes and face today.

It's time. I need to get ready for school.

"Morning, little nympho." Caden's voice is gruff as he strokes his hand down my side. Sparks follow his hand eagerly. I almost groan at how much my body craves their touch.

Luke stretches behind me. His arm tightens around my waist. "This would work better at Caden's or my house. I have a king-sized bed."

"I wasn't aware I'd have company when I was ten and got a new bed." I squeak as a hand goes between my legs. Turning over, I glare at Luke. "Not this morning."

He captures the back of my neck and kisses me with a command I'm too weak to resist. Fuck morning breath. I melt into him as he slides on top of me. His cock rests against my pussy, and for a second, I wish there weren't panties and boxers between us.

"I'm going to use the bathroom. Don't fuck." Caden chuckles as he shifts off the bed, and my bathroom door closes.

Luke lifts his mouth from mine and rubs a thumb across my lower lip. I open my eyes to his. This morning, they're soft blue, like the morning sky. He searches mine, and for a moment, it feels like he's letting me in. To see a side of him no one else does.

My heart beats a little harder. I don't know what to do. I need to get ready for school, but a part of me wants to pull him down and explore everything we can be together.

He brushes my hair off my forehead. "We need to be quiet this morning." His fingers trail down my cheek, making me shiver with awareness. "We'll need to work on your ability to not be loud, princess, but I love how noisy you are when you come."

I press my thighs together at the ache building there. My hand slides up his neck into his soft hair. "Does that mean we're going to practice this week?"

"All the time, princess." He lowers his mouth to mine, and I meet him halfway.

I should be mad at him for the way he treated me yesterday, but right now I can't seem to find the will to shove him away. There's that part of me that's so grateful for his help yesterday. And the other part that's more than willing to take anything he wants to give me.

He presses his body down on mine, and my legs part so he can settle against me fully. His heated eyes hold mine. He knows he could have me, that I would let him in to fulfill that ache he stirs.

When the bathroom door opens, Luke kisses me briefly before climbing off me to go into the bathroom. Before I can move, Caden crawls up my body, and I grin at his predatory smile. He captures my lips and claims them for his own.

These boys own me. Fully. And I can't get enough.

My breathing is heavy when he lifts away from me and sits on the edge of the bed.

I try to steady my breathing and calm down the need pulsing

through my veins. The shower turns on in the bathroom, and Luke opens the door. Completely naked. All hard, toned muscles.

Fuck, they don't play fair.

He holds out his hand to me. "Come on. Your mom will just think you took a really long shower."

I sit up. It's not like we haven't showered together, but here? Now? My mouth opens and closes. Me naked with them is a recipe for fucking.

"If we take separate showers, your mom will be suspicious, little nympho." Caden traces his finger over my thigh, right below Luke's shirt. "Luke will only take a little while, and then I'll switch out with him."

Yeah, that doesn't exactly cool down the fire burning inside. Showering together makes sense, but that ache isn't just need this morning. There's a twinge of pain ache too.

"Why do I have the feeling I'm going to be very clean today?" I scoot to the end of the bed and walk over to Luke.

"We like to be thorough." Luke's wicked grin makes my heart pound. Caden follows me into the bathroom and draws off my shirt, while Luke lowers my panties. Naked, I tremble between the two of them.

Awareness and desire flow over me, making me want to forget about the pain and dive headfirst into the pleasure.

Luke draws me into the shower. Unlike Caden's massive shower, mine is built for two people. At most. Luke is not a small guy, but there's a little room to move.

Our wet bodies slide against each other as he washes his hair. I grab my soap and rub it around his chest. His smile makes my heart beat harder. After he rinses his hair, he fills his hand with soap before rubbing his palms together.

The minute his hands touch my body, I gasp. He's as thorough as promised, touching every part of me while I try to focus on washing him. When he steps back to rinse in the shower, he draws me under the spray head and takes my mouth.

His fingers slide between my thighs and stroke my pussy. The shower door opens, and Caden closes in behind me. His hands join

Luke's on me, and I can't think. Their skin brushes mine, trapping me between them. Luke's mouth devours mine while Caden kisses the back of my neck.

Fingers thrust inside me. I'm wet, but I hiss at the slight pain.

"Sore, princess?"

I open my eyes to those soft blue ones and nod with a slight frown. I don't want to be sore.

"We'll take it easy then, little nympho." Caden's hands move up to my breasts, and I lean back against him, watching Luke with hooded eyes.

Luke continues to tease my pussy before taking my nipple into his mouth. Desire flows through me hot and heavy. When he teases my clit, my hips follow his hand, chasing my release. Caden kisses that spot on my shoulder that makes me forget how to breathe.

Moaning, I come, writhing between them. Luke smiles and captures my mouth with his before slipping out the shower door and drying off. He leans against the bathroom door and watches as Caden helps me with my hair.

In turn, I help him soap his entire body. His cock is hard just like Luke's, but he doesn't let me spend much time on it. Neither had Luke.

We rinse, and Luke holds open a towel for me to step into. Caden grabs a towel and dries himself. When Luke opens the bedroom door, we all go get dressed. The guys pull out their clothes from their backpacks while I go to my closet.

I put on soft pink panties and bra set. Then a black, knee-length skater skirt with a t-shirt before putting on Caden's jersey. I slip into the bathroom, blow-dry my hair, and brush my teeth before putting on makeup. When I come out, the guys are sitting on the end of my bed.

When Luke holds out his hand, I take it. He reels me in and lifts my skirt. His finger traces the edge of my panties. "Behave—"

"Or these will belong to you?" I raise an eyebrow. Same old material.

He chuckles and stands in my space, grabbing the back of my neck to keep me from stepping back. He leans in close to my ear, "No, princess. I'll take you into a closet and rip these from your body and fuck you until you scream."

Oh fuck, these panties are soaked. That ache is still there, and I'm not sure if it's pain or need now.

His gloating smile should raise my hackles. Instead I want to draw him back in and make him show me. Caden grabs my skirt and tugs me his direction.

"I like the way you look in my jersey." Caden slides his finger over a mark on my neck. I lean into his touch, longing for more. His green eyes hold mine. "It's like I own you."

Pretty sure he does own me. My insides soften, and fuck if I don't want to climb on his lap and let him do naughty things to me.

Caden chuckles and stands with us. "We need to get that ass ready for prime time, starting tonight."

He grabs my ass. I release a breath and shiver. Apparently nice guy time is over.

"Still not on board with the butt stuff." I shake my head and walk over to grab my backpack.

"You came so hard when my fingers fucked your ass, little nympho. You're going to love having a cock buried in it."

My cheeks burn with heat as I straighten. Yeah, I'm not pressing that particular button today. I smooth down my skirt and then look at the hulking football players in my bedroom.

"I should make sure Mom didn't stay up before you guys come out." Taking a breath, I leave my room, shutting the door quietly behind me.

The house is silent, but that doesn't mean anything. I head down the stairs and into the kitchen. Mom sits at the island with a glass of water in front of her.

"I started the coffee." She sighs wistfully. "But I need to go to sleep."

She gestures to the coffeepot.

"Thanks. Why are you still up?" I try to appear normal as I grab a coffee cup and fill it. My gaze flicks to the hallway, not sure how to tell the guys the coast is definitely *not* clear.

"Rough night. I needed to clear my head before I go to sleep." She gives me a weak smile. "How was your night? Did you sleep okay?"

"Mmhmm." I sip my coffee to keep from having to say anything else. I have to figure out how to get Luke and Caden out of my house without Mom seeing them.

"You driving today, or is someone coming to pick you up?" Mom doesn't look like she's leaving until I do. This is way too complicated. There has to be a better solution.

I make my lunch and text the guys to let them know my mom is in the kitchen and not going anywhere quick.

"Maybe I should stay with a friend tonight?" I say it but I don't know how I'm going to sell it. We can stay at Luke's or Caden's with their bigger beds and no parents to worry about finding us. Of course, I doubt Mom would be cool with me staying at a guy's house. Especially with no parents.

"Kenz?" Mom looks suspicious, with good reason. Kenz has younger siblings who are little terrors, and their house—while nice-sized —isn't big enough for their family. And Kenz is messy, like the floor may or may not exist below the things on it.

I nibble on my lip, trying to think. "I was thinking maybe Penny."

"Penny?" Mom raises a skeptical eyebrow.

"Penny Wright." I pack my lunch into my bag. "She's this girl I started hanging out with, and she said it would be okay to stay with her while you work."

"Do I know her parents?" Mom's brow scrunches as she does mental gymnastics to figure out who Penny is.

"I don't think so. We never really hung out until this year, but if you want, I can ask her for her mom's number so you can call." I cross my fingers that it will be too much trouble. Maybe Penny will cover for me, but then I'd have to figure out how to pay her back. And that would mean punishment from Eli...

Unless I prove to him it's useful to have those girls as friends.

"I should probably have her number in case I can't reach you." Mom stands and stretches. "Okay, sweetie, I'm heading to bed. Have a great day at school. Don't forget your condoms."

I choke on a mouthful of the coffee I just took a drink from. Hoping she doesn't suspect anything, I say, "Oh, think I'm going to need more. And bigger ones too."

"Ha ha. I'll see you after school. We'll talk about your nightly arrangements then." She blows me a kiss and disappears down the hallway. The stairs creak as she steps on the third one.

A knock sounds at the door. My eyebrows raise. The others wouldn't come to give me a ride with Caden and Luke here. I walk over and look out the window at Caden.

"How did you...?" I open the door, and he steps in.

"Luke's waiting in the car. You ready?" He grabs my backpack and jerks his head toward the door.

I blow out a breath and nod. Fuck it, I'm just glad I didn't have to do a weird misdirection thing to get them out. I lock the door before following him to Luke's car. "How did you guys get out?"

"Secret, little nympho." Caden laughs low. "I'm going to go down the block and get my car. You ride with Luke. And behave yourself. You don't need to be punished today."

He grabs the back of my neck and kisses me before I can protest about behaving. It's not my fault Luke finds everything I do vexing.

"Fuck, I love seeing you in my jersey. I'm totally fucking you wearing that."

Pressing my lips together, I blush and hold out my hand for my backpack.

Handing it to me, Caden grins as he backs away. "Sorry, little nympho, just being honest."

I open the door to Luke's car and slip inside. His EDM plays low.

"Ready?"

Not even a little. Today is going to be hell. "Sure."

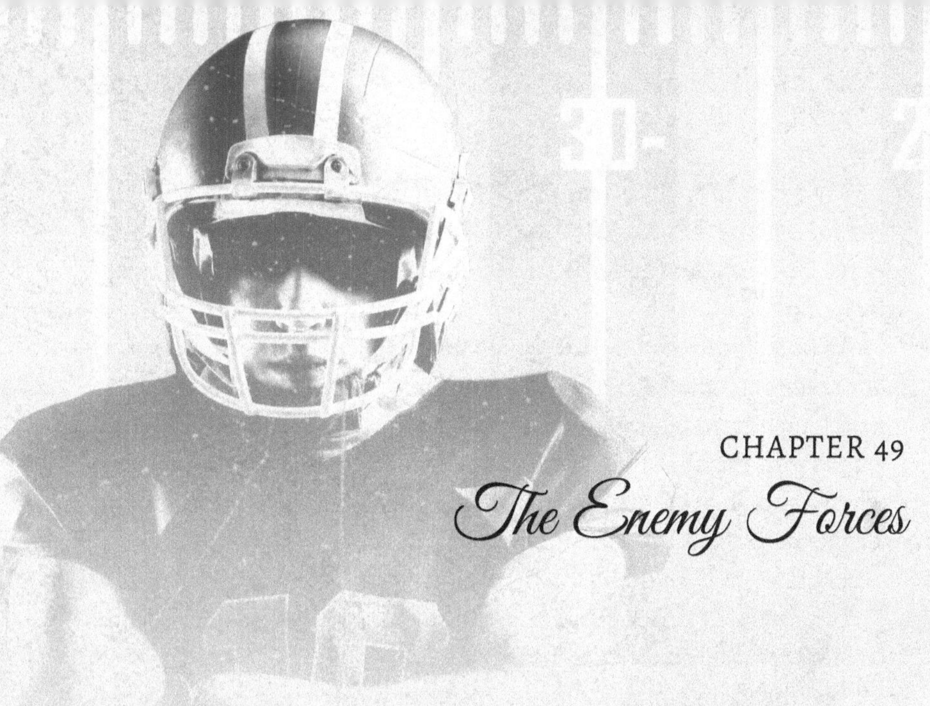

CHAPTER 49

The Enemy Forces

HARPER

When Luke and I pull up to the school, Nico, Eli, and Jack wait for us by the sign. As I move to get out of the car, Luke slides his hand under my skirt, clutching my thigh, holding me in place for a moment.

His touch makes butterflies dance in my stomach. I lift my gaze to meet his eyes.

He smirks. "I already let everyone know not to fuck you today."

My mouth drops open. What do I even say to that. Talk about needing to be in control.

"Your pussy needs to rest and heal." He strokes the inside of my thigh, making me want to straddle him and prove to him I don't need to heal, just to be defiant. But I'm also sore, so I guess I should be grateful. At least this once.

"Thank you," I say softly.

He squeezes my thigh. "No need to thank me, princess. I'm going to be pounding that pussy often and I want it in good shape to take me."

He leans across and kisses me, cutting off my protest. Heat fills me, and I worry I'll be the one to cross the sex prohibition line.

When he draws back, I nearly whimper at the heat in his eyes. This guy is an asshole, but I can't help but crave him.

My door opens, and I turn to see Caden leaning in.

"My jersey. My little nympho." He draws me out of the car and backs me against the side with his hands on my hips. The tip of his nose touches my neck, and he inhales. "My favorite smell is you and vanilla, little nympho."

My knees go weak, and all the people walking around us to get to school fade into the background. I breathe out harshly as his lips taste my neck inch by inch, until he kisses my jaw and then claims my mouth.

I fall into the kiss and let him conquer me. I don't think I'll make it a day without having one of them inside me. They all key me up and make me need them. My body knows what it wants, who it desires.

He draws away an inch. I open my eyes to his darkened green eyes.

"I can't wait to fuck you again, baby." He brushes my hair off my face, and his forehead touches mine.

I breathe in his cinnamon scent mixed with my vanilla soap. He may have marked my neck, but I've marked him too. Both he and Luke smell like me today.

Caden grins as he tugs me against his side and puts his arm over my shoulders to lead me to the others. Sitting on the sign, Jack holds his hand out to me.

When I take it, he pulls me in between his legs. He tips my head back and gives me a devastating kiss. My fingers clench his thighs as molten lava works its way through my veins.

When he lifts his head, he rubs his finger over my lower lip. "Can't wait for lunch."

What the fuck is happening at lunch? Before I can ask, Eli turns me and presses me back against Jack as he takes my mouth. Every kiss from them is different, but they all make me ravenous for more.

"Behave, kitten, we have just the game to play tonight." Eli tugs on the ring in my collar, pulling me into his hard body. The image of him naked above me, fucking me hard makes me ache. Fuck, I want to play *that* game again.

Jack strokes his hand down my neck, and a shiver ripples through me.

Nico taps Eli on the shoulder, like he wants to cut in on a dance or something. Eli smirks at Nico before he lowers his head and backs off. Nico draws me out of Jack's reach and pulls me into his arms.

"Good morning, sunshine." His kiss isn't the shy, thoughtful kiss he first gave me. It's a full-on nuclear meltdown now, making me clutch at his shirt and press my body against his.

"God, she's such a slut." The girl's voice isn't low at all, and her tone is disdainful.

"She's nasty." Another voice reaches my ears, making my stomach clench.

I draw away from Nico, tipping my chin down. He rubs my cheek as he glares over my shoulder.

"Fuck that noise, Harper. They're just jealous." Nico draws me in for a hug and engulfs me in his rain scent. I inhale and let him hold me and protect me from those insults.

The problem is, those words won't be the last. It's not a few girls who are mad or jealous today. I draw away, needing to stand on my own. I can't always expect a horseman to be there.

"Thanks, Nico." I smile, even though it's only going to get worse.

"Princess." Luke's voice makes me take in a breath before I turn to find his hand outstretched. I step away from Nico and take Luke's hand.

Just like the other days, Luke leads me into the school. The noise level in the hallway escalates as we walk through with the others behind us.

This is Nico's first day at a new school, but he already belongs to the most popular group of guys. I'm hoping at least some talk is about him, and not how the horsemen displayed me as theirs all weekend at parties.

Caden lifts me up as we reach their lockers. I unintentionally squeal, drawing even more attention. He lowers me in front of his locker and opens it with a grin.

I peek around him at the girls standing opposite us. They talk behind their hands when the horsemen aren't looking. When the horsemen look their way, they twirl their hair and strike seductive poses. Their skirts are short, and their tops show a lot of cleavage. Definitely looking to gain the guys' attention.

"Jack, you didn't call me this weekend." A blond steps out of the pack and pops her hand on her hip, giving him a disappointed look. She tips her head. The other girls watch to see what will happen.

Leaning against the lockers, Jack glances at me before smiling wide at the girl. "What was that, Bethany?"

She toys with her hair and pouts now that she has his attention. "You said you'd call."

Eli leans on Jack's shoulder as they both watch the girl.

"When did I say I was going to call?" Jack rubs the side of his lip.

"You always call, Jack." She smiles knowingly.

I glance at Caden, and he winks. My insides settle a little like I'm in on the joke. Even though I'm not.

"You sure you don't have me mistaken for another Jack?" Jack checks his phone. "Because I don't think I've ever called you."

"We should fix that then." She struts across the hallway to stand in front of Jack. "After all, you can't be getting what you need from your current options." She sneers at me before resetting her face into the seductress again.

Nico laughs from beside Luke. "Seriously is this the way girls flirt around here?"

Bethany's eyes move to him. "Who are you?"

"You don't know who he is?" Jack gasps, as if she's made a serious mistake.

"No, should I?" She checks Nico out. He's as fit and gorgeous as the others. A hint of interest sparks in her gaze. I don't roll my eyes, but I want to.

"Fuck, woman, you were just coming onto Jack and now you're eye fucking Nico." Caden shakes his head as he pulls me against his side. Warmth flows through me at his possessive touch.

"It's not like you all don't share." Her gaze flicks to mine with that same disapproving look. Like she wouldn't jump at the chance to trade places with me.

Jack laughs. "Fuck, you've got balls, I'll give you that. But next time you want to play like you know me, maybe you should actually know me."

Bethany falters for a moment. "You and I—"

The mirth vanishes from Jack's face as he steps up to look down on her. His easy smile changes to a cruel smirk. "Did exactly nothing. You flirted with me once and put your number in my phone like I'd call you."

"You might have." She lifts her chin, still trying to win this little game.

Jack holds out his hand to me. Caden gives me a push toward him. When I take Jack's hand, he draws me into his side. I'm not sure what he's expecting from me, but I press into him, enjoying the feel of him.

"Did I have time to call another chick this weekend, sweetheart?" Jack tips my chin up and searches my eyes with those gorgeous blue eyes.

Oh fuck, this isn't going to help my reputation at all. But I'm pretty sure it can't get much lower and I'm not sure what new levels of punishment might be available now.

My cheeks flush with heat. "We were busy all weekend."

He smiles before it fades as he looks at Bethany. "I honestly didn't think about you at all this weekend."

Her lips pinch. Her mouth opens like she's going to talk back, but her friend touches her elbow. She shoots me a glare before storming off.

Yeah, that won't be the only showdown in the coming weeks. Pretty sure I'll be facing off without the horsemen at my side.

"Sorry about that, sweetheart." Jack draws me into a hug and rests his chin on my head. "Some girls just can't take a hint."

The lockers behind me slam shut, and heels click on the floor. I close my eyes. It's easier when I'm just with the guys, but school is a necessity. Though Mom might be more open to homeschool if she knew who's been in my bed the last couple nights.

Luke steps in close. "If you're finished?"

I lift my head, but his question is to Jack. Jack releases me and chucks me under the chin.

"See you in second."

Luke holds his hand out, and I take it as we head to first. I don't know what today holds for me, but somehow I think I just got a taste. And fuck, is it going to be bitter.

"How are you holding up?" Kenz asks as I drop into the seat next to her in art.

I sigh. "A few *whores,* whispered *sluts,* and a lot of flirting with the horsemen."

"What?" Kenz looks confused.

"That's what I've had to deal with so far. So overall not bad for a first day as the horsemen's whore." I pull out my notebook.

"Come on, sunshine, it can't be all that bad." Nico stands next to our table with a smile. I want to tackle hug him and let him keep the mean girls away from me.

He sets his stuff next to mine and grabs a chair. He nods to Kenz. "How's it going, Kenz?"

"Good." She seems surprised and alert by his presence.

"You can relax." I laugh. "He's not a growly horseman. He's my friend."

I reach out and tug on the hair hanging into his eyes. He dips his head and grins. Little butterflies scatter in my stomach.

Penny and Nat walk in. I go still, waiting to see what they'll do. Yesterday I couldn't even meet their eyes after what happened in the bathroom.

"Hey, Harper." Penny smiles like everything is good.

Nat gives me a nod as they pass.

I blow out a breath. Guess they're doubling down. Or maybe they genuinely like me? Wouldn't that be a trip.

"What happened with the leeches?" Kenz glances back at them. Penny smiles and gives her a little wave.

"They came to the coffee shop yesterday to study. The guys ignored them. And Eli punished me for letting them use me to get to them." I squirm in my seat remembering the punishment. It reminds me of this morning. I lean into Kenz to whisper, "I might try to use Penny to stay at Caden's or Luke's instead of my house."

Tanner strolls in. His blond hair is perfectly styled, and his blue eyes fix on me before they shift to Nico. Of course, neither of us did anything wrong to him—even a perceived wrong—so I'm not sure why he glares at Nico.

What he did to Ava was so much worse than what they did to him.

He heads to the back of the class without saying a word to me, and I release the breath I held. I'm not sure I wouldn't have gone off. He used Caden's sister to get back at them and didn't own up to the consequences that never should have happened.

"All right, class." Ms. Sullivan comes into the classroom and shuts the door. Her gaze settles on Nico. "Nico Lee, correct?"

"Yes, ma'am." Nico sits up straighter.

"Glad to have you in class." Ms. Sullivan smiles and claps her hands, looking around the room. "Okay, we're splitting up into partners for the next few weeks of class."

The class buzzes with everyone asking their friends to be their partners. Nico gives me a sly smile that makes me cross my legs. Usually I'd pick Kenz.

"Not so fast." Ms. Sullivan holds her hands up. "You don't get to choose. In real life, you work with whoever you're assigned to. So you get a group project and life lesson in one."

Groans fill the room.

"So you don't think I'm playing favorites." Ms. Sullivan holds up a basket filled with paper strips. "I'll choose two names, and that's your partner."

This could be really good or really bad. There's a group of girls to the side who have been giving me the stink eye all class. That could be awful. And then there's Nat and Penny, who are at least nice to my face. It would be awesome to work with Nico or Kenz.

"MacKenzie and Natalie." Ms. Sullivan puts the papers to the side after reading them. Okay, maybe Nico?

"Nico and Angela."

Fuck.

I glance over at the girl, who preens at Nico. Angela Harris is a bombshell. Blond hair, hazel eyes, hourglass figure. Pretty sure she's slept with at least two of the horsemen. And by the way she gives Nico a little finger wave, she wants to add to that count.

"Tanner and Harper."

Shit. My eyes widen. I look up at Ms. Sullivan, but she's moved on. Shit.

Nico's jaw ticks as he glances back at Tanner. I don't think Ms.

Sullivan will care that my boyfriends hate Tanner Lewis and let me change partners. She keeps reading off names until she finishes. Dread pools in my stomach.

"Okay, now I want everyone to sit by their partners for the rest of the month. Make it quick."

Kenz and Nico stand. Kenz squeezes my shoulder before she goes back to where Penny and Nat sit. Nico doesn't move as Tanner comes up to take Kenz's seat.

"Nico," Angela calls out and waves her hand, like he couldn't see her.

"You good?" Nico's dark eyes search mine.

I shrug. I don't really have a choice. This guy threatened me. Kind of. It would be a lot to explain to Ms. Sullivan. Penny already stands at the teacher's desk, gesturing toward William Frank.

He's almost as invisible as I was. Brown messy hair and blue eyes behind black-rimmed glasses. He's a smaller guy, but still cute. As far as I know, he has no social standing. I'm not sure what Penny's problem is with him.

But hell, I'd swap with Penny.

Just as I stand to go see if I can swap, Ms. Sullivan clears her throat. "No changes. For any circumstance."

Penny sighs and stomps over to the table with William, sitting as far away as possible.

Nico squeezes my hand before he heads over to Angela. Tanner sits, facing forward, ignoring me. That works for me. I can't get in trouble with the horsemen if I don't engage with him. Not that I should get in trouble for being assigned to work with Tanner. But I'm sure Luke will find a way to make it my fault.

In fact, I'm pretty sure Luke would enjoy punishing me.

CHAPTER 50

New Information

HARPER

Ms. Sullivan explains the project, taking her time to give detailed information about what she's looking for and how she wants us to proceed. It's a series of drawings of something in nature, like flowers or trees or animals, but each one should have a piece of both artists in it.

Basically she should be able to tell I added this element and my partner added that one. We have all month to work on it in class, but the art studio will be open after school to work on it as well.

"Get to know your partner. They're going to be your new best friend for the next month." Ms. Sullivan claps her hands like everyone should be happy. Pretty sure no one is happy about this deal.

I release a breath. The guys won't be okay with this. Especially if I have to work alone with Tanner after school while they have football practice.

Glancing over at Nico and Angela, I see him introducing himself. It's hard to remember he's new to a lot of our classmates. How weird is it being back here and having to get reacquainted with everyone?

"Wishing you got to work with a horseman?" Tanner bites out.

My blood boils. I didn't see the asshole before this weekend, but now that he's shown his colors, I won't forget.

"Anyone would be better than you." I turn to Tanner and don't drop my gaze from his. I'm not about to dismiss what he said about me. He only wanted to use me to get to the horsemen. Message received. Just like Caden's sister, I'm a means to an end and I'm not about to be used that way.

"I didn't mean to come off as a dick on Sunday." He thrusts his hand through his blond hair. His blue eyes are soft when he looks at me. "Those guys just rile me up. After what they did to my sister—"

"What about what you did to Caden's sister?" I press my lips together and cross my arms over my chest. "At least your sister wanted it, and they protected her."

The softness bleeds from his eyes. Tanner's smile grows. He runs his fingers over his lips, giving me an assessing look. "They gave you the story, huh? Impressive. I figured they'd tell you to stop hanging out with me and that would be the end of it."

Fuck him. I don't say a word.

"I was sure I could charm you back into hating them with me. Maybe even convince you to give your virginity to me to thwart them. But if that didn't work out, it won't be long before one of them slips up and you'll be looking for a revenge fuck." Tanner winks, making my stomach churn. "I'm more than willing to gloat over fucking their favorite toy."

My mouth opens and closes. Ms. Sullivan is too far away to have heard him. I'll make sure Kenz knows about his threats and if I have to work late with him, hopefully she'll be here to help me.

"We should focus on our work." I take out my sketchpad. It's open to my sketch of Luke sleeping. I flip the page to a blank one.

"Nice, but he could use some devil horns. Maybe a forked tongue." Tanner leans back in his chair. His gaze flows over my body like he wants me. "Gotta get the details right."

"He didn't even do anything to you." I can't help but defend Luke this one time. He definitely didn't fuck Tanner's sister.

"Ah, but they all got me kicked off the football team and pushed me down to being a nobody." He leans forward on his desk, and his finger traces mine where it rests on the table. I jerk it away. "You know all about that though, don't you?"

"I don't know what you're talking about." I turn the page again and make a list of the things Ms. Sullivan mentioned as ideas. Anything to stop this conversation.

"If anyone understands what they can do to a person, it's you, Harper." He leans in almost too close. His cologne isn't heavy, but it's nauseating because it's on him. "You hid from them for good reason. What they've done to you so far this year..."

Shaking his head, he brushes his arm against mine. "How many people would put up with being spanked in the cafeteria and paraded around as their conquest? Don't you want to get back at them? Make them pay for what they've done to you?"

A week ago? Yeah.

Right now? No.

They wanted my body, and I've given it to them. They still want me. And I want them. It's temporary. An experience I'll never forget. Just this year. Then all of this will go away, and we'll start our lives far from each other.

"Or did they finally make you their whore?" Tanner's disdain comes through in his voice. "Did they fuck your brains and willpower out of you?"

I glare at him. I have no power though. Not really. I could tell the horsemen what he said, but then who would be the one in trouble?

Me? I'm sure Luke would find a way to punish me for being Tanner's partner in art.

Caden would rip through Tanner for what he did to his sister. If I told him what Tanner said, would it set him off?

If Caden attacked him, would Tanner press charges? Tanner has his own rich parents to help bail him out, and may not be willing to drop charges for the right price. I can't let that happen to Caden.

I need to tell Nico not to tell the others. Stop him from fueling this war. I'll do what it takes to get along with Tanner and finish the project within the classroom time.

"We need to focus on our project, and that doesn't require talking about other people. If you have a problem with that, we can go to Ms. Sullivan, and I can explain why you're the lowest piece of crap in this class."

He chuckles. His thigh brushes mine under the table. "You got a little bite now, don't you?"

Jerking my leg away from his, I shake my head and continue to write ideas down.

"I do like a girl who fights back." His words make me lift my gaze to his.

I bet he does. I see it in his eyes. The monster lurking in the deep, hiding.

He might come off as a good guy in the beginning, but I've been with monsters long enough to notice his darkness. The darkness in the horsemen doesn't scare me like the darkness in Tanner though.

He won't take no for an answer. He wouldn't let me choose. Not like they did.

"Anything to get back at the horsemen?" I scoot away from him. His entire demeanor gives me the chills. Every instinct in my body screams to get away from him.

Stay focused on the art project.

He smirks. "You have no idea."

Nico

"So you transferred back?" Angela bats her eyelashes as I try to figure out what Tanner says to Harper.

She's stiff and uncomfortable. I wish Ms. Sullivan hadn't disappeared into the back. I need to tell the guys about this turn of events. Given their reaction to Tanner on Sunday, they won't like it.

Angela's hand lands on my thigh. "I didn't know there was a fifth horseman."

"Take your hand off me." I speak in a low tone, but make it clear I'm not playing with her. The rule is we can't touch another girl. I'd prefer not to be manhandled by my art partner.

She giggles and tosses her hair over her shoulder. "I'm just trying to get to know you. You should ask Caden and Jack about me. Oh, Eli and I get along too."

"Not Luke?" I arch an eyebrow. She didn't get a chance to collect them all? Poor girl.

"Sadly, no. Sidney told me to back off." Angela shrugs. "She threatened to make me a social outcast, so I didn't pursue him. That bitch doesn't play."

I figured that out without Sidney saying a word. Those cheerleaders have a superiority complex. I noticed Hannah wore my jersey today. She didn't look happy about it. She glared at Harper in the hallway.

Guess Hannah got over whatever little crush she had on me when she couldn't get me to rise to her attention.

"So have you guys fucked Harper yet?" Angela leans into me conspiratorially. "I mean, she's a virgin, not a saint."

I lean back in my chair and study the overdone doll next to me. Her hair is curled, and she wears more makeup than Harper. Her outfit is almost a size too small for her, emphasizing her breasts and hips.

I can see why the guys would have used her to scratch an itch. She's got a nice body and if she's this forward, she'd make for an easy lay. She smiles when she notices me checking her out.

"You aren't part of the whole deal with her anyway, right?" Angela bites on the end of her pen. "After all, you weren't there the day they claimed her in the cafeteria."

"The whole deal?" I want to know what the rumor mill knows. Or what it thinks it knows.

"She's the last virgin in our class, so of course they had to make her think she's special. But obviously once the deed is done, they'll be back on the market and screwing all of us again." She pauses and gives me a pouty smile. "But not me. I'm ready for fresh blood."

Her breast brushes against my arm. I ignore it.

"Where did you get your information?" That's not the deal as I know it or as Harper knows it. Who's giving this girl those ideas?

"Hannah and Ashley were talking in gym class last week." Angela twirls her hair. "Besides, even if she puts out, she can't be as good as those of us with experience."

Yeah, I'm not going to even justify that with an answer. She doesn't seem to mind and continues on.

"Look, the girls in this school understand the pecking order. We're lucky the top bitches let us play with their men to keep them satisfied." Angela gives me a flirty look. "One girl couldn't handle the full brunt of the horsemen."

I make a noncommittal noise, neither confirming nor denying. My gaze drifts to Harper. Her head is down as she works.

Yesterday was ridiculous. Eight times. I'm not sure what the others expect from her, but if yesterday is any indication, we'll wear the poor girl out.

Angela smiles slyly when she catches me looking at Harper.

"You know there's a betting pool." She leans in close. "I'd love the inside scoop. Some girls say she gave it up last week. There was a closet incident Friday..."

I pull out a sketch pad, wanting more info, and she'll just spill it all if I let her talk.

"All four of them had her in there." Angela's cheeks flush and her eyes darken. "Could you imagine being surrounded by them?"

I furrow my brow. "Not my kind of fantasy."

Though I've been in a similar situation with everyone in the shower on Sunday morning. Everyone naked and wet, with Harper in the middle. I can't wait to have her to myself.

Angela giggles. "I wager she lost it then. A quickie in the closet to do the deed. Then they could have fucked her all weekend. The real question is which horseman did it first. There's a bonus for the person who finds out the details."

"What's the bonus?" I ask like I'm genuinely interested.

She perks up like I'm going to spill everything. She practically wiggles in her seat. "A hundred dollars. The pot is almost a thousand dollars for whoever guesses everything."

"Who's in charge of this betting pool?" I glance over at Harper working on her drawings while Tanner does the same.

"It's schoolwide, but the guy banking the money is Grant Perkins."

I have no idea who that is, but I'm sure the guys do.

CHAPTER 51

The Mess Hall

HARPER

Tanner leaves as soon as the bell rings. I can breathe easy again, but I hang back to wait for Nico.

"Come on." Nico jerks his head toward the hallway as he grabs my backpack.

"Nico, wait." I need him to not tell the others about Tanner.

I catch Nico's sleeve and tug him to the side of the hallway, out of the main traffic heading to lunch. Students turn to look at us as they walk by.

A muscle in Nico's jaw ticks as he looks down at me. His eyes are heated. I'm not sure if it's because of Tanner or because of Angela.

"Promise me you won't tell the others about Tanner being my art partner."

He opens his mouth to protest, but I press my fingertips over his lips and plead with him with my eyes. This is important.

"It will only cause trouble, and there's nothing we can do to change it." I let him see my worry for Caden and the guys if they do something and it backfires. Tanner is a wealthy guy who has nothing to lose. He's dangerous.

I might have wanted the guys to back off in the beginning, but I don't want them to actually get hurt.

"You need to tell me what he said to you." Nico glances down the hallway, keeping his voice low.

I look down at the floor before meeting his eyes.

"It surprised him the guys told me what happened with Caden's sister. He's bitter and wants revenge and will use anyone to get it." No need to sugarcoat it. "But that also means he wants a fight. He wants the guys to target him. With Caden's rage, that will only lead to bad things. Let's deal with this and keep them out of it."

"Harper—" He shakes his head.

Dammit, I'm losing him. Time to pull out the big gun.

"You and I were best friends long before they came into our lives." I press my hand over his heart, meeting his dark eyes. A reminder that if he'd stayed, we might have been more, and the horsemen would have never claimed me. We both feel it, but I won't press that button if I don't have to. It's wishful thinking and not realistic. "You owe your loyalty to me as much if not more than to them."

His hand covers mine on his chest. His gaze softens as he searches mine. Warmth fills me. "If it gets to be too much, I'll decide when to bring them in."

That just means I'll need to keep anything Tanner says to myself or Kenz. This can't ever get to the others. They promised to protect me, but I can protect them from themselves. Tanner won't actually do anything to me, so I nod.

"Show me the cafeteria." He takes my hand and squeezes it before we head down the almost empty hallway.

The cafeteria is packed as we enter hand-in-hand. A silence falls over everyone as we head to where the horsemen sit. The hair stands on the back of my neck from all the eyes on us.

I'm sure the gossip mill has done its job of spreading the arrival of the fifth horsemen. But they might not have caught on that Nico gets all the benefits. Including me.

Their eyes watch, waiting for the blowup, eager to watch my punishment at the hands of the horsemen. My anxiety wells inside me, even though I know nothing will happen. But I'm still nervous as hell in this cafeteria after years of avoiding it.

When arms wrap around me from behind and lift me off my feet, I shriek as if pirates are attacking and taking me captive. My hand drops Nico's, clutching at the arms around me. The smell of cinnamon and vanilla hits my nose, and I stop struggling.

Fucking Caden. His low chuckle stirs my insides.

Jack's laughter fills the silence as he wraps his arm around Nico's shoulders and draws him toward the table where Luke and Eli sit, talking quietly. They don't even watch the others' antics.

"You could set me down," I say over my shoulder to Caden.

His dark chuckle sends tingles through me. "Nah, little nympho. You're mine for lunch."

My cheeks heat even more. Caden circles the table to sit next to Luke and helps me sit on his lap. I cross my legs to the side of his and smooth down my skirt. When I lift my gaze to Caden's green eyes, he grins like we have a secret.

Thinking about last night, heat pours through me and my pussy clenches. We have a few secrets. At least from the student population.

"You guys have a problem." Nico sits across from Luke and glances around the cafeteria. I hope Nico isn't talking about Tanner.

Trusting Nico's problem is a different issue, I open my lunch and hand a sandwich to Caden before biting into mine. Eli holds out an apple. His smile makes me warm as I take it from him.

"What kind of problem?" Luke leans forward.

"Some guy is taking bets on when and how you all will fuck Harper." Nico's gaze flicks to mine with a slight flinch.

Huh.

Should I be shocked students in this school are betting on something, anything, the horsemen do? Including me?

I'm not. I've been here long enough to realize this is how the game is played. Taking a bite of my sandwich, I chew.

How much am I worth? It would be sad if my virginity was only worth twenty bucks. After everything I did to keep it and hide from these guys for years. Of course, I gave it up fairly quickly in the grand scheme of things, but I can't regret it.

Not yet at least.

"Who?" Luke is in his element, in control of the whole school. He doesn't even glance my way.

"Some guy named Grant Perkins." Nico looks over his shoulder. My heart quickens. "The pot is over a thousand dollars."

Shit, that's a lot more than twenty bucks. My gaze darts between all of them. Grant was the underwear guy. Is this his revenge? How does this get back at the horseman? Maybe it isn't revenge? Maybe he gets a cut?

"How did you find out?" Luke's gaze roams the room as he leans back like nothing bothers him, but there's this ticking muscle in his jaw. The same tick he gets when I defy him.

I don't like it when someone else causes it. My fingers itch to rub against it to smooth it out.

"My art partner, Angela something—"

"Harris." I draw Luke's gaze. I catch my breath at the warmth in his icy blue eyes. He looks at me like he likes me. More than just the pet some people claim I am.

When he holds out his hand to me, I don't hesitate. Drawn to this pull between us, I stand and walk over to him, taking his hand. He draws me down onto his lap, and his hand possessively grips my hip.

I rest my head against his shoulder as I look out over the cafeteria with him. Grant isn't at his usual table. I don't think he's in the cafeteria today.

Caden stands, drawing my attention. He gives me a wink before circling the perimeter of the cafeteria.

"Did Angela hit on you?" Eli asks with a knowing grin.

My brow furrows.

Nico smirks. "She said the only other horseman she hasn't been with is Luke."

Luke's grip tightens on my hip. I turn to face him, to watch his expression, to learn.

"Sidney told her to back off Luke." Nico takes a bite of his lunch.

Jack laughs. "Guess Sidney didn't tell her not to blow Luke."

What the fuck? It's like they don't even care I'm right here. A different heat floods me. It's bad enough to know they have a lot of experience.

Luke's smirk is the icing on the cake and makes me attempt to stand, but he holds me tighter. His blue eyes capture mine, and he grabs my chin to force me to stay there. "What, princess? Want to find a closet and make me forget about Angela Harris's mouth?"

The others chuckle. Like I'm one big joke. Fuck this.

I press my lips together. The guys have sexual history. While I don't, they don't need to throw it in my face. When I try to turn away from Luke, he wraps his hand around the back of my neck and lowers his head a little, like a bull getting ready to charge.

I hold my breath, waiting for the inevitable. I cock an eyebrow at him in challenge.

"Are your delicate sensibilities offended by our words?" His hand squeezes my hip.

"Maybe I don't like that you guys have gotten around. Maybe I don't want to sit here and discuss that Angela Harris fucked Jack, Caden, and Eli and only gave you a blow job. Poor her, she couldn't fuck you all."

A slow grin grows on his face. His fingers tangle into my hair.

"What?" I'm still hot under the collar and I don't know what he's so happy about.

"You're jealous." Luke leans in and kisses me, just a quick press of his lips against mine.

I rear back. "I am not."

Fuck, I so am, but I'm not about to tell Luke that.

He leans in so his mouth is next to my ear. His soft, seductive cologne weaves around me, making me lean into the heat of his body.

"Next time I fuck you, I'll make sure you forget about every other woman I've been with."

When I push against his chest ineffectively, he chuckles darkly against my ear.

"Just what every girl wants to hear." I roll my eyes.

His fingers tighten on my neck, and I stop struggling.

"I only said I wouldn't fuck your pussy today, princess. Be nice or I'll have you on your knees."

He draws his face back so his eyes can meet mine.

Narrowing my eyes, I spit out, "Wouldn't you prefer Angela?"

Fuck, I hate myself in this moment. I just handed him so much ammunition against me. Sure, they're bound to me, but that doesn't mean they can't flaunt other girls in front of me. As long as the guys don't touch them.

I swallow, but Luke chuckles and rubs his thumb along the vein in my neck. My pulse quickens. Tingles rush through my system and make me soften under his touch. Slowly he lifts his gaze to meet mine.

Like the inside of a flame, his blue eyes smolder. The whole cafeteria disappears around us until it's just him and me. That night in my bed. The quiet in his dark car. His apology last night.

This attraction between us consumes me, making me want him even though he's not good for me.

"He's not here." Caden's voice draws me out of the vortex of Luke's desire. We both turn to him.

"Not here for lunch or not here at school?" Luke's fingers massage my hip, lighting me up even more.

"Lunch." Caden sits at the table and holds out his hand to me. He raises his eyebrow at Luke when he doesn't immediately return me. Luke helps me stand and swats my ass on my way to Caden. When I put my hand over the spot, I glare at Luke.

"Remember your place, princess."

How could I ever forget? I'm their property. I'm not meant to have feelings about things beyond how they want me to be for them.

Caden's warmth surrounds me as we finish lunch, but I still feel the chill of Luke's words.

CHAPTER 52

The Cover

LUKE

Her eyes are wide when she looks back at me.

Harper Davidson.

We generally run on a catch and release program for a reason. Girls get clingy. Jealous. They think they own us, but in this case, she does. She's got us locked down tight this year unless we want to go against our word and break our agreement.

After all, she's given us what we wanted. But I'm not done with her, and by the looks on the others' faces, they aren't either. I'm not sure where Caden's and Nico's heads are, but I know they're in this for the long haul.

Caden whispers something in Harper's ear. She laughs. My fists clench. It's so fucking effortless for him. She's effortless for him. Even at night, she curls up against him. Not me.

Her dark eyes lift to mine, and I raise an eyebrow. Her cheeks flush, and her eyes darken. Is she thinking about how I fucked her? Or about how I want to fuck her?

She clears her throat and looks down at her hands, holding the apple.

"I was going to ask Penny if I could say I'm staying the night at her house." Harper glances around at everyone.

"Why would you stay at Penny's house?" Jack shovels in a mouthful of mashed potatoes.

She blushes. "Not actually to stay at her house, but to say I'm staying there. I'm pretty sure Mom would say no to an all-male slumber party, even if it's only two."

It's not a bad idea and worth considering.

"Why not ask MacKenzie?" Eli asks. "Those girls will want something in return, kitten."

Harper's shoulders fall, and she sighs. "Mom knows Kenz's mom, and besides, it's not very believable. Sleepovers happen at my house because Kenz has younger siblings and a small house."

I glance over at the table of the wannabe girls. When one of them notices me looking, almost everyone at the table straightens up and poses, like I'd pick any of them to come over here. Last year, I might have. Toward the far end is the girl who talked to Harper at the coffee shop.

Eli meets my gaze. We were just discussing the number of clingers our girl will attract when they realize we aren't exactly trolling for fresh meat. We need to talk with the others away from Harper about the girls... and the guys.

Fuck those guys who look at Harper like she's open for business. More than a few have checked her out today, making me want to claim her again. Publicly. But they know she's mine. Claiming her again would make me appear weak, and that's the last thing I want to do.

My gaze flicks back to Penny and her friends. Those girls want something from us and are using Harper to get it. They aren't preening for our attention like the others at the table, but they want something. Everyone does.

If we can figure out what, maybe we can make a deal. However, that shit takes time.

If it means Harper can stay in my bed tonight, it might be worth not knowing the cost until later. Not having to worry about her mother in the morning would be nice, and the extra room in bed would be a bonus. Caden takes up a lot of space.

"Find out what she wants in return, princess."

Harper turns to me. "What if the price is too high?"

"Does your mother know Penny?"

She shakes her head.

"We might get another girl to vouch for you." I stroke my jaw as I glance around the cafeteria. We know a lot about people. We might be able to leverage some of Jack's work in our favor.

When my gaze returns to Harper, fire burns in her eyes. I resist the urge to chuckle. She's jealous again, probably imagining what those girls might want us to do.

"I'm sure Penny will be reasonable." Harper's words have a slight bite to them.

"Jack." I nod to him. He stands with a smirk and heads over to the girls' table. All the girls are on high alert as he approaches. They give him their coyest smiles. My eyes are on Harper as she narrows her eyes on those girls.

Some reach out and drag their fingers on Jack's arm or leg. One actually tries to grab his ass before he makes it to Penny. A little growl works its way out of Harper. Caden chuckles and turns her face to his before capturing her lips.

Heat wells in me as she leans into his kiss and makes a soft noise of surrender. Caden has this bond with her I don't understand. She wanted him to be her first and gave it to him willingly. Every first I got from her, I took.

Nico clears his throat, and I look over at him. He nods toward Jack and Penny heading to our table. Caden and Harper pull away from each other, but their eyes are darkened and their breathing is quick.

Her eyes find me, and she wets her lips. My cock twitches, but I'll have her to myself this next period. I keep my gaze neutral as I turn to Penny.

"Hi, Harper," she almost sings. She practically buzzes with nervous excitement. Grinning, she glances back at the table she left.

I'm not sure what this girl will expect, but hopefully it's basic and not something we won't do.

"Hi." Harper looks to me.

My chest swells, but I don't let it show. This she gives me. When she can't speak for herself, she trusts me to speak for her. It's a start. I lean forward on the table.

"You want to be friends with Harper." It's a statement of fact, but I wait. Penny glances at me and then drops her gaze to the ground.

"Of course. She's nice." Penny smiles, and her gaze returns to Harper. "She needs a group to help with the other girls."

She's not wrong. We can't do much to the women, especially if we stay true to our word. It's easier to seduce than punish. And we won't be seducing anyone but Harper this year.

"What do you want?" I fold my hands on the table as I look her over. She has blond hair and brown eyes. Cute, but not sexy. Her crop top covers more than most girls', only revealing a little of her stomach. Her skirt goes to about mid-thigh. She's one of the girls who was off limits because she had a boyfriend in previous years.

When I glance over at the group she came from, they all have similar backgrounds. Not virgins because of boyfriends, but they also never played with the horsemen for the same reason.

She crosses her foot behind her leg. Her cheeks flush pink. "Uh..."

"This is your opportunity to ask for something before we ask you for something," I explain. "We need your help. So if you have something you want, ask for it now, or we'll assume you'll do it solely to be Harper's friend."

What I'm saying is a trap, but our girl can't have clingers constantly trying to use her. It's better if she knows who they are from the beginning.

Penny glances over her shoulder toward her friends. "We do want to be friends with Harper, but..."

Eli leans back. Some of the anger brewing in him sizzles in his eyes. He'll punish Harper for this.

This is our world. People use us to get things. We take that into account with every interaction. Harper's going to need to figure that out.

"But?" I probably look bored, because I am. Everyone wants something from us. It's the way things have always been.

She bites her lip and glances at Harper. "We want to sit with you guys at the party on Friday night."

When Harper raises her eyebrow, Penny adds, "Just sit. I swear. We won't do anything unless asked."

Penny's cheeks flare red, and she doesn't meet my eyes.

It's not a huge ask, but it will make Sidney's group insane, which might stir up more problems for Harper.

"Your group will help Harper with the other girls if we aren't around?" I want her to know what I expect.

"Of course." She smiles softly at Harper.

"Harper." I turn to her. This is her ask, not mine.

Harper straightens. "My mom works nights this week. I want to tell her I'm staying at your house, but I won't be staying at your house."

"Oh." Penny grins. "Of course, that's no problem. You can give your mom Natalie's number, and if she calls, Natalie can pretend to be my mom. Just tell me your mom's number so we know who's calling. That's not a problem."

"I don't think my mom will call, but thank you." Harper's eyes flick to me.

I can't wait to have her in my bed tonight.

Penny rises to the balls of her feet. "Even if she does, we'll have you covered. Thank you for thinking of me."

HARPER

Lunch is over, and we've stopped at the lockers. That can't be the only thing those girls want, right? I mean, it's not a huge ask to have them cover for me, but sitting with the guys at the party on Friday night?

Is it some kind of status thing?

Eli slips his finger into the ring on my collar and draws me over into his warmth. I lift my gaze to his dark eyes.

"You know the rules, kitten."

If those girls use me to get to them, Eli will punish me. Being spanked and then fucked in the coffee shop bathroom didn't seem like that horrible of a punishment though.

"Yes." My insides heat and soften, craving his punishment.

He tugs my collar again and leans down so his lips brush my ear. "Tonight when you come over to Luke's, don't wear your panties.

When you get to Luke's, you'll give the panties you have on now to me."

I press my thighs together at the ache his words cause. His cheek slides against mine as he draws back and brushes his lips against mine softly.

"You'll do as I say tonight, kitten. Everything I say."

I open my eyes to his, seeing the banked desire within, and nod. Fuck. I squirm at how wet he's made me.

Eli presses into me. His hard cock rests against my stomach. I know how he feels inside me and how he tastes. I crave him and his dark desires.

"Perfect, kitten." He slips away, releasing me from his spell.

How am I going to survive the day without more than kisses and brief touches? Releasing a breath, I let the lockers hold me up as the guys finish getting ready for their next class.

Caden tips my chin and kisses me deeply, stirring the need always waiting for his touch. He draws away with a smug smile. I touch the heat of my cheeks. My insides already feel like they're burning up.

Nico closes in on me and cups my jaw.

"See you soon, sunshine."

When I nod, he claims my mouth. I burst into flames at the intensity of his kiss. We have a history and a connection I don't have with the others. I feel him all the way to my soul. It feels safe to trust him with my feelings, but the others... I need to hold my heart away. Enjoy the experience, but leave with my heart intact.

Jack clears his throat behind Nico. "We'll be late for class if you don't let her breathe."

Nico's lips curve into a smile against mine before he presses our foreheads together.

"Soon," he whispers and holds my gaze as he backs away.

Jack lifts me against the locker until our mouths are level. I wrap my arms and legs around him, and he grins before his mouth takes mine. He grinds his hard cock between my legs, and I whimper into his mouth.

He chuckles against my lips. "We'll make sure you go to sleep satisfied tonight, sweetheart."

His tongue sweeps into my mouth and caresses mine, making me throb. He pulls away and lowers me to the ground. My knees barely hold me as he pushes me toward Luke with a wink.

Luke holds out his hand, and I take it. It's weird that this is how he claims me. We walk side by side to the classroom. He's not holding me possessively with his arm wrapped around me, but almost treats me as an equal.

That thought bursts in my head as he presses me back against the lockers next to the door. My breath rushes out of me, and anticipation tingles through me, waiting for his next move.

His hand brushes my hair behind my ear, and an involuntary shudder races through me.

"Did they make you wet, princess?"

My eyes widen at his words, and I glance around us, but no one is near. I shouldn't worry about my completely trashed reputation, but maybe there's still a part of me that does.

I narrow my eyes. "Afraid you can't do it on your own?"

My insides flip at my words. Why on earth would I challenge him like that? Why is part of me sickly thrilled at the heat and jealousy in his eyes? Maybe because I need him to feel the way I do when they talk about those other girls.

"Don't worry, princess. I'll show you exactly what I can do to you."

He releases me, and I almost grab his shirt to tug him down to kiss me, but he leads me into our classroom instead.

As I take my seat, I can't help wondering have I always liked to play with fire, or is this something the horsemen drew out of me? And what will my life be like when they're done and I'm left alone?

CHAPTER 53

The Lure

ELI

I stand in the hallway as she comes out of her class.

"Penny Wright."

Her brown eyes are wide as she turns to me. Startled, like a little rabbit. I swear she wants to bound away, but I need to make sure she's not playing games with my girl. I don't have time for wannabes.

Vicky Martinez stops behind her, looking like she's going to stay with Penny. I raise an eyebrow. Vicky touches Penny's arm and then heads down the hall to her next class.

Penny hasn't said a word and just stands there looking at my chin.

"Come with me." I don't look behind me to see if she's following. She will if she knows what's good for her. I stop once we turn into an almost empty hallway.

Leaning against the wall, I look down at her. "You want to be friends with Harper."

She nods, still looking at my chin. Girls like her make me angry. They want us to want them, but if we show them any attention, they curl up into balls or run and hide behind their mommy's skirt.

"What do you expect to gain from it?" I wait because I know it's going to take her a hot minute to open up. When I look down the hallway, I see Ashley glaring at me and Penny. She's wearing my jersey. I'm tempted to walk over and ask for it back. But that would cause trouble for Harper.

Ashley meets my gaze, and her eyes narrow before she stomps away.

For fuck's sake, that girl thinks I'm her possession.

I don't belong to anyone. Except temporarily to Harper. I never promised Ashley anything more than a rough fuck, which I know she likes. Bringing my focus back to the nervous rabbit, I clear my throat.

"I don't have all day." I let my exasperation slide into my words.

Penny trembles as she dares to lift her gaze to mine. "Harper's always been a nice girl. But she didn't want attention, so we never reached out before."

This part I know. "So what do you get out of this?"

She blows out a breath. "Until last year, we were all in relationships, which meant dates and sex, but it also meant we didn't get to go to parties and have fun. So this year…" She gestures toward me.

"You want to fuck a horseman?" I raise a brow.

"What? No." Her eyes go wide before she blinks. "I mean, maybe, but not necessarily." Penny looks down at her shoes like she wrote the answers on them. "We want to go to the parties and be single our senior year. We want to be seen with the hottest guys because that's how you become someone at this school. Doesn't everyone want that?"

"Harper fits in how?"

"She has you guys. She needs friends. We can be that for her. You don't know what the other girls are really like." Her eyes bounce up to mine for a second before looking down the hallway. Finally she sighs. "You gave the cheerleaders power, and they've capitalized on it. They control us. Keep us in our place."

I kick off the wall and step into her space. She swallows but doesn't look up at me. "You want to take their place."

She's not strong like Sidney and the others.

"Fuck no." She steps back and finally dares to meet my eyes and hold them. "We don't want their power. We just want some of our own."

I nod. Power I can understand. "You don't fuck with our girl's head, or you'll need to find an alternative way to graduate."

Penny ducks her head and nods. "We don't want to hurt Harper."

I turn on my heel and walk to class. I need Jack to dig through these girls' lives and find something we can use to keep them in line or something that could destroy them. Either way, it will make me feel better about this whole arrangement. I don't trust them.

HARPER

"Her name is Penny Wright," I say for the fifth time, like it's going to change in the last hour. Maybe Mom thinks I made up the name and will slip up. "Do you want me to pull out a yearbook and point out her picture?"

Mom lifts an eyebrow at the exasperation in my voice. "How do I know this isn't just a ruse?"

"Honestly you don't." I swallow because it is a ruse. "But I'm eighteen, and being alone in this house while you work sucks. Especially after that night. So I'm being proactive."

I also haven't been alone in this house, but she doesn't need to know that.

"I don't know, Harper." Mom sets her fork on the side of her plate. "Who is this girl again?"

Pushing my food around my plate, I sigh. "Penny. I've gone to school with her since kindergarten, just not in the same classes. We've been in art together and have gotten close. We've hung out at the football games. Do you want to see our group chats?"

I'm stretching a little, but only to make Mom feel better. It's really not that big of a deal. "It's no different than when I stayed at the party the other night."

Actually, it's exactly like that, with the exception I'll only be sleeping with Caden and Luke, not all five guys.

"I guess this is what I'll have to expect now that you run in the popular crowd." Mom pushes from the table and takes her plate to the dishwasher. "I'm not sure if I miss the days you only had Kenz or not."

"I'll be fine." Though I don't know what Eli has planned for tonight. After the previous time he played with me, I'm excited to see what he has in mind. Before Jack drove me home, everyone took another turn kissing me until I almost needed a cold shower to cool down.

"Call me if you need to come home." Mom gives me a pointed look.

Grinning, I shake my head. "How about I just come home and text you about the change in plans?"

"I guess that would work." She leans back against the counter. "What's the plan?"

"I'm going to hang out with the guys to study and then I'll go to Penny's." Not daring to look my mom in the eye, I rise and busy myself with my plate. I'm still wearing Caden's jersey and I know she knows that's his last name on my back.

"All the guys? Not number thirty-four?"

Heat floods my face as I load the dishwasher. "Yes, Mom, all the guys. We're just hanging out. It's senior week, and the guys wanted me to wear their jerseys. It's not a big deal."

Unless you ask the Cheermonsters, and then it's a huge deal.

"I'm serious, if you need more condoms and don't want to buy them, I'll get you all you could need." Mom watches me carefully now.

I straighten and look her in the eyes. "I don't need condoms, Mom."

Not a lie. Not sure the guys would use them if I asked at this point. We're clean and monogamous, so it's fine.

"One of those guys will get under your skin. Passion can be over-whelming." She's not wrong. She shakes her head. "You need to be prepared for when it happens."

"And with all the condoms you've gotten me, I will be," I tease.

She glances at her phone and sighs. "I need to get ready for work. Give me a hug."

I step into her arms, and she holds me tight, stroking her hand over my back like she did when I was little. Her coconut scent fills my senses.

For a second, I relax into the feeling of Mom. Feeling like nothing could ever go wrong. That she'll always be here to protect me.

"Don't let those boys get away with anything." She pulls back and meets my gaze.

Smiling, I roll my eyes. "Way to be vague, Mom."

"All encompassing, not vague." Mom smiles and taps my cheek. "Knock 'em dead, kid."

She heads upstairs to get ready for work, and I pack for a night at Luke's house. We need to get Nico's jersey from Hannah, which I'm not looking forward to, and I really don't want to see her in Caden's jersey for the rest of the week, but we have a deal.

I figured we'd go to Caden's again tonight, but Luke informed me earlier we'd be at his place. My memory of his place is dinner with his father.

Shuddering, I grab my toiletries from the bathroom. Mr. Foster is intimidating and cold. Just like Luke.

I pause. Well, kind of like Luke. There are moments with Luke that don't feel cold or intimidating. Little moments I want to capture and hold onto, because they're fleeting and don't always feel real even as they happen.

I grab my bag and my backpack. As I head down the stairs, I call out, "Good night, Mom. I love you."

"Love you! Be safe." Her voice comes from her room.

When I leave the house, the sky is definitely dimming. But it's still light out as I throw my things into the passenger seat. Something makes a scraping noise. My heart stops as I spin around.

Nothing's there. I clutch my keys in my hand so hard it hurts.

I'm alone out here. I scan the area, but nothing moves. The neighborhood is as quiet as it usually is.

Fuck. It's fine. Probably a small animal. I shake it off and round the car to slide into the driver's seat.

Butterflies fill my gut as I start my car and pull out of the driveway.

Once again, I'm willingly going to a horseman's house. It still feels weird and forbidden. When I pull up to Luke's house and into the open garage spot he promised would be waiting for me, I drag in a breath and press my hand to my stomach to calm my nerves.

When the garage door goes down, I jump and clutch at the steering wheel. My eyes search and find Luke striding toward me. The butterflies riot. Everything about Luke is a teenage girl's wet dream.

He's hot and confident and commanding. Everything he does has purpose. His hair is slicked back from his shower after practice. His blue eyes capture and hold mine as he opens my car door.

"Let's go." He jerks his head toward the door he came from.

Drawing in a breath, I release it. I've been alone with Luke before. I shouldn't be nervous. But of all the horsemen, he's still the one who intimidates me the most.

When I grab my things off the seat, he takes them from me before I can protest or get out of the car. As I stand and close the car door, he turns and walks.

Following, I glance all around. The garage has multiple cars, most of which have covers over them. I smooth my skirt down, self-conscious without panties on. Defying Eli didn't even pop into my head.

If Luke had commanded it, I probably would have done something like I did last time. But Eli doesn't want my defiance. I'm sure he'd punish me for it, but defiance lights Luke up better than most things. He'd prefer to conquer me than have me submit meekly.

We walk through the darkened house. I saw a little of it when I was here before, but I'm curious to see where Luke grew up. It's dark and tastefully designed with absolutely no heart in it. It's beautiful and cold. When we reach the stairs, I hesitate. I didn't think about being alone with Luke in his bedroom.

Luke stops and turns back to me. I back up a step. I'm not sure why. Self-preservation? But then his eyes soften, and he holds his hand out to me.

Little moments.

Unable to resist, I take his hand, and we walk up the stairs. He leads me down the hallway and into a room I recognize from the webcam. His scent is heavy here. It fills me, making my insides flame higher.

Luke sets my stuff on the chair in the corner and returns to me still in the doorway. "What's wrong, princess? Shy?"

It's a challenge, and everything in me wants to answer it.

"Not particularly." I shrug and look up at him through my lashes. All day they've touched me and keyed me up. This will be my first opportunity to do something about it.

Grabbing my arm, he tugs me out of the doorway. Pushing me

against the wall, he closes the door and locks it. I swallow, suddenly trapped with him and not hating the feeling.

I get wetter as he presses against me. All hard muscle and strength.

"The others should get here at seven." His hand slides into my hair and tips my chin up.

My heartbeat surges. "But you told me, six thirty."

He smirks, lowering his lips to hover over mine. "I know."

CHAPTER 54

The Kiss of Death

Harper

Oh, shit is my last thought before Luke's lips crash down over mine. My insides buzz with anticipation. He crowds me against the wall, pressing every inch of him against me, including his hard cock. I throb with need as his tongue thrusts into my mouth.

Whimpering, I grab onto his shoulders, holding on while he takes complete control of me. He conquers and tastes my mouth like we've never done this before. Curious, I slide my tongue against his and electricity zaps through my veins.

Lifting his head, he presses his forehead to mine. "Take out my cock."

His eyes are warm pools as I search them. Is this really happening? Is he going to fuck me or make me suck him off? My pussy pulses in time with my heart. I lower my hands to his jeans and flick open the button. His fingers tighten in my hair when I slide the zipper down.

I wet my lips as my knuckles brush his cock.

His other hand falls to my bare thigh below my skirt. It brands me, pouring heat through me. Even though I want to close my eyes, I bite my lip but refuse to release his gaze. It's like he's testing me, pushing me. It's a dangerous game I'm determined to win. I slip my hand into his jeans and stroke his thick, hard cock through his boxer briefs.

He sucks in a breath before releasing it against my lips. He lifts his hand beneath my skirt to my bare hip. My breath catches, wanting him to touch me more. I push his jeans over his hips, and they fall to his feet.

I haven't done what he asked yet. His boxers still cover his cock. His eyes burn into mine. I'm going slow, not to waste time, but because I want to. I want to have some control over Luke Foster.

Shoving his boxers down, I lick my lips. His gaze drops to my lips, and I almost shout in victory. He looked away first. A small smile forms. He tugs on my hair hard, tipping my head back farther, and I forget my small victory.

"I should just fuck you right now." His mouth hovers over mine. Our eyes are back to being locked.

I run my hand over the smooth skin of his cock, remembering how he felt deep inside me as we held each other's gaze. My pussy aches with the need to come.

"Why don't you?" I challenge against his lips.

His smirk is the only warning I have before he thrusts his fingers inside my pussy. My lips part at the feel of his fingers deep inside me. I clench around them, surprised I'm not as sore as this morning.

"So wet, princess." Luke licks my lips and fucks me with his fingers, rocking them back and forth, flicking his thumb over my clit, making my body scream with need.

I slide my thumb over his tip through his precum, smearing it around. "So are you."

I lick his lip before pressing up so our mouths collide. Gentleness between me and Luke isn't really a thing. There have been soft moments like yesterday when he let me take his cock for the first time. But this kiss is a clash of wills. Teeth clicking and tongues lashing each other, while we work to drive the other crazy.

Passion whirls around me like a storm, crashing over me, lifting me higher until I'm hovering on the edge.

Just as I'm about to come, Luke yanks his fingers out of me.

I protest with a groan in his mouth. His lips smile against mine.

When his hands grab my thighs and he lifts me up against the door, I grab hold of his shoulders to steady myself. Before I can even think, he slides his cock deep into me.

"Oh, fuck," I say into Luke's mouth.

I struggle to adjust to his size and let my head fall against the door, but he follows me, keeping us connected, kissing me as I throb around him. It's still new and feels odd, but so fucking good.

He slows down the kiss, making it a claiming instead of a hostile takeover. I sink into his mouth, giving in to the desire he awakens. He's all around me, filling my nose with his scent, my mouth with his taste, my body with his touch.

When I squeeze around his cock, he groans into my mouth. Power. I have it over him. I know it, but I don't know how to use it... yet.

But there's something more here.

He slowly withdraws before surging back inside me, and my brain explodes with the sensation. My insides wind up again as he continues the slow onslaught. Our breathing grows heavy, but we don't back away from kissing each other.

"Luke?" I whisper into his mouth.

"Sore?"

"No." I take in a breath as he keeps thrusting in so deep, I can feel him pressing against my wall.

"What then?" He lifts his head from mine.

My eyes open to his, and I lose my train of thought. The intimacy of this moment isn't lost on me. He has me spread open against the door, holding my hips as he slowly fucks me. My fingers clutch his hair.

How did I get here? Me, Harper Davidson? I search his eyes while he slowly drives me mad with the slide of his cock inside me. I soften my hold in his hair. His eyes close at the touch, like it feels good.

"I need more," I whisper, not knowing what to ask for because I don't know what I need. I just know he can give it to me.

He thrusts harder into me. A moan wells up inside me, spilling out my lips. Sparks float across my vision, and it feels so good.

"Like that, princess?" His blue eyes are so dark, I barely see the edge of light blue. "Harder?"

Yes, that's exactly what I need. I bite my lip and nod as he continues to thrust harder, pressing so deep. It's like he can't get deep enough, can't drive in hard enough. I want to feel him all around me.

The speed of his thrusts grows faster. I tug on his hair, so close to something fantastic.

"Touch yourself, princess," he whispers against my lips. "Slide your finger over your clit."

I touch my soft, wet skin and slip my fingers over my clit, back to where Luke's cock pistons in and out of me, stretching me open.

His grip tightens on my hips. "Rub where it feels good, princess."

I return my fingers to the hard button that makes me clench around his cock.

"Circle it. I want to feel you come on my cock. Do it, so I can fill you with my cum." Luke's eyes hold mine as I swirl my finger around my clit.

He thrusts in deep and hard, pressing on something inside that makes it hard to breathe. The pleasure swells hotter, thicker, dragging me up to a crest.

"Come for me, Harper." He leans back to look down at where I'm touching myself, and he's penetrating me like he can't stop himself. I follow his gaze.

All at once my insides explode. I cry out and tip my head back as my orgasm swells inside me. His nose nudges at mine before he claims my mouth, pistoning inside me until he groans against my lips.

Every stroke slides against my pulsing walls until he buries himself deep. I cry out into his mouth as his cock jerks, filling me. My pussy convulses around him, and I can't breathe. Slowly, his lips move over mine, exploring, bringing me back down to him. An aftershock ripples through me, and he groans again.

"Fuck." He drops his head to my shoulder as we breathe together, still connected, his cock hard inside me. Wrapping myself around him, I don't want him to pull out. I don't want to stop feeling this. Not right away.

He thrusts again, sending another ripple through me, forcing a moan from my lips.

"If you were mine alone, I'd lock this door and keep you in here all night." He lifts his head to meet my eyes. "I'd fuck you into tomorrow."

My pussy clenches around him again. I don't know what to say to that. That's not our deal. Not our arrangement. I want the others too. As much as I want Luke, I want them all.

"You make me want to misbehave, Harper." Shaking his head, he lifts me against him, his cock buried deep, my legs wrapped around his hips.

"Luke, we should clean up. The others—"

"Shh, let me pretend, princess." He walks into the bathroom and sets me on the counter between the two sinks. His cock is almost out of me before he thrusts back in deep. "I want to see you."

I don't know what he means, but every thrust builds the fire within again.

"Lean back against the mirror." He holds my hips while I follow his order. I don't even consider being defiant. I want whatever he'll give me.

He lifts my skirt around my waist. His gaze falls on the number thirty-four in blue on the silver jersey. "Take it off."

I lean up and strip off Caden's jersey.

"All of it."

With shaking hands, I lift my shirt off and remove my bra.

Luke takes his shirt with one hand and lifts it over his head, leaving him completely naked and me in only a skirt. "Fuck, you're gorgeous."

"So are you." I relax against the mirror, between the two sinks, impaled on Luke's cock. The fire inside burns brighter when his eyes meet mine.

He leans over me. His chest rubs my nipples. Arching into him, I suck in a breath at the jolt of arousal whipping through me. He captures the back of my neck and lowers his mouth to mine. "You're mine, Harper Davidson."

His lips take mine, and I fall into him.

Little moments.

Fuck me. These little moments will destroy me. He makes me want more, makes me crave more. This gentle stuff is an illusion. It has to be, because it makes me want something I know he isn't capable of giving.

He lifts his mouth from mine and leans back. Taking hold of my ankles, he puts my feet on the counter. "Stay."

His gaze drops to where his cock's buried inside me. He draws out slowly. The wet noise almost makes me embarrassed. He's so focused on my pussy and his cock. It's mesmerizing to watch him as he watches his cock fuck me, claim me.

He lifts his gaze to mine as he thrusts in deep. I catch my breath at the desire, at the possessive look in his eyes. Maybe this is what sex is always like with Luke. Maybe every woman before me felt this way. Got this look from him.

My heart clenches. He didn't keep any of them. He won't keep me either, not past this year. It's just words. It's just lust. All I can hope to be is unforgettable. A fond memory.

He presses his thumb against my lower lip and drags it down. "Suck it."

I open my mouth and draw his thumb in, sucking on it hard while his eyes hold mine. His cock thrusts in and out of my pussy. I can't help thinking about sucking on a cock while he thrusts deep inside me. Tingles burst through me.

"Touch your breasts for me." He draws his thumb from my mouth and lowers it to my clit, winding me so tight. When I don't move to grab my breasts, his heated gaze flicks up to mine. "Touch them."

I'm at an awkward angle here on the counter, my shoulders against the mirror, but I grab both of my breasts and squeeze them. Heat pours through me, making me buck against Luke.

"Fuck." Luke leans in and takes my nipple into his mouth as I hold my breast for him. Every pull tugs deep inside.

His hips move slowly in time with each draw of my breast. His thumb works my clit, making me squirm with the need for release. He supports me with his hand in the middle of my back as he leaves my nipple, spreading kisses across my chest before descending on the other.

Dragging my fingers over my abandoned nipple in time with his sucks, I rub his spit over it.

Lifting, he leans back. At this angle, I can see his cock thrusting into my pussy. How it comes out wet and glides back inside. How thick he is, and what it feels like gliding in and out. I squeeze my nipples.

"Watch my cock fuck you, Harper. Know I'm going to fill your cunt so fucking full of my cum it will be leaking down your thighs as the rest of them play with you."

His possessive words make sparks ignite beneath my skin. Part of me wants to be his, wants to be taken by him. Wants to obey him. I watch his cock sliding in and out of my pussy, building that overwhelming feeling again.

"See how greedy your pussy is? How much it wants my cum? You're so fucking tight, clutching at my cock like you never want to let go."

I can't meet his eyes, not now. Not this intimate. Yes, he's fucking me, but if I see what's in his eyes, it might change how I feel about him. This is just about sex. About getting our rocks off because it feels amazing.

But something in his voice... a longing pulls at me.

His thumb presses harder, and he thrusts deeper and faster, taking away all rational thoughts. Only the need to come remains.

"Squeeze your nipples."

As I do, my release shreds through me. I arch against him, wrapping myself around him and drawing his mouth to mine. My release seems never-ending, but he keeps fucking me through it until he groans.

His cock fills me with cum as he shudders in my arms.

I kiss down his jaw to his neck and rest my head against his shoulder as I come down, clinging to him and his warmth. What the fuck was that?

Our sweaty skin slides against each other. My skirt is the only clothing either of us has on.

When he lifts me in his arms again, my eyes flick up to his, almost afraid he's going to fuck me again and not sure how I feel about it. I mean, I like sex, but somehow it feels like I keep getting closer to Luke, and that wouldn't be good for my mental health.

He smirks, bringing me back to our reality. "Much as I want to show the guys how you look when you are well fucked, we should shower before they get here."

My skin is flushed pink, and we smell like sex. A shower is a good idea.

After turning on the shower, he sets me on my feet and lowers my skirt to the floor. I wish I could say the ache between my legs is soreness, but I know it's not. It's want. It craves Luke.

I crave Luke.

His blue eyes meet mine, and I catch my breath at the desire lingering in them. This can't last forever, right? At some point, sex will become routine. Not a burning flame that never seems to go out.

Fortunately I have almost a whole year to fuck Luke out of my system before we go our separate ways.

CHAPTER 55

Pick Your Poison

ELI

I'm the first to arrive at Luke's house. Well, second. The only reason I know is his bedroom door is locked and I can hear the shower running. Luke showered before leaving practice. Her car may not be in the drive-way, but that's so no one knows Harper's here all night.

I could pick the lock to Luke's door, something we all spent a summer learning. But I'll let him have his time with Harper, because that's exactly what I want. Time alone with our girl. I head down to the billiards room.

There's a large closet down here. Caden's isn't the only place we've played seven minutes in heaven. Luke's house may be smaller, but it's still larger than most of ours. But when he held parties, he invited a smaller, more select crowd than Caden's house parties.

Intimate is what I want tonight.

Setting my duffle down on the coffee table, I remove what I need, lining the objects on the table for everyone to see. Including Harper. I want her excited and nervous and so fucking wet.

The game I have planned will allow us each some time alone with Harper. I pause and look up at the ceiling. No sound permeates from upstairs. How long did Luke have her to himself? All I know is I'm making plans to sneak her into my bed soon. If this Penny ruse goes well, it shouldn't be an issue.

Except our leader might make it one. Sharing isn't in Luke's vocabulary. He might be a dick about it after last night.

"Hey." Caden glances around the game room. He arches an eyebrow.

I gesture to the ceiling. "In his room. Locked."

Caden grins and sits on the couch. He picks up a silk blindfold and runs it through his fingers. "Games?"

I smirk. "Always. Grab that chair and put it in the closet."

Caden takes the straight back chair and sets it inside. When he comes out, he resumes his seat and picks up the bottle of lube. Again he raises an eyebrow.

I uncover the silicone toy in the center of the table.

"Fuck." He rubs his hands together. Glancing at the closet, he jerks his head. "Do we get to watch?"

"Fuck yeah, we do." Jack strolls into the room with his computer bag. He drops it on the armchair and pulls out his laptop and some small wireless cameras.

Grinning, Caden leans back and grabs the remote for the TV. He puts on the game while Jack works to set up the cameras in the closet. I watch the monitor to help him position them correctly.

"I thought I'd never get out of there." Nico thrusts a hand through his hair as he walks in. "My mom wanted to know how my day was. How'd my classes go? Did I make any friends? I lied and said I had a big test to study for to finally get out of there."

"Does that mean you won't be able to play long?" Caden gives him a cocky grin. Like that guy needs more alone time with Harper. The bastard gets to sleep here tonight. With her again.

Nico takes a seat beside Caden and glances over the items on the coffee table. "I'm here to play as long as we can."

A low murmur of voices reaches us, and we all turn to watch the doorway. Harper pauses as she enters the room. Her brown eyes are wide and her hair damp around her shoulders. She scans the room. When she sees all of us, her cheeks flush pink.

Luke places his hand on her back and leads her forward. His hair is also damp, and he's more relaxed than I've seen him in a while. We should definitely lock those two together when they get riled up. I'm all about our leader getting fucked as long as he doesn't mess up what we have with Harper.

"Come here, kitten." I hold my hand out, and she walks to me. I love when she obeys me. Luke sits next to Caden on the couch, settling in like he doesn't have a care in the world.

When her hand slips into mine, I draw her forward to stand between my knees. She's soft and pliant right now. Today, she wore Caden's jersey. I can't wait to see her wearing mine.

"What time is the exchange?" Nico refers to swapping jerseys with the cheerleaders.

"In about twenty minutes," Luke says. "Sidney texted she'd make the exchange."

Caden stands and comes up behind Harper. She shivers as his hands find her hips and leans into his warmth.

"That doesn't leave me a lot of time." He tightens his hands on her hips. But before he draws her away, I hold up a hand.

"Wait, please." I lift my gaze to Harper's. Her eyes have darkened already. "Lift your skirt, kitten."

Did she obey me?

Her cheeks flush pink as she raises her skirt, showing me her lack of panties. Her bare pussy makes me want to lean forward and kiss it. Instead, I hold out my hand.

"They're upstairs." Her voice is low.

I glance at Caden, who slides his hands under Harper's skirt and onto her thighs. She sucks in a breath. He gives me a smirk before he buries a finger in her pussy. She moans softly, but he pulls his finger out and shows me the wetness clinging to it.

"Luke fucked you." It's not an accusation. Just a statement of fact.

She nods, and Caden rewards her. He thrusts his finger back inside her, and she gasps. Her fingers tighten around her skirt while his finger works in and out of her wet pussy.

"Sore, kitten?" I raise my eyes to hers.

With her lips parted, she shakes her head. "Earlier, but not now."

"You were supposed to bring me your panties." I pull down my athletic pants and release my throbbing cock. I've been hard since she stepped into the room. "But seeing as Caden has a time limit to fuck you with his jersey on, you can suck my cock while he fucks you."

Harper's breathing quickens.

"You like that idea, little nympho? You just fucking soaked my hand." Caden grins wickedly at me. Our girl is coming along nicely.

"Yes." Her voice is quiet, but her eyes hold mine.

I stroke my cock as he pushes in the center of her back to bend at the waist. Wrapping her hair around my hand, I bring her face to mine. "I'm going to fuck your face, kitten. If it's too much, what do you do?"

She licks her lips. "Snap my fingers or tap your leg three times."

"Good kitten." I tug her hair so her neck is arched back. "When we finish, I have a new game I want to play."

"Yes, Eli." Her words are breathless as Caden continues to thrust his finger in and out of her slick cunt.

When I lower her mouth to hover over my cock, her tongue darts out and licks the tip with a little noise of anticipation in her throat. A shiver works through me. Caden removes his hand and steps to the side as he lifts her skirt around her waist, exposing her to the guys on the couch. He slides two fingers inside her from behind as I thrust deep into her mouth.

Her throat vibrates around me as she moans. I hold her there, loving the feel of her throat trying to work around my cock while she grips my thighs.

Caden slowly works her pussy, thrusting his fingers in and out, and she rocks her hips with the motion. I follow his pace, lifting her almost all the way off my cock before sliding back in deep, nearly choking her with it. She doesn't tap out though.

"Jack, bring me the lube." Caden's words make her suck a little harder.

Jack hands him the lube, and Caden drizzles it over her asshole. She makes a noise of surprise before I thrust in deep, holding her there.

"He won't fuck your asshole, kitten. Not yet." I tighten my grip on her hair. "But he is going to open you up, because I have something for you."

She moans as he pulls his fingers free of her pussy, sliding them back through the lube to circle her puckered hole. I lift her head so our faces are level. Sliding my thumb over the sides of her mouth to wipe away the drool and brushing the tears away with my knuckles, I meet her eyes.

"Relax, kitten," I whisper. I cradle her breast in my hand, squeezing it, pulsing my hand around it to distract her from what he's about to do.

Caden eases his finger into her asshole. She pants as he slides it in a little before pulling out and then thrusting it in a little deeper. Her darkened eyes are unfocused, her lips parted.

I alternate between watching her face and Caden's finger until he has it pressed in all the way to his knuckle. She shudders and clenches my thighs.

"You ready, kitten?"

Her eyes focus on me. "Eli?"

"Caden will fuck your pussy while his finger stays buried in your ass. I'm going to fuck your face. Can you handle that? Can you take both of us?" I'm curious what her answer will be. Will she protest?

"Yes, please." She widens her stance a little, and I pinch her nipple through her shirt. She shudders at the bit of pain.

I search her eyes, but then nod to Caden. He draws his cock out of his sweats and lines up with her entrance. If Luke hadn't already fucked her, I would have told him to get more lube just to make sure she doesn't get too sore.

But with Luke's cum and as wet as she gets, she should be good to go. Caden slowly eases his cock into her pussy, just like he did his finger in her ass, letting her adjust to his size and girth.

Her eyes close and her lips part as she pants. He finally sinks all of his cock into her pussy. For a moment, he closes his eyes and breathes. Her quick breaths fan across my lips. I can't wait to feel her tight cunt wrapped around me again.

He opens his eyes and nods. His free hand slides around the front of her as I lower her mouth back over my cock. I hold her with my cock barely inside her mouth. She licks and sucks on me for a second.

As one we fuck Harper together, pulling out and pushing back in. Slowly at first, until we build up speed. Caden rubs her clit, but keeps his other finger buried in her ass, unmoving.

She moans low around my cock as her knees try to buckle.

"Fuck, you feel so fucking good wrapped around my cock." Caden grimaces as he thrusts back and forth. "I don't know how much longer I'm going to last, little nympho."

I'm not doing much better as she licks and sucks when she can while I thrust in and out of her throat. Her tears drip onto my thighs, but she doesn't tap out. Her fingers dig into my thighs as she rocks her hips in time with Caden.

She hollows out her cheeks around me, sucking me hard, and it's game over. My cum spills into the back of her throat as I hold her down over me. Her swallowing around my tip makes my balls ache as they empty.

I lift her head, and she gasps in a breath. "Open your eyes, kitten."

Her eyes meet mine while she sways with every thrust of Caden's cock into her cunt.

"Come for us again." I reach forward and pinch her nipple.

She cries out as she comes all over Caden's cock. Groaning, he releases deep inside her pussy. Caden draws his finger out of her ass before thrusting it back in.

"Ahh." Her fingers tighten on my thighs.

"Come one more time, little nympho. Come around my finger in your ass." Caden's cock is still buried inside her as he works his finger in and out of her puckered hole.

My hand in her hair holds her head up when she would have dropped it. "How does it feel, kitten?"

She pants and opens her blown eyes to mine.

"Being filled in three holes at once?" I clarify as she looks a little lost to the pleasure. "Did you enjoy sucking my dick with Caden's cock in your cunt and his finger in your ass?"

She's close to coming again. Her eyes lose focus. I tighten my hand in her hair, tugging to bring her back with pain.

"Answer me, kitten."

Her eyes squeeze shut and her mouth opens in a silent scream as she bucks back against Caden.

"Good job, little nympho." He thrusts his cock once inside her. She lets out a gasp before he pulls out and removes his finger. She doesn't move as he steps away.

I envy the others their view of her swollen cunt and the cum trickling out of it. Her ragged breath saws in and out.

"Kitten?"

Opening her eyes, she finally focuses on me. She releases her breath.

"Yes, Eli, I liked it."

CHAPTER 56

The Distraction

HARPER

Caden brings back a washcloth and cleans me up before hauling me upright. He lifts me into his arms and kisses me. My whole body is one big raw nerve.

When he lowers my feet to the floor, he takes his jersey off me, leaving me in my black shirt and black skirt. Giving the jersey to Luke, Caden takes my hand and sits in the chair, dragging me onto his lap.

"What now?"

"We wait, little nympho."

I glance over at the guys, but their attention is on the football game on TV. My gaze drops to the coffee table. A satin cloth covers something. Next to it is the lube and a length of black almost ribbon, maybe a blindfold.

Anticipation wells inside me. I'm curious what we'll do next. Luke's eyes meet mine, and heat pours through me, remembering his room. His lips tip into a smirk before he returns his attention to the football game.

Caden draws me back against his chest and nuzzles my neck. His scruff rubs deliciously on my sensitive skin. I squirm at the ticklish feeling. Jack glances our way and gives me a smile that makes my toes curl.

Now that I'm in this, having their attention is like a drug, making me high.

A chiming sound echoes through the house.

"Nico? Eli?" Luke stands with Caden's jersey. The other two stand with him, and they all leave the room.

I'm glad I don't have to go. The Cheermonsters don't like me, and the feeling is mutual, but that doesn't mean it's not exhausting keeping it up. I'd rather stay here and relax in Caden's arms.

Jack slips to the floor before me. I arch an eyebrow. What is he planning? Caden shifts me on his lap so my legs are spread wide over his. I don't think to protest when he parts his knees, spreading me even farther. Caden slides his hands up under my shirt and over my breasts, before he draws my bra cups down and teases the tips of my hardened nipples. Bursts of pleasure wind through me.

"We have to be quick, sweetheart." Jack leans in and puts his mouth over my pussy, thrusting his tongue inside.

I gasp at the suddenness and try to jerk away, but Caden holds me still, caressing my breasts. It doesn't take much for me to sink into the feel of Jack's tongue and lips feasting on the most intimate part of me.

Caden tweaks my nipples, sending bolts of lust to my pussy, and Jack shifts lower until his mouth is over my asshole. He kisses and prods me there with his tongue. Caden drops a hand to my pussy and rubs my clit.

Together, they work to push me higher and higher until I can't hold back anymore.

Crying out, I shatter and tremble in Caden's arms. Fuck, these guys are trying to kill me. I struggle to catch my breath as Jack sits back, wiping his mouth with his shirt. His hooded gaze remains on my throbbing pussy. A little aftershock ripples through me. Caden slides his finger into my pussy, then brings it to my lips.

"Taste us, little nympho."

I meet Jack's blue eyes and take Caden's finger into my mouth to suck on it. Jack's eyes darken, and I love that burst of power rippling through me. I may be at these guys' mercy, but I'm not powerless.

Caden removes his finger, and Jack kisses me, tasting me and giving me a taste of myself.

"If we had more time, I'd fuck your sweet mouth." Jack adjusts himself as he stands and returns to his seat on the couch. Caden straightens my clothes and repositions me like nothing ever happened.

The sound of voices coming down the hall tells me the guys are on their way back. It's not like the others wouldn't have watched, but I have a feeling Caden and Jack like playing separately from the others. I can't wait to explore that side of them more.

Eli

When we open the door, Sidney, Ashley, and Emma walk into the foyer.

"A bit excessive to drop off a jersey. Afraid to come on your own, Sidney?" I lean against the doorframe leading deeper into the house to prevent them from making themselves at home.

Nico steps forward with the jersey and holds it out to Emma. He's probably just as eager as I am to get back to Harper.

"What's the rush?" Emma smiles broadly. She steps forward and puts her hand on Nico's arm. "It's been ages since we played here."

Sidney steps into Luke but doesn't touch him. She's not stupid. "Word is you've fucked your little whore."

"Spreading rumors now, Sid?" Luke shakes his head and runs his hand through his dry hair. "What business is it to you?"

She smiles. "If you have or haven't is beside the point—"

"Are you going to get to the point?" Luke's tone is bored.

"It takes time to know what you like." Sidney's gaze turns seductive. "We know what you like. We have these little tradeoffs all this week. And we can be discreet."

"Is that why Hannah isn't here?" I ask. She whines the loudest about not being with Caden.

Ashley meets my gaze. "Hannah is up in her feels right now. She'll learn the new program."

"And what program is that?" I want to know how deep these girls are willing to dig themselves.

"The little virgin has to believe what you say or she might not give it up." Sidney leans back against the wall and looks at her perfectly manicured nails. "She doesn't understand how this game is played."

"What makes you think we're playing a game?" Luke smirks. "Give us the jersey and go. Unless you want to give back all of our jerseys, and we'll end this ceasefire right now."

Sidney straightens, and her eyes narrow on him. "You wouldn't appreciate what would happen to your pet."

"If anything happens to Harper, we'll come for you, Sidney." I don't move, but they feel the shift. Ashley touches Sidney's arm and shakes her head slightly. "We're busy. Do the exchange and get out. This isn't social hour. No one wants to fuck around with you here."

"Find yourselves someone else to *raise up*." Luke shakes his head. "We're content with our pet."

Emma holds out Nico's jersey and takes Caden's. Ashley meets my eyes. She's still mad about this, but there's also some resignation in hers. What we had was mutually beneficial and it wasn't about status.

"Fine." Sidney turns and walks out with the other two following her.

I step close to Luke. "When are we going to deal with them?"

"Not yet. They'll fall in line." Luke turns to head back downstairs.

"Fuck, I don't know those girls, but they don't seem the kind to back down, or you guys wouldn't have been with them." Nico rubs the back of his neck.

He's not wrong. But we can give them a chance. A small one.

HARPER

When Eli walks in, he raises his eyebrows but doesn't say a thing as he returns to his seat. Nico and Luke sit on the couch. Luke picks up the remote and turns off the TV. Now that we're all together again, I cross my legs at the ache forming there.

"We put Nico's jersey in the wash." Luke's pale eyes drag over me. Sparks ignite like he's touching me physically. "Sidney tried to push like we thought she would."

Jack scoffs. Caden rubs my leg.

"What did she try to do?" I'm not sure I want to know.

"They offered us playtime and they promised to keep it secret from you." Nico arches an eyebrow when I meet his gaze. My heart stops.

"I told them to fuck off." Luke glances my way. "I don't need them."

My insides turn to fire at the heat in his eyes. If I hadn't been here—I stop that train of thought, because part of being with them means trusting them.

"Eli." Luke touches his lip. "Tell us what you want to do to Harper."

All eyes turn to Eli. I swallow. I can't help my curiosity about what he has in store for me.

"Come here, kitten."

Caden helps me stand in front of Eli.

"Kneel. Sit on your heels."

I drop to my knees on the carpet. He stands and adjusts my posture. I take in deep breaths as he places my hands on my thighs and tips my chin down slightly. Pulling my shoulders back, he seems satisfied and returns to his chair.

"When I say kneel, I want you exactly like this." Eli puts his finger beneath my chin and tips my face up to meet his eyes. "Do you understand, kitten?"

"Yes, Eli." I note exactly how he wants me. Even though I have on my skirt and shirt, I feel exposed.

He watches my mouth, and the thought of how deep he thrust into my throat earlier makes me wetter. I didn't know if I'd like giving head. But every time I do it, pleasure rushes through my blood.

"When you do something wrong, I'll correct you. If you continue to get it wrong, I'll punish you." He grabs a long leather paddle from the coffee table. "Give me your hand."

I place my hand palm up on his, and he swats it with the leather paddle. It makes a satisfying smack. I flinch but don't pull away. It stings a little, but it doesn't really hurt. There's nothing solid in it. Not like their hands.

"Good." His dark eyes light from within. He sets the paddle down and opens the silk on the coffee table.

My breath catches at the butt plug sitting there. It's a small size. Kenz and I looked at an adult store online. We laughed and joked about the giant sizes. We both agreed we wouldn't even entertain putting those in our butts.

Honestly, I didn't even think about butt play since I hadn't even been kissed. But now...

That's going inside me. I don't know how to feel about it. Do I come when they play with my asshole? Yes. Do I want their cocks buried in there?

I scrunch my forehead as the answer doesn't come to me immediately. Their cocks are a lot bigger than a finger or even that plug.

"Tonight's game is seven minutes in heaven," Eli announces. "The rules are simple. You have seven minutes with Harper in the closet. The plug remains in her ass the entire time, but you may tug on it or fuck her with it. Cameras are set up, so we'll be watching."

Heat engulfs my cheeks. I guess I'm officially getting one-on-one time with everyone tonight. And pretty much anything goes.

This time my mother won't call to hurry me home. I'm staying the night. How long will this go on?

He nods to Jack. Jack clicks on his computer before turning on the TV screen. The screen shows multiple angles of the chair inside the closet.

Fuck, I'm starring in my own X-rated live show, apparently.

Eli clears his throat, drawing my attention back to him. "You won't be restrained, but you will be blindfolded. If the man who comes in wishes to reveal himself he can, or he can take you anonymously."

Take me? I swallow my nerves. They've all touched me. They've all fucked me. There's nothing new to worry about in that closet. Right?

"Stand."

I do as Eli says.

"Strip."

My initial response is to hesitate. Not because I haven't been naked for them, but because that's one less barrier between me and them in that seven minutes. I can't believe I'm actually consenting to this.

But when I glance over at them, I see the desire shining in their eyes, and fuck it, what they do feels good. My breathing and pulse quicken, anticipating their touch.

I'm not wearing much to begin with, so I take off my t-shirt and bra and slip my skirt down my legs. The guys are all dressed in athletic wear and t-shirts. My hands tremble.

"Caden, lie on the floor. Nico, sit in the chair with Caden's head between your feet."

My brows furrow. I thought I was going into the closet. What's this?

Eli takes my hand and leads me over to them. "Take out your cock, Nico."

My mouth waters, and my pussy tightens in response. He's hard and thick. I've only had him once, and that's not enough. I'm excited about the prospect of getting more alone time with Nico. Hell, I want to see what each of them is like individually.

Hopefully longer than seven minutes soon.

"Sit on Caden's face and suck Nico's cock, kitten. I need you ready to explode for this." Eli goes to the plug and grabs the lube. I can't tear my eyes away as he lubes up the plug that, while on the small side, is definitely bigger than Caden's finger.

Eli catches me and lifts an eyebrow, as if I'm purposely disobeying his orders. Fuck, I'm more than turned on by him. I lower myself over Caden's face. He grabs my hips and holds me above him. Anticipation makes my pussy drip and my mouth water as I lean forward to kiss Nico's cock.

He groans and threads his fingers into my hair. His dark eyes capture mine. "Hi, sunshine."

I smile at the ridiculousness. I'm about to suck his cock while I ride Caden's face, but yes, let's stop and say, "Hi."

Eli kneels behind me over Caden. The paddle smacks my ass.

"Ow." I reach back to cover my poor cheek.

"Get to work, kitten."

Get to work? For fuck's sake. I take Nico's cock into my mouth, licking and sucking the tip as Caden pulls me down. His tongue, teeth, and lips devour and explore every inch of me, setting my blood to boil.

My breath catches at how sensitive I already am. It's hard to concentrate on Nico's cock though when Caden's tongue and teeth are making a meal of my pussy. I stop moving on Nico, but he's got me this time. With his hand in my hair, Nico eases my mouth up and down over his cock. He's thick, hard, and large, filling my mouth.

Eli slides his hand down my bare back, chasing shivers through me. Too many sensations barrage me, making it hard to focus on any one thing. Caden grabs my ass cheeks and spreads them apart while he blows my mind.

Breathing out, I let go, giving myself into their hands. I relax into Caden and Nico and let them use my body how they want. It's liberating.

"Good girl," Eli whispers. His lubed fingers slide over my puckered hole, and I spin off into an orgasm. Caden tightens his hold on my thrashing hips as I suck on Nico like he's my only lifeline.

Eli draws my hair over my shoulder and kisses the place where my shoulder and neck meet. "Relax," he whispers against my skin, sending shivers of sparks dancing through me.

The tip of the plug presses against my asshole. Caden's tongue slides inside my pussy as Nico thrusts deep into my throat. I moan at the sensation as the plug eases inside.

"I can't wait to play with you on my own, kitten." Eli's voice is for my ears only as he rocks the plug in and out, pressing a little deeper with each thrust. I draw in deep breaths, trying to relax my muscles as it burns slightly, before my muscles release to let it in.

His shirt brushes my bare back. "Who will you choose to take this virginity?" He buries the plug deep inside me, and the dam releases again. Moaning, I come all over Caden's face.

Nico groans as he comes in my mouth, holding me down to swallow every last drop. Caden laps at my pussy with long strokes of his tongue as Nico lifts me off his cock. I shudder as little aftershocks rip through me. I rest my head against Nico's thigh while he strokes my hair.

Fuck, I'm not sure how much more of this I can take.

"Thank you, sunshine."

When I lift my eyes to meet Nico's, another shiver rips through me. His thumb trails over my lower lip. I kiss his thumb, and he smiles.

Standing, Eli holds his hand out to me. This is it. I can't deny I want whatever they're willing to give me. So I don't.

I take his hand, and he helps me stand. It feels weird with the butt plug wedged between my cheeks. I don't know what it will feel like if one of them fucks me with it in. I already feel stuffed full down there.

As it is, cum leaks down my leg from Caden's attention. His face is wet as he sits up, but his gaze never leaves mine, making my insides swell. He draws off his shirt and wipes his face with a wicked grin. My pussy clenches.

He's going to fuck me again. I know it and I can't wait.

Eli picks up the black silk and, holding my hand, leads me into the closet. There's a towel on the seat of the chair. Thank fuck. I'm already dripping wet, and by the time they finish playing with me, I'll need a shower. Again.

"Sit."

I follow his command with no hesitation, but hiss at the press of the plug in my ass. It doesn't hurt; it's just an odd feeling.

"Hands on your knees, kitten." When I do as he asks, he moves around behind me and quickly braids my hair. How does he know how to do that? "Close your eyes."

The blindfold rests over my eyes, and I reach up to hold it in place as he ties it. It's not completely dark, but I can't make out much beyond something right in front of my face.

The leather paddle smacks my thigh, and my hand drops to the smarting skin.

"Don't move unless told to."

The leather runs along the inside of my thigh before skipping to my stomach and then circling my breast. My breath catches as I wait for the flash of pain.

"I can't wait to test your limits, kitten." The leather disappears, and the door closes, leaving me in silence and darkness. Anticipation churns hot and heavy in my stomach. I don't know what they're doing out there, but it seems like it takes forever.

CHAPTER 57

A Taste of Pleasure

JACK

Eli comes out, but my focus is on our girl sitting on the chair. Her nipples are tight and rise and fall with every quick little breath. She's a time bomb waiting to go off, and I haven't had enough of her.

Everyone turns our attention to Eli. This is his game, so he decides how we choose the order. So many ideas of what to do to her. Fuck, I need some time alone with our girl. More than a quickie in the closet.

I'm all about sharing, but there's something intense about bringing your girl pleasure by yourself. It's easy to overwhelm a girl with multiple guys, but Harper handles it beautifully. Still, I want to have her one-on-one. No camera. No other guy waiting his turn. Just me and Harper fucking all night long.

"The bottle seems to be a good equal opportunist." Eli places it on the cloth on the table. "The timer starts as soon as the door closes. You'll have seven minutes to do what you want with Harper. Obviously the plug stays inside her at all times, but you can use the plug however you like."

He rubs his hands together. "At the end of each turn, return her to this position. If you come on her, please clean her up. We'll have a warm towel waiting."

It's easy to forget Eli can be as controlling as Luke. But I like the idea of the warm towel.

"Enough rules. Spin the bottle." I turn to the monitor, watching her. Her finger strokes her thigh as she waits. Is she even aware she's doing that?

"Fine." Eli spins the bottle, and I watch along with my friends as it slows. The opening lands on me.

I take off my shirt and slide off my pants before Eli can say a word.

"Jack…" he starts.

I stroke my cock. "Seven minutes. Do what I want. Minimal butt stuff. Got it."

Caden laughs and slaps my ass. "Hurry. It's going to be a long seven minutes for us."

I grin before heading to the door. Fuck, this girl gets in my head. All fucking day I've had a hard-on thinking about yesterday. Thinking about getting back inside her sweet, hot cunt. I can still taste her on my tongue, but I want to feel her on my dick.

When I open the door, she straightens on the chair. Eli always comes up with the best games. I turn to salute the guys before I close the door.

Seven fucking minutes. No time to waste.

"Hey, sweetheart." I drop to my knees in front of her.

"Jack," she breathes out.

"I like the way you say my name." I pick up her hand and put it in my hair. Her fingers tangle in the strands, rubbing against my scalp. When I kiss the inside of her thigh, she jolts slightly.

She lets out a nervous giggle. "I'm not sure what I'm supposed to do."

So many fucking things I want to do with her, but with only seven minutes…

I wrap my hands around the backs of her knees and tug her forward. She hisses slightly.

"Plug?" I've played with plugs before. Not all of them are comfortable to sit on.

"Yeah."

Rising on my knees, I take her breast into my mouth, sucking on her nipple while I cup and stroke her other breast.

Her breath comes out in a burst. She arches into my mouth, making me take more of her breast. My cock bobs against my stomach, eager and waiting, but I want her to want me. Not just be turned on by the others and need release.

I kiss my way to her other breast and take her other nipple, sucking, licking, tugging. I've only got a limited amount of time to work with here.

"Jack, that feels so fucking good."

I release her nipple and tug her face down to mine before claiming her lips. When she sighs into my mouth, I draw her down onto my lap as I sit back on my heels. Her wet pussy brushes against my cock.

"What do you want to do?" I ask against her lips, because while I hang out with assholes, I'm not a complete asshole. Harper lost her virginity yesterday, and both Luke and Caden have railed her so far tonight. So if she doesn't want me to fuck her, there are other ways to get each other off.

She lifts her hips and takes my cock in her hand. "Jack."

She slides her cunt down over me until we're flush together.

"Fuck," I whisper before taking her mouth. My cock pulses inside her tight pussy, but I kiss her like I'm not dying to drive into her until I come. I lift my mouth from hers and push the blindfold upward. "Open your eyes, Harper."

She blinks, then focuses on me. She brushes the curls away from my face as she searches my eyes.

"Roll your hips." I help guide her movement as she rocks on me. I could do this all night, but I've probably only got a few minutes left. If I don't get us both off before that time, I'll keep going, and they can all fuck off.

"That feels good," she whispers. Her lips part and her skin is flushed.

I roll her to her back and thrust in deep. "We're kind of on a time crunch here, sweetheart, or I'd let you chase your pleasure for hours."

Reaching between us, I rub her clit and begin a steady rhythm of thrusts. Her lips part, but her eyes remain on mine. I was right to say we should do her raw. Her pussy is the best thing I've ever felt wrapped around my cock.

Hot, wet, and tight. Even tighter with the plug in.

Panting, she arches up against me. I lower my mouth to her nipple and suck it. She cries out as her cunt convulses around my cock, dragging me into my release. I thrust deeper as I groan. My cock jerks, filling her with my cum.

I kiss her lips and lean down to her ear. "Next time, we'll take our time."

She smiles this soft smile that makes my chest ache. "Next time."

The door opens. "Time's up."

***

HARPER

I blink up at Eli as Jack pulls out of me. That fullness in my ass stays. He didn't play with the plug, but I definitely felt it when he was fucking me.

I'm not sure how this game will work. Seven minutes isn't that long. I almost feel like a fast-food place. Get in, get off, get out.

I raise up on my elbows as Jack grabs the towel from Eli.

"Give us a minute to clean up?" Jack gives me a cocky grin before saying over his shoulder, "It's not like you won't see what we're doing."

"Make it quick, Jack." Eli closes the door.

Jack grins. "That's my specialty."

"I wouldn't advertise that." I run my hands through his hair, trying to tame the curls back into some order.

"Why not? It works for you."

I laugh as he helps me sit up. He cleans us both up and kisses me sweetly.

When I sit in the chair, he brushes his thumb over my jaw before grabbing the blindfold. "If you need a break, just let us know, sweetheart."

His blue eyes search mine. This kind of attention could definitely make me fall, but I know better than to fall for any of them. They're not mine. Not really. Just temporarily.

Even so, I like Jack.

"I will." I cover his hand with mine.

He puts the blindfold back on and gives me a soft kiss. "I might be right back."

I smile. "I'll expect something new next time."

"Damn, you want me to be creative?" He chuckles.

I like that Jack lets me lead sometimes. To take the time to figure out what I like.

The door opens and closes. My hands are on my thighs as I wait for the next guy to come in. The anticipation is almost too much. The fact they can watch me sit here, waiting for someone to fuck me makes me wetter. I squirm on the chair.

The door opens, and for a second my breath hangs in the air, waiting to see what's going to happen. Not being able to see makes me turn my head, as if that will let me hear better.

The door shuts.

The smack of the leather paddle against a hand fills the space. I straighten, and my fingers tighten on my thighs. The scents of a forest and leather fill the space.

"Eli."

The leather drags across the back of my shoulders, and shivers race down my spine.

"We don't have a lot of time, kitten. I just want to gauge how you take it."

"How I take it?" The leather slides over my shoulder and down over my breast. I suck in a breath.

"Pain, kitten. You get off on it. It arouses you." The leather glides down my stomach, but I don't draw my knees together, wondering what he'll do.

My breath shudders in and out of me.

"I want to see what happens when you've had too much."

His words send shivers coursing through me. My arousal betrays me. It's thick in the air with the scent of sex.

"On your knees facing the chair, kitten. Hands on the back. Stretch that beautiful body out so I can mark it." His voice is a dark melody in the room. I do as he asks.

I'm curious. When they spank me, it makes me hornier. The leather paddle doesn't hurt as much as their hands.

Eli drags the leather from my shoulder down my spine. "How does the plug feel, kitten?"

He twists the plug inside me. I gasp. Fuck, that makes everything flutter.

"Do you know how much I want to fuck your ass with this, kitten? Watch you come from just ass play? But I've only got six minutes left." Eli sighs, and I feel his breath against my back.

The leather smacks on my ass cheek, making me clench around the plug. My cry of surprise morphs into a slight moan.

"Good girl." Eli's hand rubs at the sting. "What's your safe word, kitten?"

"Arrow." I clench my hands on the back of the chair, wishing his hand would move to my pussy.

"Don't be a hero, kitten. If you need to use it, use it. I won't stop just because you're crying." Eli's words drift over me. Fuck.

They never gave me an out when they spanked me, and that hurt. The leather paddle isn't that painful, so I'm sure I can take this.

A whoosh followed by a smack fills the room as he brings the paddle down on my ass cheeks over and over again. I lose count as he moves down my thighs. I gasp at each blow. My skin burns from the stimulation, and my breath comes out in pants as I brace for each new strike.

When he stops, I draw in a shaky breath. My fingers hurt from clenching on the chair, and my ass and thighs sting. His hand cups my pussy, and I cry out at how good it feels.

"Good girl." He kisses my shoulder, making a shiver rack through my body. "So wet, kitten."

His finger slips inside me, and I tumble over the edge into release. He thrusts his finger in and out of my pussy, keeping my orgasm going.

When his hand squeezes my sore ass cheek, I cry out as it takes me higher again.

"Mmm, that's a good kitty." He kisses up my neck to nibble on my ear. "I'm going to fuck you all night long when you sleep at my house.

Mark up your pretty pale skin until no one else's mark is visible. You'll be all mine, kitten."

I whimper because words won't form. But my pussy clenches around his finger and gushes my release.

"If I had more time, I'd fuck you." Eli's warmth presses against my back, and I want to curl into it. "But time's up."

The door opens.

CHAPTER 58

Whatever It Takes

CADEN

I swear this is my favorite show. Harper squirms against Eli on the screen. Her ass and thighs are red from his spanking. But she came beautifully afterward.

He lifts her to stand and lowers her onto the seat. She hisses at the press against her sensitive skin. Pain isn't my thing. At least not with women. I'll take a fucker out if I have to, but when it comes to the ladies, I'm good with pleasure.

My cock is so fucking hard right now after watching Jack fuck her and Eli spank her. No one's played with her ass. That's a shame. I fully intend to take advantage when it's my turn.

"Spin the bottle." Luke gestures while he takes a swig from his beer. He may act cool, but he's just as hard and wants to take our girl for another round.

The bottle spins and lands on me. Fuck yeah.

Nico sighs and slumps into the couch. I grin at him. The bottle's been an ass to me before.

"Don't worry, you'll get your turn." I stand and strip. Am I going to fuck our girl's pussy? Maybe, but I want to play with the toy everyone else has ignored. I want to make her come so fucking hard.

It's going to take maneuvering in the small space, but we'll make it work.

Eli comes out, leaving the door open. Harper sits in the chair with her hands on her thighs and that blindfold on.

"She's all yours." Eli sits on the couch and picks up his beer, drinking a swallow before his attention goes to the screen. Cocky bastard.

Grabbing the lube off the table, I walk across the room and close the closet door behind me. Quietly, I study her. Her fingers rub her thighs. She shifts slightly on the chair. I need to figure out the best way to do this.

A mirror would be helpful. I want to see her O-face. This is why I enjoy playing with Jack. I get to watch our girl while he gets her off.

"How are you, little nympho?"

She startles at my voice and turns her face in my direction. "Caden?"

"If anyone else calls you that, I need to know so I can make sure they never do it again." I lift her blindfold off, and she blinks against the sudden light.

"No one else calls me that." She blows out a breath.

She's beautiful in a subtle way. Not like Sidney and her group. They're all flashy, but Harper is pretty with her large brown eyes and full lips. Her body is fucking rocking.

"Stand."

As she follows my direction, her body brushes against me. I cup her cheek, and she leans into my touch, closing her eyes like it's the best thing ever.

This girl gets under my skin, and I don't even fucking care. She's mine. As soon as she comes to terms with it, everything will be great.

When I capture her mouth, she opens beneath me. Our tongues collide, and I could spend the entire seven minutes just kissing her. But I have something the others don't. Time and Harper in my bed all night, where I can go as slow as I want.

Besides, we have an audience, and I like to put on a show.

"You ready, little nympho?" I whisper against her lips.

"For?" She wets her lips and looks down at my weeping cock. This girl gets me so fucking worked up. She's lucky I don't rail her against the wall.

Soon, I'll have her every way I want her.

"Bend over and stick that ass out. Use the chair to brace yourself."

Her eyes widen, but she does as I ask. Her pussy is rosy and wet. Eli's spanking left her skin red across her ass and thighs. Her asshole stretches around the plug.

The plug is barely bigger than my finger. Definitely not as big as my cock. But we'll work her up to it. I squirt some lube onto my fingers. My cock brushes her ass as I lean over her to set the bottle on the chair.

"What are you doing?" Nervously she turns her head.

"Making sure you're comfortable." I smirk and trail my wet fingers down her ass crack to the plug. I smooth the lube around her stretched hole.

She sucks in a breath.

"How did it feel to have Jack's cock in your pussy and the plug buried in your ass?" I twist the plug.

"Good. Tight." Her words are breathless, and wetness trickles out of her cunt.

Holding her hip, I pull the plug almost all the way out. "Can you imagine how full and tight you'll feel with my cock in your pussy and Jack's in your ass, thrusting in and out."

I slowly ease the plug back inside before drawing it out. "You're already so fucking tight you damn near choke my cock when you come, little nympho."

Her head hangs between her arms as she rocks with my thrusting.

"Can you imagine how tight you'll be?" I line up the head of my cock with her entrance.

She whimpers as I rub my head around her wet pussy, sliding it down to her clit, while I keep fucking her ass with the toy, slow and steady. She pants with each thrust.

"Tell me, little nympho." I slot my cock against her entrance and press the tip in a little. "Do you want my cock buried inside you while I fuck your ass with the toy?"

"Please, Caden." Her words border on desperation.

I smile as I ease my tip into her before drawing back.

She makes this needy little noise that almost makes me give in to her. "Use your words, little nympho."

"Fuck me, Caden. Fill me with your cock." She grits her teeth as her hips rock back to try to take me inside her.

I thrust my cock and the toy deep into her. My fingers pinch her clit, and she shatters all around me. Her cunt and ass convulse around my cock and the toy.

"Tell me, little nympho. How does that feel?" I hold myself still.

"So good. Ah, please, Caden. Fuck me." Her words are music to my ears. She pushes back against me before pulling forward, sliding her slick pussy along my cock.

"Good girl." Growling, I grab her hips and guide her over my cock. Her fingers dig into the chair until I'm afraid she's going to break it. The plug makes her pussy snugger around my cock as it clings to me with every thrust.

I lift her leg and set her foot up on the chair, opening her up. Next thrust, I slide in so fucking deep my cock kisses her womb. She cries out as she trembles through her release.

"That's my girl." I thrust hard and deep a few more times.

Her greedy pussy milks my cock, drawing me into my release, taking every drop of my cum. I tug the plug out, sending her skyrocketing into another orgasm before pushing it back inside. She trembles against me as she tries to reclaim her breath.

"Very good, little nympho." I kiss the side of her neck.

She lets out a shaky breath. "Caden?"

I lick her salty skin before sucking on her neck. "Hmm?"

Her hand covers mine on her hip. "I think I need a break."

***

Nico

Caden opens the door and carries Harper cradled against his chest into the bathroom. When I stand to follow, no one protests. Good.

The real show is over for now. The game comes back on as I get to the bathroom and step inside, closing the door behind me.

"Relax, little nympho."

"I'm trying." Harper leans against the counter with her legs spread. Caden's fingers are between her ass cheeks.

"Need a hand?" I ask with a half grin.

Harper looks at me before her gaze narrows on Caden. "Ow."

"You're too tense," Caden practically growls. He had no trouble getting it out in the closet, so something else must be going on.

I turn the shower on. "Take a few minutes and breathe."

"I just want it out of me." She turns those brown eyes to me. "It's not like it isn't lubed up."

"She's tensing up every time I reach for it." Caden lifts an eyebrow.

I pull my t-shirt off and slide it over Harper's head, covering her gorgeous body, but hoping it will help with some of the stress. I pull her into my arms and rub my hands down her back, forcing her head down on my shoulder. She lets out an exasperated sigh.

Caden rolls his eyes but leans against the counter watching us. When she finally relaxes against me, I look down at her.

"Okay, sunshine. Let's take some deep breaths."

She looks at me like I'm crazy, but when I draw in a breath and blow it out, she does the same. I tuck some flyaway hairs behind her ear.

"Now, what are you worried about?"

She glances at Caden and then leans up and almost whispers, "What if... you know..."

I chuckle and tug her into my arms, hugging her close. Figures she'd worry about shit on the plug. I lean down and whisper in her ear. "If we do it in the shower, it won't be noticeable, but usually there isn't."

She draws her head back and searches my eyes. "You swear?"

"Swear." I brush my lips over hers. Even if there is, she'll never know. None of us would care if there was, but if we want to fuck her ass, we know better than to make her feel self-conscious.

Standing at the shower door, Caden holds out his hand for her.

She takes off my shirt and sets it on the counter. She reaches for my pants and hooks her thumbs inside my boxers to take them both down. My cock is so fucking hard for her, but I ignore it. She takes my hand and Caden's and draws us into the shower with her.

"Come here, sunshine." I turn her so she's facing me and tip her chin up.

Her eyes darken, and she wets her lips. It's all the invitation I need. I crash my mouth down on hers, thrusting my tongue past her lips. She moans against me.

When her arms wrap around my neck, I lift her against me, and she wraps her legs around my waist. Caden steps up behind her, and she makes a little startled noise before thrusting her tongue into my mouth.

Caden chuckles, and I open my eyes to see him washing the toy. Harper tugs at my hair, and my cock bobs against her pussy. Fuck, shower sex might become a habit for us.

I back her against the wall of the shower before sliding inside her. She gasps into my mouth before her hips roll on mine, taking me deeper.

I break off the kiss to look into her eyes while I fuck her. This girl is my future. I've known it since I was five years old and met her in kindergarten. When we moved, I tried to forget, but everything keeps leading me back to her.

Her lips part as we both breathe raggedly. "Nico."

The shower door closes, and I turn to see Caden drying off. Harper puts her hands on my jaw and turns me back to face her. The bathroom door shuts, and we're alone.

Finally. Slowly, I thrust in and out as she clings to me. Our eyes remain locked.

"I've dreamed about this for so long." I press my forehead to hers.

"Hopefully not exactly this." Harper tugs on my hair as a smile brightens her face.

I chuckle. "You and me, sunshine. Only you and me. You coming on my cock over and over again."

She arches into me. Breathlessly, she asks, "What else did you dream?"

"You were mine. We'd go to college together and spend the rest of our lives fucking each other." I reach between us and stroke her clit. "Say you're mine, Harper."

"Nico." Closing her eyes, she presses into me as she clutches my hair.

"Come on my cock, sunshine. You and I both know you're mine." I rub her clit in circles while pumping my cock in and out of her wet cunt, feeling the beginning flutters of her orgasm around me.

"Nico," she cries out. She tightens all around me as I keep thrusting inside her until my release finds me.

Groaning, I bury myself deep inside her, wishing I could touch her soul and write my name there.

"I'm yours, Harper." Lifting my head from hers, I search her wide, dazed eyes. "I've always been yours."

"I—" She cuts herself off and looks at the door before dropping her gaze.

"Hey, it's okay. I know you're theirs too." I smooth my hands over her hair. "As long as part of you is mine, that's all I need. I swear."

"I belong to all of you." She brushes her lips over mine.

My cock twitches inside her, and her pussy throbs around me in an aftershock.

"I'm yours," she whispers so softly I barely hear it over the water, but I'll take it.

CHAPTER 59

R&R

When Nico brings Harper back out, she's wearing his shirt. Luke holds his hand out to her. When she takes it, he pulls her down onto his lap.

"Did you like your game, princess?"

She rests her head on his shoulder and looks around at all of us. "Yes."

"Are you ready to play more?" Of course Luke's going to ask that. He may have already fucked her tonight, but he wants more. Who doesn't? We've never owned a girl before. She's taken a lot from us already tonight.

But fuck if our girl doesn't look tempted. I smirk when her gaze lands on me.

"It's getting late," Eli says and slouches on the couch to watch the game that's on the TV. "We can play more another day."

Way to shut down the party. She barely hides her disappointment as we all focus on the game playing onscreen. After a few minutes, I look back over at her, and she's asleep.

"Time for bed," I say quietly, so we don't wake her.

Luke lifts Harper into his arms. Her head rolls onto his shoulder as she blows out a breath. *Fuck, we wore her out. I'm not surprised. This won't be the last time, but now we need to take care of her.*

Luke nods, and I lead the way up to his bedroom. The others pick up the rec room. While Luke isn't expecting his dad to come home, we don't need to give him any ammunition to use against Luke.

I step into the bathroom and turn on the water in the bathtub. Harper was sore this morning, and after taking all of us again tonight, even though she's clean, a bath will help. Besides, she's ours, and we want to take care of her. After checking the temperature, I add some Epsom salt and let it fill. When I come out to the bedroom, Luke takes Nico's shirt off Harper.

She curls up on the bed and snores softly.

Fuck, maybe we're too much for one girl. That won't stop us. I'm sure Harper can handle us better than most girls could, but she looks so vulnerable.

"Bath should be about ready."

Luke nods and rises with her in his arms. She wraps around him like a koala but doesn't open her eyes.

Taking off my boxers, I sink into the warm water before holding my hands up for Harper. When Luke lowers her into the bath with me, she rouses. Her eyes open wide with panic before she turns and sees me. She comes into my arms willingly and settles against my chest in the water, straddling me.

That trust makes me feel some way.

"You okay, princess?" Luke grabs a washcloth and wipes her face almost delicately.

"Just tired." *She takes everything we give her. We could have pushed her further, but we have all year.*

I run my hands over her arms. She's going to have bruises on her hips from Eli's roughness, and especially on her ass and thighs, but hopefully the Epsom salt will sooth it and help them heal faster.

Luke finishes with her face and presses a kiss to her forehead before going over to the sink. He fills a glass with water and brings it over to her. I've never seen Luke look at anyone like he does her.

I rub her arms. "Drink, little nympho."

She opens her eyes and reaches for the glass, greedily gulping it down.

"How is she?" Eli asks from the doorway. Jack and Nico stand behind him.

"She's tired," Harper says and hands the glass back to Luke. "Thank you."

The others hang back while Eli kneels down next to the tub and cradles her face in his hands. His dark eyes take her in.

"How are you, kitten?" It's unusual for him to care, but she's not just his piece of ass this time. Plus, she's still getting used to sex.

She kisses his palm. "I'm good, Eli."

He smiles and presses a kiss against her lips. "I've got to get home. We'll have a night this week. Just you and me."

She nods, and her eyes close as she relaxes against my chest.

"Night, sunshine." Nico presses a kiss to her forehead.

"Night, Nico." She lifts a hand but doesn't open her eyes.

Jack comes in and runs his hand over her hair. "We need to work on your endurance, sweetheart."

She opens her eyes and narrows them at him with a fierce frown.

He chuckles and taps her nose. "You'll get there."

When she flicks some water at him, he laughs.

"Good night, sweetheart." He kisses her slowly, thoroughly.

When he breaks off the kiss, she sighs, a little smile on her face as she burrows back into my chest. My heart pounds a little harder at how much trust she puts in me. I want to be worthy of that trust. Luke walks the others out while I stroke my hand up and down Harper's back.

"Do you ever think about the future, little nympho?" I glance into Luke's room, thinking about the guys and our futures. Most people scatter when they leave high school. Not us. That's never been the plan.

We've been through a lot together. They've had my back, and I'll continue to have theirs.

"Mmm, college. Far, far away from here."

"Where are we going to college?" I stroke my hand over her hair.

Her braid is damp, but her hair was already damp when she came down to the basement.

"I don't know, War, where are we going to college?" she mumbles.

Her lips brush my chest as she speaks, making my body get ideas. But now's not the time for that.

"I vote somewhere far away so we can get out from under our parents' thumbs. Definitely a university, so we can all study what we want. We'll need a college that doesn't require first years to live in the dorms though, because we'll be buying a place. We won't want to be separated from you for even a year."

She lifts her head and meets my eyes. "Do you really believe that? That the five of you and I can live together for four years? And then what? We get married? Because that's illegal in most states." She closes her eyes and rests her head on my chest again. Her fingers play in the water beside us. "Besides, you guys won't even keep me for the entire school year, and everyone knows it."

"We made a deal, princess." Luke strides into the room and turns on the shower. "You're ours for the year. No backing out of it."

"Why would you think we'd back out of it?" I ask, raising her chin so she'll look at me again. Her brown eyes search mine.

"There's five of you and one of me. I'm going to need to keep my grades up and spend time with my friends and family. Not spend all my time fucking the football team." She arches an eyebrow like she knows she's right.

She pushes off my chest and moves to the other end of the tub. "I'm new and shiny. Like a toy. You'll play with me until you get bored and then throw me away for something new."

She really believes that. It's in the slight tremble to her lip and the tone of her words. She thinks we'll drop her like we're finicky toddlers. And that terrifies her.

Luke takes his boxers off and lifts Harper out of the tub.

"What are you—"

His mouth covers hers. She mumbles into his mouth before she succumbs to the kiss. Her fingers thread into his hair. I drain the tub and step out, opening the shower door for Luke.

He walks with her into the shower, and she gasps as the warm water cascades over her head. I step in and close the door.

"We need to get ready for bed." My voice seems almost too loud for the space.

Her feet touch the tiles, and he lets her step away from him. She reaches up and unbraids her hair, watching us warily. Probably because we're both sporting erections.

We have some self-control. Not much with her, but we've had our fill for the night.

I step under the shower and grab some shampoo. Pouring some into my hand, I pass her the bottle. She glances at Luke, but he's busy with washing himself.

When she moves toward the shower head, I step out of the way so she can get her hair wet. Not going to lie, I'm memorizing this shit for later if I need to jerk off. The water courses down over every curve while she closes her eyes and arches her neck, running her hands through her hair.

For the moment, we're at an uneasy truce while everyone gets clean. Neither of us touch her, because I wouldn't be able to resist backing her against the wall and fucking her again. That's the last thing we should do when she's in this mood.

She believes we won't keep her. She's in for a surprise, because I never plan to let her go. She's mine, and I'll do everything in my power to make her believe it.

* * *

HARPER

This shower is weird. It feels like gym class where we're all trying to get clean. But I don't look at the girls the way I look at these guys. I try not to make it obvious I'm ogling them. All hard sculpted muscles and large, thick cocks.

Not that they bother to hide they're watching me. By the time I'm drying off, an aching need throbs between my legs. Both Caden and Luke wrap towels around their waists and head into the bedroom.

Luke returns a moment later with my bag.

"Thanks." I take it, and he walks back out and closes the door.

The weight of his silence is getting to me. I'm not wrong. They've never claimed a girl before me. They've never shared a girl before me. It's new and exciting, but that's going to wear off. It has to.

Alone, I put on my pajamas and get ready for bed. I braid my hair into two braids since I don't want to bother drying it.

I don't understand why Luke got so upset. I was being honest.

This can't last.

I'm brushing my teeth when someone knocks.

"Come in." I rinse and spit. Luke's bathroom has a double vanity. I try not to think of Luke fucking me on this vanity. Separate water closet. Tub and shower. It's a lot bigger and nicer than mine.

Wearing his boxers, Caden wanders in and stops at the second sink, setting down a bag. He pulls out a toothbrush and toothpaste and gets to work. Our eyes meet briefly in the mirror before I put away all my things in my toiletry bag.

I put away my toiletry kit and bring my bag into Luke's bedroom. Luke's at his desk working on his computer. Okay, I'm not sure why, but it feels like they're giving me the cold shoulder.

I should be used to it. They ignored me for years before this.

Maybe I'm just self-conscious after tonight, but they took care of me. It was actually sweet how Luke carried me and Caden bathed me. We took a shower together, but no one touched me or said anything.

It feels weird to be the first one to talk. After all, I'm the one who said they'd drop me. This is more proof they only need me for one thing.

I go to my backpack and pull out my textbook. The reading isn't due tomorrow, but it's good to get ahead. I finished all my homework earlier, figuring I wouldn't have time tonight. But it's still early, and apparently Luke has homework.

I didn't really get a good look around when Luke fucked me against the wall earlier. After our shower, we were in a rush to get downstairs to the others. His bedroom is almost as large as Caden's. His king-sized bed sits against the wall opposite the bathroom. Next to the bathroom is his desk, and on the opposite wall is a small couch. His backpack is tossed on it with some clothes.

Those clothes are the only things out of place. I'm surprised, because I thought guys' rooms were supposed to be messy. Not Luke Foster's room.

Clutching my book to my chest, I head toward the bed and climb onto it. It's like a fucking cloud. I'm tempted to lie down on it, but instead I sit cross-legged in the center and open my book.

Earlier, I was exhausted, not even able to keep my eyes open, but now I'm wide awake. Aware I'm going to sleep with two guys again. Last night, we went to sleep. Is that what will happen tonight?

How many times can a guy get off in a night? Do I really want to find out?

Movement draws my attention when Caden comes out of the bathroom. He glances at Luke and then at me. His face transforms with a wide grin as he heads my way.

My insides spark to life. Guess I might find out.

"What are you reading, little nympho?" Caden crashes down on the bed beside me. I nearly tip over but stay upright.

"Homework." I'm still feeling a little put off since they went silent on me.

Caden runs his hand over my thigh and teases the hem of my sleep shorts. "We won't let you go. You know that, right?"

His green eyes look into mine. A shiver races down my spine. Part of me fears I won't be enough. Part of me is being realistic. They've never held onto anyone for any length of time. What makes me special? Because I was untouched?

And the biggest part of me doesn't want to buy into this fantasy. To hope for more. To dream bigger.

To crash and burn when they leave me in their dust.

There's determination in Caden's eyes. So maybe for a minute, I play into his fantasy. It's better than reading my textbook.

"Explain to me how this fantasy of yours is supposed to work." I set my book to the side and lean back on my hands.

Caden's gaze drops to my breasts, and they tighten in anticipation. When my nipples poke at my thin sleep tank, he licks his lips.

I need therapy, because I kind of want to go again.

Caden tugs my arm, so I fall back on the bed beside him. He doesn't roll over me or move at all. We lie there, side by side, looking up at the ceiling.

"You want our story, little nympho? Our fairy tale ending?" Caden clears his throat. "We fuck our way through our senior year.

All of us get into multiple colleges, but only one is the perfect fit for us."

"What university would be perfect for all of us?" I ask with a little attitude, because he's talking about six people here. We're in the same high school because we live in the same town, not because we share similar interests.

"One that feeds into a law school for Eli. Has an excellent engineering school for Jack. Business school for me and Luke to appease our fathers. A Division I school for us to continue to play football if we want. A fine arts school and liberal arts for you and Nico to decide what you really want to do."

He says that like it's so easy to find one that would work for all of us and admit us. "That's five different colleges within a university. Most schools excel at a few, but not all of them."

"So negative, little nympho." He takes my hand and threads our fingers together. His warmth beside me draws me, and I rest my head against his shoulder. "Dream bigger. We spend four years getting our undergrad, and most of us will do a master's in five. So it makes sense for us to buy a house or condo to live near campus for those years instead of paying rent."

"Now are we all chipping in for this condo, or are we relying on our parents to pay?" Because I don't have the money they have access to.

"No worries. My trust fund will buy it as an investment property for the future." Caden squeezes my hand. "Now, we'll wait to get you pregnant, of course."

"Of course." I roll my eyes. He wants me to have ten kids after all.

"Because you'll want to get settled into your career before taking time off."

"Who says I'll want to take time out of my career to raise kids?"

"You'll have five husbands. We'll work from home and trade off who has to stay home with the kids. You just have to take off time to give birth."

"To a football team worth of kids," I scoff.

"We can work out the number later. But think of how nice it will be to have a big family. Christmas morning with a gang of little feet creeping down to see what Santa brought them."

"I suppose you'll play Santa." I smile because his imagination is taking root in my brain and I can see a passel of dark-haired and blond children sneaking down to watch their dad putting presents beneath the tree.

It's an illusion. This perfect fantasy where we grow into adults and spend the rest of our lives together. Caden's missing one thing out of his fantasy. One thing that would hold me tighter than any vow.

Love.

We don't have it. While I can imagine falling for Nico and even Caden, maybe Jack and Eli, I'm not sure I could ever love Luke. He's cold, but there's this heat to him that draws me. I'd be a fool to give him my heart, or even any of the others, because they don't love me, and I'm not sure they can. At least not the way I could love them.

But the fantasy still plays in my mind. Caden being Santa putting presents under the tree, Nico and Jack sneaking with the kids to catch him in the act, Eli and Luke holding me while we watch. It's more than I ever had growing up. A large family. It's tempting to ignore the warning signs and just fall into the fantasy.

CHAPTER 60

The Standoff

Caden rolls over on top of me, holding his weight on his arms. "Of course I'll be Santa, little nympho. And I'll definitely remember to kiss mommy. We can practice until we get it right."

He lowers his head to capture my lips. My brain cells fry as he deepens the kiss like he's in no hurry. This isn't his all-consuming kiss. His hand cradles my head as his tongue strokes into my mouth, tasting, testing, exploring. Time loses all meaning as he doesn't make any moves to do more than kiss me.

It's an odd feeling. Except for that first week, I haven't made out with someone without the expectation it would lead to more. Caden's lips are soft but firm against mine. He tastes like minty toothpaste and something just him.

I'm not happy with him only hovering over me, not touching me. I want to feel his body against mine, so I wrap my legs around him to bring him down. Instead, he wraps his arms around me and rolls to his back, so I'm on top of him. He holds the back of my head while he continues to kiss me.

I relax on top of him and let my legs fall to either side of his body. The heat builds within me, but I like that we're just focused on making out. He isn't pressing for more, and neither do I.

Vaguely, I register Luke moving around the room. When the bed dips beside us, I open my eyes and pull away. Caden's eyes are deep green. His lips are swollen from our kiss. Mine feel swollen as well.

Luke sits beside us on the bed reading a book.

"You done with your homework?" Caden turns his head toward Luke.

"Yeah." Luke sets his book on the nightstand, next to his open computer with his webcam focused on all of us.

I rest my head on Caden's chest as I watch Eli reading a book, Nico working on homework, and Jack doing something on his other screen. It's nice they're all here. When I release a little sigh, Caden chuckles and rubs my back.

It's so easy to fall into his dream life. A future with all of them in it. But that's all it is. A dream.

We're fucking, but they don't love me. Nico wants this to be more. Caden might want more too. But all of them? That would be ridiculous. Even just having two boyfriends would probably make my mother lock me in my bedroom until I come to my senses.

My gaze goes to Luke, who's watching me with those shrewd, pale blue eyes.

"Did you want to make out with me too, princess?" He gives me a cocky smile.

I try to keep from smiling, but he can see my lips twitching. I climb off Caden and crawl up on Luke's lap, straddling his hips. That's about as far as my bravado takes me.

Luke shakes his head as he lifts one of my braids. "Such an innocent little girl."

I raise an eyebrow. "Not so innocent anymore."

"Too shy to kiss me?" Luke's eyes challenge me.

"Nah, my little nympho isn't shy. You're just intimidating." Caden slides his hand over my backside, making heat curl inside me.

Luke smirks as his gaze falls to my lips. "Am I intimidating, princess?"

My eyes narrow. Hell yes, he's intimidating. But I know he wants me to kiss him, and that helps.

My hands rest on his shoulders as I lean in until our lips are almost touching. I hold his gaze.

"You can be very intimidating, Death," I whisper against his lips before pressing forward, locking our lips together.

His hands grab my ass and haul me into him. I hiss at the sting from my spanking earlier.

"Dammit, Eli." Luke breaks off our kiss to turn to scold Eli. Fuck that.

I grab his face and bring it back to my lips, opening my mouth over his until he parts his lips. This time I'm the aggressor, but Luke could never be passive. He moves his hands up to my back as we explore each other's mouths. When he grows hard beneath me, a burst of desire flows through me.

Just like with Caden, we make out. Not even any heavy petting. But by the time Luke pulls away, I'm more of a horny mess than before.

"Time for bed, princess." Luke kisses me again before setting me between him and Caden on the bed. Finally. I'm practically soaked over here from the kisses. He turns out the light and pulls the covers over me. Then he lies down.

Oh, he means we're actually going to sleep. Caden gives me a quick kiss good night. Huh. I blow out a breath.

Rolling toward Luke, I throw my leg over his before snuggling my head against his bare chest. He releases a breath before his arm wraps around me, drawing me tight against him.

My heart skips a beat, but I ignore it. This is about sex and that's all.

***

Nico

Low moans wake me in the morning. I turn to my computer screen and watch as Caden pulls down Harper's sleep shorts and pushes her legs open before he feasts on her. Fuck.

I can't tear my eyes away as Luke lifts off her top and sucks her nipple into his mouth. I'm not the only one awake. Jack does what he does best in his tiny window, and Eli watches with that thoughtful expression like he's not hard as a rock.

Harper's face turns to the laptop with her lips parted. Her dark eyes open, and for a second it feels like she's looking right at me. But it's impossible to tell with the webcam.

Her breath pants in and out as they both work her delicious, writhing body. It's impossible not to feel envious of their ability to be with our girl. To sleep with her wrapped around them and wake up to the taste of her on their lips.

"Nico! You need to wake up!" my mom shouts from downstairs.

Fucking hell! Seriously, she worries too much.

I hit mute on my computer before yelling back, "I'm up."

I'll need a long shower with how *up* our girl has me. I unmute my computer as Harper comes. A low moan on her lips. Her body arching against theirs. Fuck. I've got to figure out a way to sneak out or sneak her in.

"See you at school." Luke closes his laptop.

Yeah, but today all bets are off. Today she wears my jersey, and she's adjusting fine if last night is anything to go by.

I take a little too long in the shower, jerking off to the memory of her lips around my cock and the image of her coming this morning.

When I make it downstairs, Mom yells from the kitchen, "Come get breakfast."

"No time." I'll miss Harper's entrance, which seriously is the highlight of my day. Getting to kiss her first thing in the morning when we wake up together would be better. Eli plans to sneak her into his room, but could I do the same?

Eli might have an easier time of it. His parents aren't worried about his transition into a new school during senior year. The attention should die down after this week. Hopefully.

"Nico, come get something to take with you then. You can't go to your second day of school hungry."

I roll my eyes and head into the kitchen. My blond-haired, blue-eyed mother scans me up and down before holding out a wrapped breakfast sandwich. To say I take after my father is an understatement. Though my skin isn't nearly as dark as his.

Mom shakes the sandwich impatiently. "If you have to go, take this. You need all the energy you can get to keep up with the other boys."

She doesn't know the half of it. I cross the kitchen and take the sandwich.

"Thanks, Mom." I kiss her cheek.

She blushes and pats my shoulder. "Off to school. Don't want to be late."

"I might hang out with friends after practice." I turn the sandwich over in my hands. "Grab something to eat with them."

"Oh." She plays with her necklace, and her disappointment is clear before she forces a smile. "Of course, you need to make friends, but you spent all weekend out. It's a weeknight, and you have to get your homework done."

I give her a cocky smile. "I always get my homework done, Mom. It's important to reestablish bonds with my friends."

She frowns and glances at the recipe book she has open on the kitchen island. "I wanted to make your favorite." She brightens. "Why don't you invite your friends over here for dinner? The lasagna would feed an army. Your dad works late tonight, so it'd be fun to meet your friends."

I hesitate, and the smile slips from her face. Disappointing my mom is a hard pass usually. It's hard to remember she's just moved back to this town herself, and Dad has been working a lot. He tries to be home for dinners, but apparently not tonight.

"Fine. I'll ask."

Practically buzzing with excitement, she grins and goes to the cookbook. "Oh, I'll need to get out the nicer dishes."

I shake my head. I doubt the horsemen will think anything about ordinary dishes, but again I don't want to disappoint her. Seeing her smile makes me happy. The past few years have been rough on her. That was the point of moving back here. Dad would work less and have more time for Mom.

"Warning, whatever you think is enough, make double. I'm bringing five teenagers home with me." If I can convince them to come. Of course, the only one I really have to convince is Harper, and the others will follow.

"Five?" Her fingers worry her necklace again.

"The guys and Harper."

Mom's smile is huge and knowing. "Harper? Your little girlfriend from elementary school?"

"She was my best friend, not my girlfriend, Mom." It pops out of my mouth from habit. Now, I don't know what to call her. But fuck it, I have every right to claim her. She's mine. "But she may be my girlfriend now."

Mom makes an *aw* face.

I wave her off and back out the door. "Gotta go. Thanks for the sandwich, and see you tonight."

"Love you, Nico."

The door shuts before I can say it back. I hope I can convince everyone to come for dinner. I get in my car and head to school. Parking next to Eli's car, I get out and grab my backpack.

"Hi, Nico." Angela Harris stands on the curb, waiting. Her blond hair glints in the sunlight. She's got just as much makeup on as yesterday and shows even more cleavage. Her skirt might be even shorter. What is with the girls at this school?

"Angela." I glance toward the school sign and see Jack and Eli talking near it. As I try to walk past her, she falls in step with me.

"So I was thinking, we should really get ahead on this art project." She smiles and licks her lips. "We could work on it at the coffee shop."

"We have weeks to work together in class. I'm sure we'll be fine." I lengthen my stride, but she keeps pace even in those ridiculous heels.

"But we could work at the *coffee* shop." She grabs my arm to stop me. If I don't want to drag her with me and make a scene, I have to stop.

Turning, I glare at her. She's working on my last nerve. Oblivious to my mood, she preens like a poodle at a dog show. Fuck this girl.

"See, everyone around here knows what happens in the coffee shop bathroom, but maybe you don't since you're new." She grabs the necklace that falls between her cleavage, probably to draw my gaze to her breasts.

"You mean fucking in the bathroom. Yeah, I'm aware. But you know I'm spoken for, so I'm not sure why you would even imply I would want that." I don't have time for these games. I gave her an out, and she didn't take it.

She laughs. "No one thinks that thing with Harper is going to last. I heard she's frigid, and that's why she's still a virgin."

My eyes narrow, and I grab her upper arm. "Who's spreading that around?"

"Ow, you're hurting me." She pouts, but her eyes sparkle with interest. "Everyone knows. I had to change my bet. But I'm hoping you guys get impatient waiting for her to give it up."

My brow furrows.

"I won't tell if you don't." She bats her eyelashes.

I shove her away. "We have a project in class together and that's the extent of our relationship. You're not my friend, and I'm not interested."

She purses her lips, but then turns and storms off into the school. Shaking my head, I walk over to the guys. Fuck, are all the girls at this school like that?

"Is that typical?" I gesture toward the door she disappeared behind.

"For Angela, yeah." Eli shakes his head. "She's always been a clinger. When one of us finished with her, she'd make the rounds until she found someone to fuck her."

"She's got a pretty talented mouth. Nice tits." Jack leans back on the sign and looks across the parking lot. "Not much else to recommend her."

I've never had trouble with women. I got a lot of interest, but nothing like the girls around here.

Speaking of... Sidney and her group stroll up to the sign and stop.

"Where's your whore?" Ashley looks Eli up and down. She's wearing his jersey with her cheerleading skirt.

Eli looks behind her. "Your mom didn't ride with you? I guess she must be on her way then."

Ashley narrows her eyes. Jack and Eli bump fists casually.

"We need to do the exchange after school. Harper can meet us in the locker room to get Eli's jersey." Sidney acts bored, but I bet they have something planned.

"We could just take it now if it's an inconvenience to you." Eli steps forward and holds out his hand.

Ashley backs up a step. When she doesn't take it off, he puts his hand down. "We've got practice and can't stop at Luke's every night this week."

"Like I said, you can give it back to us now." Eli's gaze moves past them.

Luke has his arm around Harper's shoulders as they walk toward us. Harper swallows as they draw closer. Her gaze flits from us to the cheer-leaders and back.

I'm not as attached to my number here as I was at my old school, but I have to admit, I like seeing it on Harper. She's wearing jeans today with a blue t-shirt on under my jersey. I can understand the urge Caden had to fuck her wearing his jersey. It's like she's advertising to the whole school she's mine.

"Problems?" Luke stops behind Sidney.

"They want to change the conditions of the transfer." Eli steps back and leans on the sign, casual now that Luke is here to take command. "They want Harper to meet them in the locker room after school."

Sidney turns and almost jerks back at the sight of Luke's arm around Harper's shoulders. She's practically tucked into his side. Harper doesn't look comfortable with this confrontation.

Luke's gaze narrows on Sidney. "Why would we change our agreement?"

"We have practice this week." Finding her attitude again, Sidney straightens. "Driving over to your house for a minute exchange is ridicu-lous. Harper is perfectly safe in the school locker room, and we can hand it to her there."

The *perfectly safe* doesn't make me feel better. These girls are up to something. Luke's eyes meet mine, and I step forward as he guides Harper into my arms. I draw her over to Jack and Eli. Caden remains standing behind Luke.

"You guys are being ridiculous." Emma rolls her eyes. "If we really wanted to get to your pet, we wouldn't have to try that hard."

"I'm curious why the sudden change. You seemed eager to swap the jerseys at my house yesterday." Luke circles around Sidney, breaking her off from the others. "Were you hoping more would happen?"

A brief flinch hits Sidney's face. If I hadn't been watching, I wouldn't have seen it. That's exactly what they wanted. They were hoping for a way back in.

"Is Brewster not up to your standards?" Luke steps around, stopping in front of her. "Tough shit. We had an agreement. You drop off the jersey. This isn't our problem."

Sidney's face tightens. She doesn't like the new order around here. But Luke isn't the one who will take the brunt of her anger.

"It's fine." Harper steps out of my arms and next to Luke. Her eyes meet Ashley's. "I can meet you in the locker room and give you Nico's jersey. It shouldn't be a problem."

Luke's jaw clenches.

Sidney smiles. "See, your pet can see reason. Be there after the last bell."

"Okay."

The cheerleaders turn and walk into the school. Luke's fierce eyes meet all of ours as he nods toward the school. Anticipation thrums through my veins. He's pissed.

CHAPTER 61
Apocalypse Now

NICO

"I can't back down from them or let you run them off all the time," Harper says as Luke takes her hand and drags her into the school. Her brown eyes lock with mine, pleading for help.

I don't know if she needs it, but I'm not going anywhere. Caden stops to talk to a guy. He seems familiar, probably on the football team. I'm still getting to know the other players. Luke turns down a hallway and pulls Harper into a darkened classroom.

The guy follows us. When we enter the room, he stands outside the closed door.

"Sit down." Luke points to a desk. A muscle ticks in his jaw.

"Luke, you don't—"

"For fuck's sake, Harper, do as you're told." He doesn't raise his voice, but it's clear he's on the edge.

Her eyes narrow, and her lips press into a stubborn line, but she drops into the seat.

"What the fuck was that about?" Luke turns to Eli.

"Exactly what they asked for. Nothing more." Eli glances at Harper. "Harper can make Penny and the others go with her. It will even the odds."

"That was my plan," Harper mutters, dropping her backpack on the floor.

Luke leans down with his hand on the desk and the other on the back of her chair, trapping Harper in. "What if those girls won't do it?"

She gives him a mulish expression I've seen plenty of times before.

"They will." Eli glances toward the doorway. "They want to feel what it's like to be popular. We can give them that. But if they look for more, I'll punish you, kitten."

She tears her gaze away from Luke to gape at Eli. "Why should I get punished? It's your idea, too."

"But I'm not the one who told the cheerleaders they could change the terms of our arrangement." Eli leans against the wall. "That's on you, kitten."

"If you can't get the girls to go with you, you don't go." Luke grabs the back of her neck.

"Fine," she spits out.

They look five seconds from either fighting or fucking.

"Great." I clap my hands, trying to dispel the tension. "My mom is making lasagna tonight and wants everyone to come over for dinner."

Luke straightens and looks at me like I've flipped my lid. He doesn't understand the power mothers have. But the others will.

"Dad's working late. When I asked if I could eat out, she suggested we all come over. It'll be good." My gaze goes to Harper. "She can't wait to see you."

"Her lasagna always was the best." She glances up at Luke.

"Fine." He blows out a breath and holds out his hand to Harper. She takes it, and he helps her stand. We all gather our stuff. Just as we get to the door, I drop my final bomb.

"By the way, I told Mom Harper's my girlfriend."

HARPER

Luke presses me against the locker outside of first period. His eyes search mine. "I don't like this plan."

I pat my hand on his chest. "It'll be fine. The cheerleading advisor will be there, and probably the other girls' coaches. It will be quick and painless."

I hope. I don't honestly know what to expect or why the Cheermonsters changed the plans. They hoped the guys would want to fuck them when they dropped off the jersey last night, but left disappointed.

Luke traces his finger over my lower lip, making sparks trickle through me. "Nothing is ever quick and painless with Sidney."

Is he talking about fucking her? I seriously don't want to know about their previous sex lives. My eyes narrow on his.

His pale blue eyes search mine like he knows what I'm thinking. He smirks and leans in like he's about to kiss me.

"Mr. Foster, is this going to become a habit?" Mr. Wick stands behind Luke, in front of the classroom door he's now holding open. "I'm sure Miss Davidson can find her seat without your help."

Luke breathes out. "Of course, Mr. Wick."

He takes my hand, and we walk into the classroom. I have a feeling this discussion isn't over. But by the time Luke can get me alone again, hopefully he'll have forgotten, or I'll have done something else to rile him up.

The first two classes breeze by. When I step into art, my stomach plummets. Fuck, I totally forgot about the whole project thing. Everyone shuffled seats for it. Tanner sits at my table now.

I walk back to Kenz and sit at her table with Natalie. "This is no longer my favorite class."

Kenz sighs. "I'd trade if we could. Not that you aren't great, Natalie."

Natalie waves her hand. "I understand. Tanner's a dick."

"Did you get my text from earlier?" I ask Natalie. I sent it to the group last period while Eli supervised every word.

"Yeah, I don't think it will be a problem."

I release my breath. "Good."

"What's happening?" Kenz glances between us.

"The Cheermonsters changed the handoff arrangement. They want me to meet them in the locker room after school."

"That doesn't sound like a trap at all." Kenz rolls her eyes. "I'm coming too."

I smile and relax even more. "Good. And thank you, Natalie."

"Those girls are bitches, but they rarely do their own dirty work." Natalie taps her pencil on her notepad. "We'll need to be careful."

The bell rings. I pout at Kenz and go back to my desk. And Tanner.

Ms. Sullivan comes in and turns out the lights, clicking on the interactive whiteboard. "Okay, today we'll be discussing the various methods and styles we can choose for the projects. Pay attention and note your favorite ones. You'll have a paper due on Monday discussing the art forms you chose for your projects and what drew you to them."

Normally I'd be happy to work on this, but I have to do this with Tanner. The guys don't know about our project, but it's only day two. I glance over at Nico, and he winks.

My phone buzzes.

NICO:

Wait for me after class

ME:

K

At least with the slideshow, I don't actually have to talk to Tanner. I don't even look at him as I take notes. Ms. Sullivan talks until the bell rings.

"Tomorrow, you'll discuss with your partner and start on your paper."

I don't turn to look at Tanner when I leave. He didn't say a word thankfully. Maybe this will actually go smoothly. Angela stands with her back to me as I approach Nico.

"Here's my number so you can call me to discuss the project." She holds out a piece of paper.

Nico takes it and sticks it in his folder. "We'll talk about it tomorrow. In class."

"You can use that whenever you want." She winks before turning and seeing me beside her.

"Hi." I wave, because what else are you supposed to do to a girl who's hitting on your man.

She looks me up and down before sneering and walking away.

"I don't think she likes me." I step closer to Nico.

"Probably not." He takes my hand. "Come on."

"Where are we going?" I ask as we walk out of the classroom and not towards the cafeteria. "Are we having lunch off campus? Because that would be awesome. I didn't really pack my lunch today."

"I only have you for an hour, so we're going to multitask." Nico pushes out the doors and leads me to his car.

I look back for the others. "Just us?"

Grinning, he opens his car door for me. "Just us."

A little thrill races through me as I settle into the seat. I don't know how he did it, but I'm glad I don't have to face Luke. Nico rounds the car and gets in. Five minutes later, he pulls through a McDonald's drive-through and orders us meals.

I immediately grab the bag and eat a french fry. "See, this is why you're one of my favorites."

"I should be your only favorite, sunshine." Turning up the music, he grins and drives into the hills surrounding the city. I hold out a fry to him, and he snatches it with his teeth. It feels decadent and disobedient to be out here with him.

Especially with how angry Luke was about the Cheermonsters. He doesn't understand the more he antagonizes them, the more they'll come after me. I don't want him to give in to them, because they want to fuck my men. But we can at least try to find common ground. Maybe.

Nico pulls into a secluded spot and turns off the car, setting the emergency brake and turning the music down low.

My phone buzzes with multiple missed texts. I glance over them. Panic wells inside me with each text.

"Oh, shit, did you tell them you were taking me to lunch?"

The last text was from Luke.

DEATH:

We know you left campus. Don't make us
hunt you down

Anxiety winds its way through my body, making my heart race and my hands tremble. They haven't punished me in a while, and I really don't want to be punished again. Who knows what they'll do to me now.

"Do I need to tell them everything I do?" Nico takes a bite of his burger like he has nothing better to do.

"Fuck, Nico. You won't be the one who gets in trouble."

ME:

Nico took me to get McDonald's

I hit send, but the panic rises within me. What kind of punishment will they do, especially if they don't want me to like it? There's nothing left for them to take. Well, one thing. I squirm in my seat thinking about last night.

"Eat, sunshine." Nico wipes his hands and picks up his buzzing phone.

Watching him, I unwrap my burger and take a bite while he answers his phone.

"Yes, she's with me." Nico leans back in his seat. "I didn't know I needed to check her out like a library book."

He winks, and I remember to take another bite. What if they come out to find us? Will they punish Nico too?

"The place up in the hills we used to ride our bikes to."

Why would he tell them? I can hear the rumble of Luke's voice through the phone.

"She's wearing my jersey. Of course I plan to fuck her." Nico shakes his head as he stares out the windshield.

I swallow my bite hard and grab my drink to wash it down. Okay, wasn't expecting that. I mean, I was kind of hoping but...

"No butt stuff except fingers. Got it."

Oh my god! Seriously? They should be glad I'm not the kind of girl who needs to be wooed, or they'd all be shit out of luck. Have they ever had to work for a girl before? If they did woo me, I might have been the one attacking them.

"Be back shortly." He ends the call and sets his phone on the dashboard. "You won't get in trouble, sunshine. I have as much right to you as they do."

I swallow my soda and set the cup in the holder. I arch an eyebrow. "So you brought me out here to fuck me?"

He pushes his hand through his hair and gives me a smirk. "I planned to get to that a little smoother than announcing it to Luke."

"Oh, really?" I laugh. "You didn't want to just check me out from the library?"

"Luke's got it bad." Nico shakes his head. "He wanted me to bring you back."

"He likes to be in control." Settling into my seat, I wiggle my eyebrows. "So, show me how you were going to smoothly get me to fuck you."

He moves his seat back, reclining the back all the way. "Gotta set the scene."

"Sure." Trying not to laugh, I eat my last fry. My panties are always damp around Nico. It won't take him much to have me.

"Tell me, sunshine." He smiles, and that twinkle in his eyes about does me in. It's the same twinkle that got us into trouble as kids. "Do you enjoy being ordered around or do you want to take control of your own sexuality?"

I wipe my hands on a napkin. Some of the laughter falls away. "Honestly I haven't had much choice in the matter. The guys steam-rolled me from the beginning. But I do like being told what to do."

I can admit this to Nico. He's not one of them. Well, he is, but he's mine too.

"Take off your jeans, Harper." Nico's voice rolls over me.

This feels like the night with Luke in his car all over again. Except the sun filters through the trees instead of the dark. And this time, Nico's going to fuck me. He undoes his pants and pulls them down, leaving his boxers on. My insides soften. I take off my jeans and put them on the seat behind me, leaving my panties on.

"Climb over the console and straddle me facing the steering wheel."

I swallow but carefully climb over and kneel over his legs.

"Do you know how hot you are in my jersey? With my name

claiming you, sunshine?" His hand grips the back of my neck, holding me still. His other hand trails over my panties.

"Tell me, Nico," I whisper. His hand smooths over my ass and slips between my legs to tease me through my panties. My breath catches waiting for him to do more.

His fingers slip beneath my panties and over my pussy before thrusting inside. "So fucking wet."

Gasping, I grip the steering wheel as he thrusts his fingers in and out of me, winding me up.

"I've dreamed of fucking you for years. Of sliding into this tight pussy and making it mine." Nico tightens his hand on the back of my neck. "Be glad I'm not a jealous guy when I came back and found you being hunted by my friends."

"They had me backed into a corner." I close my eyes as he winds me tighter and tighter.

"I've seen you with them, sunshine. You crave their attention. You thrive on it. Your pussy begs for their cocks." His thumb flicks over my clit, and I come all over his hand with a cry. "So fucking responsive."

He draws his fingers out of me, still holding me up as I try to catch my breath. "I should have been your first and only, sunshine."

"It's not like you kept in touch all these years." I didn't think that bugged me, but it does. He was my best friend and moved away without another word. "You ghosted me, but not them."

He jerks my panties to the side, and the head of his cock presses against my entrance. His hands take my hips, and he pulls me down on him, filling me with his cock. I moan as the sensations overwhelm me.

He sweeps my hair away from my ear and pulls me back against his chest. "If I'd kept in touch, I would have fought harder to return to you. It was bad enough seeing the guys during the summer knowing they were able to see you every day at school. At first I thought I needed to move on from you, that if I kept in contact, you would tell me about your boyfriends. As we got older, the guys could have had you, and I wouldn't have known."

His cock throbs inside me. I desperately want him to fuck me, but he holds me immobile. My hands clench on the steering wheel.

"It drove me nuts thinking about them touching you. Fucking you.

Sucking your sweet clit. And I was in New York. Without you." He kisses below my ear before sucking and biting me there, while giving me little thrusts of his hips. "Hold on, Harper."

I tighten my grip on the wheel. He raises my hips and lowers my pussy over his cock, slowly moving inside me.

"Fuck, you feel good. Do you know how good it's going to feel when I can fuck your ass, sunshine?"

I press my head against the steering wheel as he thrusts so deep inside me. His fingers rub my clit, making me pant with need.

"Nico."

He slides back inside me, so fucking slow. "What, sunshine?"

"I need more," I bite out.

"Then take it, sunshine. Grind back and forth on my cock."

Using the steering wheel as leverage, I rock my hips back and forth on Nico's cock. His tip slides against my G-spot over and over again.

His hand slides my panties down over my ass. He sucks on his finger before teasing my asshole with it. I'm already so close to the edge.

"I've been thinking about what I want to do to you. What we want to do to you. Do you have any idea how good it's going to feel to take all of us at once, sunshine?"

I whimper, unable to speak as he slides his finger inside, pressing against my sensitive nerve endings.

"One of us in your pussy." He slides his finger deep into my ass before slowly fucking my ass in the rhythm I'm working his cock. "One in this tight ass. Another in your mouth. And both your hands stroking a cock. You'll come so fucking hard you'll see stars, sunshine."

He slides his other hand around to pinch my clit. Everything inside me falls apart as I slam down on his cock and tighten all around him. My mouth opens on a silent scream. His hips rock into me until he groans, filling me with his cum.

I collapse back against him, panting. Little aftershocks make me twitch. He reaches into the center console for wipes.

"We need to clean up and get back to school before the others send out a search party." Nico cleans his hands, then lifts me and takes care of me before moving my panties back into place.

He helps me shift back into my seat and takes care of himself while I pull my jeans back on. I flip down the visor and use the mirror to make sure I don't have freshly fucked hair.

"Did I at least take your car virginity?" He gives me this hopeful look.

I smile. "I mean, it's not my first orgasm in a car. Luke and I grinded, and Caden finger fucked me. But you're the first to fuck me in a car."

He grins and straightens his seat. "Fuck it, I'll take it."

CHAPTER 62

Death on My Mind

HARPER

Nico gives me a kiss before we walk into the building and head to the lockers. When we get there, the guys glare at Nico, but he just smirks. Caden pulls me over to his locker and helps me get the books I need for the afternoon.

As I turn to face the rest of them, Eli stops and claims my mouth, kissing me like he wants to claim all of me. Sparks flood me from where his hands hold my hips and his lips meet mine.

When he backs off, Jack captures my lips in a kiss, making my head spin. I thought I'd get used to them kissing me. That it wouldn't key me up every time, but it still does. Jack grins before passing me off to Caden.

Caden draws me back into his arms. He tips my chin up, and his lips crash down on mine, giving me his best devastating kiss before pushing me toward Luke. "Behave, little nympho."

Easy for him to say. My lunch should have left me satisfied, but right now, I'm three seconds from pulling someone into a closet.

Luke takes my hand and leads me to class. The others give me nods as they head to their classes. They really don't understand punishment if that's their way of disciplining me. I might need to disobey more, because I'm buzzing from all the kisses.

As we near the classroom, Luke pushes me against the lockers and hovers over me. I figured he'd be the one who wouldn't give in easily. That he would need to lecture me about how I should behave. But he really can't complain. I was with a horseman.

Just not him.

His possessiveness hasn't been as bad lately. But I did end up skipping out on lunch, and he didn't get to lecture me more on how I shouldn't have let the Cheermonsters win this round. My hands settle on his chest, and I can feel his steady heartbeat. Anticipation scatters through me.

I meet his eyes and wait, feeling his cock pressed against my stomach. The kisses and what I did with Nico in the car already have my insides flaming hot, but Luke's nearness ignites them into an inferno.

He wraps his hand around my throat but doesn't tighten it. Sparks spread through me at his touch. When he leans in, my breath catches in anticipation of his kiss. Instead, his lips touch my ear.

"Get the bathroom pass and wait for me."

My heart pounds at the implication. Will he fuck me or punish me? Or both? Either way, my pussy throbs.

"We can't miss class." I release the breath I'm holding. I don't really mean that, but I can't just cave to Luke's demands.

"I'll make sure we get the lecture notes." His eyes search mine. That cold look barely hides the heat inside them. "Don't disobey me, princess."

I narrow my eyes. I want to disobey him and I don't at the same time. "Fine."

He releases me and takes my hand, leading me into the classroom and to our seats. I lean back in my chair and get out my notebook. What will Luke do if I don't get the pass? I glance over, and he's watching me with those eyes.

Intimidating, yes. But fuck do I feel powerful, because he wants me. Even if he punishes me, he'll get me off one way or another. Because we can't help it when we're together. We combust.

This morning, I wanted to draw him on top of me and feel him slide in so fucking deep as he fucked me hard. But then nothing. He didn't fuck me. Didn't make me suck him off.

We showered together, and this time between Luke and Caden, I got plenty of help with the soap, but that was it. Lots of foreplay, only one orgasm. It was a good orgasm, but there was all this promise of more. And nothing.

The bell rings, and Mr. Flack stands at the front of the class. He begins his lecture about Egypt and the pyramids. I take notes and try not to get distracted when Luke kicks my chair.

I want him to wait, so he can wait.

After a few minutes, he lets out a harsh breath. But before he can say anything, I raise my hand.

"Yes, Harper?" Mr. Flack stops mid-sentence. He actually seems hopeful I'll have a question.

"May I use the bathroom pass?"

Mr. Flack's face falls as he gestures to the pass.

Luke smirks as I stand, but I won't make this easy for him. Especially since I don't know what I'm getting. I grab the pass and head out the door and across to the bathroom.

I don't know what I can plan, but something.

A toilet flushes, and I freeze. Someone else is in here. Oh, fuck. I can't just go back out, they heard the door open. The door shuts behind me, and I make my way to the stalls.

The other stall door opens, and Sidney walks out. We both freeze as we stare at each other. I'm not sure what I'm supposed to do here. Just ignore her and head into the bathroom? How long before Luke comes in?

This is a mess. She's wearing Luke's jersey like she owns him. That makes my insides itch with the need to take it from her. He's not hers. Not now.

"Harper Davidson. You seem to be everywhere these days." Sidney grins and leans back on the stall. "You're a popular little slut, aren't you?"

"Yeah, I don't know what I'm supposed to say to that." I glance at the door and hope Luke wasn't able to get the pass too. My gaze drops to Sidney's hands. "Aren't you going to wash your hands?"

She cocks an eyebrow, but moves over to the sinks. Her gaze finds mine in the mirror. "You know it won't last, right? Eventually he's going to want me back."

"That's assuming you *had* him before." The words trip off my tongue like I've lost my mind. Am I trying to get into a catfight? Seriously my mom will ground me if she has to wake up and come to school to get my suspended ass because I fought in the girls' bathroom.

Sidney laughs. "You don't understand how this works, but how could you? You're just a virgin."

Not anymore, but she doesn't need to know that. "Why don't you explain it to me?"

"Luke and I have been fucking since we lost our virginities together."

Okay, that's a kick in the chest. It's not like I didn't know they had sex, but I didn't know they lost their virginities to each other. I'm not sure if that makes what they have special. It doesn't seem like something Luke would find special. Maybe it does in her mind?

"He didn't tell you?" She sounds so fucking cocky. She grabs paper towels to dry her hands and closes in on me while she talks. "There's a reason he keeps coming back to me. Over and over again. We've always fucked. I know exactly how he likes it. So while you may be something different he wants to sample, I'm who he always comes back to."

"Then you have nothing to worry about." I shrug like she didn't just squeeze my heart. I'm ignoring that, because I don't know what it means and I don't want to look too closely at that feeling.

That shit needs to be locked down, because Luke isn't playing for keeps.

She throws her head back and laughs. "Of course I'm not worried. A girl like you could never be what he needs."

Her gaze drops to take my measure. She gives me a fake sad face. "I'm sure you'll get his cock in every one of your holes eventually, but that's all you'll be to him. A convenient place to stick his dick and get off. A toy he can use and throw away."

I say nothing. This isn't news to me. But she didn't see his anger or taste his possessive kiss when I told him that last night. She didn't feel his arm around me as I snuggled against him to fall asleep.

"I'm surprised he's willing to share. But that just means he'll need some one-on-one time and not sloppy seconds." She steps back. "He likes to keep me all to himself."

She turns to walk away, but stops as we both see Luke standing next to the door.

For a second, I swear her face shows her fear, but she smiles and all traces of it are wiped away. Maybe I imagined it. His eyes never leave me. They're unreadable and cold. A shiver slides down my back.

"Looking for your toy?" Laughing, she walks over to him and dares to run her finger over his shoulder. That he lets her touch him is a slap in the face. "Let me know when you're ready to come back to a real woman."

She doesn't wait for a reply but leaves the bathroom. When the door shuts, Luke reaches out and locks it. My already stampeding pulse kicks up a notch, but he doesn't move toward me.

"What did she say, Harper?" Anger lingers in his every syllable, like it's my fault she was here.

My instinct wants me to back away. To turn and run, but there's nowhere to go and it won't change anything. He can find me. He always does. I twist the ring on my finger.

Fuck it. I've done nothing wrong. I lift my chin and step forward. A spark of desire lights in his eyes.

"That you two lost your virginities together, so you'll always go back to her." I don't need to hide what she said. If it's true, I want to know. I can't let it bother me. Even if it's trying to burn a hole in my chest, it doesn't mean anything. It just proves Sidney is a bitch.

Luke narrows his eyes and steps forward, but I hold my ground. "Yes, when we were thirteen, but that's not why I fuck her."

"Because she knows what you like?" I straighten and brace myself. It's not like he doesn't have all year to show me what he likes. He's been training me since he claimed me.

Luke shakes his head as he closes in on me slowly. "She's wrong."

But that makes sense. Otherwise why would he keep going back to her? She has to have something he likes. Of course, he's also been with eleven other women besides Sidney, and now me.

"She's surprised you're willing to share and says you keep her all to yourself. That I'm something different, but I'll never be what you need."

"And what did you say?" He stops in front of me, not touching me. Anticipation dances along my skin, waiting for his touch, craving it.

"That she has nothing to worry about then."

That soft, seductive scent he wears intoxicates me. This morning, I smelled his cologne in the bottle when he wasn't in the bathroom. It smells good, but there's something about the chemicals that react with Luke to make that scent irresistible.

"You worried, princess?" His thumb slides down the side of my throat.

I swallow as my brain liquifies at his touch. "About?"

"Me going back to her?" His head lowers until his lips hover an inch above mine. His breath caresses my lips, and shivers cascade down my spine.

"Should I be?" I whisper, wanting nothing more than his kiss.

His hand slides around the back of my neck. My insides soften in readiness. My breathing hitches as need pulses through me.

His darkened eyes search mine. "You keep questioning our deal, Harper. You keep wondering when we'll let you go."

"It's not unreasonable. You might regret committing to me for a year. You might do anything to get out of it." I don't really have an out, but the more time we spend together, the less I feel the need to break free. "All it would take is touching another girl."

He *tsks* me, soft sounds that make my pussy throb. "You're ours, princess. There's no escaping it. You're mine for as long as I want you to be."

"Just like Sidney was yours?" The bitterness clings to my tongue. I hate the taste of it, and worse, I'm sharing it with him. It's ammunition I'm willingly providing him.

He smiles. "Sidney was never mine, princess."

His lips descend. Every thought dissolves into nothingness as he claims my mouth thoroughly. Wiping away any thoughts of him with her. Staking his claim deep inside me like no one else can.

Whimpering, I succumb to the madness of being Luke Foster's. I wrap my arms around his neck, and he makes an appreciative noise in the back of his throat before he lifts me against the wall.

Wrapping my legs around his waist, I dig my fingers into his hair as I claim him back. For this year, he's mine. No other woman can claim that. If he wants me, I'm his, because whatever burns between us is too hot for me to resist.

CHAPTER 63

The Enemies' Territory

After my last class ends, I walk to Caden's locker. When my eyes meet Luke's, I blush, remembering making out during our history class. It surprised me that's all we did. But he cut it short and made me head back to class. Even more aroused than before.

Apparently Sidney took up too much of my time. Yet another reason to dislike her.

Nico pushes me against his locker and brings his mouth down close to my ear. His rain scent washes over me as he presses against me. "I could smell you on me all afternoon, sunshine. I need another taste."

I relax against the locker, putting my hands on his waist, and meet his dark eyes. Sparks ignite everywhere he touches me. He lowers his head and my insides tighten, ready for his kiss.

"We need to head to practice." Caden hits Nico on the shoulder, but Nico just continues to smile at me like we have all day.

"Who's driving me home?" I wet my lips, drawing Nico's attention to them. He could totally have kissed me during all this time. But I think he likes the anticipation, the craving.

"I've got you, princess." Luke's voice draws my attention his way.

My brow furrows. He's the captain of the football team. I thought

458

that's why he didn't give me rides home after school. The others can be a little late no problem, but not the captain.

Especially today. I have to meet with Sidney before leaving, meaning Luke will be later than normal.

He doesn't glance my way as he grabs his stuff. When he closes the locker, his gaze falls on Nico.

When I turn back to Nico, he kisses me. It's quick and leaves my lips buzzing and aching for more.

"See you at dinner, sunshine." He heads off with the others, leaving me alone with Luke.

"Is this because of Sidney?" I step closer to Luke, and he takes my hand.

"If she's going to pull something, I want to be there." Luke doesn't meet my eyes as we head toward the girls' locker room. Nerves begin to get to me, especially if Luke is worried this is a trap.

Edging closer to him, I try to keep from panicking. This is school. Coaches will be there. Kenz and the girls will be there. I'll be safe.

The Cheermonsters aren't like the horsemen. They'll get in trouble if they do anything. Even the guys know to keep fighting to a minimum at school.

Kenz, Penny, Nat, Izzy, and Vicky wait by the door of the locker room. A burst of relief floods through me. I knew Kenz wouldn't let me down, but the other girls could have ditched. They want my guys, but that doesn't mean they want to declare war on the Cheermonsters.

Luke turns me to face him. One hand grasps my arm, and the other the back of my neck. My heart pounds so hard I'm surprised he can't hear it as I lift my gaze.

"If anything goes wrong, yell." Luke's eyes search mine. I swallow. What does he think will happen?

"We've got this." Kenz steps forward and wraps her arm around my shoulders.

Releasing me, Luke ignores the others, leans against the lockers, and looks down at his phone.

I draw in a breath and take off Nico's jersey, straightening my t-shirt. With a last glance at Luke, I lead my group into the locker room.

Honestly the more I think about it, the more it sounds like a trap.

Why not exchange jerseys in the hallway? Then the guys could have come with me. Maybe that's the point.

"We're going to be fine, H," Kenz whispers as we make our way down the banks of lockers to where we can hear the Cheermonsters talking.

I nod because I'm not sure what could happen down here. And even if I yell, I'm not sure Luke could hear me. Besides, what could he really do if a bunch of girls were in a fight? Sell tickets?

Tamping down my nerves, I round the corner.

When we step into sight, the Cheermonsters quiet and take in my posse. Fuck, I have a posse. This is too weird. Sidney and the others have on shorts and t-shirts with their sneakers, ready for their practice. At least I don't have to see them in my guys' jerseys again.

Sidney gives me a knowing smile. Ashley rolls her eyes at Kenz beside me. The other two finish tying their laces, but they're aware of our presence.

I hold out Nico's jersey to Ashley. She takes it out of my hand and thrusts Eli's into mine.

"You know you're temporary, right?" Ashley leans back against the locker with her arms crossed.

"So you keep telling me." I'm ready to leave. This is the same song and dance.

Ashley smirks. "You couldn't possibly take it the way he likes. He'll get bored and come begging for the good stuff."

"Okay." I shrug. I'm not sure what she wants from me, but I'm not about to tell her Eli and I do just fine. What happens between me and the guys is not up for discussion.

"You might want to reconsider who you let get close to you." Sidney smiles at the girls behind me. "There's a reason we don't have many friends outside our group and why we each have a guy we get with. It helps maintain order."

I turn to Penny. She gives me a reassuring smile. Do I think they might try something with a horseman? Possibly, but I'm confident the guys won't let that stand. And I'm willing to take whatever punishment Eli throws my way because of it. At least I'm not down here alone.

"Noted." I turn back to Sidney. "Same time tomorrow?"

Her green eyes assess me. So far, I've agreed with everything she's thrown my way. I only popped off one time at her party and I was buzzing hard when I did. But Sidney wasn't there. If she wants to believe the guys will come back to them, I won't be the one putting up a fight.

Luke says they're mine, so I'm going to believe they're mine. Do I think it will last as long as they claim? I have no clue. I don't know what the future holds for us, but right now, I'm confident in who they want.

"Same time tomorrow." Sidney nods and glances at Emma. "You'll get Jack's for the day, then Friday you and I can switch before the game. Luke's orders. You know how he likes to order you around."

I cock my head to the side. "Of course. I wouldn't be in this situation if I didn't."

Words I can handle. I've never been in a girl fight and really don't want to be, but I'll hold my own if they come at me. I won't go crying to the guys to fight this battle unless the girls try to outnumber me.

"Good. Now be a good little pet and go tell your owner I was pleasant to you." Sidney turns, dismissing me.

Ashley watches me like she's trying to figure out my game. I guess they don't believe I'm not playing one. I'm doing what I need to survive this year. Being with the horsemen is my current lot in life. I've accepted it.

It doesn't entirely suck, but it's also not what I would have chosen. These girls chose to be with the horsemen. Maybe they don't believe a girl would want to resist them.

Kenz pulls my arm, and we walk away.

"Well, that was anticlimactic," Nat mutters, clearly disappointed.

"I prefer it that way." When I glance behind us, just in case, the Cheermonsters aren't watching. I release my breath. "Thank you guys for coming. Can you do the same tomorrow and Friday?"

Because otherwise Luke might punish me. We can't let our guard down just because it went fine this first time. That may be exactly what they expect, and Friday the guys will be occupied.

"Sure," Izzy says with a grin. "I can't wait until the party Friday night."

The others nod and smile at each other.

Eli's in my head now, because I can't help but wonder what else they'll want. I knew when Penny first approached me that they wanted to use me. I don't know if they're being honest about what they want now.

We step out of the locker room, and the girls part ways with me, saying they'll text tonight. It's kind of nice being in a group chat with them. It's different from hanging with Kenz. But Kenz is my ride or die.

Kenz hangs back when the others leave.

Luke doesn't move from his position with his phone, giving me a moment with Kenz.

"I don't know if you can trust those girls, H." She blows out a breath. "I don't think they're doing this out of the kindness of their hearts. These girls didn't give two shits about you until Luke claimed you. And I'm not confident they'll stand up to the Cheermonsters if they try something."

I nod. I'm not naive enough to think the girls just want to hang out and be friends. "If those girls try something with the guys, they'll fail or I'll be free."

"They'll fail." Luke's hand wraps around my neck and draws me back into his heat. Holy hell, I want to sink into him. It's like being cold and then someone throws a warm blanket over you.

"On that note, I should head out. Text me, H." Kenz smiles and takes off down the hallway.

We're alone when Luke begins to massage my hip. "How did it go?"

My pulse thrums in my ears as my body responds to his presence. I try to shake it off, but there's just too much of whatever binds us together swimming through my veins. I close my eyes and lean into Luke.

"Princess." His lips caress the edge of my ear as his voice weaves through me. His words are almost a growl as he says, "Answer me."

Desire pulses through me, and I whimper, needing more. Always needing so much more of all of them.

"Now."

I open my eyes to the empty hallway and try to orient myself. "They made more remarks about how you guys won't stay with me, but the tradeoff went flawlessly. We have two more trades. Tomorrow and Friday."

"Good." He turns me in his arms, and I lift my gaze to drown in the heated pools of his eyes. His thumb caresses my bottom lip. "We need to get you home."

For a second, we stand there. I want him to kiss me. This aching need for him clings to my bones.

Instead, he takes my hand and leads me out to his car. I try to calm my rioting hormones on the way to my house. Not sure I achieve much control.

"I'll pick you up for Nico's." Luke pulls into my driveway, jarring me back to reality.

My car sits next to my mom's. We drove here this morning so I could leave my car at home. I'm sure he needs to get back to practice, but part of me wants to linger in his presence just a while longer.

"Harper, if I stay any longer, I'll fuck you, and we'll both be in trouble." He leans his head back against the seat. "I'll see you in a few hours, princess."

I blow out a frustrated breath, knowing he's right. My mother is right inside. He has to get to practice. And I want nothing more than to straddle his lap and let him make me come alive.

I open the door and get out. Our eyes meet through the windshield as he backs out of my driveway. I don't understand what's going on with me and Luke. Maybe the chemicals are just too strong, but I'm drawn to him. It doesn't matter that he's an asshole most of the time.

Shaking off the feeling, I head inside and let my backpack thud on the ground.

"Mom! I'm home!" I take Eli's jersey into the laundry room and put it on the cold cycle to wash away Ashley's perfume. It's light, but I don't want to smell her on me.

When I come back into the kitchen, Mom sits at the island waiting for me.

"How was Penny's last night?" Her eyes track my movements as I pick up my backpack and set it on the table.

"Good." Keep it short and to the point so she doesn't get suspicious.

"Any issues?"

"Nope. Her house is nice, and her mom was friendly. I slept well." I give her a smile. "Much better than staying alone in the house."

"And hanging out with the guys went well?"

I sit at the table. "Yes, they were all gentlemen. We played a high stakes game of Chutes and Ladders."

Mom shakes her head. "As long as it's not hide the salami—"

"Ew, Mom." I laugh, but my heart races a little harder. How long can I really expect to keep this a secret from my mom? The dating thing is going to come up. What happens at Homecoming? Are we even going together? As a group?

"You okay, Harper?" Mom's tone dips into concern.

I blow out a breath and tuck my hair behind my ear. My gaze blurs on the book in front of me. "A lot is going on with the guys and some girls at school. I'm not used to the attention, I guess."

"Make sure you take care of yourself first, before all the drama." Mom clasps her hands in front of her. "It's fun to have that kind of attention and distraction, but if you lose yourself in it, what's the point?"

It's all new and exciting right now. The guys and I are just getting warmed up. But what happens in a month? Three months? What about when I have my period? Is this all our relationship (if you can call it that) will be? Sex?

When the guys told me their numbers of sexual partners, they said how long it had been. A week and a half, two weeks, a month. Right? So we don't have to have sex every night of the week. Maybe they're taking advantage of the fact they have access this week. Or maybe it's new and shiny.

I'm too damn curious not to take advantage.

"Hey?" Mom sounds concerned. "You faded out there for a bit."

"Just thinking." I set my backpack on the chair beside me. "I'm going to do some homework before going to Nico's for dinner tonight."

"You're having dinner at Nico's?" Mom perks up.

"Yeah, his mom wants the guys and me to come over for dinner." I open my book. Nico said he told his mother I'm his girlfriend. It's not really a lie. But it's not all of the truth.

I'm not sure what we're doing could be considered boyfriend and girlfriend. While I kind of had a choice in the matter, I also didn't. We're not exactly going out on dates and spending time getting to know each other.

No, we're rushing off to have a quickie at lunch. Which may be normal teenage dating. How would I know?

"I don't know what to think about this, Harper. I've heard of group dating, where it's a bunch of guys and girls going out together to hang out, but just you and a group of guys seems a little progressive?" She says *progressive* like she's not sure it's the word she's looking for.

"We're not dating." I shrug, though it feels like we are, but we aren't. We're definitely fucking now, but no one is trying to get to know me better. Caden talks about our future. That's about as close as we come.

We've gone to parties together. We've slept together. We're exclusive. But we're not dating.

"I honestly don't know what I'm doing," I admit and turn in my chair to meet Mom's eyes. "I like them all." Mostly. "But I don't want to date just one of them. We're all going to college next year, and everything will change."

"Then have fun this year." Mom stands and brushes off her pajama pants. "You don't have to settle on one guy. They seem to all want to hang out together. So maybe friendship is all you guys have this year. There's nothing wrong with that."

I'd laugh if I didn't think it would raise more questions. Sure, friends. "Friends would be nice."

CHAPTER 64

Hostile Environment

Nico

I wait in the living room while Mom finishes in the kitchen. I've never been this anxious about having someone over. My mom met most of my girlfriends. We even had dinner with them, but this feels different.

Harper means more than those girls.

Those girls were being introduced to my mom for the first time. Mom knows Harper from back when we were kids. What will she think of Harper now that she's grown? Now that I've claimed her as my girlfriend.

Luke made it very clear in the locker room after practice that she can be my girlfriend for my parents, but that's it. Possessive asshole probably never thought maybe Harper would like to have a title besides *ours*.

The doorbell rings, and I open the door.

"Hey." Jack walks in, followed by Caden. "Dude, it smells delicious in here."

I smile and rub the back of my neck. I never had these guys over when we were kids either. "It's the best."

Before I can shut the door, Eli walks up the steps. "Nice place."

We're down the street from Eli's house. The house we have now is a lot bigger and in a better neighborhood than the one down the block from Harper's. I miss that old house. We felt like more of a family when we lived there.

Dad didn't work all the time, and Mom didn't feel the need to escape the house and her family. In New York, we all went our separate ways. Basically had our own lives. I'm not sure what was so urgent to lead us back here, but I can't help feeling grateful for whatever it was.

We sit in the living room while we wait for Harper and Luke. It seems like we're always waiting for them.

"How's this going to work going forward?" It's been weighing on my mind. "Harper's mom doesn't work thirds all the time."

"We'll have the weekends." Caden leans forward with his hands clasped between his knees. "There are some spots at school. Lunches. Just because we can't sleep together doesn't mean we can't hang out."

Maybe it's for the best. Harper needs time outside of us. She must have had some life before the guys swooped in and took it over.

"I've got a plan for tomorrow night." Eli looks around the room, taking in everything. Mom's unpacked a lot, but a few boxes remain in the corner. "Harper's staying at my house."

Jack chuckles. "Until your parents find her and kick her out. You're better off sneaking out to sleep with her at one of the other guys' houses. Or fuck, say you need to study late and just stay the night at Caden's. It's not unrealistic for us to have a test and, with football, not a lot of time to study for it."

"We just need to be on the same page." Eli nods. "I want a night alone with her."

"When we get past the last barrier, we can make arrangements." Caden rubs his hands together. "I have a plan if we can all stay at my house tomorrow night."

The doorbell rings before he can tell us. When I open the door, Harper gives me this smile that makes me want to forget about the other guys and take her back to my room, so I can take my time and explore every inch of her. I swear my heart thumps hard in my chest at the sight of my girl.

Luke follows her in, touching fists with Eli as he takes a seat beside him.

I draw her into the living room, and my mom pokes her head out of the kitchen.

"Is that Harper?" Mom grins, wiping her hands on a towel as she looks around at the guys. "And I've seen you all on the football field, but you're a lot bigger than I remember."

"Mom, this is Jack, Caden, Luke, and Eli." I didn't have a lot of friends in New York to have over. I hung out with guys at school and at parties, but no one really meshed well with me.

"It's good to see you again, Mrs. Lee." Eli stands and offers her his hand. She shakes it.

Her cheeks flush as she looks up at Eli, and the others stand as well. "Definitely not little boys anymore."

When she turns, her gaze lands on Harper next to me. Her smile softens. "My goodness, how you've grown."

"Hi, Mrs. Lee."

Mom pulls Harper into her arms and hugs her. "I'm so glad you and Nico found your way back to each other. His other girlfriends were such snobby girls."

Harper glances over her shoulder at me, and I just shrug. I'm not with those girls now, but I liked them at the time. The truth was, they were never her. Never Harper.

Mom steps away from Harper and looks her over. "I can't imagine you without pigtails and scraped knees."

Harper smiles. "I can't wait for your famous lasagna."

"I hope you don't mind we aren't formal." Mom glances at me. "I couldn't find the dishes I wanted, and there are still so many boxes in the dining room. We can squeeze in around the kitchen table."

"It's fine, Mom. They aren't expecting a full dinner service." We follow my mom and Harper into the kitchen, and the smell in here is even better. In the center of the table is a glass dish of lasagna, brimming with cheese and tomato sauce.

"This smells fantastic, Mrs. Lee." Caden sits, and his eyes go to Harper.

But Mom has plans apparently. "You'll sit next to me, darling, and Nico can sit on your other side."

Mom releases Harper. I take Harper's hand and give it a squeeze to reassure her. We all sit down as Mom adds garlic bread to the table.

"Do you mind serving, Nico?" Mom grabs her napkin and puts it in her lap.

"No problem." I make sure everyone has a slice of lasagna as they pass around the garlic bread. Harper puts a few pieces of bread on my plate before passing it on.

We settle into our seats, and for a few minutes, it's quiet as everyone begins to eat.

"This is amazing," Jack says with his mouth full.

"Thank you." Mom blushes. "So how is everyone's school year going? What classes do you have?"

Everyone shares a few of their classes. When Harper mentions art, Mom smiles indulgently.

"At dinner yesterday, Nico told me about his first assignment in art class."

I need to stop her before she accidentally calls Harper out about her partner. "The guys don't want to hear about art, Mom."

"Nico, you don't have to be modest. He received awards in New York for his pieces. I find it interesting your art teacher divided up the class the way she did. Everyone with a partner, but you didn't get to choose." Mom smiles as she looks around the table. "It's a good idea to pair up people outside of their friend groups."

Harper's worried eyes flash up to mine. Hopefully Mom will let it drop. I didn't tell the guys about Tanner because Harper didn't want to make it a thing. But given their reaction to him the other day and Caden's story, it's a big deal.

"Weren't you saying no one was put with their friends?" Mom looks at the breadbasket and sees it's empty. "Oh, let me get more garlic bread."

"What's your mom talking about?" Luke asks quietly as soon as she's on the other side of the kitchen. His eyes don't leave Harper.

"Art class partners for a project. I'm paired with Angela Harris." I lean back in my chair, and Harper takes my hand under the table and squeezes it. "Penny got stuck with William Frank."

"Will's a good guy." Caden points his fork at me. "He's been in my art classes for years."

"Penny doesn't seem to think so," Harper comments.

She probably would have been fine if she hadn't said anything.

Mom brings the bread back to the table and sits. "Anyway, I think what the teacher did is a good thing. You don't get to pick who you work with in the real world."

"Who's your partner, Harper?" Luke's gaze never falters from her, even though she doesn't meet his eyes.

She blows out a breath and looks to me for reinforcements. Fuck, I wish I could help her with this, but she's the one who wanted to deal with it and keep the guys out of it. Besides, it's only been two classes. It won't be that big of a deal if we tell them now.

"Tanner Lewis." I lift my gaze to Caden.

He freezes for a moment. His gaze meets Harper's, and she flinches.

"It's a project that's completed during class time," she rushes out. "There was no changing partners, so I figured there was no point mentioning it."

Mom catches on to the tension. "Do we not like Tanner Lewis?"

"He's not a nice guy." Harper pushes her lasagna around her plate.

"That's a shame. Nico says Angela is okay."

Thanks, Mom. Harper arches her eyebrow when she lifts her gaze to mine.

I shrug. I wasn't about to tell my mom the chick wants to fuck me.

Mom smiles. "It'll be a good life lesson then."

Yeah, don't discuss things with my mom ever.

***

HARPER

"Dinner was lovely. Thank you again for having me over, Mrs. Lee." I'm putting off leaving. Caden is furious. Luke looks like he's going to spank me. Eli and Jack worked the whole meal to keep the tension from being obvious to Mrs. Lee.

"I expect you to be around a lot. Now that you two are dating." Her gaze drops to our hands woven together.

"Of course." I honestly hope Nico can talk some sense into Luke before he punishes me. I decided to keep it from them so it wouldn't become a thing. Caden doesn't need to be reminded of what that fucker did to his sister.

"We're headed to Luke's to do some homework, and then I'll be home." Nico kisses his mom on her cheek before steering me out the door. "You can ride in my car, sunshine."

We hurry to his car, and he holds open the door for me. Caden and Luke hang back, watching us. They're talking quietly.

"Change of plans." Luke steps forward as Nico closes my door. "We're going to Caden's."

Nico nods and steps away from the car, but I can still hear them.

"I'm there to watch him with her," Nico says. "They've barely talked. I can protect her, Luke."

"We'll talk when we get there." He claps Nico on the shoulder. "Don't think you can protect her from us."

Nico's words are lost to me as he lowers his voice. Luke's gaze grabs hold of mine, and I'm pinned in place by him. He doesn't like that I kept this from him, but my life doesn't have to be an open book to these guys.

Luke shifts his gaze to Nico, releasing me. I draw a breath into my starving lungs. Fuck. Tonight might be a shit show I'll be the center of. Wanting to avoid any more captured gazes, I purposely look away from the guys while they finish talking.

The car door opens, and Nico climbs in. "We should have told them from the start."

"Why? It's literally been a day, and nothing has happened." I throw my hands up as Nico drives to Caden's house. "Why must they know every aspect of my life? Seriously it's a fucking group project. They can't control who the teacher assigns me."

"This isn't just someone, sunshine." Nico's voice is calm as he takes the turns. "We both don't know how deep this goes, but we know enough to be wary of the guy. Who's to say he won't take advantage of this? We don't know Tanner. They do."

"She drew them randomly." I blow my hair out of my face as I rest my head against the seat.

I didn't know Tanner. Don't know Tanner. Yes, he tried to trick me to get revenge on the horsemen, but that didn't and won't happen.

And now I'm probably heading to get punished. Part of me is secretly thrilled at the prospect, since it will be a private punishment and not a public humiliation.

Nico pulls in behind Caden's car and turns off the ignition. "I can't go against the guys on this one, Harper."

I look down at my hands in my lap. "I know."

He was my friend first, but I'm not the one he saw every summer. I'm the one who hid herself away. He ghosted me and that hurt. I'm lucky I found Kenz or I would have had no one.

"Hey, I won't let them take it too far." Nico cups my cheek and turns my face to his.

"What's too far, Nico?" I bite out. It's been building in me all day with the Cheermonsters and Nico. I'm just done. "Spanking? Whipping? Torture? Where's the limit on what they can do to me and you'll be like *hey, guys, maybe we should think this over?*"

"Harper—"

"No, you chose. All those years ago, you chose them over me. And you'll continue to do that. You'll follow their edicts because you're one of them." My throat thickens, and tears press forward, but I hold them back. "For a second, I thought you were mine too, but I'm wrong. You're just another owner."

I get out of his car before he can hold me back. I'm angry at myself for thinking he could be something other than a horseman. That maybe he would be on my side. Not always, but occasionally.

He took me out for lunch so he could fuck me with his jersey on. Not because I'm special.

I swipe at the tear that escapes down my cheek. I'm not special to these guys. I'm another hole for them to fill. Somewhere along the line, I stopped believing I'm only a toy for them to use. Maybe with Caden's constant future talk, I bought in just a little.

Fuck them. I don't need any of them. They can use me as their pet until the end of this year, and then they'll be out of my life forever.

CHAPTER 65

The Defiance

CADEN

"She probably didn't want you to worry." Jack tries to convince me Harper didn't do anything wrong. "The project just started. She might have told us if it got to be too much."

But she knows the story. She knows how much I hate Tanner and why.

She's not safe where he's involved. He waited for her outside her house. He made her believe he was her friend and he could help her with us. He would have used her to get back at me.

"If he touches her, I'll break every bone in that hand." The words are a promise.

"She doesn't want you to go to prison." Jack pulls in beside Nico's car.

Nico stands beside his car, his arms on the roof, staring into the darkness around my house.

I get out, but she isn't here. Luke told me to let her go with Nico, but right now I need her in my arms. I need to know she's safe. But I'm also mad as hell at her.

"Where is she?" I growl out.

Nico releases a breath and gestures toward the house.

Luke pulls up with Eli, while I walk around to the back of the house to find my little nympho. There's patio furniture beside the door, and I find her huddled on an Adirondack chair.

Swiping at the tears on her cheeks, she doesn't acknowledge me. I'm not playing that game again. Fuck this shit.

I lift her and throw her over my shoulder.

"Hey!"

My hand clamps down on her ass to hold her there. Jack catches up to us and opens the door.

"Put me down, Caden." She struggles against me, but I hold her firm.

When the others file in, Luke gives me a nod. I can run this show, or he can. It's up to me.

Eli turns the lights on low in the rec room. Jack goes to the door to the rest of the house and makes sure it's locked, in case any staff is still here. I'm sure my parents already know I haven't slept at home for a while. They may be absent, but they keep tabs on my activities.

Nico and Luke sit on the couch as I lower Harper to her feet.

She immediately backs away, and her eyes dart around like she's expecting to be attacked. She's not wrong. I want to impress on her the seriousness of this situation.

"He can't be trusted," I bite out as I stalk around her.

She tips her chin up. "The teacher is there the whole time. I'm at school. He can't do anything to me while I'm there."

"He's a fucking blight, Harper." I stop in front of her and close the distance, so I'm practically surrounding her. "He'll use any opportunity to get under your skin. To turn you against us."

A bitter laugh erupts out of her. When I glare into her dark eyes, they sparkle with anger.

"Like you all fucking care." She straightens to her full height and stares me in the eyes like she's not afraid of me. "As long as he doesn't touch me, I don't see what the problem is. I have an assignment to do for my class. If I thought my teacher would let me change partners, I would. But she's being strict about it."

"He wants revenge on us, and he's going to use you to get it." I need to get this into her head.

"By what? Telling me his fucking sob story that isn't true? Do you think I'm naive enough to fall for a fucker like that? That I'll believe his word over yours? He's a fucking sociopath at the least, and a psychopath at the worst."

"I don't want you near him."

"I'm not dropping the class." She crosses her arms over her chest. "That's the only thing that would solve this. Ms. Sullivan won't change partners unless I have a damn good reason. While *he creeps me out and makes the guys who own me angry* are good excuses for us, they won't be for her."

"Why didn't you tell us?" I grit out. She should have come to me right away. She should have fucking trusted me with this. I've given her no reason not to trust me. I've proven myself time and time again, and I'm getting sick of always caving.

Her lips press together in a stubborn expression.

"You're a smart girl, little nympho. You knew we'd find out eventually, so why not tell us?" I use my size to intimidate people, but Harper is too damn comfortable with me.

"What would be the point? You couldn't do anything." She shoves my chest to push me away, but I don't budge. "What would you have done? Gone over to his house and beat him up? Gotten arrested?"

A flash of fear rushes through her eyes. Is she worried about me? That stops me for a second. She's not wrong. I hate the guy. Him having access to Harper will drive me mad.

How do we fix this? How do we get him away from Harper?

"We need to punish her," Luke says.

Her dark eyes narrow, and her lips press together. This is my shit to deal with. She's mine to punish.

"Do you understand why you're being punished, little nympho?" When I reach out, she flinches, but I just push her hair behind her ear.

"Because you guys are assholes." She knocks my hand away. Fuck, she's feisty tonight. Normally I'd slowly ease her out of her mood, but rage brews deep inside me. I want her to fight back. I want her to argue with me.

Tanner having access to Harper makes my blood boil. That she thinks she can decide how to handle him adds to the heat pouring through me. She's mine to protect.

"Try again, little nympho." My fingers flex, needing to make sure she knows her place.

"Okay, you're controlling dicks." She gives me a fuck-you smile.

"Strip." My voice is calm, but when she meets my eyes, she almost steps back. Almost. Her smile falls. By the end of tonight, she'll learn to not keep things from me.

She crosses her arms and would look down her nose if I weren't a foot taller than her. "No."

"Who do you belong to, Harper?" I may sound calm, but the anger festers inside me like an open wound.

"Myself, War."

"Wrong answer."

"Fuck. Off."

My hand goes to her throat, and I push her back until she's up against the wall. I don't tighten my grip, just hold her there. Still no fear in her eyes.

I can feel the guys' eyes on us. They're patiently waiting for when I need their assistance. Or if they need to pull me off her.

"You belong to me, little nympho." My other hand goes to her jeans button.

Her eyes widen, and her hands grab my wrist. "You can't own me."

"But I do. You let me in, little nympho. You became mine." Despite her efforts, I undo her button and slide her zipper down. I lower my head until my lips hover over hers. "Nothing is going to change that."

Her hot breath bathes my lips as she huffs. "It's temporary."

I slide my hand beneath her panties and thrust my finger into her soaking wet pussy. "This pussy belongs to me. Forever."

She draws in a sharp breath.

"If I want my pussy to come, I'll make it come. If I want my pussy to not come, I'll withhold its orgasm." I don't move my finger from her slick heat, feeling her cunt clutch at it. "If I want to fuck this pussy, I will. If I want all of us to fuck this pussy, we will."

Her eyes slip closed, and her hips rock against my hand. "Caden."

My name is barely a breath against my lips. It makes the anger flicker. She could easily blow out the flames. Fuck, I can't let it go out. I need to make sure no matter what she's afraid of in the future, she'll tell me. She needs to tell me so I can keep her safe.

"Eli, we need bindings." I curl my finger to stroke the spot inside her that makes her toes curl and rub my thumb in circles over her clit. "I'm going to make you come so much it hurts, little nympho, but I'm not going to stop."

Her dark eyes are hooded when she opens them to look at me. Her lips part as I wind her closer and closer to the first of many. She's so close. She'll learn my way is much better compared to Eli's. He likes to withhold, but I'm a giver.

She keeps her eyes locked with mine as her breathing grows rapid. Her fingers tighten around my wrist, but she's no longer trying to pull it away. I'm not sure she even realizes she's holding on.

"Come for me, baby."

Her eyes widen as her body arches against me. A small cry escapes her lips as her cunt clenches around my finger. I hold her by her neck and pussy and chase her release, still thrusting into her and circling her clit.

Her face softens as she squirms against me. Her darkened eyes blink up at mine.

"Jack," I call out.

She sighs against my lips as I slow down my movements.

"Go to my room and get me something to help my little nympho."

Jack's chuckle is delightfully wicked. "On it."

"The ottoman, Luke."

He'll know which one I mean. Have I ever used it for this? No, but it's perfect to keep her right where I want her.

"Are you ready to be a good girl, Harper?" I touch my lips to hers briefly.

When I lift my head, her lips press together in a stubborn line. I grin, loving that she's willing to defy me and knowing what I plan to do to make her pay for that defiance.

"Nico, come here." I draw my hand out of her pussy and swipe my slick finger over her lips.

She parts them, and her tongue comes out to taste herself. Fuck, this girl wrecks me. I'm going to fuck her until she submits tonight.

"Yeah." He glances at me and then at Harper.

She doesn't look at him, but I feel her tense beneath my touch. Her brown eyes stay locked with mine.

"Take her clothes off." I step back, still holding her by her throat against the wall.

He puts his hands on her jeans. When she reaches for his hand, I grab hers and hold it against the wall. "Unless you want me to spank you, you'll let him do what I asked of him."

Her eyes narrow, and her lips purse, but her other hand drops to her side. Her defiant gaze never leaves mine as Nico slides her jeans down her hips. He stops to remove her shoes and socks before taking the jeans off the rest of the way.

He draws her panties down her legs next, leaving her bare from the waist down. When he stands next to me, he gestures to my hand around her throat.

Smiling at her, I release her hand and cup her pussy, sliding my finger back inside her. She sucks in a breath. I remove my other hand from her throat.

Nico grabs the hem of her t-shirt. "Arms up, sunshine."

That gets her attention. She glares as she raises her arms. He winces, but takes off her shirt and then her bra. Yeah, he did something to piss her off. Maybe ratting her out to us. With his help, she could have gotten away with it for weeks.

I cup her breast, and her attention returns to my face. Good. I pinch her nipple, and she hisses at the pain.

"Get undressed," I tell the others.

Her pussy gets wetter around my finger. I pump it inside her a few times, loving that mesmerized look in her eyes as the fire gets to be too much for her.

"Undress me, little nympho."

She reaches for my shirt and gives me an impatient look.

I take my hands off her and lift my arms. She's not tall enough to take my shirt off without pressing her body against mine. The heat of her skin is exquisite as it rubs against my belly and she presses her tits into my chest.

I duck a little to help her and then straighten. "The pants too."

She grabs the waistband of my athletic pants and draws them down my legs, releasing my cock. She kneels before me to get my shoes and socks off before removing my pants.

Her gaze lifts to mine, stalling for a second on my erection. She's still angry, but her skin flushes with desire and her breasts rise and fall with each quickened breath. Her nipples are hard as she rises before me.

I step in, closing the distance between us, letting the heat of my body flow over hers, but not touching yet. I put a hand on the wall on either side of her head.

"What are you being punished for, little nympho?"

She wets her lips. "For being a rational being."

I'm sure my smile is anything but pleasant as I chuckle at her obstinance. I lean down so I'm in her face. "Tell you what, this ends when you tell me exactly why you're being punished. Not a second before."

That mulish expression crosses her face again, and I slide my finger inside her pussy, stroking it in and out while our eyes search each other's for weaknesses.

Fuck, I hope she never tells me. She shifts against the wall. Her lips part as I push her closer and closer to the edge. When her hand reaches out for my cock, it twitches at her touch.

I let her stroke up and down a few times before I remove her hand.

Her lips pull down.

"Don't worry, little nympho. I'll get mine."

Jack leans on the wall next to Harper. We still don't break eye contact.

When I slip my fingers out of her, she whimpers. I grin because that's the last time I'll leave her wanting. I hold my hand out to Jack, and he puts the bullet vibrator in it.

Palming the bullet, I turn it on and thrust my fingers back inside her tight, wet cunt, pressing the bullet up against her clit.

"Ah." Her eyes widen, and she grabs my wrist with both hands. Jack takes one of her hands, and I press the other against the wall while I thrust my finger in and out and hold the vibrator against her clit.

Jack wraps her hand and his around his cock and strokes them up and down. Her gaze loses focus as she comes all over my fingers. Her moans fill the air as her pussy squeezes around me.

She collapses against the wall, but I haven't taken the vibrator from her clit. She shifts her hips and soon she's coming again. Her breathing is harsh as she looks at me in panic. Her fingers clench around my hand.

"Caden!"

"One more, little nympho."

I curl my finger inside her this time and stroke her G-spot while the bullet rides her clit.

She groans, and her head drops to my chest as she releases, gushing around my finger. Jack groans with her as he comes.

I hand him the vibrator and lift her against me. She's lax and sighs when her oversensitive skin touches mine. I walk her over to the others, sitting her on the ottoman.

Kneeling before her, I lift her chin so our eyes meet. Hers are unfocused. "Do you want to tell me why you're being punished?"

That makes her eyes focus on mine, and her lips press together in a thin line. "For not being a simpering bitch in heat for you all."

I capture her lips with mine. She arches into me and gives in to the kiss, threading her fingers through my hair. Eli works on her ankles while I have her distracted, tying her legs to the ottoman's on either side, spreading her open.

She draws away and looks down at her ankles in surprise. I ease her back on the ottoman as Eli rounds to her head.

"Caden?" Her eyes widen and there's a question in them.

"Luke's right. You need to be punished. You're ours, Harper. If someone messes with you, we need to know about it even if you think it's insignificant."

"It's not like he arranged the assignment. It was random." She turns to watch as Eli takes her hand and ties her wrist to the leg of the ottoman. "I'm not stupid."

"But you're stubborn." I stroke my hand down over her breast and trembling stomach. "You still resist us, even when you give in."

I slide my finger over her clit as he ties her other wrist, and she tenses before she presses into my touch.

"The rules." I raise my gaze to the guys standing there naked, stroking their cocks. "Her mouth and cunt are on a first come, first served basis."

"For fuck's sake." She jerks at her hands.

"Breasts are available as long as there's space." I hold up the bullet, and it buzzes in my hand. She lets out a little whimper. "Pass the bullet to the next in line. The objective is to make her come, and often."

"I don't see how this is punishment." Her words are breathy as she strains against my finger.

I lower to lick from her entrance to her clit. She freezes, holding her breath, waiting for when I descend.

"Pleasure borders on pain, little nympho. It'll still feel really fucking good because of the chemicals in your brain, but it'll get to be too much." I release a breath over her wet pussy, and she shivers. "This ends when you confess."

CHAPTER 66

Enemy Mine

Caden

Nico steps forward with a small hand bell some decorator thought would look good on a shelf. I nod to him as he slides it into Harper's hand.

"Ring it when you're ready to confess. If you ring it before, Jack will fuck your ass."

"So much for wanting me to *give* you my virginity." She squirms against my finger, but my finger gets wetter. Maybe she likes the idea of us taking that first. Some girls don't want to admit they want anal.

Not tonight though. Not when I'm so fucking angry with her. Later, we can talk it over.

"Don't use the bell unless you're ready for one or the other, little nympho." I lower my mouth over her sweet pussy. She cries out for a second before her mouth is muffled.

Luke's got his cock in her mouth, holding her head while he fucks it. Jack kneels beside her and takes her breast into his mouth. Eli stands behind me, waiting, while Nico takes her other breast.

I get to work. Eating pussy is my favorite thing to do, especially Harper's. She doesn't fake a thing like some girls. That she gets off on it is a fucking bonus. Her body arches like a bow as I spear my tongue into her juicy cunt, over and over.

When I suck on her clit, she shatters, moaning deep and long. The vibration must do Luke in. He curses as he comes down her throat. When he backs away, Jack takes his spot. While she's still twitching from her orgasm, I rise to my knees and line my cock up with her entrance.

I slide into her tight cunt as it squeezes all around me. She groans as I sink in all the way. Fuck, I love her pussy, eating it, fucking it, just staring at it.

The bullet is on when I press it against her clit. She jolts like she's electrocuted. Her ankles and wrists strain against the ties, but the bell doesn't ring. I wait, buried deep inside her, feeling her cunt convulse around my cock.

This is where she belongs. Letting us own every inch of her delectable body. I pull back, and she whimpers around Jack's cock. I thrust in deep and steady, rubbing the little bullet around her clit.

She moans as she comes all over my cock, dragging me into my release. I continue to thrust through my orgasm as her pussy milks my cock. When my cock begins to soften, I pull out and hand the bullet to Eli before I sit on the floor with my back against the couch to watch.

Eli thrusts inside her, pressing the bullet to her clit, and Jack groans as he releases down her throat. Nico moves into place and slides his cock between her red lips.

Her body arches over the ottoman. Her nipples are hard and tight. She's so fucking gorgeous. No other girl has made me as hard as Harper does.

Luke strokes his cock slowly, waiting for Eli to finish. She moans around Nico's cock as she comes again. Her back arches, and her legs strain against the ties. We can't get enough of her, and she can't seem to get enough of us.

Jack sits beside me as we watch Nico fuck her mouth while Eli pounds her pussy.

"She won't cave easily." Jack shakes his head, even as his own cock swells again.

"She will." Because I won't relent.

Nico comes in her mouth and draws away. She pants and squirms as much as she can as Eli pistons his cock in and out of her. He rubs the bullet in circles around her clit until she screams. Her body shudders as she comes, drawing Eli into his release.

He groans as he fills her with his cum and draws out, handing the bullet to Luke. Luke thrusts into her in one stroke, making her moan as an aftershock or another orgasm overtakes her. I go to kneel before her head.

Her eyes are closed as I slip my fingers into her hair, cradling her head in my palm. Her mouth opens in silent invitation. Fuck, this girl. I slide my thumb over her lower lip.

"Little nympho, this ends when you tell me what I want to hear." I reach forward and cup her breast.

She moans and opens her blown brown eyes, focusing on mine. "You think a few orgasms will loosen my lips?"

Her eyes squeeze shut as she comes around Luke's cock. I pinch her nipple, and she cries out. Fine, she wants it rough.

I slide my cock into her mouth, and she sucks on me, licking my dick as I thrust it in and out of her, watching it disappear inside her.

"Fuck!" Luke yells as he slams inside her rapidly before burying himself in her pussy and groaning.

She moans around my cock, long. The vibrations make me see stars, but I don't come. Luke hands Jack the bullet.

Jack grins before he lowers his mouth to her pussy, licking her swollen clit. Her breath hitches, and she makes little noises around my cock, sending vibrations through me again. He's going to get both Harper and me off if he keeps doing that to her.

He thrusts two fingers into her cunt and then trails them down to her ass, sliding both of them in at once. Fucking her ass with his fingers while he eats her out. When she tenses, I pull out of her mouth as she screams through an orgasm.

He rises and meets my eyes. His chin glistens with her wetness and ours. Slowly, he eases his cock into her pussy. Her breath catches.

"Fuck, sweetheart. Are you even coming down between climaxes?" He presses the bullet to her clit while fucking her pussy and thrusting his fingers into her ass.

I lean over her and take her breast into my mouth, sucking on her nipple. She licks my cock when it bumps against her lips, making me groan. She's better than we expected, but she needs to accept she's ours.

Jack pumps into her until they both cry out. I move around to slide between her legs again, taking the bullet from Jack. My cock slides inside her swollen cunt, and she cries out. She flutters all around me as I fill her with my cock.

"Why am I punishing you, little nympho?" I hold my cock buried deep inside her and press the bullet to her clit.

"Because you don't want to admit you'd do something stupid if I told you about Tanner."

I slide a finger into her asshole, and she comes with a slightly pained cry. "Wrong answer."

She groans and haltingly says, "Because I didn't want to see you arrested for assaulting an asshole who didn't have a choice in partners either."

I slowly ease my finger in and out of her ass while sliding the bullet over her clit. She tightens around me again, moaning as sweat covers her body. No one's stepped up to do more to her, but I don't care.

This is between her and me.

"Try again, little nympho."

She moans and spits out, "Because maybe you needed protection from yourself."

"Undo her hands." Not acceptable.

Jack unties her wrists and rubs the reddened skin before helping her sit up. He wedges himself behind her on the ottoman, and she rests back against his chest.

Her tired brown eyes meet mine. I draw my cock out a little before thrusting back in. She shudders.

"You're not alone anymore, Harper. We can protect you, but only if we know what the fuck is happening."

She laughs as another orgasm swells over her. "You just want to fuck me. Use me like a fucking sex doll. Well, go ahead. But don't tell me you fucking care about me or that I'm not alone. Because I'm still alone, just in a different way. You can't protect me. None of you can."

She sighs and slides her hips against mine. "So do what you do best, War. Fuck me."

I wrap my hand around the back of her neck and draw her against me.

"I'm done coddling you, little nympho. You're mine. You're right I'm going to fuck you, but you're wrong about the rest of it."

HARPER

Shivers course through me. Caden was right, there's almost an edge of pain with each orgasm now, but I'll be damned if I give him what he wants. Jack took the bell from my hand, leaving them both free. I thrust my hands into Caden's hair and grab it. His green eyes are dark, determined, and angry. A week ago, I would have trembled before him.

Now I rock my hips, chasing the rush of chemicals that make me soar. He slides the bullet over my clit. The vibration stings even as it pushes me over the edge. I tremble as wave after wave of release tightens my pussy around his thick cock.

My legs ache from the open position because my muscles keep tightening, straining against the hold. Caden thrusts his cock in and out of me, drawing out my orgasm. I don't know how much more I can take. But I'll be damned if I'm the one to cave.

Jack slides his wet hand between my ass cheeks, stopping to thrust his fingers in and out of my ass until I cry out as I come again, pulling on Caden's hair. His head tips back, and I suck on his neck.

My pussy pulses around Caden's cock as I try to come down. The orgasms just run together now. I try to catch my breath when I can, but then I'm pushed up and over again.

Jack slides his cock between my ass cheeks, and I tense. What the fuck?

"I'm not going to bury my cock in your ass, sweetheart."

I turn, and Jack is holding my ass cheeks open around his cock. The shaft of Jack's cock rubs against my asshole as his hips thrust.

Jack grins. "But I'm going to fuck your ass cheeks."

Fuck.

"When you're ready to tell me what you did wrong, tap your finger three times." Caden turns my face toward Luke's cock before I can ask why. Ah, right, my mouth will be busy, as always.

"Open, princess."

A shudder goes through me as I part my lips. His hand tangles in my hair as he thrusts deep into my mouth. Jack slides his cock against my asshole, while Caden fucks my pussy. My nipples rub against Caden's chest as I'm sandwiched between them.

I'm surrounded, overwhelmed, and I can't stop coming. Every inch of me is sensitive to their every touch. Luke's hand tightens in my hair, holding me motionless. I stroke my tongue along Luke's cock as he pulls out and thrusts back in. I lift my gaze to his.

His thumb trails over my cheek as I suck on his cock, while my body spasms with another orgasm. Groaning, he comes down my throat. I swallow reflexively around him, never breaking eye contact.

"Fuck, princess." He pulls his cock out and leans down to kiss me. I cry out into his mouth as another shuddering orgasm rips through me. He lifts his mouth and searches my eyes. "You know what you did was wrong, Harper."

"No, it wasn't," I manage to say before another climax swells over me, making me moan and close my eyes.

Jack groans as warm cum hits my back. After a few more thrusts, he wipes it away and stands. Another warm body takes his place and slots their cock between my ass cheeks.

I cry out as another release shudders through me. Luke steps back, and Eli steps up to my mouth, grabbing my hair and thrusting inside my open mouth. He's rough, but I don't care. I want it. I need it.

Nico must be behind me. I thought I knew Nico, but I was wrong. His cock rubs against the sensitive nerves of my puckered hole. Obviously I don't need to like these guys to get off.

Caden keeps the vibrator pressed to my clit as he fucks me. The vibration is painful as it pushes me closer and closer to the edge. His huge cock stretches my pussy as I convulse around it.

I succumb to them using me. I succumb to the orgasms rocking my body. But I'll never succumb to their rule.

As another wave takes me under, I feel floaty, drunk on sex, and almost high. Sensations course through my veins. My fingers tighten in Caden's hair as the waves keep crashing over me.

Pain and pleasure merge until all I know is euphoria.

Caden slams into me and groans as he fills me with his cum. I swallow down Eli as warmth spills over my back.

They pull away except for Caden. He tips my face his way. His cock still pulses inside me, but he finally lifts the vibrator from my clit. I draw in a breath.

I rock against his still hard cock, needing the stimulation, wanting to keep this feeling flowing. It feels so fucking good. My moan escapes as I rub my breasts over his hot skin.

"Open your eyes, Harper." Caden holds my chin.

When I open them, I cry out as another release batters through me. His hot body is pressed against mine, and I just want to ride this wave. I turn toward the finger on my cheek, wanting something in my mouth, needing to suck on something.

All that matters is to keep coming and never come down.

CHAPTER 67

The Surrender

JACK

Harper takes Caden's thumb into her mouth and moans as her whole body shudders. Fuck. Her pupils are dilated. She looks drunk out of her mind. I've heard about this, but never seen it before.

"Untie her legs." I kneel beside her on the floor and untie her ankle while Nico gets the other one. I clap Caden on the shoulder. "She's never going to answer you like this."

When he slides his hand down her side, she arches into his touch.

"Subspace." I hold her upright as Caden pulls out. She curls down on me, wrapping herself around me while she makes these little needy noises that make my cock even harder. "She's blissed out of her mind."

Free from the ties, she straddles me, rubbing her pussy against my hard cock. Rising a little, she lowers her pussy over my cock, taking me inside her. Hissing at the feel of her tight, hot cunt squeezing my cock, I try to remain aware. Her mouth sucks on my neck while her hands stroke over my body. She rides me slowly.

"She'll come down, but she can come down really fucking hard." My gaze meets Caden's. He watches her fuck me with an intense look.

I meet Nico's, Eli's, and Luke's gazes while I let her chase her pleasure on me.

"What the fuck does that mean?" Luke lifts her chin and studies her face. Her brown eyes are hooded while her lips part.

"She can't distinguish between pain and pleasure." Eli steps forward. "Her high is orgasms. Her brain craves the chemical release. She definitely won't be able to tell you what you want to hear, Caden. If she speaks at all."

Caden sighs as he runs his hand down her back. She whimpers.

"She wants the pleasure. Craves it." I lick my thumb and rub it over her clit. She moans as she comes around my cock. Her tight pussy draws me in and forces me into my release. I crash my mouth down over hers as I thrust into her a few more times, and my cock jerks as I spill my cum inside her.

She tips me over, making me lie down on the floor. Her hips grind on my softening cock. It's going to take me more than a minute to get hard this time. She whimpers against my lips, not getting what she needs.

"Fuck, she needs more," Eli says.

"I've got you, princess." Luke lifts her hips off me as she continues to kiss me. She gasps in my mouth as Luke thrusts his cock into her. "She's so fucking tight."

She rubs against me like a cat as she rocks back against him. I cup her face, and she takes my thumb into her mouth, moaning around it. We've created this, fed into this. She's ours.

"Who's ready?" I ask, because she needs this, right now.

"You ready, sunshine?" Nico kneels over my head, and I guide her mouth to his cock. She slides him deep into her throat, practically purring as he fills her mouth. The vibrations make him moan.

"Take what you need, sweetheart." I stroke my hand down her throat.

Fuck, she's glorious. She's taking my friends over me, and I love watching her suck cock even when it's not mine.

I cup her breasts and rub my thumbs over her nipples. She tenses as she comes again.

"How does that feel, sweetheart?" I slide my hand down to her wet pussy and rub her clit. "What's it like being fucked by two guys?"

She moans, coming harder. Luke curses as he releases deep inside her. He caresses her hip as he falls back.

"Eli, fuck the princess." Luke rubs his lips.

Eli takes his place, thrusting into her while she's still coming. "Fuck, kitten, you squeeze any tighter and I'm not going to last."

Groaning, Nico releases down her throat. She swallows all of it before her mouth returns to mine. Sliding my tongue against hers, I circle her clit while Eli pounds into her pussy from behind. She gasps, and I open my eyes to see Eli's fingers thrusting into her ass.

She shudders as she comes. Eli keeps fucking her through it until he groans his release.

"Good girl, kitten."

Caden steps up next, easing his cock into her cunt. She pants against my shoulder as she presses back into him. He squeezes her ass cheeks and holds them apart while he slowly fucks her. This is no longer a punishment to him.

"I wish you'd rung that bell, little nympho." His finger circles her puckered hole. "I'd love for you to feel how good it is to have two cocks buried inside you, thrusting in deep."

I keep my hands moving over her breasts and her clit. She breathes raggedly.

"You got a little taste yesterday, princess." Luke sits on the ottoman beside us and lubes up a butt plug, a little larger than the one we used yesterday. I grabbed it when I got the bullet.

"Don't worry, I'll be gentle." He presses it against her asshole, slowly easing it in while we all watch her take it.

She cries out and bites my shoulder as she shatters. For a second, everyone stays still, until she squirms again, rocking back against Caden. Luke and Caden work in tandem. As Luke draws the plug out, Caden thrusts inside. While Caden pulls out, Luke sinks the plug into her ass.

Her head rests on my chest while she pants with each thrust. Her hand slides down my abs to my hardening cock. She strokes me, running her fingers over my cock, sliding down over my balls to cup them.

Her touch is slightly painful, because I'm almost tapped out. I could come again, but it would definitely ache.

When I pinch her clit, she cries out as she comes. Luke thrusts the plug in deep, filling her ass as Caden thrusts in and out. Her cry turns into a scream as another wave overtakes her. Caden grits his teeth as he comes, thrusting into her hard and fast before releasing his cum deep inside her.

"Fuck, little nympho." He smacks her ass, and she must squeeze around him because he groans. "No more."

He pulls the butt plug out and falls back. She collapses on top of me. Fuck is right.

For a few minutes, we just rest here. We don't need words to know what needs to happen. The others move around the room, doing whatever they need to do. Her breathing slows with mine.

After a few minutes, Caden lifts her from me, and she turns to snuggle against him. Eli holds his hand out to me to help me up.

"Shower." I nod toward the house door. By now the staff should have left. Everyone else has their boxers on. Except Caden, who didn't have any on before. I grab mine and pull them on.

We stroll through the empty house to Caden's bathroom. I turn on the shower. While waiting until it's warm enough, Caden holds her against him, stroking his hand down her back. Everyone else takes off their boxers.

We've done this before. Locker room showers, for sure. But last weekend with Harper, we all showered with her. While my friends are all gorgeous, I've never really crushed on any of them.

We're comfortable with each other. They know I like guys that way too, but it's never been an issue and it won't be. But I can admire their bodies for the work they put in to make them perfect. And watching them fuck Harper is fucking art.

When the shower is ready, we all walk in. Caden sets Harper on her feet in the middle of us. We alternate between washing ourselves and washing Harper. She strokes, rubs, and touches all of us, but I'm pretty sure we're all done for the night.

Caden hands out towels, and I wrap one around Harper. She leans into me as I dry her, resting her face against my chest and breathing deeply. She's tired and coming down from her high. This is when things can get tricky.

The brain stops receiving those pleasure chemicals and crashes. She might have a rough day tomorrow.

Caden pulls a t-shirt over her head and lifts her into his arms. She curls into him as he carries her to the bed and lays her down.

Her sleepy eyes meet mine, and she holds out her hand. I should go home.

But I take her hand and let her pull me down beside her. I need to go home, but I love holding her warm body against mine.

Especially when she snuggles into me. I'll just rest my eyes for a little and then head home.

HARPER

I wake up groggy and disoriented. The room is dark, and I'm pressed between two hot bodies. That part is becoming more and more familiar. I slide down the bed to go to the bathroom.

After using the toilet, I brush my teeth and wash my face. Thankfully, someone brought my bag up here. My pussy aches, and not in the I-need-to-be-fucked way.

Erotic images flood my mind. Fuck. Little nympho, indeed. I feel a little weird, not because of the sex, but almost like I'm hungover.

I sit on the toilet lid and try to sort through what happened. It's like I was there but not there. Every orgasm hit pain and pleasure at the same time, until pain and pleasure blurred, and it felt euphoric. It was a heady sensation, but now I just feel a little lost.

A tear falls onto my hand. What the fuck? I've been through a lot. Public humiliation. Girl fights that aren't actually fights. Someone puncturing my tire and freaking me out at night.

This is nothing in the grand scheme of everything that's happened. I wanted to come. I wanted them to fuck me. So why do I just want to curl up and cry?

The bathroom door opens, and Jack glances around until he spots me.

"Hey, sweetheart." His tone is soft and tender, and it makes a sob well in my throat.

I press the back of my hand to my mouth, but the sound escapes. Jack kneels before me and wraps his arms around me.

"It's okay. Whatever you're feeling, it's not permanent. It's just the crash after the high." Jack's words make sense to some rational part of my mind.

I wrap around him, lowering to the floor to be as close to him as possible. He's wearing boxers, and I don't even know where my panties are. Sex is the last thing on my mind. My pussy is sore, and wave after wave of sadness flows through me. He moves us back until he can rest against the wall.

Holding me so tight, he strokes his hand over my hair and down my back. The tears fall faster, like I have no control over them. He makes little soothing noises as he holds me close.

I swipe at the tears, aware we need to return to bed. It has to be late. We have school tomorrow.

Pulling back, I look into his eyes. "Why are you here, Jack? Why didn't you go home?"

He brushes my hair out of my face and wipes away the tears. "Because you needed me."

Tears well again, but this time I laugh. "I can't seem to stop crying."

"I know." He searches my eyes. "It'll get better."

I rest my head against his heart as he strokes my hair.

"I've never experienced subspace, but I've read about it." His voice is low to not wake the others, but it rumbles through his chest beneath my ear. It's soothing. "Like our brains shut off our pain receptors or some shit. It's dangerous during rough sex because your brain stops distinguishing between pain and pleasure. It all just feels fucking amazing, and chemicals flood your brain."

I sigh and listen to his heartbeat.

"The other side is when you finally rest and come down, your brain misses the hits it was getting. Subdrop. It can be like depression or just a down day. That's why it's important to stay close to someone after subspace."

I lift my head to look into Jack's pretty blue eyes. "Is that why you stayed?"

Suddenly it's the most important question. I need to know the answer. Yes, these guys are all assholes, but they don't always treat me like their personal sex toy. My heart stalls as I wait for him.

"Yeah, Harper. I stayed for you. To make sure you were taken care of, and because you reached out to me. It's not like I'll get in trouble. I'll tell my folks I fell asleep at Caden's watching a movie." Jack cups my cheek and searches my eyes again. A little crease forms between his brows.

I take a deep breath, knowing he's seeing more than I want him to right now. He's seeing the gaping loneliness that loves that these guys pay attention to me now. That their sole focus is on me.

"That whole thing with Caden..." Jack sighs.

I start to draw away, but Jack holds me.

"You're important to him. I know you don't believe me, but I've known him all my life. When he claims you, that's it for him. He's loyal and fierce. And he claimed me a long time ago, and the other guys, but he's never claimed a girl before. He's never wanted just one girl. You may think he's doing this to have sex with you, but he's all in."

My heart pounds against my ribs at every word spilling out of Jack's mouth.

"Tanner is a problem. He won't go away quietly like some guys. He's angry and bitter."

"You don't think I know that—"

"Of course I do, but what you aren't seeing is how he affects Caden. We've kept him out of Caden's path to make sure he doesn't break."

"That's what I was trying to do." I move in close to Jack. "I couldn't do anything about the assignment, but I could try to protect Caden from finding out. I could keep Tanner away and make sure Caden didn't get arrested. I saw how angry he was that day at my house. If I could, I'd beat up Tanner myself, but that's not an option."

Jack smiles and shakes his head. His finger brushes the tears off my cheeks. "Not an option. We want to protect you. But we knew when we claimed you, it made you a target. You make us vulnerable, because we'll do anything to make sure no one hurts you."

I draw in a breath. Everything he says makes sense, but I don't know if it's because I'm so damned emotional right now. He sounds sincere, like he's not blowing smoke up my ass.

My cheeks flush with heat. I meet his eyes. "Would you have?"

"What, sweetheart?" Jack tips his head as he looks at me.

I take a deep breath, not sure I want the answer. "If I rang the bell and didn't answer Caden, would you have fucked my ass?"

He releases a breath. "No, sweetheart. Consent is important. And yeah, I could make an argument you ringing the bell is consent, but you're ours. You're mine."

My breath catches as he presses a kiss to my lips.

"While we've claimed you, you're still Harper Davidson. You have a right to your own thoughts and the right to decide when you're ready to take the next step." He grins mischievously. "Even if we enjoy pushing you to make those decisions. I need you to feel safe with me. To know that I'll protect you from the outside. That when you're ready, I'm fully prepared to take that ass, but not until you beg for it."

Like gears shifting inside me, something falls into place as I search Jack's eyes. It's too much. I can't let myself believe they're mine because, when it comes down to it, I'm just their toy. Nico proved that earlier. I don't have the bond they have as teammates, as friends, as brothers.

I snuggle into Jack and let him comfort me because I need this. I take the comfort, though it's fleeting. That feeling of someone caring for me. That feeling of belonging. But then I'll tuck it all away, because I can't have it. Not with these guys.

I want them, but not just a piece of them. That's all they have to give me. If I believed these guys could love me, maybe I'd be willing to open my heart. They give me little glimpses of something more, but I'm not one of them.

A piece of me wants more and won't settle for less. But for this year, I've agreed to be theirs. At the end of this, I'll have to find a way to move on. Without them.

CHAPTER 68

The First Shot

HARPER

Hope is such a fickle bitch. A few days ago, I had hope this might be something more, and now it's gone. Now they're just the assholes who own me. Who toy with my heart whenever it helps them get what they want. I'm on my own.

Today is just another day. I wake up, shower, and get ready for school... alongside three guys. Who, while they aren't being grabby this morning, are definitely touchy. I'm sore, which isn't surprising given how many times they fucked me last night.

There's this dull ache inside, and my heart hurts, but I can't let them know I'm a little broken today. Jack doesn't mention me crying last night to the others.

Caden keeps giving me dissecting looks, but Jack maneuvers me away from him. We didn't finish what we started last night. I apparently checked out before he got what he wanted. Though I wouldn't have given him those words.

I didn't do anything wrong. They're just controlling asshats who need to know my every move. And I was doing it to protect *him*. Fuck that.

Luke is almost pleasant this morning, which is kind of freaking me out. It's little things, like handing me a towel and caressing my hip.

Though everyone had plenty of orgasms last night, so maybe he's just satisfied. For now.

He watches me like any moment I'm going to break. It's disconcerting.

"Come on, sweetheart. You're beautiful." Jack leans in the doorway while I finish putting on my makeup. I'm wearing Eli's jersey and a skirt I wish was jeans right now. This is the problem with packing before knowing what the evening would bring. I wish I had a chastity belt instead, because I have a feeling this aching pain won't go away anytime soon.

My gaze locks with Jack's in the mirror. I swallow at the kindness in his eyes. It's a lie. This is all a lie. I have to keep telling myself that. I have to make myself believe it.

Grabbing my stuff, I pack my bag. Tonight, I'm sleeping in my bed. If they want to camp out in my house, so be it, but I'm sleeping alone.

Jack's hand catches my hip as I try to slip past him. I stop and wait for whatever he's going to do. He tips my chin up and searches my eyes.

"You okay?" He says it so softly tears choke me.

I swallow them down, refusing to cry anymore. Even as this emptiness threatens to consume me whole, I force a smile. "I'm good."

His thumb rubs my jaw, and his eyes narrow like he can see through my bullshit.

"Let's go," Caden calls out, breaking Jack's attention.

I walk past him into the bedroom and head toward Caden's voice. His house is still a maze, and I swear I'd get lost if one of them didn't direct me.

Luke waits for me in the hallway and walks next to me. His hand falls on the small of my back, and he guides me the correct way to the kitchen. I ignore the sparks dancing through me from his fingertips. My messed up hormones make me want to lean into him and take comfort. From *Luke*.

That's pretty fucked up.

Caden sits at the large table with a breakfast spread that would feed a small army.

He kicks out the chair next to him. I'm tempted to go around to the other side and take a seat there. Just to be stubborn. But Luke doesn't let me veer off course.

I drop into the seat and look at the various baked goods set out. My stomach growls angrily, but I don't reach for anything. Luke sits next to me and grabs a few things for his plate before setting a couple on mine.

Sighing, I relent to my stomach. When I look down, what's on my plate is exactly what I would have chosen. My heart bursts with a weird feeling of warmth, but I don't let my surprise show. So what if Luke paid attention when we've eaten together before. He's a smart guy. That doesn't make him a nice guy.

Jack drops into the chair across from me. He's dressed for school in clothes I know he didn't bring here. My lips part to ask, but instead, I shove a Danish in my mouth. It's none of my business. I'm just a toy to them.

"You'll tell us everything he says to you." Caden's voice is rough. "If he touches you, even accidentally, you tell me."

Caden reaches out for me, and I flinch. I didn't mean to. My eyes widen as I lift them to his. His brow furrows, and I swear hurt flashes in his green eyes. He withdraws his hand and sets it on the table between us.

Fuck, why did I do that? I'm not afraid of him. I swallow the delicate pastry like it's a lump of coal. My appetite is gone. "Can we go to school now?"

Luke stands. "You ride with me, princess."

Nodding, I rise and avoid looking at the others as I grab my stuff and follow Luke out of the house. Today is going to be hell.

I DON'T KNOW IF PEOPLE CAN SENSE NOT TO MESS WITH ME today, or if the guys make them stay away. Either way, I'm glad that, for once, I can focus on school.

Unfortunately third period comes way too soon. Caden walks me to class, but Tanner isn't in the classroom yet.

Caden tips my chin up and blows out a breath. "I don't want him to hurt you, little nympho."

His green eyes are soft as they search mine. Tanner hurt his sister. I've never forgotten that fact, but I'm not his sister. I'm not young and naive enough to believe Tanner's bullshit.

"I won't let him, War." My voice is low and soft.

He leans down, and my breath catches in anticipation of his kiss. He's still searching me, still trying to get inside me. I need him to know I'm not afraid of him. I lift on my toes and press my lips to his.

When I pull away, his hand grabs the back of my neck, and his mouth claims mine. He aims to conquer me, claim me, make me his. As his tongue slides against mine, my traitorous body softens, melting into him. I grab his shirt to keep him close.

A low growl rumbles in the back of his throat as he presses me up against the lockers. The noise of people chatting and racing to their next class disappears in a haze of desire I'm not strong enough to fight off.

"Caden?" Ms. Sullivan's voice breaks the spell woven around us.

Caden lifts his head. Our eyes lock for a second, and his longing makes my insides clench. A dull ache thrums through me, reminding me of last night. He turns to Ms. Sullivan as his grip loosens on me.

"Ms. Sullivan." Caden doesn't turn toward her, probably to conceal the erection pressing into my hip.

"We miss you in art." She smiles like he isn't the fiercest guy in school. She also doesn't acknowledge we're still wrapped tight together.

"If I could have fit it in my schedule..." He gives her a half smile.

"It's a shame." She shakes her head. "We miss your energy."

Now it's my turn to look at Ms. Sullivan like she's lost her marbles. Dark, growly energy? She misses that?

"I should get into class," I say. Caden lets his hands fall.

Ms. Sullivan gives me a smile like she just noticed me. "You two would have made great partners on this project. Your creative energies complement each other."

Caden's eyes turn thoughtful as he watches me walk backward into the classroom. I'm not sure what he's thinking, but it makes my chest tighten.

"See you at lunch, Harper." Caden turns to talk with Ms. Sullivan, but I'm out of hearing range now. I turn and see Tanner sitting at our table. Fuck.

He must have passed Caden and me kissing. It's not a secret the horsemen own me or that they kiss me. Everyone in school must know that by now. But it's still a little unnerving he walked right past us and I wasn't aware of it. Was Caden aware?

Shaking the thoughts from my head, I sit in my chair and pull out my sketchbook.

"Enjoying being their whore?" Tanner's voice is low enough I'm the only one who can probably hear him.

I glance over at Nico, but Angela has him distracted. Good, I don't need him running off and telling the others what Tanner says. Especially when he's trying to provoke them.

"Do you miss being beaten up?" I turn to him with a curious look. "I mean, you're pretty enough without bruises discoloring your face, but if that's what you want."

I shrug like it doesn't bother me. Tanner is a pest.

"It won't last. Your pussy won't be enough to keep them from straying." He opens his sketchbook to a nude woman he's working on.

I roll my eyes. "Why do you care?"

Honestly it shouldn't matter to anyone how long the horsemen decide to keep me. I'm not permanent. Eventually they'll tire of playing with me and move on. So what? Tears well against the back of my eyes.

Fuck, not this shit again. I refuse to cry in front of this particular asshat, so I choke the tears down the best I can. It's what Jack called subdrop. The emotional letdown from the euphoria. I can handle it.

"I don't care if they drop you. But while you're theirs, I can fuck with them by fucking with you."

My gaze collides with his devious blue eyes. He smiles like the cat that ate the canary. A shiver of dread rolls through me. Maybe I should ask my mom for that Taser.

"I'm going to be honest with you, Harper."

"That would be a change."

His chuckle is dark. "I don't care what it takes. I want to destroy them, and you're the tool I'll use to do it. It won't matter how they try to protect you. I'll hurt you to hurt them."

Evil. That's what I get from Tanner Lewis. Pure, unadulterated evil. A chill races down my back, knowing I'm the target of all that hate.

The door slams, and I jump. Ms. Sullivan comes into class.

Tanner returns to his drawing and acts like he didn't just drop a bomb in my lap. Here's the thing. He wants me to take that back to the guys. He wants them on high alert. I don't want to give him that satisfaction.

But I know I can't handle him on my own. I need to figure out a plan to deal with whatever Tanner throws my way without involving the guys. As Ms. Sullivan begins her lecture, I can't help thinking why.

Why am I protecting the horsemen? Maybe Tanner distracting them is a good thing. It would definitely make them let up on the constant attention and give them someone to fight instead.

They want to know everything or they'll punish me. A little thrill rushes through me at how well they punished me last night, but I ignore it. Tanner wants a war. Fine, I'll give him one.

ELI

When Caden draws Harper down on his lap at lunch, she winces and doesn't relax into him like she usually does. Her punishment last night probably did more harm than good. Physically and emotionally. She's a seething kitten.

I hold out an apple to her.

I get why the others wanted to fuck her wearing their jerseys. I've been hard every time she's near me in mine. But I'm sure her cunt is sore today. Still, a little extra pain doesn't bother me. I can use it.

She takes the apple without fussing and sets it down beside her hot lunch Caden bought for her.

"Hey." Nico falls into the seat next to me. "What did Tanner say to you in art, sunshine?"

Her brown eyes are cold when she lifts her gaze to him. "That he'll use me to get to you guys."

The shift in expression on Caden's face is so subtle, I doubt anyone but us noticed. His gaze scans the lunchroom, but Tanner doesn't come in here. He's not stupid enough to face us together.

"That won't happen." Luke leans back in his chair. "He's one guy, and as long as he doesn't have access to you, he won't be able to make good on his threat."

"What exactly did he say, kitten?" I prop my elbows on the table while I search her eyes.

"That he wants to destroy you, and I'm the tool he'll use." She shrugs as if it isn't a big deal and picks at her food with her fork. "He plans on fucking with me, so that sounds exciting."

Tanner Lewis was supposed to fade into the background after we eliminated him as a threat and took away all his power. We never underestimated him, but we didn't know we'd be claiming a girl like Harper.

"We can discuss what we need to do tonight." Luke gestures to our food. "Eat."

Strategy, we need one for dealing with Tanner. Harper picks at her food before setting her fork aside after a while. Her gaze wanders the cafeteria, taking in everything. When her brown eyes clash with mine, I stand.

"Come on, kitten. We have business to attend."

She cocks an eyebrow, but Caden sets her on her feet. When she reaches for her backpack, Caden stops her.

"I've got your bag, little nympho."

I hold my hand out to her, and she draws in a breath before coming around the table and taking it. I briefly meet Ashley's angry eyes as I lead Harper out of the cafeteria. There are plenty of places to disappear in the school, but I won't take Harper to any of the ones Ashley might know.

She's becoming a thorn in my side, and if she doesn't get in line, I may have to pluck her out.

Jack follows us out of the cafeteria. Harper glances over her shoulder at him. When we get to the closet we lured her into before, I open the door and gesture for her to go in.

She hesitates, and her cheeks flush red. "I'm sore."

I close in on her and tip her chin up. "A little pain doesn't scare me, kitten."

When I back her into the closet, Jack closes the door for us. Now it's just me and my kitten. Her breathing is loud in the dark space.

"Do you remember how it felt to have us surrounding you?" I

whisper as I wrap my hand around her throat and press her against the wall. My other hand trails up her thigh under her skirt.

"Yes," she whispers. Her voice trembles slightly, giving me that edge of fear. My cock hardens painfully.

"Next time we bring you in here, we'll fuck you to climax and leave you dripping with our cum." I slide my fingers over her panties and feel the damp heat of her pussy. "But right now, kitten, you belong to me."

CHAPTER 69

Reprieve

ELI

I tighten my hand slightly around her throat as I press my fingers against her entrance through her panties. A slight gasp escapes her. She wraps her hands around my wrists, but she doesn't pull either of my hands away.

"Good girl." I pulse my finger against her pussy. Her breath catches in the silence.

"Unbuckle my belt, kitten." My whispered words sound loud in the dark.

Her hands tremble as they work on opening my belt. Her fingers brush against my hard cock where it strains against my jeans. When she moves to my button, I grab her wrists, holding them in one hand.

I pull my belt from my jeans and loop it around her hands, pulling it tight. Her breath shudders in and out, and her hands tremble in mine.

"You remember your word?" I kiss her cheek beside her ear.

"Arrow," she whispers.

"Good. Use it if you can't take it, kitten." I smile in the dark, knowing she can't see it. I love having her at my mercy. Mine to do with what I please.

She can blame Sidney for me fucking her at school. I would have waited until this evening, but then she won't be wearing my jersey. Of course, since yesterday got a little out of hand, I'll need to postpone my night with her.

"Such a good kitten to wear a skirt." I lift her arms over her head and put my hand back on her throat. Her swallow moves against my hand, making me want to tighten my hold, to make her gasp for breath, to feel her struggle against me. "Spread your legs."

"Eli, last night was a lot." Her voice trembles.

I squeeze her throat slightly, just enough for her to feel that little catch of breath, so she knows I can cut it off if she doesn't obey. "Spread your legs, kitten. I won't ask again."

Whimpering, she does as I ask. Brushing my cheek against hers, I slide my hand into her panties to cup her warm, wet pussy. So fucking wet. Always ready for me. This girl was made for us. Time to experiment and see what her limits really are.

I rub a finger over her clit. "Are you sore here?"

"No." Her voice is breathless. Her hips rock against my hand while I work her little clit, stroking it in small circles. When she quivers beneath my hand, I slide my finger back to circle her entrance, slow languid circles like we have all day.

I press my mouth against her ear. "How about here?" My voice is barely a whisper.

She shakes her head.

I *tsk* and squeeze her throat. "Use your words, kitten."

"No, Eli."

I slide my finger inside her. She releases a breath and tenses.

"Here?"

"Yes." She squirms to get away from the ache.

"Hmm." I press against her walls, massaging them with my finger, feeling them tense and relax beneath my touch. When her noises become needy, I slide my finger in and out a few times as she moans softly. Her wetness coats my finger.

I squeeze her throat. "Do you want more, kitten?"

"Yes, please," she pants as her hips follow my finger, chasing her release.

Drawing my hand out of her panties, I press my finger against her lips, coating them in her wetness. She opens and sucks on my finger, tasting herself. I pull it out. So fucking responsive. I can't wait to spend a night torturing her until she begs me to let her come.

"Should I leave us wanting, kitten?" I suck her earlobe into my mouth. Her breath catches.

She hesitates in the dark. I wish I could see her face. It gives away her every thought and feeling. Soon, I'll blindfold her and have her stretched across my bed, and play with her until she squirms beneath me, craving release.

"No." She sighs.

"Do you want me to use your mouth?" Releasing her throat, I thrust my fingers into her mouth and slide them against her tongue, pressing down. She sucks on them, and my cock jerks. As much as I love her mouth on my cock, I want to bury myself in her sweet, aching cunt. "Well, kitten?"

She shakes her head, and my cock throbs. Since my fingers are in the way, I allow it.

She whimpers as I take them out and undo my pants, pulling them down enough to release my cock. I stroke her spit over me. She's plenty wet, but it's going to hurt her in the best way.

Using both hands, I lift her until she wraps her legs around my waist and her bound wrists drop behind my head. She tenses against me, probably expecting pain.

"Relax, kitten." Pushing her back against the wall, I slide her panties to the side and thrust my cock deep into her cunt in one stroke.

"Eli," she cries as she clenches around me. Her cunt pulses around me in a small orgasm. We can do better than that.

I remain buried deep inside her, letting her come down and adjust to my size. "You're ours, kitten. I gave you a choice today, but I won't always. If I want to be inside this tight pussy, I have every right to fuck you."

Moving my finger over her clit, I circle it until she relaxes against me.

"If I want to give you pleasure, you'll take it. If I want to give you pain, you'll thank me." I pull out before thrusting back in hard. "If I want you to beg, you'll beg."

A muffled cry escapes. I almost shake my head. Silly kitten. She's holding back her cries now, probably worried someone will hear us. I lean in and kiss her, finding her teeth pressing into her bottom lip.

"Kitten, no biting." I pinch her clit.

She cries out as I cover her mouth with mine, thrusting into her while my fingers work her clit. Her cunt tightens around me as she comes. When I bite her lip, she screams into my mouth. Her walls squeeze my cock so fucking hard.

It just makes me more aroused. Her pain. Her pleasure. It's almost unbearable.

Her cunt milks my cock until I can't hold back anymore and spill my cum deep inside her, thrusting a few more times before burying myself deep. I hold her close as my cock jerks and pulses within her. Her breathing is ragged in the silence of the closet. My mouth claims hers as we both come down. When I suck on her lip, an aftershock rocks through her.

Chuckling, I pull out and straighten her panties. Using the wall to hold her, I put my cock away before lowering her legs to the ground and ducking out from under her arms. She slumps against the wall while I slowly unwrap my belt from her wrists and rub them in the darkness.

"You okay, kitten?"

"Does it matter?" She turns her head away from me, even though I can only see her shadow in the dark.

This girl. I grasp her chin and turn her to face me. "Yes, it matters."

"I'm fine." The tone isn't the greatest, but it's not snippy, so I let it go.

I put my belt on and lightly knock once on the door. Jack knocks back twice to let me know it's clear. He opens the door, and Harper brushes out past me and heads to the girls' bathroom.

"She okay?" Jack asks.

"I don't fucking know." I run my hand through my hair. That's the problem with fucking in the dark, I couldn't see her expressions. Maybe she's sore. Maybe she's an angry kitty. Maybe she hates all of us. I shake my head. "She's not good though."

"You think it's subdrop?" He rubs the back of his neck as he stares at the door she disappeared behind.

"Maybe. I think somewhere we fucked up." I pat Jack on the shoulder. "We should definitely talk tonight."

HARPER

"Are you spending the night at your friend's tonight?" Mom's voice draws me away from stirring the pasta on my plate.

My mind is so full right now. Sex with Eli was only a little painful, but I barely noticed the pain as he pushed me over the edge and then made me come again even harder.

After cleaning up, the afternoon went by slowly. Classes dragged. The guys almost left me alone, but they were right there. Even the Cheermonsters were quiet when we made the swap.

Of course, they got in their usual sneers and called me a pet, but overall, not what I expected with the exchange. If they have something planned, it's not this, apparently. Maybe it really is for their convenience.

I put Jack's jersey in the wash when I got home. Then I showered and changed into the most comfortable sweats and sweatshirt I have. Now I'm picking at my dinner. My mood is still low, and I've lost count of how many times I've almost broken down into tears today.

"Harper?"

I lift my gaze to Mom. "Yeah?"

Her fork clatters on her plate. "What's going on, sweetie? You've barely eaten, and this is the second time I asked you a question and you didn't hear me."

"Just boy nonsense." I shrug, not wanting to go into detail because once those floodgates open, I don't think I could stop at just telling her what's currently happening. I'd tell her the whole thing. Every last sordid detail. And part of me desperately wants to tell her, because she might help me figure this out.

"Maybe you should stay home tonight." She reaches over and covers my hand. "Call Kenz and see if she can stay with you."

I nod, feeling those stupid, weepy tears pressing forward again. Today has been less than stellar, and this weepiness is beyond annoying.

"Yeah, maybe I will. Not sure her mom will let her. She got in trouble, I think."

Did Kenz say she was grounded, or was it just that day? Fuck, I used to know Kenz inside and out, and lately we barely have time to talk.

"You should." She picks up her fork and takes a bite. She arches an eyebrow. "Which one of the football players is on the outs?"

I blow out my breath and shake my head. "All of them? None of them? I don't even know anymore."

"Harper, you can talk to me, but it sounds like you need a girlfriend right now. Let me call Kenz's mom and explain what's going on. Maybe we can get around the trouble."

That makes me feel slightly better. My mom is my hero. "Thanks, Mom."

She waves it off and talks about her work the night before. She's always careful not to name names of people who come in, but that doesn't stop her from telling me about the crazy shit that landed them in the hospital. By the time we do the dishes, I feel marginally better. I head up to my room and work on my homework.

The doorbell rings, and I tense. Which dick has come to pick me up? I've barely heard from them tonight. Luke dropped me off after the exchange, but he was in a hurry to get back to practice.

My bedroom door opens, and Kenz walks in, closing the door and dropping her overnight bag in the corner.

"What's up, my bitch?" She holds her arms wide, and I tackle hug her. She laughs, rubbing my back. "Miss me? I mean, I just saw you with the Cheermonsters so..."

A sob rips from my throat as the tears I pushed back all day flow down my cheeks.

"Oh, H." The sympathy in her voice makes me cry harder. She leads me to the bed, and we sit on the edge. She hands me the box of tissues, and I grab a few, trying to wipe the tears away. "What's going on?"

"I don't even know where to start." I shake my head.

"Can you name which asshole is being a dick, or is it the whole lot?" Kenz takes a tissue and presses it to my face. Her worried look has me holding back a fresh wave of tears. I love Kenz and don't have to worry about her loyalty. It will always be me she chooses.

Taking a breath, I tell her about last night. How Nico's mom outed Tanner is my partner in art, and Nico didn't back me up. Then how angry Caden was, and the sex. Fuck, the sex.

"Holy shit, H." Her eyes are big. "I mean, it sounds... it sounds..."

"Hot?" I laugh. "I mean, I'm happy to come as many times as they want me to, even when it hurts a little. If they were aiming for punishment, they missed the mark."

Kenz touches her lips. "I mean, yeah, but one after another?"

My pussy pulses in memory of the slide of their cocks inside me. It was like having a never-ending erection. I blow out a breath and shake off the memory.

"Jack says I went into subspace. I need to look that up tonight." I haven't had a chance yet. My cheeks burn remembering the need, the craving. "I couldn't get enough."

Her eyebrows raise as her doubtful gaze drops to my lap. "How's the vajayjay today?"

"Sore, achy. And then Eli fucked me hard at lunch in the closet." I close my eyes, remembering his words and the way he touched me, like he knew my body better than I did. He made me want it.

They all do.

"At school?" Kenz shakes her head. "You know about the betting pool, don't you? I just found out about it."

"Yes, Grant Perkins. I'm surprised no one has claimed it yet. We haven't been that secretive. I mean, there was the whole study session at the coffee shop." Maybe I did the exit wrong and should have made a circuit of the shop, giving everyone high fives.

"You'd think someone would catch on." Kenz rolls her eyes. "Grant's a prick."

"It's the horsemen claiming a virgin. Anything they do calls attention to them. It probably didn't help they stuffed underwear in his mouth." I smile. They did it because he harassed me, but maybe I'm looking at it with rose-colored glasses. In reality, it was probably to maintain their power or solidify their claim on me.

My smile falls. Everything they do is for them. I need to remember that. I bury my face in my hands. "What am I doing, Kenz?"

"Having the fucking time of your life." Her grin is obvious in her tone.

"Am I?" I flop back on the bed. "Is it really better than hiding?"

"Hell yes, it is." She lies down next to me on her side with her head propped on her hand. "H, you can go to parties, dances, study sessions. You don't have to live in fear of the guys realizing you exist."

"But I have to deal with the guys." I pout. "They're all bossy and demanding in their own way. Every time one of them seems nice, they do something dickish that tips the scales back toward assholes."

"What was the problem last night?" She flops down next to me and holds my hand as we stare up at the ceiling. "Besides the multiple orgasms."

"Besides Nico totally feeding me to the lions and not defending me? I thought he was my friend, but I should have known the horsemen come first. Then Caden and his stupid need for me to know what I did was wrong. When I was keeping it a secret to protect him. And Luke telling Caden to punish me. I swear he gets off on punishing me." I blow out a breath, letting the anger overwhelm me a little. "Eli was fine last night, but in the closet—" I stop as I remember. It's all so fucking confusing. "He wants what he wants whether or not I want it, but he makes me want it, which is frustrating as hell."

"And Jack?" she asks.

"Jack." I blow out a breath. "Last night must have been his turn to play nice guy. Jack stayed the night and held me while I cried in the bathroom."

"Why were you crying?" Kenz squeezes my hand.

I roll my head to face her. "They keep making me feel like this could be more, then they do this shit and I realize I'm not one of them and I never will be. I'm just a toy for the year."

Maybe that's what stings the most. I'm not part of their group. They own me. I'm no better than a toy to them. They haven't even called me tonight, probably because they know I'm not up to having sex. Therefore, they have no use for me.

"They're pretty tight with each other. You're more in than any other girl has ever been. They've claimed you, Harper. They've never done that before."

I turn on my side to face her fully, putting my hand under my head. "They just want me for sex. The novelty of a virgin they can do anything they want with. Someone only they have touched."

A shiver works through me. There's more to it though: Caden's dreams of the future, Luke's possessive streak, Nico's friendship, Eli's coaxing and promise to protect me, and Jack... I rub at my chest, not sure what to feel about Jack right now. He's always let me lead. He lets me explore before he takes. "There have been moments, but..."

"You don't have to fall in love with them, H. Appreciate you're getting an education most of us couldn't dream of. A chance to experiment and enjoy yourself without worrying about the tangle of emotions." She mirrors me on the bed and reaches out to move some hair off my face. "Just think how confident you'll be in your first genuine relationship. The horsemen may have had your body, but you'll still have your heart to give to some lucky guy."

"Maybe." I release my breath. "Okay, enough about me. How are you and Brandon doing?"

She grins, and her whole face lights up. "Girl."

My heart unclenches, knowing she's about to tell me a good story. She doesn't judge me.

"I've missed you so much." I breathe out.

"You're always my girl, H." She takes my hand and presses her forehead to mine. "If you need me, I'll always be there for you."

"Thank you," I say quietly. "Okay, tell me about what you've been up to."

With a smile, she starts a story about this closet they found at school. I listen and smile at the appropriate spots. Part of me is still heartsick after last night. She and Brandon fell in love before they started having sex. Now I'm having sex with no hope of love. As long as I remember that and don't let myself slip, I can just have fun. Maybe that's good enough for now.

CHAPTER 70

Strike Team

NICO

"She texted to say Kenz is staying the night with her." Jack slides his phone back in his pocket before focusing on his laptop.

When I came back to Sherman High School, I never imagined I'd be outside someone's house, dressed head to toe in black, waiting for Jack to finish making sure the coast is clear. The guys crouch beside me. Everyone has on a black mask completely covering their features.

It's late in the evening. But this needs to be done. We're all in agreement about that.

"Okay, his parents are out, but we need to keep this contained." Luke meets all our eyes. "He needs to know not to mess with us or our girl."

Caden grunts in agreement. At practice, he was a beast. Unstoppable. They had to walk a sophomore off the field after a particularly rough tackle during a scrimmage. Ever since Harper dropped that little nugget about Tanner at lunch, the anger radiates off Caden.

The lights are off in the house, meaning the guy's already asleep or maybe watching something in the dark.

Jack closes his laptop and slides his mask down over his face. "We're good to go."

We huddle together and look to our quarterback to lead us.

"You all know what your job is. Let's put this asshole back in his place." Luke holds out his hand, and we all pile on top of it before breaking with a low *hooah*.

Eli leads us across the lawn. We all stay low to make sure someone glancing out their windows won't see us. His house is roughly the size of Harper's. Not enormous, but not small.

Jack lowers to his knee in front of the keypad on the door. I glance back across the lawn to make sure no one saw us. The air is still, and the only sound is the pressing of buttons.

The lock clicks, and Jack turns the knob, gesturing for us to follow. The others go through, but I continue to watch our backs before slipping inside the house. We spread out.

Eli showed us the layout of the house. The bedrooms are on the second floor, and there are two sets of stairs leading up to it. One is narrower and more winding, but definitely a way to escape if he hears us coming. Jack and I head to the narrow one, while Caden, Eli, and Luke sweep the downstairs before going up the main staircase.

The stairs are creaky as we carefully climb them. Houses this age usually have pops and creaks, even when there aren't football players converging on your location. We reach the upper hallway and check out a bathroom and a guest bedroom before waiting outside his bedroom.

After a few minutes, the others join us. Eli clears the primary bedroom before we all stand outside the door. Luke holds up three fingers as Caden puts his hand on the doorknob.

Luke lowers one finger, another, and then the last. Caden throws open the door, and we circle Grant Perkins on his bed.

"What the fuck!" He shoves his laptop away, and the headphones disconnect. The sounds of moans and grunts fill the room. I glance at the screen, and two guys are fucking a woman.

Caden grabs Grant's arm and drags him from the bed. He's naked with his hard cock jutting out from his hips.

"I don't have any money."

Luke chuckles darkly. "We don't want your money, Grant."

"But we want to give you a message." Eli steps forward.

I'm sure if Grant weren't hard, he'd be wetting himself. Jack comes forward with rope to tie Grant's hands.

"I didn't do whatever you think I did. I've stayed away from your girl. Honest. I haven't even talked to her." Grant's voice gets high pitched as Jack tightens the rope.

"Instead, you chose to bet on her." I get a good look at his terror-filled eyes in the light of his computer.

"It's just a pool. If you guys want in, I can give you a cut."

"What we want is for you to learn a lesson about what can and can't be wagered on." Eli claps his hand against the side of Grant's face, and Grant whimpers.

"We're going to do a little friendly wagering of our own." Luke steps back. "See, I'm confident you're going to wet yourself or cry after an hour of being tied up outside the high school."

"What?" Grant shrieks. This guy isn't even a worthy opponent. He needs to be made aware of that fact apparently.

"I'll bet a dollar he doesn't make it until morning before he cries," Jack adds as he claps Grant on the shoulder.

Grant's erection goes down as fear gets the better of him.

"I'll bet you a dollar he won't cry until the first girls laugh at him tied up to the flagpole." Eli gestures to Caden.

Caden grabs Grant's arm and drags him to the door.

"Wait. Wait. You guys can have the money. It's a lot." He drags his feet on the ground. "This isn't funny."

"Do you hear us laughing, Grant?" I stop in front of him. "She's ours. Not yours. Not even for your betting pool." I step to the side so Caden can escort Grant out. I add, "I bet a dollar he pisses himself before we even tie him to the flagpole."

"Dude, that's my car." Eli winces.

"Put him in the trunk on a plastic sheet," Jack says. "There's an extra one in the trunk."

"Grab a towel from the bathroom." Luke gestures to me. "If he struggles, I'm not getting piss on me."

I grab a towel as we pass.

"Guys, I didn't mean to do it. Fuck, at least let me put on boxers."

"That was your decision, Grant." Luke leads the way. "You couldn't control yourself, and now you have to face the consequences."

Jack lets out a whoop before he rushes ahead, probably to get the trunk ready.

"Come on, guys. It was just a little extra money, and no one's won it. There's speculation, but no one's offered any proof you've done the deed yet." Grant's tone turns pleading. "I'll return everyone's money in the morning. I swear. I'll say there's no way to know who won."

"Not good enough," Luke says, opening the back door. "You need to be made an example of for those who might try to follow your lead."

"Can't you just rough me up a bit?" The whine in his tone almost makes me want to rough him up. I hate guys who can't own up to the shit they do.

"Don't worry. We'll get the message across." Caden lifts him and puts him into the open trunk. I toss the towel over his flaccid dick.

"Watch your head." Jack sounds almost giddy. "And remember, we could do a lot worse if you make trouble for us."

"Fuck." The trunk closes on Grant, and he doesn't make a sound.

We get into the car, and Eli drives us to the school. No one says anything. We can't be sure if he can hear us and we don't need him to know anything about our situation.

He doesn't live far from the high school. We park and file out of the car. Jack works his magic on his laptop, making sure the cameras won't have any evidence to point our direction.

Sure, they might get Grant to talk, but probably not. If he thinks this is bad, he should have heard the other options. Caden opens the trunk.

"Fuck," Caden mutters and glances at me. "Looks like I owe you a dollar."

The towel is wet, and the smell of piss fills the air.

"Good thing we put him in the trunk." I help Caden get him out, and we all head to the flagpole.

"What else should we bet on, Grant?" Luke stands in front of him while Caden and Jack tie him to the pole. "Should we bet on when someone will let you down? Maybe you'll get lucky, and the janitor will untie you. Do you have any friends, Grant? Because maybe they'll release you."

Eli steps back and pulls out his phone.

"Guys, be reasonable. It's cold."

"It's sixty-five out. Grow a pair." I shake my head.

When Caden and Jack step away, Eli's camera light comes on, alerting us he's recording.

"Seriously?" Grant struggles against the ropes. "I'm sorry. Okay? You've had your fun. Now untie me."

Eli stops recording. "It's not okay. Most likely someone will help you out before the whole school gets here in the morning. But don't worry, at eight a.m., everyone in school will have seen you tied up naked to the flagpole. One way or the other."

We all turn and head toward the car.

"Guys, come on. Fuck. I said I'm sorry. You don't have to do this. Fuck."

We get in the car, and Luke turns to us from the passenger seat.

"We'll take turns watching him to make sure nothing bad actually happens. Caden and Jack, you're on first watch. You two good to sneak out?"

Eli nods. When Luke's gaze falls on me, I nod.

"Good. I'll relieve you after an hour. Then I've got some guys on the team lined up to take shifts until morning." Luke glances out the window at Grant.

He knows who did this to him. I can't help but ask, "Will he talk?"

"Not if he doesn't want my fist in his face." Caden practically growls.

"What about the game tomorrow night? Coach will be upset if we don't get sleep." Jack leans back.

"We'll each get plenty of sleep." Luke blows out a breath. "We need to talk about Harper and Tanner."

"She's not happy with us currently." I know my sunshine. She's off and definitely mad at me, if not all of us. In this case, I disagreed with her trying to handle Tanner on her own.

"She still thinks we're using her," Jack says quietly. He glances toward the school. "It's easy to see why she feels that way."

Last night was something else. Watching her come over and over again, feeling her hot mouth and tight cunt wrapped around me... She was amazing.

"She can't keep secrets from us," Caden growls.

"At least she did it to protect you." I yank the black mask off my face. She's right. I'm supposed to be her friend, but I can't be both. My loyalty will always be divided between them and her, and when push came to shove, I chose them.

"Why didn't you tell us earlier?" Luke lifts his black mask. His eyes spear me, but I'm not afraid of him.

"Because she asked me not to." This tug-of-war back and forth between the guys and Harper might be too much. "She was my friend before you guys."

"I think that's part of our problem." Jack sits forward. "There shouldn't be an us against her thing. If she's ours, then she's ours all the way. No more dicking around."

Luke glares at Jack. "Of course she's ours."

He laughs. "No, she's our pet. We claimed her. She has very little say in her relationship with us. Fuck, she doesn't even think we have a relationship."

Luke scowls but says nothing. Jack's not wrong. Yes, she gave in to us willingly, but I wasn't here to wear her down with the rest of them. She seemed eager to take whatever we could give her. Still does, but that doesn't mean she feels like an equal.

"Fuck that. I've told her she's mine." Caden folds his arms over his chest.

"Exactly. We own her. She's not a part of the group," Jack says.

"He's right." Eli hits his hand on the steering wheel. "She's willing, but that doesn't make her part of us. She's holding herself back."

"Fuck. I'm done talking about feelings. She's ours. She'll deal with it." Luke jerks his head toward the others. "Jack and Caden, stay here with Grant. We'll bring one of your cars over. We need sleep so we can win tomorrow."

LUKE

The house is quiet. Harper's asleep, but I couldn't resist coming here. I lay in my bed for almost an hour before giving in to my compulsion. My bed was too big, too cold, too empty. Fuck, she's already in my head.

I push her door open and see Kenz first. She and Harper share the bed, each curled away from the other. On silent feet, I round to Harper's side and draw the covers away from her body.

She's wearing shorts and a tank top. When I lift her into my arms, she barely wakes before rolling her head against my chest. Something settles inside me at having her in my arms.

I don't mind sharing a bed with one of the guys on Harper's other side, but I draw the line at her friend. There's a guest bedroom right next to hers we can sleep in. Last night was a lot for her, but all I want tonight is sleep.

Pushing open the guest room door, I balance her against my shoulder to pull the covers down and chuck the decorative pillows on the floor. When I lay her on the cold bed, she shivers and curls into herself.

I tug off my shirt and ditch my jeans before sliding in behind her. As soon as I pull her into my arms, she sighs and settles. I draw in a deep breath of her and exhale.

Fuck. I shouldn't need her in my arms to sleep, but my body instantly relaxes.

It doesn't matter if she believes we're using her. She's mine and that's not changing. I understand what Jack said. Nico is a prime example of why keeping a *her versus us* mentality will cause problems.

My arm traps her against me, but she doesn't struggle to get free. Instead, she snuggles back into me. Her vanilla scent surrounds me. Her warmth draws me down into sleep.

A scream wakes me up, and I tighten my arms around Harper, but she's not the one screaming.

"Let me go, Luke." She pries at my hands. "Kenz."

I release her and roll out of bed. "Stay here."

Opening the door, I glance over and see Harper's bedroom door open. Harper touches my back. Of course she followed me. Fuck.

"Get the fuck out of here!" Kenz yells. A dull thud follows, and someone grunts.

I don't have time to force Harper to stay back. When I rush to her doorway, someone dressed all in black with a ski mask turns to me. He charges me.

I shift back and press Harper into the wall to keep the guy from accidentally running into her, and he tears down the stairs.

I turn, and Harper's wide eyes meet mine. "Get in your room. Lock the door."

She grabs my arm before I can take off. "What are you going to do?"

We need to know who this fucker is. I kiss her before pushing her toward her room. "I'm going after him."

The story continues in THEIR CRUEL PLAY

Meet C.S. Berry

C.S. Berry is a combination of my love for writing and my love for reading. She began as an experiment and took off into something I absolutely adore. It's not often you can do what you love and it works as a career. As for me, I love reading and romance and heroines seriously getting railed. I assume since you've read my books, you do too.

If you want to discuss books or anything with me, come join my Facebook group, C.S. Berry's Spicy Executive Suite. And you can always catch me on Instagram @csberry.

Oh and me, I have a lovely family who aren't allowed to read my books. But are so proud, they keep leaking my pen name. My dog and cats don't care about my writing as long as I sit still long enough for them to snuggle.

XOXOXO,

C.S. Berry

Keep up with C.S. Berry
View the shop: csberrybooks.com
View the Patreon: patreon.com/csberry
Join her Newsletter on her website
Join the Facebook Group:
https://www.facebook.com/groups/csberryreaders
Checkout her Website: csberry.com

www.ingramcontent.com/pod-product-compliance
Lightning Source LLC
Chambersburg PA
CBHW061338190726
48288CB00005B/1499